Praise for MiJa

D1438014

'I found MiJa incredibly engrossing. Some of this. I think, is due to the vividness of the writing, as well as attention to historical detail. I genuinely felt like I was there.' **Julia, Book-Sirens Reviewer**

'Loved it! Rich storytelling that spans generations ... Atkinson's writing is digestible and thoroughly enjoyable ... his characterisation of MiJa's mother, Boknam, is sublime.' **Kristiana, Reedsy Discovery**

'Beautifully done historical novel ... I really enjoyed the plot and am excited to read more from Mark Atkinson.' **Kathryn, Booksprout Reviewer**

'Love a good historical novel. This one has a lot of history and is hard to put down. Good read.' **Rhonda G, Booksprout Reviewer**

'A compelling story ... this book deserves wide readership.' **Morag, Booksprout Reviewer**

'Wow, just amazing. This story is the best I have read in a long time. It was so well written that I was hanging on the author's every word. I really couldn't put this book down. It's definitely been a long time that I have been this invested in a novel, and I read a lot of books. This story was so sad, emotional and atmospheric it almost felt like a true story. It's certainly a story about resilience. It really shocked me in places. It is also inspiring, if MiJa can get through all life threw at her then so can we. I really can't recommend this book enough. It's a fantastic historical fiction set in South Korea. The story goes through so many changes within the country. Through civil War, occupation, failing crops, school changes, kidnap and death. It's certainly a roller coaster ride. This story will stay with me for a very long time. I know we are only in the end of January, and I will probably read another 400 books. But this book is definitely likely to be book of the year. It will take a lot to knock it off my top spot. I was totally engrossed in this book and read it all in one sitting. The characters were amazing and well developed. Only the highest of praise goes out to the author and publishing team for creating the most perfect novel. I really hope this author writes more books. I will certainly keep my eyes peeled.' **Claire, Netgalley Reviewer**

'A historical fiction story about Choi MiJa. We follow along on her journey from childhood to adulthood. A difficult adventure that will pull at your heartstrings and root for her survival. A beautifully and poignant story.' **Intriga, Book-Sirens Reviewer**

'You write beautifully and when you describe a setting it's absolutely great. It makes the novel a pleasure to read ... it's extremely cinematic ... a great piece of work.' **Development Editor, Jericho Writers**

MIJA

MARK ATKINSON

book mark

PUBLICATIONS

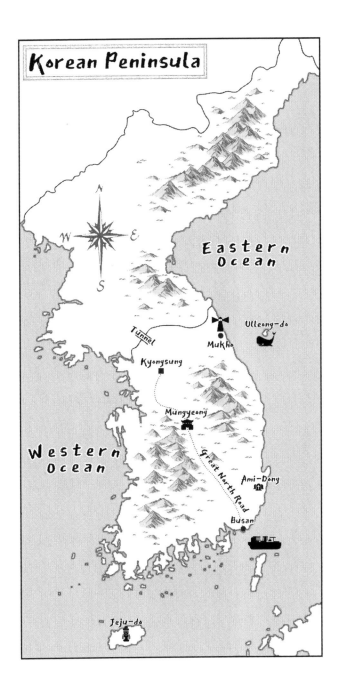

MUKHO

29 FEBRUARY 1960

Mukho is a great place to hide if you don't mind the smell of dried squid permeating your life. If you catch the slow train up the east coast of the South Korean peninsula until you can go no further and walk ten miles or so towards the Eastern Ocean, you will arrive at the small fishing village. It borders the demilitarised zone with North Korea, so not many people go there, and the few that do are either lost or running away from something. That was the route I took in the summer of 1954, although I was unaware of it at the time.

This winter has been the coldest in living memory. I don't know how we survived. A sudden and irreplaceable loss plunged me into a dark depression that was difficult to escape but, somehow, I managed it. The last thing I want to do now is go outside, but I have no choice. The charcoal won't last the night. I must go to the market or we will freeze to death. I strap my son to my back with my podaegi, a small, quilted blanket, and take the last of the money from its hiding place under the vinyl floor. I stare at it before scrunching it into a ball in my fist. If my husband doesn't come back soon, I don't know what we'll do. His threadbare coat still hangs where he abandoned it, so I throw it around the both of us so that it rests on the top of my head and fasten the top button under my chin. It still smells of him.

The market is only a brisk hour's walk away, but today it feels much longer; perhaps it's because of the biting cold that cuts like a whetted knife or the fact that I've been house-bound for so long. I pull the old coat closer to my body to keep out the groping icy fingers of air and, eventually, we arrive. The market is the usual bustle of activity. The hawkers yell in my face and urge me to try their wares; they thrust free samples of steamed silk-worm larvae, roasted chestnuts and rice cakes under my nose. Huge aluminium cooking pots boil vigorously under hissing propane burners, filling the air with steam and the aroma of anonymous pig parts, garlic, ginger and cinnamon. The cloying smell reminds me of better times and sets my stomach grumbling. Temptation calls, but I ignore it and head over to the charcoal seller.

'Azuma. It's your lucky day,' he shouts. I wince. He is as black and dusty as the pile of briquets stacked in front of him. Lucky day, indeed. That will be a first. I have no husband, no money, and a young child to raise. And where did all the years go? Not that long ago, I would have been addressed in public as a young woman, not an old mama. I'm only thirty-three years old. The upsetting part is that I know he is telling the truth, but I could do without the reminders.

The hawker beckons me to come closer and whispers, 'I have a special offer. Just for you. Forty-five hwan for ten briquets. You can't beat that. Top quality charcoal. How many would you like?'

I pick up one of the heavy cylinders, the size of a paint tin, and inspect the holes drilled radially around the centre. 'It's not that imported Chinese rubbish, is it?'

The hawker pulls a face as though deeply offended. 'Of

course not. As I said, this is top quality. It's made right here, in this very town.'

'It feels damp. That last lot I bought from you crumbled before I even got home, took ages to dry out, and when I finally did manage to light it, it hardly gave off any heat.'

'There's plenty of other customers.'

'I'll give you twenty hwan for six briquets.'

He flashes his best salesman's smile. 'Has old age made you deaf, Azuma? Do you have dementia? If you remember, I have just told you that it's forty-five hwan for ten briquets.'

'Well, I've only brought twenty hwan with me. I left the rest of my cash at home in case I was robbed. It looks like I made the right decision.'

The charcoal seller laughs. 'I won't be able to feed my children if I sell at that price. I can let you have four briquets for fifteen hwan. Take it or leave it. That's the best I can do.'

We both know I have no choice. 'If that's the best you can do for a poor old Azuma, Then I guess I'll have to take it,' I say, knowing full well that I can only manage to carry four briquets anyway.

The hawker stacks two cylinders on top of each other and threads some twine, made from plaited rice straw, through the holes. He makes a loop in each end so I can carry one in each hand, and I hobble over to the Hae-nyeo. The Hae-nyeo, or Sisters of the Sea, make a living free-diving for octopus, conch and abalone. They had taken me under their wing when I first arrived in Mukho, and I knew I'd never be able to repay their kindness. I would pay my respects and maybe, just maybe, they would have something left over.

I find them huddled around a brazier, trying to keep out the evening chills. Their faces are lit up in the glow, each one the texture of wrinkled leather that had been used hard and put away wet. Faces never lie; they always reflect the type of life you lead. There's a row of large plastic buckets, the colour of a shiny terracotta, standing along the quayside and one of the women breaks off from the group to pour fresh seawater into it.

'Sisters, look who is here,' she says. The other Hae-nyeo wave. Most are in their sixties or seventies, and all had outlived their husbands by a good many years. They have been diving and harvesting the sea for decades, and their fitness and steely determination have been the stuff of legends. It was rumoured, mainly by fishermen who never left the safety of their boats, that even the sharks feared them.

The matriarch stretches out her arms and says, 'Come on. Give him here.'

'He's sleeping.'

'Give him here. You need to rest after all you have gone through.' She unties my podaegi and takes my son over to the brazier. I can smell the aroma of fish stew bubbling away on the top. One of the sisters is still in her wetsuit. She is squatting on the ground, and she suddenly grasps a writhing eel, pushes its head onto a nail set into a wooden board, skins it alive with a sharp knife and chops it into bite-size pieces. She puts the still squirming mass of pink flesh on the grill. The sound and smell of searing fish waft my way, and I deeply inhale the aroma.

I already know the answer, but I ask anyway: 'Do you have any live fish left?'

The Hae-nyeo laugh, 'Of course not. Not at this time.'

My son is fully awake now and starts whining. The head Hae-nyeo digs around in the coals and retrieves a soot-blackened sweet potato. She peels back the charred skin, breaks off small pieces, and blows on them until they are cool enough to feed to him.

'You are more than welcome to join us for dinner,' says the woman in the wet suit, and she nods to the pot. 'There's plenty.'

'I would love to, but I have to get home before it gets too dark. Besides, my husband will be back tonight. Can I have five hwan of whatever shellfish you have left?'

One of the sisters takes a plastic bag and puts a generous scoop of whelks into it.

'That's far too much,' I say, embarrassed by their generosity.

'How are you feeling? Back to normal?'

'Yes, I think so. Thank you for all you have done for us. I don't know what happened to me. It must have been the sudden shock of —'

'Hush. Don't say another word. We understand.'

'I'm sorry I can't stay any longer, but I will come back soon. I really must get going.'

The head Hae-nyeo helps me to strap my son to my back, and as I bend down to pick up a charcoal bundle in each hand, she slips a large, fat flounder into a plastic bag and ties it to my podaegi. It flutters in protest, and my heart does the same. As I'm leaving, she whispers into my ear, 'I hope he's there when you get home.'

'Come back soon,' they urge.

'I will,' I reply, but I know I will not. Not until I have some money, and who knows when that will be? I glance back at the harbour. The first electric lights flicker into life, and their soft light diffuses through the orange soju tents that fringe the quayside.

The journey home seems much quicker, and my son falls asleep on the warmth of my back. I can hear him gently breathing over the crunch of my snowy footsteps. The flounder flutters on my breast until its protests grow feeble and they eventually stop altogether. It freezes in an icy patch over my heart. It's only then that it occurs to me that the head Hae-nyeo must have been saving the flounder for her dinner but decided to give it to me instead. Maybe the charcoal seller was right: perhaps this is my lucky day? I feel sure my husband will be waiting for me when I get home. I could make sashimi for him or even a fish stew now that I have plenty of charcoal. He always likes that.

It's dark when I arrive home, and the snow starts to fall in a fierce flurry. The temperature plummets, and my exposed hands feel frozen solid from carrying the charcoal. But, even in the dark, there is no mistaking my home: a rough stone shack that had once been thatched but now has a rusty corrugated iron roof that gives it a unique silhouette against the night sky. There's no light on inside, and my heart sinks. I put down the charcoal to avoid breaking it, and I catch sight of something out of the corner of my eye: a parcel wrapped in rags that somebody has left on my doorstep. There's a label attached to it with the words, *Up to You? Feb 29, 1960*, scrawled on it. I decide to leave it on the doorstep.

The shock of finding the parcel has taken the edge off my appetite so I put the flounder and the whelks into a bowl of cold water and put a new briquet on the heater with the charcoal tongs. My head is spinning. What should I do? The neighbours must have seen somebody leave it so I couldn't just abandon it. I bring the bundle in and place it on the floor. I remove an old rag from a crack in the wall, and an icy blast of air whistles in. That should be cold enough, I think.

I hug my son under my yo, a thin mattress topper, and press my body against the warmth of the floor. Once or twice, my son wakes up, and I let him have my breast until he nods off again, but the sleep I crave will not come. My mind is a jumble of thoughts, and every time I nod off I am stabbed awake by a prick of conscience. I feel betrayed and abandoned with only my silent sobs and salty tears for company. Occasionally, my anger gets the better of me and I stick my foot out of the yo and nudge the bundle closer to the icy draught.

That night seems the longest of my life, as if the morning

would never come. And sometimes I hoped that it never would, but of course it did. I must have dozed off at some point because when I awake, all is silent. A fresh batch of snow has fallen and cast a blanket over the world that soaks up all the sounds of humanity. It's a bright, eerie morning and I'm so scared I keep my eyes tightly shut and listen. The only sounds I can hear are the sounds of my son softly snoring and my pounding heart reverberating off the hard floor. There's no sound coming from the bundle in the icy corner of the room. Not a whimper. The silence of the dead. Good, I think. It worked. Anyway, there's nothing I can do about it now. It's too late. The foundling must have frozen to death in the night.

PART ONE

THE JAPANESE OCCUPATION

CHAPTER 1

MIJA

Choi MiJa was born in Korea, in 1927, with a gold spoon in her mouth, but it was her fate to be burdened by the old Chinese curse, 'May you live in interesting times.' Nobody could remember who actually muttered the curse but, many years later, when the curse was proven beyond all doubt, everybody agreed that it was probably her mother, Park Bok-nam.

Her father, Choi Gil-soo, was the nineteenth generation of the high-born Yangban caste that owned large tracts of arable land around Mun-gyeong. He had inherited the fruit orchards, barley fields, a ginseng farm and numerous rice fields from his father, but he made most of his money when he ventured into trading rice. To make sure nobody would underestimate his wealth, he extended the ancestral home until it was a sprawling complex of ninety-nine rooms arranged around a central courtyard. A high wall made from rough, undressed stone surrounded the entire complex. He hired the finest craftsmen and used only natural, local materials to build in the traditional wooden post-and-beam frame style. Each building had wattle and daub walls, coated with fine kaolin clay that dried to a natural off-white colour, and an upswept roof made from intricately carved slate-grey tiles — the expensive kind, usually reserved for temples. He was quite sure that things were settled forever and that his wealth and name would last another 500 years.

In the female quarters, Bok-nam sat on the edge of her bed and stroked her swollen belly. In her hand she held the letter from the local Japanese governor. He wanted to know why MiJa had not registered for school yet. She had been putting it off for as long as possible, but now she had no choice. She cursed under her breath, folded the letter and put it back into the envelope. What was the world coming to? she thought. She didn't believe in educating girls. *She* hadn't received any education and look how well she had done. All a girl had to do was learn how to count money, write her name, marry well and bear healthy sons. But the Japanese had mandated it, so that was that. It didn't make any sense to her. Sons need educating; that much is evident to all, but why girls? Her eldest daughter, Mi-soon, had received an education, and all she ever got from her was backchat.

Bok-nam felt a kick in her belly. It was a strong kick, a boy's kick. It had better be, she thought. Two girls are enough for any family, and her husband would think about taking a concubine if she bore him another daughter. She stroked her belly and said under her breath, 'Good morning, my precious son.' Something she did every morning without fail. Then she yelled to the out-of-sight servants, 'You can wake MiJa now and give her a bath.'

A few moments later, the head of the female servants appeared and kowtowed. Bok-nam handed her a bar of soap that she kept under lock-and-key. 'Make sure that she is scrubbed clean, but don't use too much of it,' she said. 'It's from Italy and made from olive oil.'

'Yes, Ma'am,' said the servant and headed off to repeat her

orders to the kitchen staff.'And don't forget to bring it back as soon as you've finished. It's expensive,' yelled Bok-nam.

The kitchen staff had been up since dawn preparing breakfast and fetching water from the well. The water was heated in a vast cast-iron pot on the kitchen stove. When it was hot enough, two of the servants scooped up the water and poured it into a huge bathtub, made from a series of oak staves held together with black iron hoops, like a truncated beer barrel.

'Why do I have to get a bath anyway?' said MiJa, rubbing the sleep out of her eyes. 'I had one last month. For the Lunar New Year. Don't you remember?'

'Ma'am insists. You are to go to school today.'

'Really?' asked MiJa, now wide-eyed and fully awake. She had been nagging her mother for months to go to school. She wanted to be smart like her elder sister, Mi-soon. She tentatively dipped a big toe into the water to test the temperature and jerked it back out. 'It's still too hot,' she said, so the servants scurried back to the well to draw more cold water and pour it into the bath until it was to MiJa's liking. MiJa closed her mouth and squeezed her eyes shut as the two servants poured water over her head, washed her hair, and tried to scrub her skin off, armed with only rough cotton flannels and the expensive Italian soap.

'Can I wear my favourite dress again? The pink one I wore for the Lunar New Year?'

'Yes, we are getting it ready.'

The servants brought more hot water to rinse the soap off MiJa. They wrapped her in a warm towel, dried her hair and combed oil, made from the seeds of camellia flowers, through it then tied it in braids. The servants dressed her in her casual house clothes and led her across a gravel courtyard. Outside the kitchen area, an army of dark-brown earthenware pots stood guard against hunger. Each was large enough to fit MiJa inside and contained different vintages of kimchi, assorted pickles, soy sauce, chilli paste and fermented bean paste that would meet their needs for many years. Bunches of dark-red chillies and Chinese cabbage leaves hung from the exposed rafters to dry out over the bone-dry winter. MiJa let her hand trail in the ornamental pond and hoped that one of the koi carp would nibble at her fingertips. She liked the sensation of their soft leathery mouths and still imagined them to have been somehow accidentally splashed with red and orange ink.

'You have just had a bath. And don't dawdle. Your mother wants her breakfast,' said the servant.

When they passed the reception hall, MiJa glanced up at the enormous wooden sign that hung from it. It was the house name, *Mae-jook-dang*, carved in Chinese characters. She tried to remember the meaning of each of the characters. One represented plum blossom, another was bamboo, and the last character meant house. Mi-soon had explained to her that it was how the family had managed to survive for so many generations. Plum blossom could survive the harshest of winters, bamboo always grew straight, was evergreen, and more importantly would yield to the wind instead of resisting it and breaking.

When MiJa arrived at the female quarters, her mother and her older sister were waiting for her.

'Serve the breakfast now,' Bok-nam shouted to the servants. She glowered at MiJa. 'You took your time. I thought you wanted to go to school? You really should be more considerate, MiJa. Especially to your *mother*. Especially in *my* condition.'

'Sorry, Mother,' said MiJa.

'Good morning Little Sister,' said Mi-soon.

'Good morning, Elder Sister. I'm going to school today. I'm going to be smart like you.'

Bok-nam laughed and looked around, anxious for her breakfast to arrive. Two servants brought in a heavily lacquered zelkova wood table laden with plates of fried fish, bowls of steaming white rice, a bowl of hot soup made from freshly picked dandelion greens, and side dishes of beansprouts with toasted sesame seeds, assorted pickles and a plate of fermented kimchi.

Mi-soon was hungry, but she knew she could not start eating until her mother picked up her spoon.

'When is Father coming back?' asked MiJa.

Mi-soon kicked her sister under the table, taking care that her mother could not see her.

'Soon,' said Bok-nam, much to Mi-soon's relief. 'Now, let's eat.'

Bok-nam's husband, Gil-soo, had been summoned to the Korean capital, Kyongsung, to discuss important business with Japanese land officials. All the Korean landowners had been ordered to the capital by the Governor General of Chosen. Gil-soo should have returned yesterday but had sent a message that he would be late.

After breakfast, Bok-nam ordered the servants to dress MiJa for school. 'Make sure you bring her to me, so I can inspect her before she steps out of the door.'

In MiJa's room a maid was ironing MiJa's hanbok: a traditional Korean dress made from a pink, full-length bell-shaped skirt. On top of this, she would wear a dark green bolero jacket with multi-coloured hooped sleeves. When the servants had finished dressing MiJa they tied long pink ribbons at the end of her braids, made sure that her silk shoes were fitted correctly, and took her to her mother for the inspection.

Bok-nam looked her daughter up and down and asked MiJa to turn around. Then she said, 'She is acceptable. Dol-soi will take you to school.'

'Thanks. See you later, Mother,' said MiJa and bowed. Her mother nodded back.

'See you later, Little Sister,' shouted Mi-soon. 'Enjoy your first day at school.'

Dol-soi, the head servant, led MiJa through the courtyard and down a set of granite steps, across a manicured lawn, to a large wooden gate that was reinforced with black iron bands and set between two stone pillars. On one of the pillars, MiJa noticed that the plaque, engraved with her father's name, was slightly crooked; she asked Dol-soi to straighten it. They joined the Great North Road, an ancient route that started in Busan on the southern coast and finished in Kyongsung. The town of Mun-gyeong was located about halfway and formed part of the mountain pass that cut its way through the Sobaek mountain range; local legend said that the mountain pass was so high that even the birds could not reach the summit. The town had grown fat from the bounty of the traders, scholars and pilgrims that followed the road north in their quest for money, knowledge and spiritual enlightenment.

It was a beautiful clear spring day, and MiJa delighted in watching the flycatchers dart in and out of the hedgerows, busy making their nests and singing a song about the promise of summer. She looked down the road in both directions and was pleased that her long shadow cast on the road made her look taller, but the butterflies in her stomach would not settle.

'What if nobody likes me?' she asked Dol-soi.

'I'm sure they will.'

'What if nobody wants to be my friend?'

'Of course they will.'

Then a few moments later, 'Are you sure they will like me?'

'I'm sure.'

About thirty minutes later, they arrived at the town entrance. A fortified wall, the colour of pale honey, encircled the town and was initially built to keep out brigands and strangers. Above an archway stood a guardhouse with the swept-up eaves of a temple roof.

'It's not far now,' said Dol-soi as they slipped through the archway. MiJa noticed how cool and shadowy it was in the tunnel, and when she emerged into the bright sunshine at the other end she gasped. She had never seen anything so beautiful in her life. Ahead of her lay a long avenue of cherry trees, in full blossom. She let go of the servant's hand and ran towards them, straining her neck backwards to stare at the solid canopy of pink-tinged clouds, with sunlight poking through. Suddenly, a gust of wind fractured the cloud into a million pieces, and the spring sky filled with a flurry of pink blossoms, each fluttering in the breeze like a tiny butterfly. MiJa was afraid they would vanish forever, so she ran like crazy with her pink dress billowing in the wind and her hair ribbons fluttering erratically in the wind until she was indistinguishable from the clouds of blossom. She leapt with feline grace, clutching at the petals, with both hands, until she could hold no more. She opened her hands, expecting to have captured their delicate beauty and faint perfume, something she could always keep and treasure: instead, all she found was a crushed brown mess. She sniffed at them, but their delicate bouquet had vanished, replaced with something acrid and bitter. She threw them on the ground, disappointed that something so beautiful could be lost so quickly.

The sign above the school gate read: *The Good Citizen Elementary School*. MiJa was excited about her first day at school and full of pride that she was almost a schoolgirl, nearly an adult in her mind, so she pushed back her shoulders, marched through the gate, and stepped into a different world.

CHAPTER 2

THE GOOD CITIZEN ELEMENTARY
SCHOOL

A large crowd had gathered on the packed-earth courtyard outside the school and slowly shuffled towards the registration hall: a modern, squat, brick building designed for functionality rather than aesthetics. MiJa had never seen such a crowd and felt nervous. She had seen large gatherings before at birthday parties, and Chuseok when the harvest was celebrated, but this was different: all the social castes had been thrown together. It was as if the Japanese had swept away a thousand years of tradition.

Members of the Yangban class — civil servants, politicians and landowners — rubbed shoulders with the scientists, engineers, doctors and musicians from the Jungin caste. The craftsmen, fishermen and labourers of the Sangmin class mingled freely with the Baekjong caste, the untouchables — the butchers, funeral directors, leather makers, shoemakers, entertainers, prostitutes and shaman priests; anybody who dealt in death or was unclean.

Everybody seemed to be talking at once, and when they became frustrated at not being heard, they raised their voices even louder. MiJa was confused by their coarse, thick accents and wasn't sure if they were even speaking Korean. She was shocked by their strange attire, but most shocking of all was the smell.

Nearly everybody was clothed in rough, undyed and unwashed hempen cloth. Bare limbs poked out of the ragged arm and leg holes and these, too, were unwashed and streaked with mud. Had these people no shame? White was the colour associated with death; it was worn at funerals.

MiJa glanced around nervously, looking for anybody that looked normal, and was relieved to see a small splash of colour against the enormity of the dirty blank canvas. She saw two girls in traditional hanboks; one was in aquamarine, the other purple. A handful of boys wore their traditional garb: grey baggy pants, pastel-coloured silk waistcoats and black hats. There was even one in a jacket and tie, western style. MiJa whispered an incantation under her breath, 'I hope I am in the same class as those girls,' and repeated it ten times to make sure it came true. She wasn't worried about being in the same class as the boys because that was simply unthinkable.

The registration hall opened, and as the crowd surged forward MiJa was nearly shoved into the girl in front of her. She backed up slightly and smoothed her dress by her side to fill as small a space as possible. She stared at the girl in front of her. She wasn't wearing any shoes, and her hair looked like it had never been washed or combed. She had mud caked on the back of her neck that looked so deep, you could plant mooli radishes in it. When the crowd moved forward again, MiJa grabbed Dol-soi's hand and pulled on it to lift herself slightly so she could walk on tiptoe and avoid soiling her shoes, and with her other hand, she held her perfumed braid under her nose and inhaled the sweet camellia oil.

As they got closer to the registration hall, MiJa peeked

inside. A short, thin man with a balding head, spattered with beads of sweat, sat behind an oversized mahogany desk as if he was trying to compensate for his lack of stature. He beckoned them forward with a slight wave of his hand.

'Name?'

'Dol-soi, sir.'

The registrar took off his glasses and looked up at the servant as if he was the village idiot. He grimaced, shifted uncomfortably in his chair, and said, 'What is your family name?'

'I don't have one.'

The man interlocked his fingers and sat up straight. It was going to be a long day. 'Are you her father?' he said and nodded to MiJa.

MiJa covered her face to hide her blushes. She had never heard anything so ridiculous. How could a servant be her father?

'No sir. She is my master's daughter.'

'Why didn't her father bring her? Is he ashamed of her?'

'No sir. He had to go to the capital, Kyongsung —'

'Yes, I know what the capital is called,' said the registrar, and he shook his head in disbelief. He turned to MiJa and asked, 'Can you tell me your father's name?'

'Choi Gil-soo,' said MiJa. She watched the registrar sort through a pile of papers on his sweat-stained desk until he found the right one. He read through it, nodded, and gave it the official stamp.

'Welcome to our school,' he said to MiJa and handed her the stamped paper. 'Please wait over there with the others. You will see the nurse next.'

As they turned to go, the registrar said, 'Not you, servant. You can wait outside the school gates until we have finished, er .... processing them.'

The nurse was an elderly, stout woman, as broad as she

was tall, with her hair tied in a severe bun that pulled her sagging skin taut over her face. Her mouth had lost its fight with gravity and drooped downwards giving her the impression that she was in a permanent sulk; she was. 'Stand up tall,' she said to a boy as she measured his height and squinted through her Coke-bottle glasses. 'You're not very tall for your age are you?' she said to the boy as if it was his fault. The boy didn't answer. 'Does your mother feed you?'

'Yes, Nurse.'

'Well, obviously, she doesn't feed you enough, or you would be taller. But don't worry. We will feed you well.' She wrote something on a piece of paper, handed it to him, and shouted, 'Next.'

MiJa handed the nurse her registration paper.

'Stand up against the wall. Back straight.' MiJa stood on tiptoes under her dress, and the nurse wrote her height and 'uniform size 3' on her registration paper. 'Join those over there,' she said and pointed to where MiJa should stand. 'You will get your name next.'

MiJa joined the queue and wondered why she needed a new name. She already had the one that her father had given her. She watched as the children were taken one by one into a room, only to emerge a few moments later with a smile on their face and a piece of yellow cotton cloth clutched in their hand.

Standing in front of MiJa was a boy with a parcel wrapped in waxed paper, tied with string, tucked under his arm. Something that looked like blood seemed to be dripping from it. He was holding hands with a girl who had protruding teeth. They were called into the room together and MiJa strained her ears to listen. She could only just make out the voices inside the room.

'Name?'

'Baek Un-yeon, sir,' the girl replied.

'Wrong.'

The girl hesitated. 'That is what my father calls me.'

'That may well be, but from now on, your name is Usagi.'

'Usagi? What does that mean?

'It's Japanese for Bunny.'

There was a slight delay, and the girl said, 'This is my younger brother.'

MiJa heard the boy say, 'My father asked me to give you this, sir.' She could hear the rustle of a parcel being unwrapped.

'Ah, you must be the butcher's son. Can you tell me your name?'

'Baek So-dong, sir.'

The man put down his pen. 'Please thank your father for the gift. He must be quite a comedian. He calls your sister Un-yeon (No Name) and he calls you So-dong (Cow's Arse).' The man laughed, not understanding that the poor had no reason to name their offspring. Instead, they gave them self-deprecating nicknames in the hope that the jealous gods would overlook their children and spare them the worst.

'I think you will like your new Japanese name much better. It is Gomasuri.'

'Thank you, sir,' said the boy and he slowly repeated, 'Go-ma-suri.' Japanese for ass kisser.

They left the room a few moments later, clutching their cotton name tags and repeating their names over and over so they didn't forget them.

The registrar summoned MiJa next.

'Stand there, on the yellow cross, with your arms by your side.'

MiJa did as she was told and straightened her back for good measure.

'What is your name?'

'I don't know sir.'

The man put down his pen and stared up at MiJa. 'You don't know your name?'

'No sir.'

'Why not?'

'You haven't given it to me yet, sir.' MiJa noticed that his left eye gave an involuntary tic. He smiled.

'What is your Korean name?'

'Choi MiJa, sir.'

'You are Yoshiko from now on. It means beautiful girl. The same meaning as your Korean name.' He wrote her new Japanese name onto a yellow cotton label. 'Ask your mother to sew this onto your school uniform, then everybody will know who you are. Without a Japanese name, you are nobody. Understand?'

'Yes sir,' said MiJa, and she bowed deeply to show that she did understand.

The lobby was buzzing with excitement as the children discussed their new names. MiJa heard one girl tell a group of children that she was delighted with her new Japanese name.

'My name is Shimai,' she said with a puffed-out chest like a pigeon. 'I'm the youngest of six girls. My oldest sisters are called Geum-ju (Gold), Eun-ju (Silver), and Dong-ju (Bronze). Then came Soon-ju (Not So Bad) and Geut-ju (Last Daughter). I think my father had had enough of girls when I was born because he called Mal-yeon (No More Fucking Girls), but now I'm Shimai.' She proudly waved her name label above her head, not knowing that Shimai means, The End.

'And you still don't have any brothers?' asked one of the boys.

'Last year a baby brother arrived.'

'And what's his name?' asked the boy.

She grabbed her crotch and said, 'Bo-seok, of course, because he has got the crown jewels.'

Some of the children laughed but most didn't understand.

MiJa blushed and followed them to the next stage of the process. She could hear a faint buzzing behind the closed door that sounded like a distant wasps' nest, but there was so much talking going on it was hard to make out what it was. MiJa noticed that many children went into that room, but nobody ever came out. Suddenly the door opened, and a man dressed in a white coat emerged, accompanied by a strong whiff of disinfectant. He yelled, 'Next!'

MiJa entered a long corridor, harshly lit by fluorescent lights. A row of chairs stood on either side, facing the wall. On the left sat the boys, all with military-grade buzz haircuts. On the right, the girls with identical short bobs. There wasn't a single mirror in the room, but most of the children were crying. They saw the severe haircuts on the other children and could imagine them on themselves.

'Sit in the chair,' said the man with the white coat and slicked-back oily hair. He wrapped a large cloth around MiJa's neck and fastened it with a clothes peg. MiJa took a sharp intake of breath as she felt the press of cold metal against the nape of her neck. She heard the snipping of shears behind her, and then suddenly, she felt lighter, as if a huge weight had been removed from her shoulders. She felt herself rise in her chair, caught the faint whiff of camellia oil, and then everything went dark, as her hair fell around her face like a pair of black velvet curtains.

A short while later, the barber removed the cloth, shook the hair out of it, and moved on to his next victim. MiJa stared at her bunched-up silky braids lying on the floor, still tied with her pink ribbons. She bit her tongue, determined not to cry in front of the other children. They reminded her of the camellia flowers that her father grew in his garden and had often wondered why they fell as complete flower heads and not petal by petal. She stooped down, picked up the braids, and sniffed at them; the perfume had faded already. She gently stroked them as if saying goodbye to a lifelong pet, removed the pink ribbons from the braids and let the dead hair fall to the floor.

'You look like a mop,' said a voice behind her. MiJa wiped her eyes and turned around. It was the boy she had seen in Western dress.

'Well, you look like a monk,' she said.

'All the boys look like monks, but I think I'm the most handsome. I'm Kim,' he said. 'Kim Jung-sik.'

MiJa ignored him. She was too embarrassed to talk to a boy she didn't even know.

'Don't worry. It'll grow back,' he said.

'Then they'll cut it again. Won't they?'

Eventually the children were disgorged back into the schoolyard dressed in their school uniform. The boys wore a military uniform: black trousers and a black tunic with gold buttons and a mandarin collar. They hid their crew cuts under a peaked military cap emblazoned with the school badge. The girls were less fortunate and had to wear white long-sleeved blouses, fastened with a ribbon tied in an asymmetric bow, and black skirts that only came down to mid-calf. The girls tugged at their skirt hems, trying to make them longer and MiJa blushed at the thought of revealing her bare ankles in public. She was glad she had stood on tiptoes because her skirt was longer than the others. Some of the girls were embarrassed that they hadn't washed their once hidden limbs and were now trying to wipe off the dirt with spit and frantic rubbing.

On the way home, Dol-soi carried MiJa's traditional silk dress over his arm. She looked at her beautiful hanbok and compared it to her plain school uniform. She had traded her beautiful braids for a mop haircut, but she was a schoolgirl now and would learn about all the wonders in the world. It was a price worth paying, she decided.

When they were almost home, Jung-sik, who had been following behind, shouted, 'I will see you tomorrow morning.

We can walk to school together.' He pointed to his house and said, 'I live over there. What's your name?'

MiJa ignored him. She was staring at the gatepost outside her house. The plaque engraved with her father's name was missing.

CHAPTER 3

JUNG-SIK

'Ichi, ni; san, shi; go, roku; shichi, hache; kyuu, juu.'

MiJa heard them before she could see them, but soon a red flag tied to a bamboo stick fluttered over the horizon, followed by a cloud of dust and a column of children marching in 2:4 time. It was the first day back at school for the older children, and the column had been arranged in rank and file, boy, girl, boy, girl, with the tallest at the front.

'Fall in at the back,' bellowed the head boy with the flag.

MiJa did as she was told, the order to advance was given, and the children marched along the dusty road like a uniform multi-legged organism.

'We will learn to count to ten in Japanese, one number for each step. Repeat after me: Ichi — Ni.'

'Ichi — Ni,' replied the children.

'San — Shi,' said the leader and so on until he got to ten and returned to the beginning. It was effective, and by the time they got to Jung-sik's house, MiJa had already memorised how to count to ten in Japanese.

'Good morning,' said Jung-sik. MiJa rolled her eyes and

pretended something interesting had caught her eye and looked the other way.

'No talking in the ranks,' shouted the leader, and he gave the command to set off marching again.

After a while, he got fed up counting to ten and moved on to the Japanese National anthem. 'Repeat each line after me after me.'

> *May your reign*
> *Continue for a thousand,*
> *Eight thousand generations,*
>
> *Until the pebbles*
> *Grow into boulders*
> *Lush with moss.*

MiJa mimicked the other children and repeated the words parrot-fashion. She didn't understand their meaning, but she could feel her spirits sink as the lively bouncing marching rhythm was replaced with a solemn dirge, devoid of any emotion, and she felt more like she was going to a funeral than school.

At the school gate they were confronted by a platoon of prefects who checked that each pupil had their Japanese name tags sewn onto their uniforms in the correct place and turned away those that didn't. The boys were told to stand up straight, button their tunics and straighten their caps. MiJa focussed on the two girl prefects, armed with wooden rulers and scissors. She could hear one of them say, 'Hair should be four centimetres below the ear and skirt hems should be ten centimetres below the knee.'

MiJa watched them check the girls with their rulers. If the hair was too long, they cut a notch out of it with the scissors, at the regulation length, and told them to get it cut after school. MiJa rolled up the waistband of her skirt to shorten it.

A temporary wooden stage had been erected in the playground, with stairs on either side. Centre stage was a man dressed in the gown of a schoolmaster, with iron-grey hair that stood erect like the bristles on a wild hog. When he held the megaphone up to his mouth, he revealed that far too many yellow teeth had been crammed into far too small a mouth. He held onto the podium with his free hand and addressed the school with a high-pitched nasal whine.

'Good morning, children. I am your headmaster, and my name is Kitamura. I would like to welcome you all to The Good Citizen Elementary School.'

MiJa copied the other children and said, 'Good Morning, Kitamura san,' and bowed deeply. Some of the children were slow to respond, so their form teachers gave them a tap on the head with a long stick as a timely reminder.

The headmaster continued, 'We have much to do on our first day, but before we separate you into your form classes, I want to say something about why you are here. I come from the Glorious Empire of Japan. The head of our country is Emperor Hirohito, and he has decided to educate the people of Korea, for free. The first duty of a good citizen is to worship the Japanese Emperor.'

His voice cracked, and one of the teachers handed him a glass of water. He took a drink and cleared his throat before continuing. 'When I first arrived here, I was shocked to see how backwards Korea was. Your farmers still rely solely on the weather, so we decided to build a series of irrigation canals and drag Korea into the twentieth century. Even now, we have a team of Agricultural Officers mapping the country and making a list of who owns all the land. The survey will allow us to manage the land more efficiently, which means more food for you to eat.

'We will help Korea build the first factories and construct the first railway system, and soon this part of Japan will have a modern economy, just like the Motherland. That is where you come in. We need workers to achieve all of this. If you work hard and listen to your teachers, you will learn much here, and when you graduate you will become productive citizens and perform an important job for the Empire of Japan.'

When they were sure the headmaster had finished speaking, the prefects started a round of applause. This was followed by a rousing rendition of the national anthem before the pupils were led to their allocated classrooms.

The form teacher opened the sliding door to the classroom and read out the names from a list. MiJa noticed that the shortest girls were called in first and allocated seats at the front of the room. Each desk seated two students, and the desks were arranged in three rows.

MiJa looked for the girls she had seen dressed in the traditional dress, but now everybody looked the same in their uniforms. The girl with protruding teeth was there, and she was called in next. MiJa was very pleased with herself for having the foresight to stand on tiptoes. At least she wouldn't have to sit next to a butcher's daughter. When MiJa's name was finally announced, she was allocated a seat in the middle row. The seat next to her was vacant, so she turned to her left and smiled at Bunny.

The boys were called in next and started filling up the right-hand row of desks. When that row was filled, they started occupying the central row, and it slowly dawned on MiJa that she was going to be seated next to a boy. This was an outrage. She felt nauseous and tried her best to ignore the stares and jeers thrown her way, and just when she was thinking it couldn't possibly get any worse, a familiar voice said, 'I think it's our destiny to be together.'

It was Jung-sik. Not him again, thought MiJa. Maybe I

can ask to be moved, or he will sit somewhere else tomorrow? She didn't know what to say to him, so she just smiled, blushed, and looked away. At least he looked smart dressed in his school military uniform, and when he sat down, he didn't smell too bad either.

'Settle down, children. Settle down. I am your class teacher, and my name is Yamamoto.' The teacher wrote his name on the blackboard in large Japanese letters.

'When I say good morning class, you will say, good morning, Yamamoto San and bow like this.' He demonstrated how the children should bow to a superior, with the body bent at ninety degrees.

'Now, let's all give it a try. Good morning class.'

The children all stood and said, 'Good morning, Yamamoto san,' and bowed deeply.

'Good, now all sit down and take a long look at the person sitting next to you. They will be your study partner for the entire year.'

Jung-sik gave MiJa a broad smile, and her heart sank.

The teacher scrawled three headings in Japanese characters on the blackboard. 'These are the subjects you will learn this term.' He tapped the first heading and said, 'First, the Japanese language. It is essential to learn the Japanese language to fit into cultured society and find useful work when you leave here. The second topic is Japanese history. You will learn about our common history so that you can understand where our people come from and what makes us special. Finally, you will learn about the Shinto religion. The Shinto priest will teach you directly at the Shinto shrine every Friday. Does anybody have any questions?'

A murmur of excitement filled the classroom, and everybody started talking about visiting a temple.

'Any questions?' asked the teacher. 'No? Good. Then we

will start our first lesson and learn about the Japanese alphabet. Quiet!'

The morning seemed to drag on forever, and MiJa was glad when the bell rang for the lunch break. In the afternoon, they had their first history lesson.

'Does anybody know where our great Emperor came from?' said the teacher.

The class remained silent until MiJa raised her hand and said, 'From Tokyo, sir?'

'That's correct, Yoshiko,' said the teacher straining his eyes to read her name tag. 'That's where he lives now. But where did he come from originally? How was he created?'

Total silence.

'Nobody? Then I will tell you,' said the teacher, and he sat down on the desk and began his story.

'A long time ago, a God called Izanagi took a wife called Izanami, and together they created the islands of Japan. Unfortunately, Izanami died in childbirth and was taken to hell, which the Japanese call Yomi.'

Jung-sik raised his hand, and the teacher said, 'Yes, Ryosuke. What is it'

'Why did she go to hell, sir? What did she do wrong?'

'The Japanese believe that everybody goes to hell. But Yomi is not like the hell you may have heard of. There is has no punishment in Yomi. We believe that there is no punishment in the afterlife for any sin committed on earth.'

The teacher continued with his story. 'Izanagi was greatly upset by this, so he tried to bring his wife back from the underworld, but he failed in this task, and when he got back from hell, he felt dirty and polluted. You see, Yomi is a very grimy and filthy place, a bit like Korea.' The teacher paused for the laughter, but when nothing happened, he continued.

'Whilst washing his eyes and nose, he created three gods. From his left eye, he washed out Amaterasu, the sun goddess, and she illuminated the whole of heaven. From his right eye, he washed out Tsukuyomi, the moon god. And from his nose sprang Susanoo, the god of storms and the sea.'

'Ugh,' groaned the class in unison.

'All was not well in the kingdom. As I am sure you know already, brothers are jealous of their sisters and fight all the time. The constant bickering tried the patience of Izanagi, so he banished Susanoo from heaven. But before Susanoo left, he paid a visit to his sister, Amaterasu, and set her a challenge. Each would take a possession of the others and make something from it. Whoever made the best thing would win. Amaterasu made three women from Susanoo's sword, and Susanoo made five men from Amaterasu's necklace. Amaterasu claimed that the men were hers because they were made from her necklace, and since men are superior to women, she had won the contest. From that moment on, all her children would rule Japan until the end of time.'

'Is that why you have a sun on your flag?' asked MiJa. 'To represent Amaterasu?'

'That is correct, Yoshiko. But it is *our* flag. Korea is part of the Japanese Empire.' The teacher explained that Emperor Hirohito is directly descended from the Sun God, Amaterasu, and the Emperor rules according to her wishes. Anybody who challenges him will be struck dead by the sun goddess.

When the school bell rang to mark the end of the day, the children formed their marching column and paired off with their study partners. Jung-sik was surprised when MiJa asked, 'What do you want to be when you grow up?'

Jung-sik thought about it for a while and said, 'I don't know. I haven't thought about it. Maybe an emperor.'

MiJa started laughing. 'He was made from snot, wasn't he?'

The two set off on a giggle fit and, after a while, MiJa told him her Korean name.

'Well, MiJa. What do you want to be when you grow up?'

'That's why I want to go to school. So, I can find out what I want to do. I want to be smart like my sister. Girls just seem to get married and have children, but I want to be somebody.'

'My father says Japan is a great country,' said Jung-sik. 'He said Korea will be great too, one day. What do you think?'

'I don't know,' said MiJa, and she shrugged her shoulders. 'But I will ask my sister, Mi-soon. She knows everything.'

CHAPTER 4

MI-SOON

MiJa found her sister squatting on the floor in front of a traditional cob oven made from mud and straw, shaped like four mini-igloos melted together. A large black iron cauldron was set into the top of each one so that only the top third protruded. Mi-soon was placing kindling wood into the arches, underneath.

'What are you doing, Elder Sister? Where are the servants?'

'Oh good, you're back.' Mi-soon's eyes grew as wide as saucers, and her dilated pupils were flecked with the flickering orange from the fire. 'Word arrived that Father will be home tonight. I've sent the servants away because I want to cook his favourite meal.'

'Can I help?'

'Yes. In fact, I've been waiting for you to come home. I have got just the job for you.'

She led MiJa to a shady corner of the courtyard and handed her a bamboo pole that was at least twice as tall as MiJa. A net was attached to one end.

'Which one?' asked MiJa.

'How about the ohgolgae?' said Mi-soon and she pointed

to a large, black chicken that had puffed up its feathers in annoyance at their intrusion.

'I don't know,' said MiJa. 'It looks a bit fierce. Let's pick another one.'

'No. I want that one,' said Mi-soon

'Why that one?'

'Because we use that type of chicken for special occasions ... and it's also the biggest ... and it's also the tastiest.'

'Let's get it,' said MiJa.

'Here's the plan. I'll wave my arms up and down like this,' said Mi-soon and demonstrated the movement. 'When we corner the chicken against the fence, *all* you have to do is catch it in the net. Got it?'

'Yes,' said MiJa, but she didn't feel too confident. 'I don't like the way it's looking at me.'

Mi-soon laughed, pushed her little sister into the coop first, and shut the gate behind her.

Any onlooker that day would have been amazed to see two young Korean girls, one dressed in school uniform and the other dressed in traditional dress, chase an angry black chicken all over the coop. The chickens scattered everywhere, and the air filled with clucks and squawks, screams and shouts, angry feathers and flying limbs. The taller girl ran around like a crazy woman, waving her arms in the air, whilst the smaller one swung an unwieldy net through the air as though she was trying to catch butterflies. Once, the girls had it cornered, but the smaller girl was too slow with the net, and there was an angry exchange of words. Then, the taller girl stumbled into a pothole and fell over. The younger one tripped over her, and both got entangled in the net. Eventually, by chance or poultry fatigue, they netted the ohgolgae.

'I've got it! I've got it!' shrieked MiJa, and when everything quietened down, she said, 'What do we do now?'

'I'm not sure,' said Mi-soon. 'When we take it out of the net, you hold its legs, and I'll hold its head.'

'Hurry up,' said MiJa. 'Its claws are sharp.' She hated the scaly roughness of its legs and its violent struggles to free itself.

'Hold on tight.'

'I am. I am,' said MiJa, and she looked away and screwed her eyes tightly so that she didn't have to look. But her ears were open to every squawk and every crack of the neck bones. The chicken twitched for a while, but a few moments later it went limp in her hands, and she opened her eyes with relief. 'That wasn't so bad, was it?'

Mi-soon was speechless and just stared at her sister. She didn't want to let MiJa see her gut and pluck the chicken, so she sent her to get the key for the storeroom. Ownership of the storeroom key was one of the few powers entrusted to a woman in a male-dominated Confucian society and was passed down the generations, as precious as any heirloom. Their mother hid the key, but Mi-soon knew that she kept it in her jewellery box.

When MiJa returned, she stared at the naked chicken perched on the table. 'Ugh. Its skin is black too. Has it gone bad?'

'Oh, no. That is the way it is. Its bones are black as well.'

'I don't believe you. You're fibbing.'

'I'm not. You wait and see.'

'Did you get the key?'

'No. Mother wants a list of the ingredients you want to take from the storeroom,' said MiJa.

Their father's favourite dinner was samgyetang: poached chicken with ginseng and medicinal herbs. Mi-soon wrote out the list of ingredients she needed for the recipe and said under her breath, 'I don't know why she wants this. She can't even read.' She handed the list to MiJa, 'Give this to Mother.'

'Why do I have to do all the running about?'

'Because I am nearly fourteen and you are only eight, but before you go, you can help me with the lid.' They could not lift the heavy cast-iron lid, so they slid it aside. The escaping steam stung their faces, and they instinctively pulled them away with a jerk of the head.

When MiJa returned with the key, her sister was ladling boiling water onto the chicken skin and removing the last of the stubborn feather shafts with a pair of heavy-duty tweezers.

'Some girls use these to pull the hairs out of their eyebrows,' said Mi-soon.

'I don't believe you. You're lying,' said MiJa with a bewildered look on her face. She tugged on her eyebrow hair. 'It hurts.'

'It's true. I read all about it in *Brand New Woman* magazine. They do it to make themselves look beautiful.'

MiJa laughed. 'You're crazy. I'm not ever going to do that.' She pulled on her eyebrows again. 'It hurts, a lot.'

'I'll try it on you,' said Mi-soon and snapped the tweezers open and closed in front of MiJa's face.

'I'll tell.'

Mi-soon stuck her tongue out, handed her sister a large bowl, and said, 'Right, Little Sister. Let's go and get what we need.'

The storeroom was the size of a small grocery store. Mi-soon unlocked the door, and the girls entered silently and tried to think only pure thoughts as though they were entering a cathedral. The room was crammed full of tables that bowed with the weight of the fresh produce piled on top, enormous earthenware containers full of rice, and cupboards stuffed with every available exotic ingredient. Mi-soon went over to a collection of wooden boxes labelled with their vintages. She found one marked *Ten Years* and removed the layer of damp moss from the top. An earthly aroma of freshly dug soil, dampened by fresh April showers, filled the air.

'Do you know what this is?' said Mi-soon. She held up a large, gnarled root, still caked in its original soil.

MiJa snorted in disgust. 'Ginseng. I'm not stupid. Father grows it.'

Mi-soon put some ginseng roots into the bowl, and they moved over to a lacquered Chinese medicine box that smelled like an apothecary's shop. She opened one of the drawers. 'How about this?'

'I don't know,' said MiJa.

Mi-soon smiled. 'Really? I am surprised because it's written on the front of the door.'

'Yes, in Chinese.'

Mi-soon smiled. 'It's called astragalus, and it boosts your energy levels, just like ginger.' She added the astragalus, a stem of knobbly ginger root, and a choice piece of liquorice root to the bowl. 'To cleanse the blood,' she explained.

'It smells like medicine,' said MiJa.

'That's because it is, but over time people have learned to like the taste of the medicine.'

They moved over to a bank of shelves stacked with earthenware ginger jars, and Mi-soon foraged for the dried fruits she needed. 'These help you to sleep,' she said and added jujube and goji berries to the bowl, handling each ingredient as though it was a priceless holy relic.

'I need ginkgo fruit too,' said Mi-soon. 'Ah, here it is.' She removed the lid from the jar and sniffed it. 'Yuk. Disgusting.' She handed the jar to her sister. 'Here, what do you think?'

'It smells like the poo hut in the back garden,' said MiJa. 'I don't want any if you're going to put that in.'

'I think it has gone bad, so we'll leave it out,' said Mi-soon, not realising that it was the natural aroma of fresh ginkgo fruit.

'The bowl's getting heavy,' said MiJa. 'Have we got everything?'

'Nearly. Ah, here is what I was looking for.' She put a prickly branch with a bulbous head and a stem full of evil-looking thorns into the bowl.

'What is that for?' asked MiJa.

'To scare away ghosts.'

'I have never seen a ghost.'

'It proves it works then, doesn't it?' Mi-soon added some garlic cloves, sweet rice and dried chestnuts to MiJa's bowl. 'That's it,' said Mi-soon. 'Just let me check the list one more time ... Oh, I nearly missed something. Don't worry, it's not heavy.'

'What is it?'

'A magic ingredient.' Mi-soon opened another cupboard and brought out a packet. 'This is very expensive and has magic powers.'

'Magic?'

'Yes, magic. And precious.'

'What is it?' asked MiJa again.

Mi-soon read from the packet, 'Mono. Sodium. Gluta-mate. The cook said it makes everything taste better.'

'It must be magic, with a name like that. I can't even say it.'

'That's why everybody calls it MSG.'

When they got back to the kitchen, Mi-soon washed the sweet rice to remove any small stones. Then she stuffed it into the chicken cavity along with some dried chestnuts, and tied its legs up with strong cotton thread. She put the chicken into the pot with the other ingredients and made sure that its head and feet were fully submerged in the liquid. Mi-soon showed her sister how to regulate the oven heat by adding more kindling sticks, and they both squatted in front of the ovens and let the warm glow from the fire slowly spread across their faces.

'How was school?' asked Mi-soon.

'Survived, so far.'

'Well, that's a start. I think short hair suits you.'

'I like it because I look like you. I've got a Japanese name too,' said MiJa and pointed to her name badge on her uniform. 'It says, Yoshiko.'

'Yes, I know. I can read Japanese.'

'What's your Japanese name?'

'I don't have one.'

'Why not?' asked MiJa.

'When I went to school, I had a Korean teacher and he refused to give us Japanese names. One day he disappeared and was replaced by a Japanese teacher and I haven't been back since. But before he left, he gave me something. Something precious.'

'More precious than MSG?'

'Far more.'

'What? What is it? Tell me,' said MiJa and tugged on her sister's skirt.

'I'll tell you later. I might even show it to you at bedtime.'

'I can't wait that long. Tell me. Please.'

'Give me a hand with this lid,' said Mi-soon, and they slid the lid aside, taking care not to get steam-cleaned this time, and the delicious aroma of stewed chicken and medicinal herbs filled the kitchen. Mi-soon scooped the scum off the top of the stew and checked the seasoning.

'Did you make any friends?' asked Mi-soon.

'Not yet. I've only just started.'

'Who are you sat next to?'

'Jung-sik.'

'A boy!' Mi-soon stared at her sister and made a scandalous face.

'I know,' said MiJa, 'and it looks like I will be stuck with him all year.'

The sisters chatted for the next two hours. MiJa told her

sister all about the emperor-God who lived in Japan, the headmaster's speech, her teacher, what the other children were like and about her upcoming visit to the Shinto shrine. Mi-soon listened patiently and regulated the heat of the fire so that the liquid barely simmered because she didn't want to make the chicken tough. Their timing was perfect because when the samgyetang was ready, they heard the head servant announce their father's return.

CHAPTER 5

A KOREAN HISTORY LESSON

'Welcome home, father! Welcome home!' shouted the girls as they rushed towards him and clung to his legs. Gil-soo put his arms around his daughters and tried to suppress his anger. They had lopped off the beautiful, silky braids of his youngest daughter and dressed her in the drab school uniform, identical to all the other children. He recalled when the same thing had happened to Mi-soon, and it was like picking a freshly-healed scab.

'It's good to be back. I missed you both,' he said in a cracked voice that betrayed his hatred for the Japanese.

'We have a surprise for you,' said Mi-soon trying to hide her concerns. Her father had only been away for one week, but she was shocked by how much he had aged. The iron-grey hair on his temples looked even thinner, his face was deeply wrinkled, and the skin had lost its suppleness and hung loose with a sickly sallow hue.

'Oh, what is it?' asked Gil-soo.

'You must be hungry after your long journey,' said Mi-soon.

'We made your dinner,' said MiJa, stealing her elder sister's thunder.

Mi-soon carried the small serving table laid out with the bowl of samgyetang, a selection of side dishes, a silver spoon, and a pair of silver chopsticks. MiJa followed behind, carrying a smaller table, set with a bottle of Sapporo beer that had been cooling on ice, an empty tumbler and a bottle opener. The bottle tottered and tinkled against the empty glass with every hesitant step. MiJa opened the bottle and poured it into the glass. She handed it to her father, taking care to use both hands and bowed deeply. Her father looked at the glass full of beer foam and laughed. It was good to be home.

Bok-nam surveyed the food. 'Is that all there is? It took you all day...' She didn't finish the sentence, her husband's scowl silenced her.

'We made your favourite,' said Mi-soon.

'Thank you very much, girls. It looks and smells wonderful. Are you sure you cooked it all by yourselves? Without any help from the servants?'

'We even killed the chicken,' said MiJa.

'What brave girls you are,' said their father and wondered how it had come to this. His daughters shouldn't be butchering animals. That was a job for the lower classes. Times had changed, and not always for the better. 'Thank you, girls, but please leave the killing of animals to the servants next time.'

'Please eat, Father. Before it gets cold,' said Mi-soon. 'It will help you recover your strength after your long journey.'

'I'm sure it will, but there is rather a lot here, so why don't we share it?'

Bok-nam smiled.

'But we made it for *you*, Father.'

'I know, I know, but wouldn't it be lovely to eat dinner together? Besides, I want to catch up on all the gossip.'

Gil-soo spooned portions of stew into four serving bowls and, for a while, they ate in steamy, contented silence. The meat fell away from the bones like hot butter, and the fatty broth was delicious, healing and nutritious.

MiJa pulled the flesh off the bone with her chopsticks and dipped it into a small dish filled with rock salt and toasted sesame seeds. She was surprised: her sister had been telling the truth about the chicken's bones – they were black.

'My name is Yoshiko,' she said, as she smoothed her name badge on her uniform.

'Do you like your Japanese name?' asked her father.

MiJa nodded her head.

'Why is that?'

'Because it is longer than MiJa. I can write it in Japanese characters already. Shall I show you? I can count to ten in Japanese too. Ichi, Ni ...'

MiJa talked all through dinner until finally their father pushed his bowl away and said, 'Thank you, girls. That was the best samgyetang I have ever tasted.'

Mi-soon smiled.

Bok-nam frowned.

MiJa said, 'Can we open our presents now?'

'Who said I had brought you presents?'

'You always bring us presents when you visit Kyungsong,' said MiJa. 'Me first. Me first.'

Their father handed a present to each of his daughters. MiJa removed the lid on hers and gasped at the pink, patent-leather Mary-Jane shoes inside.

'Do you like them?' asked her father.

'Oh, thank you, Father. I love them. Can I wear them for school tomorrow? Please?' She put them on and strutted around the room, holding her foot at different angles so she could see the different views. 'Do you like them, Elder Sister?'

'They're gorgeous,' said Mi-soon.

'And they have got straps, so they won't fall off when I'm running,' said MiJa.

'Do you like your gift, Mi-soon?' asked her father.

Mi-soon nodded her head and choked back her tears. 'They're beautiful,' she said. She was thrilled to receive her first shoes with kitten heels and wondered if she could walk in them. She was dying to find out, but she was much too mature now to prance about the room like her little sister.

'You are a young lady now, so I thought you should have something appropriate.'

'Thank you, Father. I will cherish them.'

The other boxes contained Swiss chocolates and English butter biscuits.

'They're to share,' said their father. 'Do you think you can do that?'

'Of course,' said MiJa, knowing full well that her sister would let her have the lion's share.

Bok-nam was anxious to know what happened at the meeting with the land agent, so she suddenly announced, 'It is getting late. And MiJa, you must get up early tomorrow and go to school. Time for bed, girls.'

'Aw, do we have to?' asked MiJa.

'Yes. Now. And no backchat.'

The sisters lay on top of a thin mattress called a yo. It was about two inches thick and stuffed with cotton wool. A blue silk sheet had been laid on top, folded back over the edges, and stitched into place to create a silk border. Their blanket was a thinner version of the yo but covered with cream silk cloth, embroidered with purple orchids and grey-crowned cranes. The girls were silent, enjoying their chocolates and shortbread until MiJa pulled the blanket up to her chin. A pair of kitten-heeled shoes and a pair of pink Mary-Janes hung over the edge of the yo. They both laughed. Mi-soon rummaged around under the yo and pulled out a dog-eared book.

'This is it,' she said. 'The secret I told you about.'

'That's it?' said MiJa, not even trying to conceal her disappointment.

Mi-soon opened the book as though it was a priceless manuscript. 'It was written by a Korean professor and used in all the schools, but now it's banned. If the Japanese ever found me with this, they would kill me.'

MiJa sat up. It was starting to get interesting. 'Really? What's in it?'

'The truth,' said Mi-soon.

Her little sister looked at her and rolled her eyes. 'Will you read some of it to me?'

'No, I don't think I should.'

'Pl-eeease. Pl-eeease.'

'Well, maybe just one story, then,' said Mi-soon and she flicked through the pages until she found what she was looking for: 'For hundreds of years, the Japanese had been sending fleets of fierce pirates, known as Waegu, to raid the Korean coast and capture the men and women. They took them back to Japan to work as slaves or teach the Japanese how to make Korean pottery.

'In the 1590s, Japan got a new Daimyo. His name was Hideyoshi, and he was greatly feared and managed to unite all the warring factions. By 1592, the whole of Japan was at peace, and the Samurai warriors had nothing to do. Hideyoshi feared an uprising, so he sent the Samurai warriors to Korea and told them to kill as many people as possible.

'This Hideyoshi was intelligent, and he didn't trust his soldiers, so he ordered them to bring back the head of everybody they killed as evidence.'

MiJa slid under the blanket and pulled it tight to her body for protection.

'Are you alright?' said Mi-soon. 'Do you want me to continue?'

'Yes, I'm just a bit cold. Carry on. What happened next?'

Her sister continued, 'The Samurai had taken so many heads that they wouldn't fit into the ships, so guess what they did?'

MiJa shrugged her shoulders.

'They cut off their noses and ears as proof.'

'Is that true?'

'It is. They still have shrines full of Korean ears and noses, and they worship at them.'

'Really?'

'Hush,' said Mi-soon. She could hear their parents arguing.

'What are they saying?' said MiJa.

'Be quiet,' said Mi-soon. She put an index finger on MiJa's lips and whispered, 'Hush. I want to listen.'

'It had better be a son this time. When I die, I don't want these Japanese fuckers stealing all my possessions because I don't have a legitimate heir. We have owned these ancestral lands for as long as anyone can remember, and I am not going to be the one that loses them.'

'How did the meetings go?'

'It was a complete waste of time, just as I expected. The head spokesman for the landowners is a Japanese ass-kisser just like the Kim family in the next estate.'

'Keep your voice down. The children will hear you. I think MiJa is in the same class as Kim's son, Jung-sik.'

Their father continued in inaudible hushed murmurs until his anger got the better of him, and his volume increased again. 'They're sending an Agricultural Officer to survey the land and the tax rate is going up to sixty per cent unless we sign the land over to them, then it's only ten per cent. I don't see how we can make ends meet.'

There was silence for a while until their mother said, 'Maybe we should sell the land to the Japanese and pay the ten per cent rate.'

'What to those thieves and brigands? Never. I would never betray my ancestors. My land has been handed down generation after generation through the male lineage. I'm the nineteenth generation. They have even taken my name plaque from the gate. The bastards.'

'I'm scared. I mean, look what the Japanese did to my family,' said Bok-nam.

'I won't be the one that lets the family down. Curse that son-of-a-bitch Prime Minister Lee Wan-yong. He handed over the country to the Japanese, and for what? A Japanese lordship. He'll get his comeuppance, mark my word. Him and all the other Japanese collaborators that infest the police, the civil service, and the army.'

'What are they talking about?' asked MiJa.

'Oh, it's nothing,' said Mi-soon. 'Go to your room and sleep now.'

'Can I stay a little longer?'

'No. Go to your room.'

'But I'm not tired,' said MiJa, rubbing her knuckles into her eyes. 'I'll go after another story?'

Mi-soon sighed. 'Just one more, then, but after that, you have to go.' She lit a fresh candle, retrieved her history book from under the yo, flicked through the pages, and began. 'Queen Min was the wife of the twenty-sixth King of Korea. As Queen, she was expected to keep the peace amongst the King's concubines, host parties and set the fashion for the court ladies. But Queen Min was different: she wasn't interested in those kinds of things. She decided to educate herself, so she studied the sciences and politics and started to take an interest in her husband's duties as King.

'When Japan won the war with China, it started telling the King of Korea what to do. He was weak and always did what the Japanese wanted, but Queen Min was not. She wanted to modernise Korea and use Western technology and ideas, so she invited a team of Russian diplomats to come to Korea to give her advice. The Japanese didn't like that one bit, so they sent a group of ronin to kill her —'

'What's a ronin?' asked MiJa.

'A samurai warrior without a master. The ronin bribed the Korean guards and gained access to the Queen's chambers. The ronin dragged Queen Min and her four servants by their hair. Then they raped them and cut them into pieces with their swords so that their bodies would never be found.'

'What's rape?' asked MiJa.

'You don't need to know. You're too young,' said Mi-soon. 'But it's really bad. After that, they burnt Queen Min's body and spread the ashes in a nearby wood. All they ever found of her remains was one small finger bone.' Mi-soon held up a crooked little finger. 'Like this.'

'Why didn't the King have the guards and ronin executed.'

'He ran away, like a coward. Then the Japanese burnt down the Royal Palace.'

'Is that it?'

'For tonight. Go to *your* room now.'

MiJa shook her head. 'I'm scared. Can I sleep here with you, Elder Sister?'

Mi-soon sighed. 'Only for this one night,' she said and blew out the candle.

MiJa stared up at the ceiling and tried to go to sleep, but it was impossible. She was too scared, and once or twice she thought she heard the crunch of a footstep on the gravel outside. She saw shadows slip stealthily behind the paper screen windows, but she told herself it was only her imagination. She edged closer to her sister and moulded herself around her warm body and tried to think about something distracting. She thought about wearing her new shoes tomorrow and the visit to the Shinto shrine, but nothing seemed to work.

Her head was swimming with questions. Why was what she had learned at school different from what her sister had told her? Who should she believe? Her sister wouldn't lie to her, but neither would her teacher. It was all so confusing. Why didn't everyone tell the truth? Then an idea formed in her mind. When they visited the Shinto shrine in the morning, she would ask the priest because a priest wouldn't lie, would he?

CHAPTER 6

THE SHINTO SHRINE

A large torii gate, carved from wood so gnarled and ancient that it looked older than time, marked the entrance to the Shinto shrine. MiJa thought it looked like a giant bird perch, and she scanned the sky and the treetops, half expecting a huge phoenix to sweep down and perch on top of the gate.

She was still panting from the strenuous trek up the mountainside. The resinous tang of the pine forest had caught in her throat, and she needed a drink. The gurgling sound of a nearby mountain brook sharpened her thirst, and she imagined the icy cold water flowing over the cool riverbed pebbles and onto her tongue. She threw a small rock at Jung-sik, and when it hit him on the back of the head, she looked the other way, towards the Shinto shrine.

The shrine was a sleepy wooden structure. Debarked tree stumps painted ochre red and carved with Japanese characters supported a roof of cedar shingles that had tarnished to the colour of ancient pewter. It gave the overall appearance that it had magically sprouted straight out of the fertile earth, grown organically, and slumbered for centuries. In the dappled light of the forest, it was difficult to tell which was shrine and which was jungle.

Something disturbed the bamboo wind charms that hung from the eaves, and their eerie hollow knocking sound announced the arrival of two men. The eldest was the strangest looking man MiJa had ever seen. She nudged Jung-sik to get his attention, but he was already under his spell.

The man looked older than the mountains, as though he had been made from the bits of wood and rock that God had leftover when he created the earth. His face was the colour and texture of old tree bark, and a thin, dry wispy beard drooped from his chin like a piece of old lichen drained of all its colour and vitality. A baggy tunic hung from his skeletal frame, covered his grey baggy trousers and came down to a pair of shiny black platform clogs. On his head he wore a conical hat.

He looked like he had stepped straight from the pages of a Chinese mythology book, and the children watched every tottering step as if enchanted by a magical spell. They watched him make his way down the pock-marked granite steps, supported by his assistant, and in his hand he held his badge of office — a wooden mace called a shaku that resembled a giant, wooden shoehorn.

The morning sun backlit him and created an aureole around his entire body that made him seem otherworldly, and when he stretched out his arms to welcome the children, he revealed armholes that drooped so low that a wizard would have been proud of them. When he addressed the children, they believed God himself was speaking.

'Welcome, children,' he said. 'I am the Kannushi for this Shinto shrine, and I will teach the lesson today. But before you can enter the Shinto shrine, you have to follow a strict purification ritual. My assistant will show you what to do. Watch him and repeat everything he does because we don't want to upset the Kami spirits that live here, do we?' He turned to leave, and the children watched him melt back into the depths of the shady shrine, his platform clogs click-clacking on the stone steps. They were left wondering if what they had just seen was real.

His assistant led the class to a small, thatched pavilion that contained a rough stone trough full of cool, clear water. An ingenious contraption of bamboo pipes and guttering had been lashed together with vines to divert the mountain rill. The assistant took one of the bamboo ladles that hung from the rafters and dipped it into the trough. He poured the water over his left hand, transferred the dipper to his left hand, and poured the water over his right, then he filled that hand with water, rinsed his mouth and spat it on the floor.

'Now it's your turn,' he said. 'Do not let the ladle touch any part of your unwashed body.' He handed MiJa the dipper and sat on a nearby log to watch the children perform the purifying ritual.

MiJa plunged the dipper into the water and washed her hands as shown and took a mouthful of water. She was startled at the sight of a water dragon carved into one of the rafters and swallowed the water.

'I've swallowed the water by mistake,' said MiJa and repeated the ritual. She took another drink to quench her thirst. When the entire class had completed the purifying ritual, the assistant led them over to the torii gate.

'When we walk through the gate, we will leave the world of people and enter the world of the Kami, the spirit world.' He made a delicate bow and walked under the gate. 'Be sure to keep to the outside. The central path is reserved only for the Kami.'

When MiJa crossed the threshold, she noticed it was significantly colder. A chill ran up her spine, and the foisty smell of decaying wood, mushrooms and damp soil from mouldering graves replaced the freshness of the pine forest.

The assistant led the class up a short flight of wooden steps, slimy with moss and rotted by time and wood-boring insects. Ferns and creepers jutted out of the natural fissures between the rocks of the low limestone wall that surrounded the temple, and two stone mythical lions guarded the entrance with faces ugly enough to scare off any evil spirits that might be lurking nearby.

The assistant demonstrated how to worship Emperor Hirohito at the shrine.

MiJa nudged Jung-sik. 'Can you see any?' she asked.

'Any what?'

'Kami.'

'Shut up, or you will get us into trouble,' said Jung-sik.

'Yoshiko. Pay attention,' said the assistant. 'You can go next.'

MiJa walked up to the shrine and peered inside. She expected to see a god, or at least the figure of a god, but there was nothing. Only a set of dusty shelves that contained some old, gnarled pine branches and an assortment of small rocks assembled into cairns. MiJa doubted that any of the relics housed any spirits.

She pulled on the bell with both hands, to get the attention of the spirit world. Then she bowed deeply to greet the spirits, clapped her hands twice and made her prayer. She wondered what to pray for and whispered: 'I am MiJa from Mun-gyeong.' She wanted the gods to know who she was and where she lived so that there could be no mistake in granting wishes. 'I would like a baby brother. A brother, not another sister because I have got one of those already.' Then she bowed deeply to say goodbye to the spirits and went to join the other children.

At lunchtime, she joined Jung-sik in a pool of cool shadow that was cast by a tall clump of verdant bamboo. They ate in silence and laughed at tiger-stripe shadows that fell on their faces until MiJa said, 'What did you ask for?'

'Ask for? When?'

'At the temple.'

'I don't think you're supposed to ask for anything. You're supposed to worship the Emperor.'

'What's the point of having a god if you can't ask for things?' said MiJa. 'I asked for a baby brother.'

'A baby brother?'

'I've already got a sister.' Then she said, 'Can you keep a secret?'

'Yes. Of course,' he said, raising both eyebrows in surprise that she'd confide in him.

'Somebody I know has a book. I can't tell you who, but she's not supposed to have it. It's a Korean history book, and it's banned. If they find out about it. They will kill her.'

'If who find out?'

'The Japanese,' she whispered and covered her mouth with her hand.

'You had better keep it a secret then.'

'Do you think the Japanese are here to help us?'

'My father says they are.'

'My sister says they aren't. I'm going to ask the priest.'

'I want to ask a question too,' said Jung-sik. 'I want to know why we pray to a Japanese god? I think Koreans should pray to a Korean god.'

'I'll ask first,' said MiJa.

After lunch, the Kannushi returned, and all the children stood and gave him a deep bow. He sat on the top step and looked down on them.

'Please be seated,' said the priest. 'There's plenty of room at the front. Don't be afraid. I won't hurt you.'

Jung-sik and MiJa made their way to the front so he could hear their questions. They were so close to him now that they could smell him. He smelled like the shrine: of mud and old hemp rope that had rotted away in a garden shed for far too long.

'Does anybody know what Shinto means?' said the priest. Without bothering to wait for an answer, continued, 'It means, the Way of the Gods.'

The children remained silent, still bewitched by the mythological priest.

'Shinto tells us how we should live our lives. I like to think of it as a three-legged stool. The three legs are called Kami, Creation and Purification. If you remove just one of these legs, the stool will fall over.'

The children laughed at the image.

'Hush. It is no laughing matter,' said the priest. 'The first leg is Kami. Take a good look around you, children. At the stones. The water. The trees. Everything that you can see contains a spirit. You and I also contain the Kami, but it is strongest in the Japanese people.'

'The second leg of Shinto is Creation. Your teacher taught you how the Emperor was created as a living god yesterday. You must worship Emperor Hirohito at every opportunity you get, and the best place to do that is here.'

MiJa raised her hand to ask a question, but Jung-sik pulled it down.

'Not yet,' he whispered.

The priest continued: 'The third leg of Shinto is Purification. You know how to purify yourself before entering the shrine. You must not enter the shrine with impure thoughts.' The old man smiled, 'Shinto is as simple as that. Any questions?'

MiJa and Jung-sik raised their hands at the same time.

'Yes,' said the priest and pointed to Jung-sik. 'What is it?'

'Why don't we pray to a Korean god?'

The priest frowned, and Jung-sik thinking that the priest

didn't understand his question, elaborated. 'We are in Korea, so why do we have to pray to a Japanese god?'

'It is a simple matter. A question of faith. You can choose to believe what I tell you, or *I* can make you believe,' said the priest.

Still puzzled, Jung-sik said, 'How?'

The priest beckoned his assistant and whispered something in his ear. The assistant walked over to the bamboo clump, cut a thin culm of green bamboo, the thickness of his finger and the length of his arm. He dragged Jung-sik to the top of the steps and made him face the shrine.

'Roll your trousers up and hold them up,' said the Kannushi.

Jung-sik heard the thin bamboo swatch whip through the air with a crack. He flinched and glanced nervously behind him.

'Keep still and fix your eyes on the shrine,' said the priest.

Jung-sik waited for the pain to come, but it didn't. He heard the bamboo slicing through the air at least two times, but he didn't dare turn around. The anticipation was unbearable, but eventually he felt the cane bite into his bare calves, and he yelped out, lost his balance, and fell off the step. He furiously rubbed the back of his legs to try and take the sting away.

'Get back onto the step,' said the priest, 'and stop snivelling like a girl. We will clean those impure thoughts from your mind. Keep holding your trousers up. I won't tell you again.'

The fourth stroke was another deliberate miss, and Jung-sik flinched his shoulders when he heard the bamboo slice through the air. The waft of air stung his red-raw legs, and the anticipation of waiting for the next stroke was agony.

'Keep still. Eyes front,' said the priest. The next stroke bit Jung-sik's calves, followed by a loud thwack. He tried his hardest not to cry in front of the class but could not stop the flow of hot tears as they ran down his cheeks and dripped onto the steps. He could taste the salt in his mouth and began to sob heavily.

MiJa could see angry red welts raised in relief on his skinny legs, and a trickle of blood ran down his right leg and soaked into his sock. She was temporarily dumbstruck with the horror of it, but then snapped out of it and ran over to the shrine and began to frantically ringing the bell as loud as she could. Everybody was now staring at her. She bowed twice, clapped her hands twice, and made a prayer. When she saw that the priest had stopped delivering his punishment, she stopped.

'What the hell do you think you are you doing?' said the priest, purple with effort and rage.

'I wanted to tell the great Japanese Emperor God not to look. I thought he would be angry watching this happen at his shrine.' She bowed her head towards the ground, held her breath, and awaited her punishment. It never came. The Kannushi's rage had subsided, and he threw the bloody bamboo cane onto the floor and dismissed the class.

The walk home was long and slow. Jung-sik found it hard to walk and, even though MiJa had strapped his backpack to her front and put an arm around his waist to help him stand, the pair fell even further behind the marching column until they were alone.

'I have to stop for a rest,' he said.

MiJa lowered him onto a rock at the side of the road. She removed both backpacks and said, 'Hold on, I am going to look for some medicine,' and disappeared into the lush vegetation growing by the roadside.

She returned a few minutes later, accompanied by the aroma of freshly-cut vegetation, and fingernails stained green with plant matter. In her hand, she clutched a fistful of wilted herbs. 'I could only get the small ones,' she said. 'It's still too early for the good stuff.'

'What is it?' asked Jung-sik.

'Mugwort,' said MiJa. 'It will help ease the pain.' She pounded the leaves on a rock to release the active ingredient and spread the herbal poultice onto his bloody calves.

'Ouch.'

'I know, I know. It stings, doesn't it? That means it's working.'

She pulled up his socks to hold the poultice in place, but they wouldn't stay up, so she ripped one of the ribbons from her school blouse and tied up his socks with it.

'Can you walk?' said MiJa. 'We must get going. It will be dark soon.'

'I'll try,' said Jung-sik. MiJa helped him to his feet, put both backpacks on, and put her arm around the small of his back, and they hobbled off.

After a while, she said to him, 'I'm glad the priest chose you first.'

'Why?'

'It could have been me.'

Jung-sik laughed at her honesty. I think I'll let you ask first next time. Tell me something, why did you start ringing the bell?'

'I prayed to the great Emperor Hirohito that the priest would stop beating you.'

'You believe in the Japanese Emperor god?'

MiJa laughed. 'It worked, didn't it?'

'Yeah. I suppose so,' he said and smiled.

When they were nearly home, dusk had fallen, and an eerie flickering, orange glow hung over the town.

CHAPTER 7

THE SCHOOLTEACHER

The Presbyterian Church of Korea clung precariously to the side of a limestone crag that overlooked the Great Northern Road. It was a plain church for plain people with freshly painted wooden clapboard cladding, a louvred bell tower and a tall steeple surmounted by a large wooden cross. A recently repaired cedar-shingled roof had faded in the sun until it complemented the colour of the limestone crag and lent the church an air of belonging; it didn't.

Inside the vestry the Reverend Han was adding the finishing flourishes to his sermon. Recently there had been a noticeable surge in his flock and he was expecting a full house tonight. He wasn't stupid or vain enough to believe that the congregation came to Evensong for his sermons; they came for the free food or to protest at being forced to worship State-sponsored Shinto. It was the same story all over Korea; the church had become a hotbed for the Korean Nationalist movement.

He stepped outside because he liked to watch his flock arrive and personally greet each member. 'Good evening Mr and Mrs Park. It's lovely to see you both again, and you have brought all your wonderful children? How many is that now?'

'We have been blessed with six, Reverend.'

'Wonderful, wonderful, the more the merrier,' said the reverend and recalled how much they had eaten last week. 'The Lee family, isn't it? It's so good to see you all again. Welcome. Welcome.' All three generations had turned up this week. As he shepherded the last of his flock into the safety of his church, he felt like somebody was missing and he racked his brain until it came to him. It was usual for a member of the local police force to be present — their job was to count the collection and make sure the majority went to the Japanese — but he gave the matter no further thought and swung the heavy oak door behind him.

The inside of the church was spartan. A row of naked electric lightbulbs hung on long pendants from the dusty open rafters. They swayed in sympathy with the disturbed air as the Reverend walked the well-trodden oak floor, between the regimented rows of plain oak pews stained dark by sweat and patina. There was no unnecessary church paraphernalia — no icons, no stained-glass windows, no brass ornaments, no relics, no stone statues, not even any prayer books — there was no need. This congregation knew their scripture by heart.

The murmur of the congregation fell silent as the Reverend took up his position behind the lectern and said, 'Please be seated. Let us pray.' The mumble of prayer filled the church as the congregation's hopes, thoughts and wishes floated heavenward towards the rafters.

'Amen,' said the congregation.

'Amen,' said the Reverend. 'Hallelujah, may God be with us and guide us through this service. Our first hymn this evening will be Psalm 23, The Lord Is My Shepherd.' He glanced over to the dusty old organ with a wheezing bellow and nodded to a dusty old organist, with wheezing lungs, who brought the contraption to life. The hymn filled the church:

The Lord is my shepherd; I shall not want.
He maketh me to lie down in green pastures:
He leadeth me beside the still waters.
He restoreth my soul:
He leadeth me in the paths of righteousness for his name's sake.

Outside, the Chief of Police gave a hand signal, and a truck advanced and pulled up a short distance from the church. Two officers jumped down from the tailgate and crept into the shadows, taking care to avoid the soft pools of tungsten light that soaked the ground under the windows. They threaded a heavy chain through the iron hoop handles on the church door and padlocked it. Then they unscrewed the caps on their jerrycans, doused the wooden building with fuel, and waited.

Inside, the congregation was oblivious to what was happening and continued with their hymn.

Yea, though I walk through the valley of the shadow of death,
I will fear no evil: for thou art with me;
Thy rod and thy staff they comfort me.
Thou preparest a table before me in the presence of mine
enemies:
Thou anointest my head with oil; my cup runneth over.
Surely goodness and mercy shall follow me all the days of my
life:
and I will dwell in the house of the Lord forever.

At the allotted time, the police sergeant gave the hand signal. Zippo lighters sparked in the dark, followed by a flash of light and the rush of air as a giant fireball engulfed the church. The fire spread quickly, fuelled by the dry timbers, and the steeple acted like a chimney and drew more air into the raging inferno. The paint began to blister, and thick black smoke seeped out of the gaps between the wooden clapboards. The police officers surrounded the church and raised their rifles in readiness.

Inside the church, the panic spread even faster than the fire. The doors rattled and banged as the families hammered on them, trying desperately to escape. 'It's locked,' somebody screamed, followed by, 'We're trapped.' There was more screaming and pleas of, 'Let us out! Let us out!' Then more hammering on the door. 'Please, please,' somebody begged.

The Reverend shouted to make himself heard over the chaos. 'Don't panic. Everybody remain calm.' Nobody was listening, and some of the congregation picked up the pews to use as battering rams, but the doors held firm. The roof space started to fill with smoke and crept downwards like a blanket of death. It edged steadily downwards, and some of the younger children succumbed to the heat and fumes and lay, unconscious or dead, in the arms of their parents. The Reverend Han kneeled beside them, clutching their hands, and reciting the Lord's Prayer. The fire took a firm hold on the infrastructure, and time was running out. Somebody yelled, 'The windows, break the windows.' Some brave men fought their way through the choking smoke and stood on the stacked pews to break the windows. Fresh air rushed in from the outside and into the hungry maw of the insatiable inferno. The fire raged upwards, taking the low-level smoke with it, and temporarily clearing the way. It was their last chance, and the men tried to lift the women and children to safety, but the heat was so intense it burned their sensitive nasal passages, blurred their vision, and shrivelled their ears as the skin contracted. Some of the women and children miraculously managed to make it to the window ledge and were on the verge of escaping but were thrown back by a hail of bullets. Finally, the screaming stopped, and an eerie black silence fell over the church.

Two men emerged from the shadows and moved into the light cast by the sickly orange glow from the fire. One of them casually lit a cigarette and offered another to his colleague.

'Do you believe in God?' said the Colonel.

'I believe in worshipping Emperor Hirohito,' said Mr Song and put the cigarette in his mouth, unlit.

The Colonel studied Song's face. 'No, I mean this Christian God. Do you believe in Him?'

Song lit his cigarette and thought for a moment before replying. He knew that this was the final test, and he must pass to advance his career. The Colonel had brought him here to witness the butchering of his people. Innocent people. It was a price he was willing to pay; he didn't want to remain an elementary schoolteacher for the rest of his life.

'This Christian God didn't even save his son, did he, so how can he be a true god?' said Song. 'This white American God is nothing but a fake. He is a foreigner, and we can't have foreigners interfering in the running of our country. I think we both know that the true God sits on the Chrysanthemum Throne in Tokyo.'

The Colonel smiled and flicked his cigarette away. 'I think we understand each other. I have managed to get you enrolled at Changchun Military Academy in Manchuria.'

'Thank you, sir. You won't regret it.'

'I know. I recognise ambition when I see it. A man like you can make a name for himself in Manchuria.' The Colonel knew that such ruthless, ambitious men like Song were useful idiots and easy to control.

Song was delighted. When he was eighteen, he had started his teacher training and soon realised that he had made a mistake. He hated the school. He hated the pupils. Most of all, he hated the countryside. The never-ending rice fields. The mud. The thatched hovels, and especially the farm labourers that lived in them. They were a constant reminder to him of how backwards Korea was. He was stuck in a remote backwater with no future and longed to get back to the city and civilisation. He had always believed he was destined for better things. Then, one day he met the Colonel, a military attaché, whose role was to scour the schools for suitable officer cadets for the Imperial Japanese Army. Song grabbed his chance with both hands and nurtured their friendship. He wanted to drag his country into the twentieth century and modernise Korea just like Japan had done under the Meiji Emperor, and nobody was going to stop him. So what if he had to kowtow to a few Japanese assholes along the way? All the months of kissing the Colonel's ass, learning the ropes, and trying to determine which way the political winds were blowing had finally paid off. He would be an officer in the Imperial Japanese Army and had got his foot on the first rung of his career ladder, and who knew where that would lead? All he had to do now was give the end-of-term speech at the school. After that, he would change his Korean name to a Japanese one, become a fully-fledged soldier in the Imperial Japanese

Army, and swear an oath of allegiance to Emperor Hirohito. Only time would tell whether his chosen path would lead to glory or the grave.

CHAPTER 8

THE BUSHIDO CODE

The late afternoon sun beat down from the heavens like a pressing weight, and a hazy vapour of hot air shimmered and hung lazily above the cracked, hard-baked earth. The children were restless. Every child was impatient for the summer break to start, and their heads were full of the dreams of summer: the long hot endless days, of fishing and swimming in the cooling riffles of the river, and a few animated their thoughts and had already started to make a paddling action with their legs. But first, they had to endure the agony of the end-of-term speech.

They had assembled in the schoolyard in military squares, with the form teacher standing at the head of each square. All eyes were on the central staging, where the headmaster languished in the deep shade of a canvas awning with the guest speaker. It seemed to take forever, but eventually the headmaster approached the podium and pressed the loudhailer to his mouth.

'Attention,' he said. 'Today, I would like to invite our guest speaker, Mr Song, to say a few words. He has an important message for all of you, so please listen carefully.'

He handed the loudhailer to Mr Song, who gripped the podium with his left hand, raised the loudhailer to his mouth, and squeezed the trigger. An ear-splitting high-pitched screech forced the children to cover their ears. Mr Song shrugged his shoulders and looked at the loudhailer as though it had deliberately conspired against him. He pressed the trigger again and cleared his throat a few times for good measure.

'I would like to thank the headmaster for allowing me to speak today,' he began. 'As I am sure you all know, it is only through the generosity and wisdom of our great Emperor in Japan that you attend this school, free of charge.'

A patter of applause rippled through the pool of children, and Mr Song basked in the limelight and let the clapping die down before continuing. 'How should we live our lives? Once again, we should look to the Japanese for the answer. Look how much they have achieved in such a short time. How did they manage it? I believe the answer lies in the Bushido code. The Bushido code was developed a long time ago by the ancient Samurai warriors. Bushido means the Way of the Warrior.' He paused. Some of the children had started to fidget, shifting their weight from one leg to the other.

MiJa whispered to Jung-sik out of the corner of her mouth, without moving her head, 'I thought we were supposed to live the Shinto way: the Way of the Gods, now it's the Way of the Warrior. I wish they would make their minds up.'

'I am not asking any more questions,' said Jung-sik, and they couldn't suppress a giggle, even though their form teacher told them to shut up with silent, threatening eyes.

Mr Song continued in a louder voice. 'There are seven Bushido virtues, as follows: loyalty, courage, compassion, respect, honour, integrity and honesty. What do I mean by loyalty? A warrior must always be loyal to his master, just as we must always be loyal to the emperor, but loyalty is also a friend that stays true to you, even when you are not there.'

He took a sip of water.

'It is obvious, I hope, that a warrior must have the courage to face his enemies, but courage does not only apply to warriors. There is no point hiding from life like a turtle in its shell. You must overcome your fears and emerge from your shells. Compassion means being kind to others —.'

One of the girls fainted and fell in a heap on the ground, and the form teacher gently slapped her face until she woke. He propped her back into place and ordered her study partner to support her and make sure she did not fall over again. Mr Song's face contorted and reflected the bitter taste in his throat; he made a mental note to weed out the weak. 'Respect means that you must always consider the feelings of others, especially your elders. A person has honour if they always do what they believe. A person has integrity when he always does the correct thing, even when nobody is watching, and last but not least, we have honesty. You must always be honest, especially to yourself. Does anybody have any questions?'

Everybody remained silent, anxious to start their holidays.

'If you work hard in your lessons and follow the Bushido code, you will become a good citizen and serve the Japanese Empire well.'

After a few moments of contemplation, the headmaster led a round of applause and declared the school closed for the summer holidays, to a great cheer.

The children dawdled home along the Great North Road, discussing everything they would do in the holidays. They made the same grand plans every year, and none of them ever came to fruition. Some of the poorer children looked glum and wished they could stay at school: they would have to help their parents with their chores for the entire vacation.

'What is wrong, MiJa?' said Jung-sik. 'You are so quiet.'

'Oh, nothing. I was just thinking about what Mr Song said in his speech.'

Some of the boys had cut bamboo canes about an inch thick and three feet long from the roadside verges and were busy play-fighting with their makeshift katanas. One of the boys ambushed, MiJa. 'I am going be a samurai warrior when I grow up.' He shouted, 'Koshi,' and landed a two-handed blow to her ribs followed by a direct hit to the top of the head with a shout of 'Atama,' to confirm the target.

'Stop it. Stop it!' said MiJa. 'I haven't got a weapon.'

'You can't have a weapon. You can't be a samurai warrior,' said her assailant. 'You're just a girl, and girls can't be warriors. I bet you can't even fight.'

'I can, and I will fight you if you want,' said MiJa. 'When I grow up, I will be a braver warrior than you.'

'My father says that girls are good for nothing,' said her assailant. 'Girls are not even strong enough to work in the fields. That's why nobody wants to have a daughter.'

'That's not true,' said MiJa. 'Is it, Jung-sik?'

'Boys are better at everything,' said her assailant.

MiJa started to get angry. 'No, they're not.'

'Well, name one thing, just one thing, that girls are better at?'

A group had gathered around MiJa and Jung-sik to see what all the commotion was about and started chanting, 'Fight, fight, fight.'

MiJa looked at the girls for help, and one of them whispered, 'Maybe, cooking.'

MiJa sighed, 'Having babies,' she said, and immediately regretted it.

'You can't argue with that,' said Jung-sik.

'Is that all? Boys are much more important,' said her assailant. 'If a father doesn't have a son, the family name dies.'

'That's true,' said Jung-sik.

'Bushido is not just about fighting,' said MiJa. 'I can have loyalty and courage .... even as a girl.'

That seemed to end the argument, and the crowd wandered off. A few moments later, Jung-sik cut some bamboo swords from the roadside. 'Take this,' he said to MiJa. 'In case they try to ambush us again. We will be ready next time.' They caught up with the group of boys ten minutes later, but they had thrown their swords aside and had formed a line on a high embankment. They were pissing into the bushes, seeing who could get it the furthest.

'You can't even do this,' shouted one of the boys, and they all laughed.

CHAPTER 9

THE AGRICULTURAL OFFICER

The agricultural officer for the Mun-gyeong district arrived at the Choi family home in late summer 1935. He was a slender Japanese man, seemingly constructed from mainly skin and bone with a bit of piss and vinegar thrown in for good measure. A few wispy strands of facial hair hung limply from his angular face, and he had too many teeth crammed into too small a mouth. He leaned back in the rattan chair and sucked on his cigarette, pulling his cheeks deeper into his skull, gazing at the world through his thick round spectacles like a startled goldfish. He checked his wristwatch for the umpteenth time and said to his Korean land agent, 'Go and see if you can find him. I haven't got all day.'

The Korean agent found Gil-soo in his living quarters, bowed respectfully and said, 'The agricultural officer is waiting for you in the reception hall.'

'Yes, I know, I know,' said Gil-soo. His servant had already informed him that they had arrived, but he had decided to keep them waiting.

'Could I have a word first?' asked the agent.

Gil-soon frowned. He hated dealing with odious syco-phants: it was a well-known fact that the agent, even though he was Korean, represented the Japanese first and foremost and would sell his own wife, daughters and grandmother for the right price. It was also well-known that his hand emptied directly into the hand of the agricultural officer, and he scraped a living from the crumbs that stuck to his tacky palms. He ignored him.

'I might be able to help,' said the agent.

'I doubt it,' said Gil-soo, turning to gaze at him directly.

'The Japanese plan to build a new road that will pass through your land. I may be able to persuade him to —.'

'How much are they offering?' asked Gil-soo. This was news to him. He thought they were here to record the land acreage and assess the taxes.

'Sir, may I suggest that you give them the land, free, as a goodwill gesture? After all, the land they need for the road is poor agricultural land.'

'Never.'

'If you cooperate, I could ask for a reduction in your taxes. I may be able to negotiate a reduction from sixty per cent down to ten per cent. I could smooth the way with a little offering. It won't be much, just a token gesture.'

Gil-soo held up his hand, and the conversation was over; he wasn't going to offer this dog a bone. 'Take me to your Japanese master.'

The reception hall resembled a large gazebo: open on all sides, with a roof supported by eight columns. Gil-soo could see that the agricultural officer was slouched back in his chair, smoking a cigarette, and he checked his anger.

'Sorry, I am late, but I had some *important* business to attend to first,' said Gil-soo as he entered the reception hall and sat in a chair opposite the officer.

'Fine weather this year,' said the agricultural officer, not bothering to get out of his seat. He tapped out another cigarette from his pocket and put it in his mouth, unlit.

Gil-soo was offended by his social ignorance and arrogance. So, it is going to be like that. He called for his female head servant, 'Unyeon.'

His eldest daughter, Mi-soon, appeared a few moments later. 'Yes, Father?' she said.

'Where is Unyeon?' said her startled father.

'I don't know, Father. Is there anything *I* can get you?'

'Could you bring two glasses of water, please?'

The officer lit his cigarette and kept his eyes fixed on Gil-soo. 'It looks like we will have a good harvest this year,' he said, in an excitable high-pitched voice that reminded Gil-soo of a mouse that had just got a whiff of fresh cheese.

'If you are referring to the weather, then yes, it has been good. We were blessed with a long warm summer and enough rain to prevent the rice fields from drying out. The weather has been good ... so far,' said Gil-soo.

'I expect it will be a bumper crop,' said the officer.

Gil-soo knew that a bumper crop would mean bumper taxes and that the Japanese would take the majority and ship it to the Japanese mainland. 'We haven't brought in the harvest yet, and who knows what the future will bring? We could get hit by a typhoon, like the one that hit Japan recently.'

The officer shuffled in his seat as if it was suddenly too hot for comfort.

Gil-soo continued, 'The last typhoon made a direct hit on Japan and ruined their harvest, I believe.' He snapped open his fan with a loud *chack* and fanned himself, making sure that the officer could see his Korean family name and motif embroidered in gold on the red silk fabric. 'Then there are the losses due to pestilence. You know what pests are like: they breed like crazy when food is abundant and fill their greedy bellies with food that isn't theirs.'

The officer stubbed out his cigarette with harsh, jagged movements as though trying to stab the ashtray. He was about to launch into a tirade when he was interrupted by Mi-soon sashaying up the stairs with two glasses of water balanced on a tray. She served the officer first and wondered why her father didn't like him: to serve plain water to a guest was an insult.

The officer watched Mi-soon's every move, the way a snake watches a mouse. When she leaned over to place the glass onto the table, a gap opened in the V-neckline of her jacket and revealed the silhouetted form of her breasts. The officer smiled at her, and his pulse quickened. He tracked her movements as she walked over to her father. 'You have a beautiful daughter. How old is she?'

'Fourteen,' said Gil-soo and immediately regretted dignifying his question with a reply. Gil-soo thanked his daughter and dismissed her. He took a drink from his glass and noticed a slender willow leaf floating in it. He got the message. His daughter had placed it there on purpose, and its meaning was clear. He should not gulp his water but sip it gently. Stay calm. Stay in control. 'Tell me, why are you here? What is it you want from me?'

'Why haven't you changed your name to a Japanese one yet? The officials in Tokyo are becoming very annoyed. I will give you some free advice: it is in your best interest because soon it will not be possible to own any land, or even work, without a Japanese name.'

'Or even go to school,' said Gil-soo.

'Have you even thought about choosing a Japanese family name?'

'How about Hirohito?' said Gil-soo, deliberately picking the same name as the Japanese Emperor. He smiled when he saw the anger break the calm surface of the Japanese officer's face.

'Enough of these games.' The officer slapped down a sheaf

of documents onto the table and placed a pen on top. 'You will sign this.'

'What is it?'

'A compulsory land sale order. The Emperor needs a small portion of your land to build his new road.'

'How much are you offering?'

'Nothing. It is an enforced land order. For the good of the Empire.' The officer smiled.

'I won't sign it,' said Gil-soo and pushed the papers back towards the officer.

'We will see about that,' said the officer and pushed the papers back towards him. 'I am also here to assess your taxes. The charge this year will be sixty per cent.'

'Don't you think you steal too much from us?'

The agricultural officer laughed and leaned forward. 'You can't steal from yourself. All this land belongs to Japan now, and you cannot complain. We are not so different from you, Choi Gil-soo. The Yangban have stolen from the poor for years. Those days are over. We are in charge now. Understand?' He leaned back in his chair and flashed him a nicotine-stained smile. 'You would only have to pay ten per cent tax if you sign the document.'

Gil-soo stood up, snapped his fan closed, and whacked it on the table. 'Damn mosquitoes. We need to crush them. They spread disease everywhere and don't even care whose blood they suck, as long as they have a full belly.'

The agricultural officer flinched in his chair, and his eyes grew large behind his jam-jar-bottom glasses as he focussed on the table, trying in vain to search for the squashed insect. There was nothing there, so he lit another cigarette and watched the smoke spiral upwards. 'I will give you three days to think about it. After that, I will return to collect the tax payment *and* the signed land transfer papers.'

Gil-soo watched the agricultural officer leave with the

Korean agent. They were arguing about something. Probably about the agent not getting his bribe money. Gil-soo smiled, but his thoughts soon turned to his own problems. He didn't have any choice in the matter. The Japanese would eventually bleed him dry, and he cursed the spineless Korean politicians and the other Yangban who would not stand up to them. He thought about his unborn child. If he was blessed with a son this time, he could not bear to tell him that he had squandered his inheritance. After nineteen generations, he wasn't going to be the one that lost the family land. He would pay the tax to buy more time and hold on to his land for as long as he could. He would borrow the money from a distant relative in Kyong-sung. There was no time to lose. He ordered Dol-soi to pack their bags, and that afternoon Gil-soo and Dol-soi set off for the capital. But he did one more thing before he left. He fixed a new name plaque onto his gatepost.

CHAPTER 10

THE BIRTH

Later, in the wee small hours of the morning, the whole household was jolted awake by the sound of Bok-nam screaming. An ear-splitting cry of 'Unyeon! Unyeon!' echoed around the house. It was soon followed by shouts of, 'Get in here. Hurry up. It's time.'

MiJa arrived first on the scene, peered into the room, pinched her nose at the strong smell of urine, and gawped. The head servant was running around the room like a headless chicken, and her mother had kicked off her covers and was laid on a wet stained yo.

A few moments later, Mi-soon poked her head around the door and said, 'What's all the commotion? Oh my God. What is happening?'

'Mi-soon do you know where the Halmum lives?' yelled the Unyeon.

Mi-soon nodded her head.

'Well, go and fetch her, and be quick about it.'

She returned an hour later, carrying a heavy, beaten-up leather bag slung across her shoulder. Hobbling behind her was a wizened old prune of a grandmother, clutching a long gnarly blackthorn walking stick that looked like an extension of her arm. She was clucking away to herself, sucking in the air across her crusted lips and a ragged mouth of gums, and she wore eyeglasses that were too large for her, so she had to keep shoving them back up her nose with her free hand.

The whole town referred to the woman as the Halmum or midwife, but she had no medical qualifications of any sort. What she did have, however, was lots of experience. She had given birth to eight of her own children and had successfully delivered hundreds of healthy babies into the world; nobody had bothered to keep a tally of the unhealthy ones.

'We need more light, she said. 'Bring more oil lamps and get plenty of water on the boil.' She directed the servants to bring lots of fresh towels and sheets.

'Hurry up, Halmum. It's coming,' said Bok-nam with panted breaths.

The midwife lifted Bok-nam's nightclothes to check her dilation and smiled. 'Not yet, dear. Not yet. You should know by now. It is not your first time. Mi-soon, please bring my bag over here.'

The Halmum rummaged in her bag and removed a small cast iron bowl and the largest pair of scissors that Mi-soon had ever seen. She tried the action of the shears in the air, and Mi-soon's eyes widened at the metallic snip-snip sound of the thick broad blades.

'What are those for?'

The midwife laughed. 'To sever the cord.'

She handed Mi-soon the cast iron bowl and told her to get the servants to fill it with hot charcoal from the kitchen. The servants returned five minutes later with the bowl full of red-hot glowing charcoal. The midwife inserted the scissors onto the glowing embers of charcoal and said to Mi-soon, 'Give me a hand with these sheets. Roll two of them lengthways and tie them up there.' She pointed to the rafters that overhung the bed. 'Let them drape down so your mother can grab onto each end.'

Mi-soon watched her mother wrap the ends of each sheet around each of her forearms and grip the loose ends tightly in her fists. She could see the fear in her eyes.

The midwife put a gag into Bok-nam's mouth and tied it at the back of her neck.

'Is that so she doesn't bite her tongue?' asked Mi-soon.

'Yes,' said the midwife, and whispered under her breath, 'and to shut her up.'

The servants brought bowls of boiling water and bundles of clean towels, and in all the commotion, nobody noticed that MiJa had slipped into the corner of the room. She had no intention of leaving; she wasn't going to miss any of the action.

'How often are the contractions?' asked the midwife. 'Eh? Eh? I can't hear her. What did she say, Mi-soon?'

Mi-soon undid the gag a little.

'I. Don't. Know. But. He. Is. Coming.' said Bok-nam between shallow pants. Beads of sweat formed on her brow, and Mi-soon mopped them up with a facecloth.

The midwife checked the dilation and could see the head crowning. She said to the servants, 'Tighten the gag so she can't spit it out and grab her feet. Mi-soon dismissed one of the servants and said, 'I'll hold this one.'

'Don't push. Give your body time to adjust,' said the midwife.

Bok-nam let out a groan. The contractions were too powerful, and the urge to push was irresistible. She pushed. The sheets bit into her forearms, and the rafters groaned in sympathy. Sensitive skin began to tear, and the room filled with muffled screams and profanities that the sisters had not heard before, but neither of them could bring themselves to look away.

If anybody had bothered to glance into a small corner of the room, they would have seen the blood drain from MiJa's face until it matched the colour of freshly laundered sheets. She felt nauseous with the smell of blood and promised herself she would never have a baby.

The midwife did her best to help ease the baby into the world. She could see a bloody mess of matted, black hair. 'Don't push,' she screamed. 'Do you hear me? Don't push. The umbilical cord is wrapped around its neck. Do — Not — Push.'

Bok-nam nodded and took shallow breaths to control her contractions. She gripped the sheets, and her white bony knuckles glistened under a thin layer of sweaty, transparent skin.

The midwife quickly untangled the cord from around the baby's neck and wiped the blood and guts from her hands that left a bloody smear on the towel. 'You can push again,' she said. By now, Bok-nam had no choice in the matter, and suddenly she let out a huge groan, and the baby plopped onto the mat with a loud squelch.

MiJa held her breath and stared. She was wide-eyed, not daring to blink, in case she missed anything. Her mouth was bone dry. There was something wrong. This baby had a blueish tinge to its skin and was streaked with blood and shit. Its face was covered with a thin veil of white skin that looked like snot, and it was silent. MiJa knew that babies always cried. And then she saw something that shocked her even more: attached to its stomach was the writhing bloody snake that was pulsating as though it was alive. She wanted to vomit and could taste the bitter bile in her mouth. She held her nostrils to block the nauseating smell of urine, shit, sweat and blood. She gagged and swallowed the bitter pre-vomit bile that filled her mouth. She wanted to leave the room, but it was too late: her legs wouldn't move.

The midwife picked up the scissors and dipped the cutting blades into the heat of the charcoal bowl for a few seconds, then she grabbed the writhing snake and cut through it. MiJa jolted her head backwards as a spurt of hot blood shot across the room. The midwife tied the cord and removed the caul membrane that had formed a veil over its face. She wrapped the baby in a towel and rubbed some life into it, slapped its bottom until it started bawling its lungs out, and handed it to the mother.

'Is it a boy? Is it a boy?' asked Bok-nam.

The midwife just smiled and said, 'I think the Choi family name will live on for a while.'

'I have a brother,' said Mi-soon with a big grin on her face.

MiJa was about to slip out of the room before she was noticed but then realised that the show wasn't over. Her attention was riveted on the midwife again as she grabbed the bloody snake protruding from her mother and started pulling on it gently.

'Tell me when you have your next contraction,' said the midwife.

'Now,' panted the mother, and the midwife pulled on the cord and out popped an organ, the size of a brick and the same deep red colour, but this one was dripping in blood and mucus. The midwife gave the afterbirth to the head servant and told her to wash it and clean it. Later, she would put it in the jar she had brought with her for that purpose and bury it one auspicious day to ensure a long life for the new-born.

Before passing out Bok-nam said, 'Don't forget to hang the golden rope at the entrance to the house. I want the whole world to know that I have a son.'

It was 15th August, 1935.

CHAPTER 11

THE GOLDEN ROPE

The journey to Kyongsung normally took two days but it seemed to get longer with each visit, thought Gil-soo. The shortest route to the capital was to cross the mountains on foot and catch the train at Jumchon station but, with each passing year, the hills got a little steeper, the ground a little harder and his breath a little shorter. His lungs gasped, and his heart pounded, and his thigh muscles quivered on the ascents. His knees creaked on the descents and, even though it was mid-summer, the mountain air still had a bite to it and the wind ploughed furrows into his face. His skin felt clammy and cold, and he ignored the tightening in his chest: it was the altitude or the rarefied air in the Sobaek Mountains, he told himself, or perhaps it was simply indigestion. His host had been insistent, and he had felt obliged to overindulge in his last night in the capital; it would have been rude not to.

His host was also from Yangban stock but had sold his ancestral lands to the Japanese and invested his money in a business importing foreign goods. He never seemed short of cash and had willingly lent him the money. Maybe he should do the same? He would need to have a series of good harvests to pay the loan back. All he had achieved was delay the inevitable, but at least it was over until next year. His mood darkened when he considered his options. Once you have solved one problem, you forget all about it and move on to the next one. That's life, he thought. The problems seemed to grow more numerous and more complex with age and an image of a clear spring day flashed into his mind as though it were only yesterday.

He was young and full of hope for the future. It was the first of March, and he was demonstrating in Pagoda Park against Japanese rule. He could hear Chung Jae-yong's voice reading aloud the Korean Declaration of Independence, and it still rang true after all these years. Where had the time gone? Would Korea ever get its independence back? He didn't think he would see it in his lifetime. He was too old now, but at least the journey was nearly at an end. He snapped out of his daydreaming and wondered if anything had changed during his week of absence.

'Not long now, Dol-soi.'

His servant, who was walking a respectable number of steps behind him, was out of breath too, so he just nodded. When the house finally came into view, Gil-soo suddenly stopped in his tracks. Some movement had caught his eye. He must be seeing things, so he waited until his servant caught up with him. 'Do you see that?' said Gil-soo and pointed to his house with a trembling finger.

'I don't see anything, sir.'

'Right there,' said Gil-soo. 'Right there! Are you blind?' He guided his servant's eyes to something fluttering above the gate and said, 'It looks like ... No, it can't be?' He had already started to run.

'Wait for me,' said the servant.

When they got nearer, Gil-soo said, 'It is. Look. Can it be

true? Tell me I am not dreaming.' He fell to his knees and started laughing, 'Tell me, I'm not seeing things.'

'You're not,' said the servant. 'I can see it too. Congratulations, sir.'

A simple rope was hanging above his gate, made from braided rice stalks with a left-hand twist, and woven into it were dried red chilli peppers, pieces of charcoal and small twigs of needly pine. The red chilli peppers represented the penis, the charcoal was there to kill any germs, and the spiky pine needles discouraged any evil spirits that might be lurking nearby.

Gil-soo stared at it intensely, as if he had never seen anything like it before. It could only mean one thing. He had a son. He sprinted into the house, still not daring to believe that such a dream could come true. He burst into his wife's living quarters. She was asleep with the baby at her side, so he crept forwards in his stocking feet and gently removed the covers. He loosened the baby's clothing to make sure it was a son. It was true. He had a son. He fell to his knees and stared up to the heavens with his hands clasped together in prayer. He prayed to his father's ancestral spirit until his eyes welled up and overflowed with hot tears that ran down his cheeks. He whispered, 'Thank you, Father. Thank you.'

'What do you mean by showing up at my house at a time like this?' Gil-soo yelled at the agricultural officer and his Korean agent. Every Korean knew that the golden rope festooned over the gate signalled a new birth and that nobody was allowed to visit the house for twenty-one days to avoid passing on any infections to the new-born. 'Didn't you see the golden rope? You are not supposed to visit.'

'I have no time for these primitive superstitions. We are

living in the twentieth century now. You know why I am here. Do you have the money?'

Gil-soo threw the envelope on the floor, 'Here take it and leave,' he said.

The agricultural officer instructed the agent to pick up the envelope and count the money. 'It's all there,' said the agent, with an astonished look.

The officer raised an eyebrow, 'The land transfer deeds?'

'I will not sign them. You will leave now. But before you go, I want you to know one thing.'

'Oh, and what's that?' said the officer.

'You will never have my land. I have a son now, and he will inherit everything I have.'

The agricultural officer pocketed the envelope and smiled. He issued Gil-soo a writ and said, 'The Emperor has confiscated your land, and the construction of the road will begin in one month.'

CHAPTER 12

THE FORTUNE TELLER

15 AUGUST 1936

Gil-soo picked up a photograph of his son and fondly recalled the trip to the photographic studio, the only one in the town, on 23 November 1935, the exact day his son was one hundred days old: an auspicious day in the lives of all Korean children. His son had been posed in a wicker chair, completely naked, like a fat, wrinkled toad, with his legs akimbo so all the world could see that he had a son. Gil-soo's chest heaved with pride as he looked at his Little Buddha, and he dabbed a tear from his eye with his sleeve. He had fulfilled his first duty to his ancestors: he had produced a strong son that would carry the Choi name into the next generation, and today was a special day. It was Choi Yung-soo's first birthday party.

Gil-soo had risen early to collect the choicest fruit from his land. He chose only ripe unblemished fruit: Asian pears, apples, watermelons, and the small hard yellow melons unique to Korea. They had been neatly stacked in piles on the table, along with towers of Swiss and Belgian chocolates. In the centre of the table was a rainbow cake made from layers of glutinous rice and sugar, each layer a different colour. Gil-soo

sat at the head table with his wife by his side and his son
cradled in his arms. His son was wearing the regalia of a mini-
Mongol emperor: baggy silk trousers and a navy-blue waist-
coat, embroidered in gold brocade. On his head, he wore a
black silk bandana secured with a silk scarf. He had to look the
part because today, he had a life-affirming job to perform. He
would determine his fate.

They were expecting more than a hundred guests, so they
had enlisted a small army of farmwives to do the cooking.
They stood guard over the makeshift kitchen that had been
assembled in the open, adjacent to the regular kitchen. MiJa
watched one of the farmwives wipe the sweat from her brow
and scoop a batch of Korean pancakes from the giant frying
pan she had made by turning the cast-iron domed lid of a cauldron upside down. The cloying smell of hot pig fat sizzled and
spat in the cast iron pans and saturated the air, adding to the
heat of the day. MiJa tore a ragged piece from the crispy edge
of the pancake and popped it in her mouth.

'Wait. You will burn yourself.'

'But, it smells so good,' said MiJa, blowing in and out to
try and cool down her mouth.

'Well, how is it?'

MiJa savoured the pancake, made with strips of beef, leeks
and mushrooms and said, 'It's my favourite. Can I have some
more?'

The farm wife shooed her away, so she moved to the next
cooking stall. She had been visiting each one in turn and had
counted ten different types of pancakes so far. Whichever she
tried last was her favourite. She had tried pancakes made from
fish, squid, wild garlic, minced pork and other ingredients she
couldn't even identify. She had even visited Mi-soon in the
house kitchen and tried the fried fish and the galbi: a beef stew
made from short ribs.

The first guests arrived at about ten o'clock, and Dol-soi

accompanied them to the reception hall and presented them to Bok-nam, as she had instructed. A farm labourer with a wife and two small children in tow handed Bok-nam a small red envelope with gold writing on it. He bowed and said, 'Thank you so much for inviting us, and congratulations on having such a beautiful son, Ma'am.' He was surprised to have been invited, and it was a struggle to get enough cash together for the gift.

'Thank you,' said Bok-nam. She took the envelope and put it on the table. She knew that the cash in the envelope would not cover the cost of their food and drink and could not understand why her husband had even bothered to invite them. She directed Dol-soi to seat them on mats at the rear of the grounds, as far as possible from the reception hall and open to all the elements. The area where the poor, the unwashed and the unwelcome were seated.

A Yangban-class family arrived next. They made their salutations, complimented Bok-nam on having a fine son, and presented her with a handsome gold ring. Bok-nam placed the gold ring in the palm of her hand, weighed it carefully, and placed it on the display table. They must have fallen on hard times, she thought. So sad, but that wasn't her problem. She instructed Dol-soi to guide them outside to sit with the labourers to teach them a lesson. She hoped she would have more luck with the next family. They certainly looked wealthier.

The husband was wearing baggy trousers, tied at the legs, a long, over-jacket, fastened with a sash, and a tall black felt hat. His wife wore her hair up, secured with an elaborate hairpin made from red fire coral, the latest fashion from the capital. Hanging from her waist on silken threads were trinkets made from semi-precious stones, corals, and jade. The daughters bowed, and their dresses rustled and billowed in a cloud of topaz blue and lime green. This is more like it, thought Bok-nam.

'Congratulations on a fine son,' said the husband and turned to Gil-soo. 'You must be so pleased now that you no longer have to worry about your future, and your ancestors can finally sleep peacefully in their grave.'

Gil-soo laughed and nodded in agreement.

The guest handed Bok-nam a large solid gold figurine of a toad to bring good luck. Bok-nam beamed. She placed the golden toad in her hand and pretended to admire the intricate carving. It must have weighed fifteen don, she thought, about the same weight as a large chicken egg. She gave a slight nod of the head, and Dol-soi seated the guests in the reception hall.

Their neighbours the Kim's arrived next. Bok-nam was shocked by their appearance and did not know where to look. The husband was wearing black and grey striped pants that were a tailored fit, and she could see the shape of his legs. He wore a long black coat with tails at the back, and on his head, he had a tall silk black hat. But most shocking of all was his wife. She was wearing high-heeled shoes, a floral pattern dress that showed most of her legs, and on her head was the biggest floppy hat that Bok-nam had ever seen, adorned with bird-of-paradise feathers. Their son, Jung-sik was wearing the same western-style suit and tie that he wore on his first day of school, but the trouser legs were so short that his socks were showing.

'Hello Jung-sik,' said MiJa. She rushed over with a welcome drink for them as soon as she spotted him.

'Not just now MiJa,' interrupted Bok-nam. 'I am sure that a handsome young boy like Jung-sik doesn't want to be wasting his time with a plain girl like you. Go and serve the other guests.'

'You also have a handsome son now,' said Kim and smiled. 'Please accept our humble gift.' He handed Bok-nam two solid gold figurines: a toad and a turtle. Bok-nam estimated that each must have weighed 50 don as she placed them in the centre of the table. They were clearly doing well, even if they dressed ridiculously. She had been right. They should have cooperated with the Japanese. It was all her stupid husband's fault. The obstinate fool, stuck in the old ways. Bok-nam nodded to her servant, and he escorted the guests to their seat in the reception hall, next to the head table. When all the guests had arrived, Bok-nam nudged her husband to begin the proceedings.

'Thank you all for coming to my son's first birthday party. I know that many of you have left behind important work in the fields to be here, and some have travelled far and wide. I hope you all have a great time, and I would like to thank you for all your most generous gifts ...' When he had finished his speech, it was time for his son to determine his future. He set Yung-soo down on the edge of a woven straw mat in the centre of the reception hall. On top of the straw mat were a collection of objects: a calligraphy brush, a bow and arrow, a spool of thread, a bronze medallion, and a bunch of coins with square holes punched in the centre. Whichever his son chose would determine his future.

Yung-soo stared at all the faces staring at him and froze with stage fright. His face cracked, and his bottom lip quivered as though he was about to cry. His father put him into the crawl position and offered him encouragement with a pat on the bottom, and off he went at breakneck speed towards the objects. His hand hovered over the coins, and Bok-nam smiled. Gil-soo frowned; he wanted his son to select the medallion with a horse imprinted in the centre to secure a government position. Mi-soon wanted her brother to have a career as an academic and hoped Yung-soo would select the calligraphy brush. Whilst MiJa wanted her brother to live an active, outdoor life and wanted him to choose the bow and arrow. Suddenly everybody started shouting out which object they wanted Yung-soo to choose as if they had wagered on it. Yung-soo was startled and lost interest in the money, and he picked up the spool of thread and put it into his mouth. All the guests cheered, and Gil-soo picked up his son and carried him back to the head table.

Maybe that was the best choice, thought Gil-soo. The thread symbolised long life, and the name, Yung-soo meant the same. Not every child made it to their first birthday, and now that his son had, he stood a good chance of living to adulthood, but it had been a close-run thing. He thought about the many sleepless nights he had spent nursing his son. A measles epidemic had hit the town hard and robbed many a family of their sons and daughters. When Yung-soo developed a fever, he had prayed to his ancestors that it was not measles, and in the end, it turned out to be just a regular fever. There was no known way to protect children from disease, and if it wasn't the measles that sealed their fate, there was always whooping cough, pneumonia, and the whole gamut of infectious diseases that silently lay in wait: one in three new-borns died in their first year.

Gil-soo snapped out of his daydreaming and ordered the servants to bring the food. Bok-nam looked down at a bowl of birthday soup and sighed; she hated it. Every Korean mother had to eat it three times a day for the month after their pregnancy to boost their iron content and purify the blood. It was also served on everybody's birthday in celebration. She chased the slippery pieces of kelp around the beefy broth with her spoon, hoping she didn't catch any and sniffed at the broth: it smelled of the sea, at low tide, and tasted like rock pools. After a few minutes, she pushed the bowl away.

MiJa and Mi-soon helped serve the guests ice-cold Sapporo beer and ceramic pots full of jung-jong, a type of Korean wine, served warm. The band started up, and a cacophony of drums filled the air. Dancers flew amongst the guests, wildly gyrating their necks, to send the long ribbons attached to their conical hats swirling through the air, whilst Bok-nam made a careful inspection of each gift on the display table, and she had calculated that they would make a tidy profit.

CHAPTER 13

THE FATE OF EMPERORS

It is said that even the fate of emperors is determined by the weather. The spring of 1937 arrived too early; tender young shoots sprang forth in the rice and barley fields, the fruit trees were full of blossom, and Yung-soo was sprouting up faster than a young bamboo shoot. The omens were good, the weather gods were smiling, but all that was about to change.

One morning the Gil-soo found the head servant slumped in a chair, sobbing. When he asked what had happened, Dol-soi couldn't find the words or the courage to express his feelings. He just shook his head in disbelief and pointed in the direction of the orchards.

Gil-soo was devastated by what he found. An overnight frost had frozen the delicate fruit blossoms, and every last one had fallen to the ground and carpeted the earth in pink and white. A gentle breeze stirred the air and scattered the precious petals to the wind, and Gil-soo cursed as he watched his profit disappear. There would be no fruit this year.

Things went from bad to worse: the rainy season was late. Gil-soo rose with the dawn and scanned the skies for the slightest sign of rain but saw nothing but blue, barren skies. Once his spirits soared when he thought he saw the faintest whisper of a cloud, but it soon evaporated, along with his hope. Dusk till dawn, the servants filled buckets from the stream and hauled them to the cracked fields. It wasn't enough. He cursed the Japanese: they had not even started to build the irrigation canals, even though they had collected the tax for it a long time ago. Eventually, the stream ran dry, and they had to draw water from the well they used for cooking. But even that was not enough to save the crops. July came, but the rains didn't.

It got worse: summer arrived with a fiery vengeance, and the rice paddies dried up and the barley fields baked in the hot sun until the earth lay cracked and broken. Gil-soo even joined the other farmers and kowtowed to the weather gods, but it was no use. The crops slowly withered and died, and the once fertile, black soil turned into barren dust.

The road was the final death-knell. It hadn't taken up much acreage, and the land the Japanese had stolen was poor agricultural soil anyway. The problem was that the road brought a steady stream of trucks, carrying workers and new ideas. It was only natural that people would start to ask questions. Where were all those people going? The Korean agent told them of the steel mills, the hydroelectric power plants and the chemical plants springing up in the north. The agent told them they would earn far more money in a factory than toiling away on the farm for a Yangban master, that times were changing, and nobody wanted to live in the countryside anymore. He told them that everything they could wish for was available in the city, and he could help them get a job in one of the new factories for a small fee. The servants began to trickle away from the land until they became a flood, and more and more farm work needed to be done, with fewer and fewer people.

His distant relative in Kyongsung called in the loan, so Gil-soo sold all the family gold that his children had received as gifts on their first birthdays except for Mi-soon's necklace. Ever since she was big enough to wear it, she had refused to part with it and always wore it hidden under her clothes as a protective amulet. He also sold the family silver, the spoons, and the chopsticks, but when autumn came there still wasn't enough to pay his tax bill. The agricultural officer delighted in telling Gil-soo that the Emperor had confiscated all his land. But it wasn't all bad: as an act of compassion, the Emperor had allowed him to keep a small field so he could grow enough food to feed his family.

Gil-soo had held back some of his money to buy rice — the first time in his life that he had to buy rice — and there were still some dregs of kimchi left in the storage pots. With luck and strict rationing it should last them over the winter period, but when spring arrived they would have no option but to grow all the food they needed to survive.

In the spring, he used the last of his money to buy rice seedlings from the Japanese and for the first time in his life, Gil-soo farmed his land. He learned the hard way where his wealth came from nineteen generations ago. He felt the sting of the rain on his face and the warmth of the sun on his back. He felt the earth under his feet and the rough calluses on his hands.

On the most auspicious day in the farming calendar, Dol-soi showed Gil-soo how to plant the rice seedlings. Mi-soon and MiJa held a taut string line across the flooded field as a straight-line guide.

'Not like that master,' said Dol-soi. 'You must plant the rice seedling vertically, not at an angle.' Dol-soi demonstrated the correct technique, yet again. 'Push it deep into the earth until your wrist is fully submerged.'

MiJa was getting bored holding the string and scraped at

the soil lodged under her chipped fingernails with her index nail on her other hand. 'Can I have a go? This is so boring.'

'If you want to donate your blood to these,' said Dol-soi, and he removed a blood-sucking leech from his leg and threw it towards MiJa.

'I'm fine here,' said MiJa as she looked with disgust at the swollen, black, segmented worm writhing on the ground.

Dol-soi had decided to stay with his master out of loyalty and because he knew nothing else. For as many generations as he could remember, his family had always been head-servants to the Choi dynasty, and it would seem like a betrayal to leave them now. He knew the family would struggle without his help, but he also knew that the land allocated to them was not large enough to feed them all. He had only expected it to last a year, but somehow it had stretched to two, and he had seen his Yangban master and his two daughters work in the fields until they were weather-beaten and bronzed, just like him, and it saddened his heart.

'You are not to visit her anymore. Are you listening to me, Jung-sik?'

'Yes, Mother,' said Jung-sik, but he wasn't listening. He had heard enough already and was sick of his parents constant nagging. They didn't want him associating with MiJa; the Choi family had bad luck, and they didn't want their bad luck rubbing off on him; they should have swallowed their pride and cooperated with the Japanese as they had done. But no matter how many times they told him to stay away, he didn't. Without fail, whenever MiJa was absent from school, Jung-sik went to see her that very evening and go over the school lessons that she had missed.

For MiJa, the farming life was full of excitement and a new adventure, but her fondest memories were of Jung-sik's visits.

When she looked back at those couple of years, the springs were full of hope, the long hot summer days, full of laughter and birdsong, the autumns full of endless green fields as rich as butter, as they slowly turned to gold, and the winters, a time for rest and learning.

But for Mi-soon, the farming life brought only sadness. The years dragged on and she noticed that her father's shadow seemed to grow smaller, fainter and more stooped with each passing season, as though he was bending ever closer to his grave. In the winter of 1940 he became more introverted and forgetful. When she asked what was on his mind, he would give her a faint glimmer of a smile, nod his head, and drift off to some past foreign land.

For Gil-soo, farming represented failure, and the changing seasons reminded him of his life: the spring of his life was all-but-forgotten, a distant land populated by his wandering youth that now seemed like a dream. The summer of his life yielded many bitter fruits, but occasionally he found a sparkling gem, especially when he thought about his children. Autumn arrived with much still too much to do, and then, suddenly before he knew it, winter had him in its clutches. His dreams withered on the vine as the world had moved on and left him behind. It had taken a lifetime to get to know the rules, and then they changed, and he felt like he no longer had a place in this world. The old ways had gone forever, never to return. He tilled the earth and felt like he was digging his grave. He felt so tired. All he had to do was lie down and go to sleep. He fell to his knees.

'Father are you alright?' said Mi-soon as she dropped to her knees beside him and placed her hands on his bony shoulders. She was shocked at how thin and fragile they felt. She held both his hands and stared into his eyes. 'Father, I want you to sell my gold necklace. The one I received for my first birthday. You can use the money to see a doctor.'

Gil-soo hung his head in shame. He could not even support his own family, and yet here was his daughter offering to sell her only possession in the world so that he could see a doctor. And he realised, for the first time in his life, what love was. His life had been empty, and it had taken him this long to find out. He wanted to say so many things to his daughter, but the words clogged in his mind and stuck to his tongue. Instead, he broke down and cried.

CHAPTER 14

A PROCESSION

MiJa trailed a long way behind the procession. Her eyes watered, and the cold, dry air nipped at her extremities and wicked the moisture from her lips until they cracked. She could no longer feel her toes. Her shoes, specially made for the occasion from woven rice stems, had kept her feet warm for the first mile or so, but now they had soaked up the damp and had started to freeze. They crunched under her feet and slipped on the snowy ground, but occasionally a patch of rocky scree or a stray pinecone poked through the surface and gave her some traction up the mountainside.

She hugged her thin burlap dress closer to her body, tightened the thick plaited straw belt, and trudged on, trying to catch up with the rest of her family. Every intake of breath was laboured, and the faint tang of ozone in the mountain air caught in her mouth and filled her lungs. The only thing that broke the silence was muffled sobbing and the rhythmic chant of the shaman.

'E Je Ga-myun. Un Je Oh-na?' *(Now you are going. When will you return?)*

'Aye-go. Aye-go. Aye-go,' wailed the followers. It was the traditional lament, used when plain words were insufficient to express the grief one felt.

On they went, threading their way along the mountainside path that led through a stunted pine forest. Once, they came across a passer-by cutting firewood. He removed his hat, bowed deeply, and watched the funeral procession pass. He wondered if the departing spirit had lived a good life and would return as human again or whether the opposite was true, and he would return as an inferior animal.

The shaman priest led the way and rang a small bell to set the rhythmic gait. Behind him, eight men, dressed in natural un-dyed burlap, swayed under the heavy load and with each plodding step, their hats, shaped like truncated cones, flapped from side to side.

'E Je Ga-myun — Un Je Oh-na.'
'Aye-go — Aye-go — Aye-go.'

Four pallbearers stood on each side of the wooden bier: a raft-like structure made from heavy logs. All had worked for Gil-soo. They supported the weight of the bier with heavy ropes slung over their shoulders. An elaborately decorated coffin sat on the top of the bier. Above it was a white canvas canopy which was decorated with silk flowers and red and blue silk banners, fluttered in the light mountain breeze. Behind them marched the rest of the male mourners, each desperate not to show any emotion. Last of all came the women.

On they went, the pallbearers panting heavily, struggling under the load like beasts of burden with steaming breath and burning muscles. They climbed higher and higher until the trees became sparse and grotesque, shaped by the prevailing winds.

Mi-soon slipped and fell onto the snow, and one of the

male mourners called out for the procession to stop. 'She's fainted. Stand back. Give her some air.'

MiJa ran to her side, 'Elder Sister, wake up,' she said, but there was no response. The family had spent the last five days in mourning. Their mother had fallen into a state of shock at the loss of her husband and couldn't even manage to look after her son, so MiJa cared for her baby brother, whilst Mi-soon was left to make the funeral arrangements. The coffin was placed on a trestle and hidden behind a large, folding screen. In front of the screen stood a console table and on the table was a red lacquered tablet engraved with the name, lineage, title, and generation of the deceased. On either side of the tablet stood a burning candle. On the right of the table was a brass thurible filled with sand and a box of incense sticks. On the left was his last meal. Mi-soon had done her best to prepare the meal but still felt saddened by the meagre offering: a plain bowl of steamed rice, with a spoon, stuck vertically into it, and a side dish of kimchi. A pair of chopsticks bridged the two to guide the spirit through the meal. The only fresh fruit she could find was apples and pears, and she had laid the red apples on the east and white pears on the west of the table, as tradition demanded.

The family had received mourners from far and wide, and Mi-soon had prepared food for them all. When the mourners arrived, Dol-soi would escort them to Gil-soo's room. Bok-nam, Mi-soon, MiJa and Yung-soo had to be present each time a mourner entered the room, and they could show up at any time of the day or night. The mourner would kowtow twice to the coffin, take an incense stick, light it with the candle, and place it in the thurible. The mourner and each family member would kowtow to each other, and Mi-soon would leave the room to feed the guest until the next one arrived. The guests ate well, but the mourning family was not supposed to eat, and by the end of the week, Mi-soon felt faint from the lack of food. The only people who had bothered to pay their respects were the ex-farmers who had worked on the land. No Yangban turned up at all.

When Mi-soon recovered from her fainting fit, the funeral procession continued. As they approached the gravesite, the shaman rang his bell faster and faster and louder and louder to drive away any evil spirits that might be lurking at the gravesite. The Choi ancestral burial plot was a sunny glade cut into grass terraces, one for each generation. The graves were shaped like domed hummocks so that the spirits could keep watch over their ancestral land.

Bok-nam looked at the freshly dug gravesite. It was the last available plot apart from the space next to it, reserved for her. She clutched her son closer and shuddered at the thought of the cold ground waiting for her. She stared at the older generation of Yangban wives, buried next to their husbands, and cursed them. Their spirits were supposed to protect the family. She thought about her duty as a wife and the ridiculous ranking system for widows. A widow of the first rank was supposed to kill herself when her husband died. A second-rate widow would spend seven years dressed in mourning and gradually starve herself to death. For what? They would build a shrine for her to let all the world would know what a faithful wife she had been. No thanks. A third-class widow would wear mourning clothes forever and never see a man again as long as she lived. To be a married woman was no more than being an incubator for her husband's children. She would never be integrated into the Choi family and would always be a Park. Her children would carry the Choi name because they had their father's blood and if anything happened to her they would be looked after by the Choi family.

Bok-nam wore the mask of mourning, as was expected of her, and it looked genuine enough on the outside. She dabbed at her eyes with a handkerchief and shed a few tears, but they were tears of anger, not grief. She pounded her breast and tore at her hair. What was she to do now? How was she supposed to survive now that her husband had died? She thought about her son. He should have inherited the land, but now she had nothing. The Japanese had robbed her son of his birth right, and there was nothing she could do about it. The world was upside down. Even her ex-servant was better off than her: he was still living in his old quarters but had left their service to work in the Japanese textile factory and was earning a good salary. She stared at her gravesite and felt uneasy. Was she next? No, not just yet, she thought, and the seed of a plan formed in her mind.

The front pallbearers dipped the bier three times and set down their load. The shaman produced a knife in his hand and danced erratically all around the gravesite, carving up the surrounding air and ringing his bell to make doubly sure that any loitering demons would flee the scene. He jumped into the prepared gravesite, recited an incantation to exorcise any evil spirits that might have been lurking in the grave, and gave the order to lower the coffin. The family gathered around the coffin, and the shaman threw some heavy clods of soil onto the lid with a loud thud. He lowered himself in and trampled down the earth, and each mourner followed suit in order of seniority.

Bok-nam swooned a few times on the return journey, and she would have fallen into the snow, but Dol-soi always seemed to be at her side to catch her. He took her son from her arms and carried him, and Bok-nam smiled under her veil. Darkness was beginning to fall when they approached the family home, and Bok-nam could see the glowing funeral lanterns that hung on either side of the main gate. By the time she could clearly define the Chinese characters written on them, symbolising death and sadness, her plan was complete.

CHAPTER 15

A MIDNIGHT VISITOR AND A FAREWELL

On a January evening, in 1940, shortly after Dol-soi had loaded the furnace with logs and retired to bed for the night, he thought he heard the soft sound of a door sliding in its tracks. He must be imagining things, he told himself. The servants had left long ago, and nobody had a reason to visit at this hour. He pulled the blanket around him, closed his eyes, and strained his ears for any sound. There was nothing, so he convinced himself that it was just his imagination and fell into a deep sleep; a short while later, the soft pad of feet pitter-pattered across his bedroom floor.

He awoke with a jolt. Something didn't feel right. Was he having a nightmare? No, that wasn't the reason. He was definitely awake because he became vaguely aware of hot breath ruffling the hairs on the back of his neck and making them stand rigid. Then something touched him. Something warm. Something alive. His heart raced. Something had slithered under his blanket and was now preparing to feast upon him. He froze in terror and cautiously clutched at the covers, not even daring to exhale. Something fleshy ran down his back, and with a single movement he leapt out of bed and wrapped the blanket around himself for protection. He lit the oil lamp and stared down at the bed in disbelief. There in *his* bed was his Bok-nam, wearing only a smile.

'Ma'am. What are you doing here?' said Dol-soi, his mind in turmoil, and he was not quite sure if he was still dreaming. He tightened the blanket around himself.

Bok-nam laughed, 'Isn't it obvious?' she said and batted her eyelashes.

'You shouldn't be here,' said Dol-soi, not knowing where to look. 'You could have waited until the morning ... if you wanted me to do something.'

'Hush. Don't be scared, Dol-soi,' said Bok-nam. She propped herself up on her arms, raised her legs and let her knees open slightly. 'Don't you want me?'

Dol-soi's terror intensified. 'Ma'am, don't do this to me.' It made perfect sense now why she asked him to stay in the servant quarters after the funeral. 'You should go now. Please leave,' he said and tried to avert his eyes.

Bok-nam was annoyed. His reaction was unexpected. She thought it would be a straightforward affair, like giving candy to a baby. She played her final card and burst into tears. 'I have nobody to turn to,' she sniffled. 'At the funeral, I realised that it is you who cares about me the most. You have always been by my side, even after all these years, and now I need you.'

'But, how can I help?' said Dol-soi. He feared a trap, but he couldn't think straight as the blood diverted from his brain.

Bok-nam smiled. 'I'm cold,' she said, and when Dol-soi handed her the blanket, she latched onto his arm, mantis-like, and guided her prey down onto the bed. She drew him nearer and kissed him softly on the lips, and when she was sure that he had swallowed the bait, she struck and whispered into his ear, 'Don't you understand Dol-soi? I always wanted you as a man.'

Bok-nam woke up in the small hours and listened to the

sound of her servant snoring softly beside her. She liked the sound of that: her servant. The old fool was back in servitude again, and he didn't even know it. She smiled. Everything had gone to plan. He was in the palm of her hand now. She had snared a grafter who was not afraid of physical labour, someone who knew how to grow the crops to feed her and someone who drew wages from the textile factory. He would not dare refuse her now, or she would scream rape, and who would the police believe? A poor grieving widow, of course. Nobody in their right mind would willingly submit to their former servant. When the forty-nine days of official mourning were over, she would marry her ex-servant and to hell with the village gossip. She smiled again at her ingenuity, wrapped the blanket around her, and returned to her chamber. She had to get ready for her appointment and put the second part of her plan into operation.

In the afternoon, Bok-nam received the Korean agent in the reception hall. 'Thank you for coming at short notice,' she said.

'Sorry, I didn't make it to the funeral,' said the Korean agent. 'You have my deepest sympathies —.'

'It's of no consequence now,' said Bok-nam.

Somewhat taken aback by her coldness, the Korean agent raised his open palms and said, 'How can I help?'

'I want you to help my daughter find a job,' said Bok-nam. 'One that suits her education and breeding.'

The agent was surprised that Bok-nam wanted to use her daughter this way. Poor Korean families lived off their daughters when times were hard, but not the Yangban class. When he had suggested such a thing to her late husband, only last year, he had bluntly told him that he would never live as a parasite. The agent thought for a while and said, 'As you know, the Japanese Empire is at war with China, and we are always looking for healthy young women — to train as nurses. Would that be of interest?'

'A nurse? How much do they earn?' said Bok-nam.

'Which daughter? The youngest or the eldest?'

'The eldest, Mi-soon.'

'How old is she?'

'Seventeen.'

'Did she finish her education?'

'Yes. She received the highest quality education and passed all the exams.'

'In that case, I could go as high as fifty dollars.'

'Fifty dollars? Is that all?'

'It seems like every house has too many daughters these days. You know, the cost of feeding them, only for them to disappear when they marry. The cost of the dowry. Do I need to go on?'

Bok-nam nodded.

'We pay you the fifty dollars in advance. We also pay a basic monthly wage.'

'Which is what?'

'Five dollars a month.'

'Five dollars! That wouldn't even buy a bag of rice.'

'We take care of our nurses and provide all the accommodation, food and training.'

'Ten dollars would be more appropriate for an educated, Yangban girl. Can you arrange to send the money directly to me?'

'That is nearly twice what I pay for the other girls.'

'After all, I am losing a daughter. I need some form of compensation.'

'Agreed,' said the agent knowing full well that she would never receive the monthly income. 'What about the youngest one?' said the agent. 'MiJa, isn't it?'

Bok-nam pretended to think about his offer, but she had

other plans for MiJa. MiJa would look after her son, do the housework, and help on the land. Without MiJa she would have to do the manual work, and that was beneath a lady of her class and breeding. She had never done a stroke of work in her life, even when they lost everything, and she had no intention of starting now. She also knew that MiJa would earn more money if she finished her education first.

'Isn't she a bit young for that? She's only thirteen.'

'No. Not really. Other families send their daughters to us at an even younger age, some as young as nine or ten,' said the agent. 'The younger we get them, the sooner we can start their training.' He smiled and added, 'It's easier that way.'

'I will think about it, but for now it will just be the eldest,' said Bok-nam. 'When can I expect the money?'

'Next week when I collect your daughter.'

'Next week!'

'A ship leaves for Fukushima every Wednesday.'

The following Wednesday, early in the morning, MiJa knocked on Mi-soon's bedroom door. There was no reply, so she slid open the door.

'Elder Sister. Are you there?'

'Come in,' said Mi-soon. She was cramming the last of her belongings into an old leather bag that once belonged to her father. She saw at once that her little sister was standing with her hands behind her back, trying to conceal something. 'What have you got there?'

'Where?'

'Behind your back.'

'Nothing.'

Mi-soon could hear the rustle of paper each time MiJa moved to prevent her from seeing what was behind her. 'It sounds like something to me.'

Unable to contain her secret any longer, MiJa smiled and blurted out, 'I made you a present.' She handed her sister a crumpled paper bag.

Mi-soon was surprised by the weight. 'This is heavy. It must be expensive.'

'It's a necklace,' said MiJa before her sister could even open the bag. 'To replace your gold one. Mother said we must call Dol-soi father now.'

'Did she? Well, I never will,' said Mi-soon as she opened the bag.

'Me neither,' said MiJa, anxious to copy everything her big sister did. She watched Mi-soon open her present.

'Thank you,' said Mi-soon with a startled face. She held up a heavy stone pendant with a hole drilled in the centre, threaded with an old pair of tattered leather shoelaces.

'I made it myself. It's not gold, though. Aren't you going to put it on?' asked MiJa.

'Of course,' said Mi-soon and hung it around her neck. 'I have seen the Hae-nyeo divers wear something just like this.'

'Really?'

'Yes, they wear them as diving weights to help them sink faster.'

They both laughed, and MiJa said, 'Look. I scratched my name on it, so you won't forget me.'

Mi-soon turned the necklace over and examined the scratch marks. 'No chance of that sister,' she said and hugged her.

'Do you like it?'

'It's lovely. It must have taken you ages to make. It's more valuable than a real gold one, and I shall always wear it.'

'You will?' MiJa wasn't sure if her sister was kidding or not.

'Yes, of course. Except when I am swimming, though — or in the bath. I don't want to drown.'

'I don't want you to go. I'm going to miss you,' said MiJa. She bit her lower lip to stem the tears.

Her older sister said, 'I will miss you too. But this is a good chance for me. Maybe, it will be my only chance in life — a chance to really do something with my life and help you and Yung-soo. Do you understand?'

'No,' said MiJa and could not stop the tears.

Her sister wiped the hot thick tears away with her thumbs. 'I've always wanted to be a nurse,' she said and had long dreamed of meeting a handsome medic, settling down, and having children of her own.

'Do you think Mother will send me out to work too?'

Mi-soon let go of her daydreams. 'No, I don't think so.'

'Are you sure?'

'Yes. I will make enough money to look after you and Yung-soo.'

MiJa nodded and dried her eyes.

'I want you to have this,' said Mi-soon, and she handed MiJa her Korean history book.

MiJa was dumbstruck: she knew that it was her sister's most treasured possession. 'Really,' she said. 'You are not going to take it with you?'

'No, I know most of the stories by heart now. You can have it, but always remember to keep it hidden.'

A horn sounded outside. Mi-soon took a deep breath, picked up her leather bag with one hand and grabbed her sister's hand with the other, and together they marched outside. A Yokohama cab truck stood waiting with the engine running. Mi-soon scanned the bench seats, hoping she would know somebody. She didn't want to travel alone, but she didn't recognise anybody. Some of the girls looked far too young. Were they really training nurses that young? She glanced at her mother standing by the gate, cradling Yung-soo in her arms, and chatting to the Korean agent. She saw him hand her a fat brown envelope. Tradition held that she should kowtow to her mother, but it was also a tradition that she should mourn her father for at least forty-nine days, and her mother had not let her do even that. To hell with tradition.

'Promise that you will look after yourself and Yung-soo until I come back,' said Mi-soon and she held up her little finger.

'I promise,' said MiJa and she interlocked her little finger with her sister to stamp the deal.

Mi-soon let go of her sister's hand and said, 'See you soon.'

MiJa grabbed her sister around her waist from behind and interlocked her fingers so that her sister could not leave. 'Goodbye Elder Sister. I am going to miss you.'

Mi-soon had to prise her fingers apart to escape and take her place on the truck. She was one week shy of her eighteenth birthday when she waved goodbye to her little sister, and she wondered when she would see her again.

CHAPTER 16

THE GAKSEORI

The 8th of February 1940 heralded the Chinese New Year: the year of the Golden Dragon. That year after the official mourning period of seven weeks was over Bok-nam married her ex-servant. The town was abuzz with vitriol, stabbing tongues, shaking heads and caustic accusations: his body was still warm when she re-married, and the yellow chrysanthemums on his grave had yet to fade. Gil-soo will rise from his grave when he hears about the affair. She started it when he was still alive. She is short of money. Did you hear that she sold her eldest daughter?

Bok-nam didn't care one jot. They could say whatever they liked, and she had heard it all before. She wasn't going to play the part of a grieving widow forever. How could she when she had a son to raise? They were right about the money, though. When Yung-soo was born, she kept MiJa off school to look after him: not for her all that nappy changing, feeding, winding, sleep deprivation and endless whining. But now, her son was a toddler, and if MiJa finished her education, she would be worth more and might even fetch the same price as her eldest daughter. So, one spring morning, a week after the new school term had started, Bok-nam asked MiJa if she would like to go back to school.

MiJa's eyes lit up, but she didn't say anything initially, fearing a trap. 'Really, Mother?' she ventured.

'Yes, really, but I don't know how I will manage with all the housework.'

'I can do that after school,' said MiJa. 'I promise.'

Bok-nam smiled. 'Good, that is settled then. You can go to school tomorrow.'

'Thank you, Mother.'

'One more thing, MiJa. I nearly forgot. You will have to take Yung-soo to school with you. I couldn't possibly cope alone.'

'But —.'

'No buts, MiJa.'

'Whatever you say, Mother.'

MiJa took her old school uniform out of the wardrobe. It was in desperate need of a good wash and iron, but there was no time now. It wouldn't be dry by the morning. It would have to do. She tried it on, but it was too small, far too small. Her forearms poked out of her sleeves, and the skirt was so short that it exposed her knees. She hunted around for any material she could use to extend it, but all she could find was the silk sheet sewn to the bottom of her yo. She removed the sheet, cut it into strips, and attempted to lengthen her sleeves and skirt. It took all night because MiJa had never used a needle and thread before, and her mind kept wandering. Had she missed too many lessons? Was her Japanese good enough to follow the lessons? Would they still accept her? And her baby brother?

When she had finished altering her clothes, it was late, and she still had to cut her hair to the regulation length. It was way too long, so she took the kitchen scissors and cut it herself, half asleep and in the dark. That night she couldn't sleep. She felt anxious at the thought of seeing Jung-sik again. In the morning, she overslept, and by the time she had cooked the family breakfast and got her brother washed and dressed, she didn't have any time for herself, but she didn't want to be late, so she grabbed her brother's hand, crammed on the first pair of shoes she could find and dashed out of the door.

'Hurry up. Get a move on, or we will be late.'

'I'm walking as fast as I can.'

'Do you want a carry?'

'I'm not a baby. I am five.'

MiJa recalled her very first day. The fresh, spring day. The birdsong. The sunshine and the clear blue cloudless sky; the only clouds that day were from the cherry blossoms. Today was different. It was a bleak, leaden day, and the threat of snow hung low in the clouds. No birds sang, and a thin layer of hoar frost still covered the road. She could feel the ridges of mud that had frozen solid under the soles of her shoes. She only then realised, in her panic, that she had chosen the straw ones she had worn at her father's funeral. Should she go back and change them? There was no time, she decided.

The houses that fringed the roadside that had looked so airy and inviting on that first day were now brooding and menacing, and once or twice MiJa thought she saw dark, prying shadows at the windows. She half expected somebody to slide open a door and yell, MiJa, why are you wasting your time going to school? You should be at home helping your mother with her chores. She yanked on her Yung-soo's hand until he was skating along the icy road.

Eventually, they arrived at the town gate. The stone walls looked steep and imposing, and the guardhouse hung over the dark archway. The only rays of sunshine were the ones on the imperial Japanese flags draped over the city walls. The cherry trees wore their winter attire: bleak and bare, with no signs of life, their gnarly limbs intertwined and formed a dark tunnel.

When MiJa entered the tunnel, she felt uneasy as if it was closing in at the far end. The branches seemed to grab and probe at her with tiny claws, hunting for any sign of weakness.

'Come on, we are really late,' she said and scooped up her brother, threw him onto her back and ran the rest of the way to school.

'Don't squeeze so tight. You're choking me,' said MiJa, but Yung-soo was too scared and tightened his grip. The schoolyard was lifeless. A limp Japanese imperial flag clung to the flagpole. MiJa made her way to her classroom with her brother still clinging to her back, took a deep breath to settle her nerves, and slid open the door. There was a loud scraping noise as the classroom door groaned in its tracks, and the entire class turned to see who was late.

The class stared in unified horror at a bedraggled young girl with tanned skin and unkempt windswept hair. They looked her up and down: she was wearing a worn-out school uniform that had been patched with remnants of cloth in clashing colours, and she had baggy gipsy frills on the ends of her sleeves and skirt. She wore the remnants of home-made straw shoes, and most alarming of all, a pair of startled owl eyes peered over her shoulder. There could be no doubt. It was a Gakseori: a type of vagabond that went begging from door to door. All that was missing was a gourd begging bowl and spoon. The classroom erupted into howls of laughter.

'Be quiet,' said the teacher, 'What do we have here?'

MiJa stepped into the classroom, and between pants of breath, she said, 'I am MiJa, but my Japanese name is Yoshiko.'

'MiJa is fine. We don't use Japanese names anymore. The teacher didn't explain that the Japanese had complained that second class citizens like Koreans should not have a Japanese name.

'Welcome back,' said the teacher, who was laughing along

with the rest of the class. 'And who do you have on your back?'

'This is my brother, Choi Yung-soo. He can sit under my desk. He won't be any trouble. He never cries.'

She looked around the classroom to see if she could see Jung-sik. Another girl was sat in her seat, a beautiful girl, and her heart sank. She wondered why she had come back at all. She should have stayed at home, and she saw now how foolish she was to think that she could return and expect things to be the same.

'Why can't your mother look after your brother? He is too young to attend school,' said the teacher.

MiJa shrugged.

'Very well then, but if your brother disrupts the class, you will have to leave.'

MiJa nodded.

'You can take one of the vacant desks at the back of the classroom.'

MiJa took her seat, sat her brother under her desk, and tried to ignore the murmur of disapproval that rippled through the class.

'Now, where was I?' said the teacher and continued with the lesson entirely in Japanese.

MiJa struggled to understand, and it didn't help that she was distracted by the smell emanating from the brass lunch tins that sat warming on the stove in the centre of the classroom. Her stomach grumbled and reminded her that she had forgotten to make her lunch.

When the bell rang for lunch, the children dashed over to their lunch boxes and started complaining that their food was too hot. MiJa could hear them blowing on the food and wafting the smell of steamed rice to every corner of the classroom. There was nowhere to hide.

'Sister, I'm hungry,' said Yung-soo.

MiJa led her brother over to a quiet corner, and they sat facing the wall pretending to study whilst they waited for the others to finish their lunch. She was hungry too and cursed her stupidity. A hot tear ran down her cheek. She brushed it away in anger before anybody saw it.

'I'll make you something to eat when we get home,' she said to Yung-soo. 'It won't be long.'

'But I'm hungry now,' said her brother.

'Why are you not eating MiJa?' taunted one of the children.

'I'm not hungry,' she replied, not bothering to turn around, but she could sense their smiling, jeering faces.

'Well, your brother seems to be,' taunted another voice.

'If you stand on a table and sing and dance for us like a Gakseori, we might share our food with you.' The children started to clap, dance, and clown around, mimicking a Gakseori beggar, but they fell silent when a voice said, 'Shut up, all of you. You act no better than dogs.'

MiJa recognised the voice, and her heart skipped a beat.

'MiJa, why don't you come and sit at my desk and share my lunch?' said Jung-sik. 'There is more than enough.' He opened two bento boxes: one contained steamed rice with a fried egg on top, and the other kimchi, fried anchovies, and shredded beef.

After school had finished, MiJa waited for Jung-sik at the school gate. She wanted to walk home with him, but he was taking too long, and she wanted to get home before it got too late. The first flakes of snow started to fall, and she watched them see-saw through the air. Her brother started shivering, and she could wait no longer.

'Let's go,' she said to her brother.

After a short while, her brother said, 'Can I have a carry?'

'I am tired too,' said MiJa. Their progress slowed to a snail's pace, and the snow started falling thick and fast and transfixed the children with its mesmerising dance. They tried to catch the flakes on their tongues but soon tired of the game, and after a while, her brother said, 'Sister, my feet are hurting.'

'Stop complaining like a baby,' said MiJa. 'I thought you said you was all grown up.'

'I am, but my feet are still cold.'

'Well, walk faster then,' said MiJa. Her straw shoes disintegrated in the wet and the slush, and she threw them to the side of the road. The initial sharp sting of the snow soon abated as her toes, and then her feet, turned numb, but at least it was soft underfoot, and with each laboured step, she spread her toes wide to grip the snow. She gazed at the heavy white clouds that filled the sky. Dusk was near, and if they continued at this pace, it would be dark before they got home. She feared getting lost and could already hear her mother's scornful tongue. The two sets of footprints in the snowy track became one, and the only sound was the squeak of her feet cutting through the crisp fresh snow and the soft snoring behind her. The snow came thick and fast, and each snowflake, the size of paper doily, sashayed through the air and settled onto the thick blanket already lying on the ground.

When they were nearly home, MiJa let out a deep sigh of relief, followed by a curse as she felt a warm wet patch spread on her back and the faint whiff of urine. Great, she thought and shook her head and laughed at her misfortune. MiJa had only known thirteen winters, but her fourteenth would be the longest, the coldest, and the most bitter. On Sunday, the 7th of December 1941, Japan attacked Pearl Harbour and dragged Korea into World War II.

PART TWO

THE WORLD WAR

CHAPTER 17

THE ARMY MEDIC

BURMA, 20 MAY 1943

T he summer monsoon came early that year. Great black storm clouds swept across the Bay of Bengal and released fat globules of tepid rain onto the camp. The rain drummed on the tents, and the canvas sagged and billowed, buffeted by the wind until the pooled water ran off in intermittent muddy gushes. It was like living in a flushing toilet, thought the medic, and he laughed inwardly. That image seemed appropriate enough for this cesspit of a country: a country rife with disease — and he was sick of it.

When he had first arrived in this godforsaken country, and that seemed so long ago now, he was glad to see the onset of the monsoon because it would mean an end to the fighting. The resulting flash floods created a filthy network of raging rivers and that, coupled with lush, dense vegetation, made the hilly terrain impassable, or so their British commanders had told them. But nobody had bothered to inform the Japanese, and those fanatic bastards hacked their way through the jungle and ambushed them at every opportunity. He pulled the last dregs of nicotine from his cigarette, flicked the stub away into the swirling rain, and pulled out the crumpled letter from his pocket.

PO 54394
Royal Army Medical Corp
Burma India Command

18 March 1943

Hi Darling

I was so happy to receive your letter. I hope that you have bucked up a bit and are feeling better. I wake up every morning when I hear the postman open the rusty gate, jump down the entire flight of stairs, and almost hit the floor before the post does.

I went to the flicks with Jean on Saturday to see Casablanca. I thought it was rubbish, but she liked it. I showed her my hand with the ring on my finger, and she was so jealous. Everybody keeps asking me when we are going to get married.

They also showed a British Pathé newsreel. They are bombing Berlin almost every night, and the Russians defeated the Krauts in Stalingrad. There was nothing about South East Asia Command, though. I think they have forgotten about you lot, but I haven't. I miss you terribly, so please come home soon. I worry about you so much. I hope you are well and giving the Japs hell. The feeling in Blighty is that the tide has turned, and the war will soon be over. I do hope so.

That is all the news I have for now. Love you till the camels come home on skis and the desert turns into the ocean.

Valspar xxx

p.s. Please write soon and send me another photo. I loved the last one you sent — the one in Gibraltar with the Rock Apes. They remind me of you. Ha-ha.

He thought about home. It had seemed like a good idea to enlist at the time. The impatience of youth; he wanted to do his bit before the war was over. A shot at glory and the chance to return to England and a hero's welcome. He snorted at the folly of his youth. It hadn't taken him long to work out that war heroes came from other theatres of war, not operating theatres. Now he was damaged goods. He couldn't un-see the things he had seen and wished he had never left. He should have stayed in Cheltenham and finished med school. He would be a qualified doctor by now, working as a GP in one of the leafy avenues in the Home Counties. Start work at nine, dole out a few aspirins, antibiotics and anti-depressants to the elderly and hypochondriacs, and be on the golf course by mid-afternoon. No risk. But he had chosen this life, and his life now was the field hospital.

The field hospital was nothing more than a large green canvas marquee furnished with meagre and inadequate supplies that had to be hand-carried through the dense, steamy jungle or dropped by parachute from a Dakota C47. He paused at the tent flaps to the hospital and took a deep breath. He knew what to expect, but it still caught him by surprise. The stench hit him squarely on the nose and raised his gorge: the smell of damp, mildew, sulphurous shit, disinfectant and death.

In the sixty hospital cots, laid on rubber sheets, were the sorriest bunch of ragtag men anybody was likely to see, this side of hell. Hung at the end of each bed was a triage label, colour-coded for easy identification: black meant that you were going to die; red for urgent medical attention; yellow for close observation, and green was reserved for the walking wounded. All the patients knew the code. It wasn't combat that claimed the most deaths, it was disease, and the medic wondered if they had really moved out of the shadow of Scutari. The warmth and humidity suffocated the country and turned it into one large petri dish, the perfect medium to incubate disease and death. In the monsoon season, the latrines would overflow, run into the rivers and streams and pollute the only source of drinking water. In the evenings, the men were under constant attack by clouds of aggressive mosquitos. Too much work and too little food weakened their resolve and lowered their resistance, and dysentery, malaria and cholera set ambushes for them at every corner.

'Morning, medic. A beautiful day, isn't it? I was thinking of going for a walk later,' said his first patient, an emaciated sapper who was no more than a bag of skin and bones, inflated with a dry sense of humour. That was another thing the medic could never get used to, the indefatigable sense of humour that flowed through these dying men. Last week, he had strapped this patient down and helped the doctors amputate his right leg. The sapper had only received a minor cut to his thigh, but it had become infected, and when the gangrene got in, there was no alternative. He was only twenty-four years old, the same age as the medic.

'Morning,' said the medic as he changed the dressing on the still angry stump. There was no sign of infection and no smell of rotting flesh. That was good. It was as much as he dared hope for, but it didn't quell the anger he felt at the waste of it all. He knew the sapper would be sent home soon to be thrown on the scrap heap, ignored by his own countrymen, his sacrifices soon forgotten and as faded in the public conscience as the medal ribbons on his chest.

Most of the patients had dysentery. It was easy enough to

treat, in theory. You just had to rehydrate the patient and give them enough time and rest to recover, but it wasn't quite that simple: nothing ever was out here. If the patients remained dehydrated for a long time, they would lose vital vitamins, and open ulcers would form on their skin. In this climate, that meant disaster. His next patient had deep leg ulcers that never healed in wet conditions. Flesh-eating bacteria had formed a black skin on the surface of the ulcer, and below that was yellowish skin that was slowly being eaten away and exposed white shin bone. Poor bastard, thought the medic. They had run out of painkillers, but he couldn't let the wound fester anymore.

'Here, take these,' he said to the patient and handed him two Sulfa tablets. Sometimes they worked, sometimes they didn't, but that is all they had to combat infection. He had read about a wonder drug called penicillin in *The Lancet*, but they could not make it in sufficient quantity yet.

'Here, bite on this,' said the medic, and he handed the patient a thin wooden dowel that he carried in his pocket. 'I'm sorry, but this is going to hurt like Billy-O.' He sterilised a spoon, irrigated the wound with Dakin solution, and scraped off the dead skin and pus the best he could. He could feel his patient's body convulse with each scrape of the spoon and his weak fingers clutched at his forearm.

It was unpleasant and frustrating work, and the job he liked least was checking the bedpans. Not just because it was foul work but because of the fear of what he might find. If the patient defecated a watery discharge, the colour of rice water it meant cholera. A death sentence and the victim knew it. He remembered his first case last year, and he would never forget the look of terror in the victim's pleading eyes, but there was nothing he could do. He knew the procedure: affix dog tags and immediately isolate them in the quarantine tent. The dog tags were necessary because they would be unrecognisable in the morning. They would violently evacuate body fluids out of every orifice as the body tried in vain to rid itself of the bacteria. There was no hope for these unfortunate victims, and when he visited the forlorn figures the following morning, the skin on their hands and feet had wrinkled and turned a pallid, bluish-grey, and sunken eyes stared out of a living corpse. Mercifully it was usually over very quickly, sometimes just a matter of hours.

In the afternoon, the deep guttural splutters of twin radial engines announced the arrival of an RAF Dakota. The medic watched the plane eject its cargo, and his heart filled with joy as each parachute filled with air and drifted safely towards the ground. When the mule team recovered the supplies, they returned to base camp, accompanied by an advanced column of long-range penetration soldiers returning from one of their lengthy forays behind enemy lines. They were an unshaven bunch, many were without trousers, and they wore mud-splattered khaki smocks stained with blood, sweat and toil. Over their shoulders were slung their Bren guns, and strapped to their backs was a heavy metal-framed rucksack that looked like it was the only thing holding them together; remove it, and their limbs would start to fall off. These were the Chindits.

He was no longer shocked by their appearance. When he first arrived in Burma, he asked a young corporal why he wasn't wearing any trousers and was told, "You stop wearing trousers when you shit them four times before breakfast, sir." He still blushed at his naivety. The only water they had access to was from the mountain streams. It was just a matter of time before dysentery would rear its ugly head. They lined up outside the hospital tent, and he called in his first patient. He could tell from his uniform that he was a young corporal in the Royal Engineers, and he also wore the Chindit logo on his arm: a mythical beast, half lion, and half gryphon, that guarded the Burmese temples.

'Have you been taking your Atabrine?' said the medic. The anti-malarial drug of choice was quinine, but its supply had dried up when Japan had captured Java. They managed to get some Atabrine from the USA, but one of its side effects was that it turned the skin a bright yellow.

'Yes, sir,' said the young corporal and saluted.

'There's no need for formalities,' said the medic and asked him to remove his top. He pressed his stethoscope to a ribcage that resembled that of a starved corn-fed chicken. His breathing was shallow, but there was no rattling. He had some bleeding from his gums but no fever.

'So what was it this time?' he asked the sapper.

'We were sent north to clear a landing strip for the gliders, up near the Patkai hills. The Gurkhas cut a path through the thick, teak jungle, interlaced with bamboo. It was hard going and like a sauna in the daytime and a fridge at night, even at 3000 feet. Some days, we only managed to cover about two miles.'

'Uncle Bill's tactics are working then?' asked the medic. Lt General Will Slim had recently taken over the Burma Command.

'Yes. We have turned the tide now. We can stand our ground if we receive supplies from the air and have started to advance into Burma. We have just captured Paungbyin, a village just east of here.'

The medic issued him with a rehydration pack and an anti-malarial, 'Here, take these,' he said, 'and drop your uniform off at the DDT tent.'

'That's it, Doc?'

'Yes, you are fine. Nothing a good rest and a square meal can't cure. I think you are in luck. Tonight it's bully beef and hardtack, washed down with hot tea.'

'You make it sound like the Savoy Grill or Simpson's in the Strand.'

The medic laughed. It was always the same meal.

'Next,' he shouted.

After his shift was over, the medic collapsed into his bed, still wearing his boots, and fell into the sleep of the dead, only to be resurrected what seemed to him like a few moments later. It was already morning.

A senior officer stood by his bed and said, 'Get your kit together. Your presence is required in Paungbyin.'

CHAPTER 18

THE CHINDWIN STAR HOTEL

Paungbyin village was little more than a jumble of wooden-stilted houses thrown together on the east bank of the Chindwin River. The military escort had used the river to navigate, and they had tracked its leisurely meander: a chocolate brown ribbon that threaded its way through the verdant, virgin jungle. They marched up a dusty road, lined with swaying toddy palms and ancient Burmese teak, and the tree canopy offered some welcome relief from the beating sun. Pools of cool emerald shadow spilt on the ground, splashed here and there with smears of golden sunlight. At random intervals, bell-shaped stupas punctured the tree canopy with their golden domes and spires, and the natural and spiritual world seemed in perfect harmony.

On the outskirts of the village, they came to a large two-storey house with jalousie shutters. Above the entrance, somebody had scrawled on a signboard *The Chindwin Star Hotel*. A Gurkha rifleman stood guard at the door. He saluted the military escort and let them pass.

When the medic stepped inside, a familiar foe embraced him: the putrid smell of suffering, death and decay. It looked like the hotel had been converted into a makeshift hospital. Rows of grubby pallet beds spaced no more than a foot apart had been pushed up against the walls. He counted forty beds on the first floor alone, and each bed contained a dead body covered with a manky sheet, threadbare and stained with yellow patches. Every sheet had a dark bloodstain around the abdomen area. What use was he here? He slammed his Gladstone bag onto the floor and raised a thick swarm of glossy black flies. They struggled to get their fat, bloated bodies airborne, stupefied by their drunken orgy of congealed blood.

He donned his gown and face mask, snapped his rubber gloves on in a puff of chalk, and unleashed his anger. 'Why have they brought me here? There is nothing I can do here. I'm a fucking doctor, not God. They should have sent for the padre.'

He pulled back the first blood-stained sheet and took a step backwards. The body of a young girl, pre-teen in his estimate, stared back at him with accusing eyes that seemed to be asking, why? He closed her eyelids and checked her pulse and her breathing, but he knew in his heart that it was a lost cause. She was dead. He examined her body. She was completely naked and tied to the bed, bound at the ankles and wrists. She had suffered a wound to her abdomen that was about an inch wide, and she had bled to death. Puzzled, he checked the sheet; it had tears in it, and so did the mattress. He covered her with the sheet and moved on to the next bed. It was the same. Like a maniac, he pulled back the sheets from each bed and threw them on the floor in disgust. Each bed contained the corpse of a young girl, some looked so frail and small they could have been children, and all had their wrists and ankles tied to the bed frame. Every sheet had the same blood stains, either in the abdominal area, the breasts, or the womb. It dawned on the medic that this was no makeshift hospital; this was a brothel, and these girls had been executed, bayoneted whilst they lay helpless in their beds.

'Up here,' shouted a voice from above. 'I think one is still alive.'

The medic rushed to her bedside and checked her pulse and breathing. 'She is,' he said, 'but only just.' Her pupils were dilated and failed to respond to the light: she was in a coma. He tilted her head back and inserted an endotracheal tube to keep her airways open. He hooked up a saline IV drip to keep her blood pressure stable. He pulled back the blood-stained sheet and revealed an abdomen wound. He winced. It looked like somebody had bodged a Caesarean section. He was puzzled: she was too thin to have been pregnant. It was a recent scar, and the stitches had failed to heal and still wept. The skin had started to turn black where necrosis had set in. He checked her temperature. She was running a fever and had all the signs of chronic disease: her skin was sallow and her face sagged and was etched with the furrows of pain, making it difficult to assess her age. He cleaned the abdominal wound, applied some Steri-strips to keep it closed, and loosened her bindings. He inspected the sheet, but there was no hole in it. He had to save her. If he could keep her alive, she could tell him what happened here.

'She needs emergency surgery in Imphal. Get on the radio and find out when the next Dakota arrives.'

He gave orders for the Gurkhas to dig a mass grave in a patch of grass at the back of the hotel. One by one, the medic untied their hands and wrists and made sketches of their wounds and any other distinguishing marks in his diary. He wanted these bastards caught and punished; somebody had to pay for this atrocity. He searched the hotel for any documentation to identify the girls but found nothing but a few charred embers in the reception area. The girls were washed, wrapped in the sheets they died in, and carried to the mass gravesite. He conducted a short burial service and was determined to show them a bit of dignity in death that they were so cruelly denied in life.

The medic pulled up a chair next to his patient to monitor her vital signs and waited. She was still comatose, but once, her eyes opened. There was no pupil response to his flashlight. The medic knew that the last of the five senses to deteriorate was hearing, so he arranged for a Japanese speaking Gurkha to be brought to her bedside to see if he could reach her, but after a few hours of trying, he dismissed him. He worried that what had happened here would remain unpunished.

In the late evening, her eyes flickered open briefly, and she mumbled something in Japanese before drifting back into the abyss.

'Interpreter,' shouted the medic. 'Stay here with me. If she wakes again, we need to record everything. It could be our only chance to find out what happened.'

The next time she woke, she started shaking violently and screaming something in Japanese. The medic handed her some water, and she cowered in terror. The interpreter explained that it was only water, and they were not there to hurt her, but when the medic attempted to approach her, she screamed and kicked.

'Don't touch me,' she yelled in Japanese and started sobbing helplessly.

'Tell her that we are here to help and that we are enemies of Japan,' said the medic. 'And that she must drink.'

He passed her the water again. It seemed to work, and when she had calmed down, she sipped the water and sobbed intermittently.

'What is your name?' asked the medic.

There was no reply, and she lowered her head as though she was ashamed of something.

The medic worried that she would bury the mental

trauma deep inside her, and it was important she told him what had happened here. She was the only living eyewitness.

'I want to kill them. I want to kill all the bastards,' she said and started shaking with anger.

The medic tried to comfort her, but she shied away and started crying again. After a while, she recovered and said, 'I was supposed to be a nurse.' She gave a hollow laugh. 'That is what they told me. They lied. They tricked me: tricked me with soft words and promises. I was supposed to be a nurse, but they beat me over and over until I did what they wanted.'

She screamed and pulled at her hair until a clump came out at the roots. The medic had to grab her hands to stop her from doing more damage. He asked the interpreter to tell her they wanted to catch these men, and she must tell them everything, no matter how difficult it was. Explain to her that if she told them everything she knew, they may be able to catch the people responsible for this and punish them. He'd record everything in his diary.

She sobbed and nodded her head. 'Where are my friends? The other girls.'

The medic couldn't find the words to reply.

'It's all we have had these last few years, each other. They were my friends.' Her face contorted and cracked with the pain of the memories.

'Please tell us what happened here?' said the medic. 'Did they bayonet all the girls? And why?'

'Yes, all of them.'

'Tell us exactly what happened to you?'

'I was pregnant. I was in labour for hours. They said the baby was upside down, and they would have to cut it out. The wound wouldn't heal and leaked blood onto the sheets, and when they started butchering the girls, I played dead. They thought they had already killed me. I am so ashamed.'

'There is no need to be.'

'Am I going to die?'

'No,' said the medic and turned a new page in his diary. 'Can you tell me your name?'

She was reluctant, but eventually, she hung her head low and said, 'My name is Choi Mi-soon.'

'You're Korean?' said the interpreter. 'Not Japanese?'

'All the girls were Korean. I got on the truck with other girls. Everybody was excited. We thought we were going to Japan to train as nurses. They took us to Kyongsung and locked us all together in a small room. We knew something was wrong, but we were so tired from the journey and in the heat of the small room, we nodded off, one by one. I was woken in the middle of the night by a man. He grabbed me by the hair and dragged me out of the room. He took me somewhere dark and tried to rape me. When I refused, he beat me until he broke every bone in my body. But he still raped me, and when he had finished with me, he tossed me to the other men like you would throw scraps of meat to a dog. They all raped me. All of them, over and over, every day, until I accepted it.' She glanced downwards to avoid looking into his eyes.

'Can you continue?'

She nodded. 'I just wanted a job, so I could help my family. I was innocent in the ways of the world and had never left my small village. My bloody mother. I hope she knows what she has done to me. I will never, ever forgive her.'

'The same thing happened to all these girls?' asked the medic.

'Yes.'

'You were all forced to work as prostitutes for Japanese soldiers?'

Mi-soon laughed. 'Not *prostitutes*.' She spat out the word. 'Prostitutes choose to do it and get paid. I was supposed to be a nurse, but instead, they forced me to be their sex slave.

Comfort women, they called us, to hide the reality of what they did.' She laughed. 'Comfort women! A cowardly name, made up by those who could not or did not want to face the truth.'

'When were you brought here?' asked the medic.

'I don't remember, but it must have been more than a year ago. We were taken to many places in Korea and then put on a ship and brought here. I cried and prayed that somebody would take my pain away, but nobody did; nobody came to wipe away my tears, and eventually, they dried on their own. The other girls gave me comfort. It meant I wasn't on my own. We had to look after each other because we got sick all the time. Sometimes we had to serve thirty men or more whenever they wanted. It didn't matter if we were eating or sleeping. They just took us.'

'Did the men wear protection?' The medical officer knew that syphilis and gonorrhoea were endemic, and probably all the girls were infected.

'They were given condoms but most didn't use them,' said Mi-soon. 'They didn't care if we were sick or not. When we got sick, we still had to work, wash uniforms, or cook for the soldiers until we recovered, and it would all start over again. They even continued to rape the girls even when they were pregnant.'

'And you received no treatment when you got sick?'

Mi-soon laughed. 'When I first got sick, I begged the brothel manager for medicine. Every single day I pleaded with him, but he just laughed in my face. They had the medicine. The soldiers used to get it, but they sold it on the black market. We never had any money to pay for it.'

'What happened to the babies?'

'They were mostly stillborn. The ones that survived were diseased and soon died. The few healthy babies that were born disappeared, and we never saw them again.'

The medic was struggling to contain his emotions and took a deep breath. 'Who was in charge of this place? Who was responsible?

She shrugged her shoulders and said softly, 'I don't know.'

'Can you tell me the names of the other girls?'

Mi-soon told him the names and ages of her friends, and the medic recorded it in his diary and was shocked to learn that some were as young as twelve.

'How many men were garrisoned here?'

'Too many.'

'Do you know any of their names?'

Mi-soon was silent for a while, 'A man visited once, dressed as a Japanese officer, but I knew he wasn't. Everybody saluted him and used his Japanese name, but I knew him as a teacher at my school. His name was Song.' She started crying again and said, 'I want to go home.'

'A Dakota will arrive here tomorrow morning. It will fly you to the hospital where you will receive the treatment you need, but for now, take these. Do you understand?'

Mi-soon nodded, and the medical officer gave her some Sulfa tablets to fight any sexually transmitted disease, some codeine for the pain, and a sedative. 'I'm so tired. I want to sleep.' Before she fell asleep, she muttered some words that were so faint that the interpreter had to lean over her to hear. 'They stole my life and broke my dreams,' she said and clutched at his forearm. 'Promise me you will make them pay for this?'

'I will,' he said. 'I will tell the whole world what happened here.'

'I dreamed about becoming a nurse,' she said, 'but now look at me. Look at me.'

The medic sat watch all through the night. He monitored her breathing and heartbeat at regular intervals, and he made two promises to himself. The first was that the world must know what had happened here; those responsible must pay for this atrocity. The second was that when war was over, he would go back to England and qualify a doctor: he was out of his depth and should have been able to do more.

The following morning, the interpreter found the medic kneeling beside a freshly dug grave, reciting the Lord's Prayer.

'What happened?' said the interpreter.

'Mi-soon is dead,' said the medic. 'She died last night.' He had made a simple wooden cross and carved the date of her death, 18 July 1943, on it; he handed the cross to the interpreter, and he added *Choi Mi-soon* in Japanese characters into the cross and placed it on the grave.

'When she died, she was clutching this,' said the medic. He held up a stone necklace strung with a leather bootlace strap. 'It has some writing scratched onto it. Can you read it?'

The interpreter examined the childish scrawl scratched onto the rough stone pendant. After a while, he said, 'It's Korean. A name, I think: *MiJa*.'

CHAPTER 19

THE SEVEN ANGELS WATERFALL

Mija thought Jung-sik looked resplendent in his military uniform, all starch, spit-polish and shiny brass. His rounded boyish looks had recently hardened into that of a handsome youth, and she felt proud that he was her friend and that he had achieved the highest grade in his year. But the award should have been hers: she had always beaten him in every exam, but she had to miss a few this term and her attendance record was poor.

It was the last day of half-term, and the school had assembled for the award ceremony. MiJa applauded with the others, but her thoughts were elsewhere. Jung-sik was nearly eighteen and would graduate at the end of next term and go to high school. She knew that her mother would never send her to high school, and she was worried that he would slowly slide out of her life.

After school, they walked home together. Jung-sik enjoyed this time together, especially since MiJa's little brother had made school friends of his own and did his own thing. He noticed that she no longer walked like an awkward, ungainly girl; she had developed the graceful gait of a confident young woman. Even though they had grown up together and he was comfortable in her presence, he was nervous about asking her on a date. She was on the verge of womanhood now, and that changed everything. He had to be brave, he told himself. A faint heart never won a fair maiden. What if she said no? He would look like a fool. So he surprised himself when he heard his voice say, 'Do you want to go to the waterfall tomorrow?' He blurted it out so fast that it was unintelligible, and he regretted saying it almost before he had finished.

'Did you say something?' asked MiJa?

'No.'

'I'm sure you did.'

His heart sank. Why do girls have to make it so hard? It was torture. Do they do it on purpose? He had nothing to lose now. 'I was thinking of going to the Seven Angels waterfall tomorrow. I don't suppose you would like to come along? No, I thought not.'

'I would love to,' said MiJa.

'Really?'

'Yes. Really,' said MiJa. Why are boys so stupid, even ones that come top of their year?

'Do you know where the Seven Angels waterfall is?'

'Of course.'

'I will meet you there, at nine.'

MiJa wondered why they didn't meet first and walk to the waterfall together, but she was so delighted Jung-sik had invited her that she kept quiet and walked the rest of the way home as though she was floating on air.

After dinner, MiJa plucked up enough courage to ask her mother for permission to go on the date; she had learned the hard way that it was always better to ask for things when her mother had a full belly.

'MiJa, the garlic needs harvesting. It will go to seed if it's left in the ground for too long. Sometimes, I wonder what they teach you at that school.'

'But mother, one more day won't make any difference, and I promise I will do it the day after.'

'Why do you want a day off anyway? Where are you going?'

'Nowhere.'

'Nowhere? You don't need a day off work to go *nowhere.*'

'Jung-sik asked me —.'

'I see. Then the answer is definitely NO! You stupid girl. Even if he likes you, do you think his parents will approve? They won't. Do you think they want him associating with a poor girl like you?'

'But, it's not fair. I have to do the housework, make the meals and —'

'Life is not fair, MiJa. I told you that going to school would fill your head with nonsense.'

MiJa bit her lip, 'Please, Mother.'

'No, MiJa, and that is final.'

MiJa decided that she would go anyway and suffer the consequences. She wanted to look her best, so she took all the clothes out of her wardrobe and spread them on the floor. They were all hand-me-downs from Mi-soon: the ones her mother could not sell, either because they were too old or too old-fashioned. She wanted to wear the pretty summer dress, but it was grubby, so she washed it and hung it in the kitchen to dry overnight.

In the morning, she woke at 5:00 am and was excited at the thought of spending all day alone with Jun-sik. She would usually make the family breakfast, but today she decided she wouldn't. She didn't want to wake anybody, and she planned to slip away before they got up. She felt her dress. It was still damp but it would have to do. She would arrive early and dry it in the sun, long before Jung-sik turned up. She put a kitchen knife into her school backpack and tiptoed out of the house.

'Where are you going?'

MiJa froze and thought her heart would seize. She turned around, dreading the worse, and saw her brother, dressed in his pyjamas. He usually slept until late. Just her luck, she thought. She put her hand over his mouth and hissed at him: 'I am not going anywhere. And be quiet, or you will wake everybody up.'

He mumbled through her fingers, 'Why are you wearing your backpack then? If you are not going anywhere.'

MiJa released her fingers and gave him the hush sign.

'I'm just going for a walk.'

'Can I come?'

'No way. Go back to sleep.'

'But I want to come with you.' Her brother sensed that his sister was up to no good, and he wanted to be part of the adventure.

'You can't,' said MiJa. She wondered how she could explain to Jung-sik why she had brought her baby brother on a date.

'Take me or I will scream'

MiJa saw that she had no choice, so she grabbed his hand and roughly dragged him out of the door. She didn't want to arrive empty-handed, so she made a detour to the family orchards. They belonged to the Japanese now, but they wouldn't miss a few pieces of fruit, and besides, nobody would be up this early in the morning. She told Yung-soo to stand guard.

Yung-soo was delighted: it was the most important task he had ever had, and he kept a vigilant watch whilst his sister picked the choicest peaches and ripe plums. He watched her inspect each one and carefully put it in her backpack. Then she stooped down and struggled to pick up something heavy with both hands. The next thing Yung-soo knew, MiJa sprinted past him.

'Come on,' MiJa shouted, and they ran down the road as fast as they could, not daring to look back. She clutched in her arms a massive watermelon. It was too heavy to carry, so they stopped, and MiJa cut it in half and said, 'Do you want some breakfast.'

'Yes, I want some rice.'

'You want rice?'

'Yes.'

'Well, go home and have some rice then.'

Yung-soo looked at the severity of his sister's face and said, 'Watermelon it is then.'

'Go and fetch a piece of bamboo, about this big,' said MiJa and gestured to Yung-soo with her hand. When Yung-soo returned, she cut the bamboo diagonally in half to make two scoops and gave one to her brother. 'We will eat it camping style.' They sat together on the ground with the hemisphere of watermelon between them and scooped out all the sweet pink flesh. When they had scraped out the last remnants of the watermelon, she dried the empty rind and placed it on Yung-soo's head.

'Sister, what *are* you doing?'

'It's an army hat.'

Yung-soo smiled at his sister and knew he had made the right decision, today was going to be fantastic. What an adventure they were going to have.

'Ready to march to the waterfall, soldier?'

'Yes, sir. Hold on,' said Yung-soo, and he scoured the bushes looking for a length of bamboo that would pass for a rifle. When they arrived at the waterfall, Yung-soo slinked off into the undergrowth, seeking contact with the enemy. His dark green and ochre striped helmet blended in perfectly in the dappled light and shadow of the forest, and the peaceful morning calm was broken, here and there, by the sound of imaginary gunfire.

MiJa found an open sunlit glade and aired the last of the dampness from her dress: she stretched her arms wide and ran up and down the clearing with the wind blowing through her blouse and the sun beating on her back. She lifted her skirts and whirled around and around until she was dizzy and had a giggling fit. She had to stop and catch her breath. In her mind, she was still a young girl, wild and carefree, but she was also glad that nobody was watching.

Jung-sik also set off early that morning. He wanted to select the best spot for the surprise picnic and lay out the food before MiJa arrived. He had suggested an early start so that they could spend some time alone before anybody else turned up, but when he had nearly reached the waterfall, he halted in his tracks, crestfallen. Somebody was already there. They had beaten him to it. Why had they come so early? In a sunny clearing, next to the waterfall, running around like a headless chicken, was a crazy woman with her hands stretched wide apart. He watched for a while, hoping that she would leave, but she just carried right on, whirling around with the grace of a ballerina dancing with an invisible partner. Things weren't going to plan, thought Jung-sik, but it got even worse: some-body was hiding in the bushes. It looked like a young boy, who appeared to be wearing a watermelon on his head. He was sneaking through the undergrowth with a length of bamboo and shouting: 'Bang! Bang!'

Jung-sik wasn't sure what to do, so he tucked himself into the foliage and watched for a while. Then he would make up his mind. Had he made a mistake? Had he accidentally planned his date to coincide with a day release of the local mental hospital? Just his luck, he thought. Should he go back and warn MiJa before she arrives? He sneaked closer to get a better look, and then he got the shock of his life. The crazy girl looked like MiJa. Wait a minute. It *was* MiJa. What was she doing? He grabbed his picnic basket and sprinted towards her with his arms outstretched.

'MiJa. Sorry, I'm late,' he said. 'What on earth were you doing, just now?'

MiJa stopped dancing, and her face flushed. 'Good morning,' she said. 'I was performing Tai Chi. I do it every morning. Have you ever tried it?'

Jung-sik had, and whatever MiJa was doing it wasn't Tai Chi, but at least they could spend some time alone, at last.

'Stick 'em up,' said a voice behind him.

Jung-sik slowly turned around. 'Hello Yung-soo,' he said, trying his best to conceal his disappointment. 'I haven't seen you for a long time.'

Yung-soo was pointing his bamboo gun at him. On his head was a lopsided dark green and yellow watermelon. Streaks of sticky red juice had run onto his face and pyjamas as though he had taken a headshot. Jung-sik put his picnic hamper down slowly and raised his arms. 'Don't shoot.'

'It's only a stick,' said Yung-soo. 'My sister made me an army hat from a watermelon.'

'Sorry, but I had to bring him,' said MiJa.

Jung-sik raised an eyebrow.

'He ambushed me as I was leaving the house.'

When Yung-soo had routed the invisible enemy and won a breast full of medals for bravery, he got bored with his army games. A squadron of hornets started showing a hungry interest in his sugary scalp, so he stripped off his clothes and jumped into the pool under the waterfall.

'Look at me, sister. I can swim.' He stood underneath the waterfall and pretended to scrub under his arms as though he was in the shower. 'Are you coming in?'

MiJa laughed. 'What — naked like you? No, I don't think so.'

Jung-sik blushed as he imagined a naked MiJa bathing in the waterfall, and it reminded him of the legend. He removed his shoes, sat on the edge of the pool, and dipped his feet into the cool water. 'Hey, Yung-soo. Do you know why they call this the Seven Angels waterfall?' he shouted over the clatter of the falls.

Yung-soo cocked his head to one side and knocked the water out of his ears. He did the same with the other side and sat down in the shallows with his arms propped behind his back. 'No,' he said, but he could sense a good story. 'Tell me all about it.'

Jung-sik's face lit up when MiJa sat next to him. She even bared her feet and dipped them into the water, and he began his story:

'Once upon a time, they lived a wise old man with a wispy white beard that came down to his navel. He lived in the spirit world and was attended to by seven beautiful angels, who had wings sewn into their clothes. Every night they would swoop down from heaven and look for the best places to bathe. One night they chose this very waterfall.'

Yung-soo's eyes widened, and Jung-sik looked at MiJa and smiled. She laughed and laid back to listen to the story, dapping her feet on the surface of the water.

'A woodcutter used to live in the forest, not far from this waterfall. He was an ugly-looking man, so much so that nobody wanted to marry him, and the thought of never having any children filled his heart with sadness. One evening he found a young deer caught in a trap. He managed to free it and stroked it gently to calm it down and lost himself in the gaze of its dark, innocent eyes. He had never seen anything so beautiful in his life, and when he let it go, much to his surprise, it didn't run away. It kept stopping and turning around as if it wanted the woodcutter to follow. The deer led him to this very spot, and the woodcutter stared in amazement at what he saw. The moonlight revealed the seven most beautiful women he had ever seen, bathing naked under the waterfall. He wanted to keep one forever, so he hatched a plan and stole a set of winged clothes, hid them in an earthenware jar, and buried it deep in the forest.'

Jung-sik leant back and laid next to MiJa and soaked up the warmth of the sun. His arm brushed against hers, but she did not pull it away; he felt her warm skin against his own, silky soft, and noticed that the down on her arms stood erect and caught the sunlight.

'What happened next?' asked Yung-soo.

'Six of the angels changed into their clothes and flew home, but the one who couldn't find her clothes had to stay behind. She married the woodcutter, and they had a son together every year for three years. After three years, the woodcutter convinced himself that she truly loved him and would stay with him forever, so one day, he returned her clothes.'

'Then what happened?'

'She put on her clothes and flew back to heaven, cradling her three sons in her arms. The woodcutter was devastated with grief. He consulted a shaman who told him about a secret place in the forest where a rope hung down from heaven, and if you were strong enough, you could climb the rope and enter heaven. The woodcutter never stopped searching for that rope and refused to give up. Then many years later, when he least expected it, he found it. He was so frail and old he feared he was not strong enough to climb the rope, but his belief made him strong, and it carried him all the way to heaven and reunited with his family.'

'Is it a true story?' said Yung-soo.

'Of course, it is,' said MiJa.

'So if you want to go home, you had better put your clothes back on,' said Jung-sik

'Not yet,' said Yung-soo and dived back into the pool.

MiJa and Jung-sik sat in silent contemplation, lost in their dreams. They basked in the warmth of the sun and paddled their feet in the cool water, taking care to make sure that their feet playfully kissed. Yung-soo continued splashing and diving, lifting the blurry underwater rocks, and searching underneath for minnows and bullheads until hunger drove him from the water.

Jung-sik found a flat rocky outcrop, spread the picnic blanket, and put the hamper on top. He opened the three tiers.

'Wow,' said MiJa. 'Somebody has been busy.'

'The servants,' said Jung-sik, feeling embarrassed at mentioning the servants and realising that MiJa would not have had such expensive food for a long time.

'I have only brought some fruit,' said MiJa.

'That's fantastic. I forgot about dessert,' said Jung-sik.

They ate lunch in silence, and for dessert they shared some fruit and the last half of the watermelon. Jung-sik put the watermelon skin in the sun to dry.

'Will you go to high school?' said MiJa.

'Yes, I expect so. I will be eighteen soon and my father expects me to go, but it depends on the Japanese, he said. They are taking a lot of boys to work in Japan, to work in the factories.' He saw the concern on MiJa's face. 'It won't apply to me though because my father has the right connections. Father says that the Japanese will lose the war now they have lost the battle of Midway. They have no aeroplanes left, and the Americans are bombing the Japanese mainland already.'

MiJa frowned. The thought of losing him when he went to high school was too much; if he left Korea, it would be unbearable. She watched the shadows lengthen and fall across the pool. The day would soon be over. She didn't want it to end, not ever.

'A penny for your thoughts?' asked Jung-sik.

'Oh, nothing. I was just thinking about my father. His grave is not far from here. I should take Yung-soo to go and say hello. Do you mind?'

'Not at all,' said Jung-sik.

MiJa led them down a well-trodden track that meandered in and out of the pine forest. The boys played soldiers in their watermelon hats. Yung-soo was ambushed, took a fatal head-shot, and staggered about in a prolonged death scene that was worthy of an Oscar. MiJa collected wild Naki lilies and Korean Angelicas and tied the stems together with a strip of grass to make a bouquet of vivid orange and brilliant white to place on the grave.

Jung-sik collected some clover flowers and formed them in a daisy chain fashion by piercing each stem with his thumbnail and threading the next flower through the slot. He made a ring and bracelet and slipped them onto MiJa's ring finger and delicate wrist. She smelled the delicate fragrance and felt intoxicated.

'They're so pretty,' said MiJa, admiring her wrist. 'They have a natural beauty and small all of their own.'

'Like you,' said Jung-sik and blushed.

Yung-soo groaned, and MiJa blushed too. She didn't know what to say and was confused about her feelings. Nobody had treated her like this before. 'It is so hot today,' she said and fanned her red face with her hands.

They crossed a babbling mountain rill and climbed the rocky scree to the gravesite. 'It's not far now,' said MiJa. When they reached the gravesite, the boys removed their helmets, out of respect, and they all kowtowed twice to the grave. MiJa fell to her knees and burst into tears. The unkempt grave was overgrown with weeds, and some had even blotted out his name on the headstone. How soon he had been forgotten and abandoned by those he had given life to. She started to trim the overgrown grass and briars with the kitchen knife.

'Give me the knife. I'll do that,' said Jung-sik.

'No. I must do it,' said MiJa through blurry eyes. 'Yung-soo, you should be doing this. It is your duty as the twentieth generation Choi. Watch how I do it. As the eldest son, you are supposed to do this at least three times a year: at lunar New Year, Chusok, and on the anniversary of his death.' When she had finished tidying up the grave, and her tears had stemmed to mere sniffles, she laid the wildflowers at his grave and put one peach and one plum on his graveside table, and said a prayer. She promised her father that she would visit the grave more often, and then she beckoned Jung-sik to come forward.

'Father, this is Jung-sik,' she said. Jung-sik bowed twice.

'Look what he made for me.' She showed her father the clover ring and bracelet and made a silent prayer that the war would end soon, then Jung-sik would not have to go to Japan, and Mi-soon would come home.

The journey back home was carefree. MiJa spirits lifted a little, and soon they were all laughing and skipping and talking at once. It was the best day of her life, and she didn't care about the punishment that was waiting at home. However painful it was, it was worth it.

A week passed, and MiJa never heard from Jung-sik, so one evening, when she had finished harvesting all the garlic, she decided to visit his house. The head servant answered the door, and when he returned, he said that his master had told him that she should go away and never darken this door again. She had brought bad luck to the Kim household. 'Jung-sik gave this note to me before he left. He said I was to give it to you.'

MiJa ran away with teary eyes until she could run no more. She tore open the note with trembling hands and read it:

Hi MiJa, this is Jung-sik.

When I got home from the picnic, the Japanese were waiting in the house. I must leave at once, so I have only got a minute to scribble this note. I just wanted you to know that today was the best day of my life, and for a long time now, I wanted to tell you how I feel about you, but I could never find the right words.

I love you, MiJa. Today, when we visited your father's grave, I asked him if he would accept me as his son-in-law. I must go now. They are taking me to Japan to work in the Mitsubishi factory in Hiroshima. I will write as soon as possible. Please take care of yourself until we meet again.

See you soon. Your Jung-sik.

CHAPTER 20

DESTROYER OF WORLDS

T wo years, eleven days, and seven hours had passed since Jung-sik was taken to Japan. MiJa had not heard a word from him since then. Every weekend she returned to that same hill that overlooked the Seven Angels Waterfall. What she was looking for, she did not know or care. It was just enough that she was there. Maybe she was reinforcing her memories of Jung-sik so that they would never fade, or perhaps it was because of the calm she felt when she was there, and she half expected Jung-sik to come running over a sunlit glad still clutching a picnic hamper in his outstretched arms.

She smiled wistfully at her thoughts and opened her Korean history book. It always fell open at the same page: the one where she had pressed the clover ring and bracelet that Jung-sik had made for her on that perfect summer day. She sniffed at them, and they still smelled as fresh and fragrant as that first day. She held the book to her beating breast, and the tears came, dripping onto the pressed flowers for a moment seemed refreshed and alive. She stayed until dusk, and the ritual always ended the same thought: Jung-sik did not return today, but he would tomorrow. She was sure about that.

6 August 1945 was a date burned into her mind forever. It started with the excitable, shrill voices of the street urchins, 'News. News. Read all about it: Americans bomb Hiroshima.' They only bothered to print the news leaflets when something monumental had happened, so MiJa ran into the street and grabbed one. When she read it, she was dumbstruck. What should she do? Her mouth was dry and her heart was pounding. On impulse, she ran to her mother.

'Look, Mother.'

'What is all the fuss about?' said Bok-nam.

MiJa put the leaflet on the table and smoothed it flat. 'The Americans have bombed Hiroshima. The war will soon be over.' The front page carried the Oppenheimer quote as the headline: '*Now I am become death, destroyer of worlds.*' Underneath the quotation was a photograph of the destroyed City. Nothing remained but a desolate wilderness as though the city had never existed at all.

'Nothing could survive that,' said Bok-nam. 'He must be dead.'

'Who must be dead?'

'Jung-sik, of course. So, you can forget all thoughts of him. I told you, but do you ever listen to me? You should have married that other man when you got the chance. I will find you another match. You need to get on with your life instead of moping around in the past all day.'

MiJa looked directly into her mother's eyes, searching for a glint of compassion, but they were as empty as her soul. Her poisonous mouth uttered some other cruel barbs, but MiJa has stopped listening. She turned away so her mother could not see that her eyes were full of tears and her heart full of hatred. How could she be so cruel to me? she thought. My own mother.

'How dare you say that Jung-sik is dead?' she said. 'How can he be? He must come home and marry me.'

MiJa felt sure that if he had died, she would have known. She would have felt something. Every night she had the same dream: it was the day of their wedding and Mi-soon was there with a big smile on her face. It was her destiny. She would run away as soon as she was twenty-one but until then she was still a child and must do as her parents say. MiJa was so cut off from reality she did not notice the world unravel before her very eyes.

On the 8 August 1945, the Soviet Union declared war on Japan and marched towards the Korean peninsula.

The next day fate smiled kindly on the Japanese City of Kokura: cloudy weather diverted the B-29 Superfortress, Bockscar, to Nagasaki, and the world witnessed the first hydrogen bomb.

Two days later on the 11th August 1945, the USA and USSR agreed to divide Korea at the 38th parallel. The Americans promised the 'Prompt and utter destruction of Japan. If Japan refused to surrender, they could expect a rain of ruin from the air, the like of which has never been seen on this earth.'

On the 15 August 1945. Emperor Hirohito, a living god descended directly from the sun god Amaterasu, was defeated by mere mortals; the ingenuity of man had created a far more powerful and destructive artificial sun. Japan surrendered unconditionally.

World War II was over.

CHAPTER 21

THE COCKROACHES COME HOME

Cockroaches have remarkable resilience; they are one of the few creatures that can survive the fallout of a nuclear war. Nobody knows how they manage it, but it is believed they hide underground until the danger has passed. Once it is safe to return home, they emerge from their hiding places, as if by magic, and scuttle back to gorge on the detritus of war until they are fat and slick.

In mid-October 1945, the personal aeroplane of General MacArthur, *The Bataan,* touched down at the Kimpo Air Base, just outside Seoul. The old capital, Kyongsung, had been renamed Seoul: a new name for a new beginning. The Lockheed Constellation contained a man who was little-known in Korea even though he was Korean and claimed royal lineage. The man was called S M Lee. As a young boy he had been struck down with smallpox and nearly blinded, but an American pastor, who also happened to be a doctor, managed to cure him. In his youth, he campaigned for an independent Korea, and the Japanese imprisoned him, but he managed to escape and make his way to the USA, where he decided to sit out the war and wait for his chance. His chance came after

Pearl Harbour, and he grabbed it with both hands. The Americans thought him awkward, unreliable, and a troublemaker, but he had their backing because he was fiercely anti-communist, spoke English, and was educated at Harvard.

Also making his way home was Mr Song, the ex-schoolteacher from Mun-gyeong. His career had advanced rapidly in the Imperial Japanese Army. In Manchuria, he worked in military intelligence and spied on Korean insurgents fighting for independence. He served in Burma, and when the Japanese surrendered, he joined the nascent Korean Military Academy, newly established by the Americans, and graduated top of the class.

All over Korea, people dreamed of a better future. It was a time to dream, a time of golden opportunity. Roosevelt, Churchill, and Chiang Kai-Shek met in Cairo and promised Korea freedom and independence. The Korean people had dared to dream, not the airy dreams of the impossible but real dreams — ones that might come true, given time, providence, hard work, and luck. They had thrown off the yoke of Japanese oppression, and all over the Korean peninsula in every city, town and village, they arranged a local committee to govern their affairs.

Then anger raised its ugly head; anger that had been suppressed for far too long and bottled up until the pressure built and built until it erupted in a bloody fountain. The Korean people dug up the body of Lee Wan-yong, the Korean Prime Minister who signed over his country to Japan, and brutally dismembered it. They razed the Japanese Shinto shrines, and Japanese collaborators were ruthlessly hunted down and executed without trial. The hunt for the guilty continued and they ruthlessly persecuted the Yangban class, who had led them into this mess. One cold evening in November, four men barged into the Choi family home and demanded to see Bok-nam.

'Mother, some men are here to see you,' said MiJa as she instinctively shielded her brother behind her back.

'Park Bok-nam?' shouted one of the men.

'Yes. Who wants to know?'

'You have to come with us.'

'Who are you?'

'Never mind who we are. You are to appear before the judge in the People's Court.'

'Why? I have not done anything wrong. I am not going anywhere.'

Two men grabbed her, one on each arm, and dragged her out of the house. She screamed, 'Let me go. Why are you doing this? You are making a mistake.'

CHAPTER 22

THE PEOPLE'S COURT

The facilities at Mun-gyeong police station were basic: no-frills, no lawyers, no jury and definitely no justice. Bok-nam had spent a sleepless night locked in a cramped police cell that was sparsely furnished but full of darkness, fear and body odour. In the harsh cold light of the morning, she reflected on her situation as she struggled to get up from the hard glazed floor and stretch the aches and cramps out of her body.

She slumped down into the solitary steel chair, bolted to the floor and glanced around the cell: a thick cluster of flies moped around a naked electric lightbulb, and the strong smell of urine wafted from the steel bucket in the corner. She tried to ignore the smell, but it was impossible: the choking stench was the first thing she noticed when she arrived at the police station, and it clung to her wherever she went, as though it had seeped into the very fabric of the building.

A dark-red stain on the far wall of the cell caught her eye: a translucent smear on the surface of grimy white tiles that looked like blood, and she tried not to think how it got there, but her imagination filled in the gaps. She flailed around for pleasant thoughts but drew a blank, and after what seemed like days but must have only been a few hours, the cell door was unlocked, and a man in a sweat-stained police uniform shouted, 'Park Bok-nam.'

She nodded.

'The judge will see you now.'

The court official ushered her into Court Number One, and she saw her accusers for the first time: a man in his mid-forties, with short-cropped hair and a fogged-over lazy eye, was dressed as the judge. She thought she had seen him before. He looked a lot like the butcher in the next town, Sangju. On closer inspection it was him, and he was flanked on both sides by two uniformed officers that she also recognised as her former farm labourers. She looked around the courtroom. A motley crew of the great unwashed had gathered, the Baekjong, the Sangmin, and the Jungin classes of this world. They leered at her with gap-toothed grinning faces and shouted and jeered — a baying mob who had no interest in justice. All they wanted was revenge, and the rising murmur of discontent in the crowd urged the judge to deliver it.

'Are you Park Bok-nam, wife of Choi Gil-soo,' said the judge.

'I am, but my husband died.'

'You are here because you are a Japanese collaborator and a traitor to your country.'

'I am not —'

'How do you plead?'

'Not guilty,' said Bok-nam. 'I may be many things, but I am not a traitor.' The lunatics had taken over the asylum, she thought, and it wasn't right that a woman with her pedigree and breeding should be forcibly dragged here and put on trial by the dregs of society.

The judge continued, 'Do you remember the agricultural officer for the Mun-gyeon district?'

'No.'

'No, Your Honour, and I find that hard to believe that you didn't know him. After we expelled the Japanese Army, we hunted everywhere for him, but alas, we were too late, and we found him hanging from a tree with his tongue cut out and his guts spilt on the floor.'

'That was nothing to do with me, Your Honour.'

'Maybe not, but we did manage to capture his Korean agent, and before he died a horrible death, he gave us a list of all the people who had collaborated with the Japanese. One of the names on that list was yours.' The judge referred to his papers and said, 'It says here that you sold your eldest daughter, Choi Mi-soon, to the Japanese.'

'I never. I only found her a job in Japan. Is that a crime?' said Bok-nam.

'Anybody who took money from the Japanese or helped them in any way has committed a crime.'

'My late husband was forced to pay his taxes to the Japanese because he had no choice. Is that a crime too? I never even received any money from Japan,' said Bok-nam.

The judge scribbled some notes down and tapped the bottom edge of the papers on his desk to align the top. 'It says here that you received money every month.'

'It's a lie. I swear.'

'Also, your late husband was a landowner, part of the Yangban class that sold Korea to the Japanese.'

'Is everything a crime now? I cannot choose which family I was born into, no more than you can. Did you choose which family you were born into?'

The judge ignored her. 'Will anybody speak up for this woman before I pass sentence?'

Dol-soi stood up. 'Your honour, she is wy wife now. I was once her head servant, but she still chose to marry me. That is proof that people can change and that she is a reformed character.'

'You claim to be married to this woman?' asked the judge.

The crowd tittered.

'Yes, Your Honour.'

The judge rifled through his papers again. 'There is no record here of any further marriage after the death of her husband, Choi Gil-soo. You are her ex-servant, you say, and you admit to having a sexual relationship with this woman.'

'Yes,' said Dol-soi and hung his head.

'Please appear before me tomorrow morning.'

'Yes, Your Honour,' said Dol-soi, and stunned into silence, sat down.

'May I speak?' said a voice from the gallery. The crowd turned to see a young girl with an infant in tow.

'Who are you?' asked the judge.

'I am her daughter, Choi MiJa, and this is my brother Choi Yung-soo.'

'Then you are part of this Yangban family too, and I suggest you are careful what you say to this court.'

'All his life, my father stood up to the Japanese, and he paid for it with his life. We are not traitors to Korea and never have been. You say we are Yangban class, but we do not live as they do. My late father always respected the farmers who worked for him and treated them fairly. When the Japanese took everything from us, we had to grow our own food, and there was barely enough to survive. I say we are no different from all of you gathered here.'

The judge was startled that this young woman was addressing him so directly. 'Is that all, young woman?'

'No, that is not all. You have the power of life and death over our mother, but what will happen to him?' She pulled her brother closer to her. 'How is he supposed to live without his mother? He is innocent. Why should he be punished? Korea is a free country now, and we have a chance to build a new country. A new future. What does that future look like? Shall we build a new country for all, or just a few? We must stand together and stop our squabbling between the classes because we are weak if we are divided. If you want evidence look to our history: first, it was the Chinese that took advantage of our differences, then it was the Japanese, and now it is the Americans. When will it end? We need to put our differences aside and do what is right. I beg you for mercy. I beg you to be wiser than the Japanese, and wiser than the Yangban of old and perform a noble deed and set our mother free.'

By now, the crowd was in an uproar, arguing about what the future should look.

'Order! Order!' shouted the apoplectic judge. When the rabble subsided, he said, 'I have listened to what you have said, but I am afraid that my hands are tied. Rules are rules, and traitors must pay for their acts. We cannot just forget the past, and there must be a deterrent for criminals, especially traitors.'

He addressed their mother next. 'Park Bok-nam, the People's Court finds you guilty: you are guilty of treason because you collaborated with the Japanese, and you are guilty of being a member of the Yangban class and therefore a Japanese collaborator. I have no option but to sentence you to death.'

Bok-nam felt faint, but before she collapsed, she summoned the strength to shout, 'I am innocent. I am innocent, I tell you. What right do you have to judge me? On whose authority?'

When she recovered, Bok-nam pleaded for her life with the judge. He let her stew for a while. 'There is one thing,' he said. 'If you agree to transfer your house and land to the Korean people, the sentence may be commuted. What do you say?'

'What will happen to my children? Where will they live without me?'

'If you sign over the deeds, I can see that you are set free. You will live on a local farm and undergo a re-education programme. Do you agree?'

'Yes, but what choice do I have?'

'Then please leave your old house immediately. I want it vacant by tomorrow morning. Is that understood?'

'Yes.'

'Yes, Your Honour.'

'Take the prisoner away.'

Dol-soi scrounged an old handcart, a two-wheeled contraption like a rickshaw, with a steel pulling bar at the front. It was dusk when they had finished packing their things, and MiJa was glad of the cover of darkness to hide her shame. Dol-soi pulled the handcart through the streets like a beast of burden, whilst Bok-nam, MiJa and Yung-soo trailed behind carrying as much as they could. They were all glad of something to hide their faces behind from the ever-watchful neighbours that had lined the streets to watch them depart.

When they arrived at the farmhouse allocated for the re-education of Bok-nam, they were shown to a hayloft, perched precariously over eight rickety stilts.

'This can't be it,' said Bok-nam.

'It is,' said Dol-soi. 'It will look better in the morning.'

Nobody believed him. The access to the hayloft was via a flight of shoddy steps, but first, you had to cross a filthy pigsty guarded by an angry old sow. Yung-soo found some rotten apple cores and threw them into the corner of the pen to divert the sow whilst they climbed the creaking staircase. Dol-soi pushed open the trapdoor, and the musty smell of old straw bedding, soaked in stale animal urine, fell out. Everybody groaned and gagged. Dol-soi poked his head through the trapdoor. It was dark, but a little moonlight forced its way through the chinks in the wooden clapboards and cast bars of light onto the walls and floor that made it feel like a cage.

'I don't want to stay here,' said Yung-soo. 'It stinks of animals.'

'Be quiet,' said MiJa, and she looked around the room, and as her eyes adjusted to the dark, she could see that it was bare except for three makeshift beds made from the scraps of old wooden pallets. She tried to move and cringed when her shoes stuck to the tackiness of the floor. She glanced down and noticed she was standing over a small trapdoor that opened directly onto the pigsty below.

'The toilet,' said Dol-soi.

'Ugh,' said MiJa and struggled to fight back the tears. It was going to be impossible to live here, and it wasn't just the filth. Summer would be stiflingly hot, and plagues of dengue-fever-carrying mosquitoes attracted by the pigs would move in with them. The winters would be bleak and mind-numbingly cold. All-year-round it would always sound and smell like a pigsty, but little did she know that one day, in the not too distant future, that cantankerous old sow would save her life.

CHAPTER 23

THE RE-EDUCATION OF BOK-NAM

The re-education of Bok-nam began early next morning long before dawn, when she was jolted awake by a loud knocking sound on the floorboards that disturbed motes of dust and roused hidden barnyard aromas. Even the hayloft objected by shaking on its stilts.

'Get up, you lazy Yangban. You must work for a living now,' shouted one of the farmwives, as she thrust her wooden staff upwards and dislodged another floorboard. Some of the straw bedding fell through the gaps in the floorboards and fluttered onto the ground below.

Bok-nam could hear them laughing. She hadn't slept a wink, and on the few occasions when she did drop off she was woken by a snuffle, a grunt or a squeal. She would never get used to that smell, the smell of failure. 'Bloody hell. What time is it?' she said as she tried to open her matted eyes.

'Never mind what time it is. Get up. You have to go and fetch the water,' shouted a stern voice from below.

MiJa and Yung-soo looked at each other and could barely suppress the smirks spreading slowly across their faces. Their mother was going to do some housework for the first time in her life, and they didn't want to miss a thing.

The farmwives were manoeuvring a large, galvanised steel bath into position. Dol-soi made the mistake of trying to help them.

'Aren't you expected before the judge this morning? First thing?' said one of the wives. 'I wouldn't be late if I was you. He hates that.'

When Dol-soi had left in a panic, one of the wives said to Bok-nam, 'You have to fill this tub every morning. Make sure you fill it with enough water for all your cooking and washing needs.'

'How do I do that?'

'We will show you.' Beside the tub lay some large earthenware pots and several small mats made from woven straw, shaped like a doughnut. Bok-nam copied the other women and picked up one of the pots and a doughnut-shaped ring. Yung-soo tried to help his mother, but one of the wives, the one with the skin of a leathery reptile and a filthy cackle in her voice, told him that his balls would fall off if he ever attempted to do women's work. He watched the women walk off in single file, and when they were safely out of sight, he slipped his hand into his pants and checked.

When the women arrived at the well, one of them broke the ice from the galvanised well bucket, lowered it into the well and started to fill her earthenware jar. When it was full, she put the straw doughnut on top of their head, secured it by putting the loose end of the straw into her mouth, and lifted the pot on her head in one fluid movement. 'Now it's your turn,' she said to Bok-nam.

When Bok-nam tried, her fingertips stuck to the cold metal bucket, and she had to blow on them to prise them off. Her muscles burned from winding up the heavy bucket from the well, and she had to stop halfway for a rest. The farmwives give each other a knowing look and exchanged tuts. When Bok-nam finally managed to fill the large earthenware pot, it was too heavy to lift, so she poured some of the water onto the ground to lighten her load. The air turned blue with a chorus of profanities and angry gestures. Bok-nam put the straw doughnut ring on the top of her head, knelt and tried to lift the pot onto her head with both hands. She just managed to get it to her head, but it dislodged the ring. The second time she remembered to put the loose end of the woven straw in her mouth to stop then ring from sliding off and managed to lift the pot to her head, but the condensation on the outside made it slippery, and when she stood up she lost her grip, and the earthenware pot fell and smashed to pieces.

Dejected, she followed the single file of women back to the farm. She felt foolish because she had failed her first simple task, and the fact that MiJa had managed it her first attempt made it so much worse. She watched the line of women plod on. In the sunlight, she could see their faces clearly for the first time: with their weather-beaten and wrinkled skin, sullen watery eyes, and heads sunken deep into their shoulders under the heavy load, they looked like a bale of turtles marching to the sea.

When Bok-nam finally managed to lift a full pot onto her head, she received a round of applause. She managed to get all the way back without breaking it, but when she tipped it into the bathtub, she found she had spilt most of the water. The women laughed, and one of them said, 'At this rate, it will be dark before you fill that bathtub.' They cackled some obscenities and left them to it.

In the late afternoon, miraculously, the bathtub was full of water. Bok-nam and MiJa were busy cleaning the hayloft when Yung-soo appeared with a lovesick puppy trailing behind him.

'Where have you been?' asked Bok-nam.

'Playing with my new friend. Can we keep him? Please?'

'He already belongs to somebody. Look, he has a collar,' said MiJa. 'Somebody has tied a blue ribbon, with a tiny silver bell on it around his neck.'

'He's called Silverbell,' said Yung-soo. 'Can we keep him?'

'Do you think there's enough food to feed one more mouth?' said Bok-nam.

'I will share my dinner with him,' said Yung-soo. He had already decided to keep him.

When Dol-soi returned in the evening, he had the second biggest shock of his life. His wife emerged from a cloud of fragrant steam carrying a large bowl of steamed rice. He grinned and said, 'Did you cook dinner?'

Bok-nam smiled. 'We get a weekly ration of rice. It's not much so we must be careful.'

'What happened at the court. I thought the judge —'

'He offered me a job.'

'What!'

Over dinner, Dol-soi told them how the judge had asked him to join the committee, and then he explained what their plans were. The People's Committees were going to rebuild Korea and every village and town would get whatever was needed. They were going to build the irrigation ditches that the Japanese had promised and failed to deliver on all the farms. They would pool their knowledge and offer advice to farmers on land management and the latest techniques. They would bulk buy to get the best prices. They would sell directly to the market and cut out the agents. The school would be refurbished, be free for all and follow a Korean syllabus. They would even construct a new public bathhouse. It was a much better system than the old ways: they would cooperate on all the projects, and not compete. A new way of thinking.

Dol-soi spooned some rice into his mouth, chewed it thoughtfully and said, 'What is this called?'

'Nothing special, it's just steamed rice.'

'Well, I think we should call it three-layered rice.'

'Really?'

'Yes, because the bottom layer is burnt crisp, the middle layer is still wet, and the top layer is uncooked.' They all laughed and finished the meal in silence, except for the occasional grunt from the old sow. If it was waiting for any leftovers, it would be disappointed.

The family settled into their new life: Yung-soo started the Korean school, much to his annoyance, but every evening Silverbell would wait for him outside the hayloft, and they would go on one of their adventures. Bok-nam knew that she would never be accepted as one of them, and the taunts continued. One evening, in the summer of 1947, Bok-nam and MiJa went to wash the clothes in the river.

'Look sisters, is that the Queen of the Yangban, washing her clothes in the river!' shouted one of the washerwomen as she beat the living daylights out of her laundry with a large, narrow wooden paddle.

Another shouted, 'Don't damage your soft pretty hands.' Then they would cackle, caw and curse until they'd had their fill and returned to their gossip. They were talking about the public bathhouse. The latest rumour was that it would be ready for the Lunar New Year.

Bok-nam tried to splash her tormentors with the river water, but they were too far away. MiJa told her mother to ignore them. Bok-nam ignored her and scoured the river for the heaviest rock she could find and lobbed it at her tormentors. It fell short with a mighty splash, but it soaked the women. Bok-nam smirked with satisfaction, lost her footing on the mossy rocks, and crashed straight into the river to an uproar of laughter and the shaking of tearful heads.

'You are supposed to take your clothes off before you wash them, you stupid Yangban,' shouted one of the washerwomen and sat down and slapped her thighs in hysterics. Bok-nam took her anger out on the laundry. She grabbed the first item and soaked it in the river, making sure she held it under the water long enough to drown. She flung it on a flat rock with a loud wet slap and flayed it with a bar of hard soap. Then she beat it within an inch of its life, with a flat elongated wooden paddle, drowned it again, and wrung it until her knuckles turned first white and then purple.

CHAPTER 24

THE YEAR OF THE RAT

The Year of the Rat fell on 10 February 1948. It was a lucky year for rats; some of them even managed to get elected. The public bathhouse had opened on time and there was great excitement on the farm. Everybody was eager to visit to scrub away last year's grime and start the Lunar New Year afresh.

MiJa wanted to arrive early before the mob dirtied the water. She removed her shoes and put them in the pigeonhole shoe rack at the entrance. She recalled the last time she had been to a bathhouse and somebody had stolen her shoes, so she'd gone home shoeless and hung around outside the house, afraid to tell her mother what had happened. That was one of the benefits of being poor, she thought. Nobody was going to steal your shoes.

She went through the door to the female changing rooms. Two old Azumas were sitting on a wooden bench. They were both completely naked, yakking away unselfconsciously with their fleshy arms flapping away in excited animation. One was seated with her legs akimbo, and the other was breastfeeding her son. MiJa felt embarrassed and looked the other way. She went to the furthest changing locker, tucked away in the far corner of the room, where she had a little privacy and wouldn't have far to walk far to the hot tub.

As she undressed, her eyes fell on a pair of jiggling breasts as a young woman was bent doubled-over, drying her hair with a towel. She locked the locker, tied up her hair with the elastic band used for a key fob, and covered her modesty as best she could with a towel the size of a face flannel. Then she made her way over the slippery, wet tiles to the hot tub room and slid open the door.

She was disappointed. Through the fog of chlorinated steam and whiff of cheap soap, she could see that the hot tub was full already. Women were packed tightly together like beansprouts in a pot. Hot water gurgled from two taps that were left continuously running so that the bath overflowed onto the tiled floor and carried with it the dirty soap, suds and scum down the drain. Around the perimeter of the hot tub was a tiled shelf that acted as a seating area. There was one space left.

MiJa collected two plastic bowls and sat on the seat. She dipped the smaller plastic bowl into the hot tub and doused herself. She washed her body with the cheap bar of soap, inserted onto a metal spike in the wall to stop the customers from stealing it, and rinsed off the suds, waiting for her turn in the hot tub. It seemed to take forever, but eventually somebody got out of the tub, and she gingerly lowered herself into the scalding hot water until it came to her chin. She sighed and let her worries evaporate with the steam.

After twenty minutes of being softened up, she was ready for the next stage of the cleansing process. Around the entire perimeter of the room ran a trough full of clean hot water, but again there was no space and MiJa expected to wait but a kind Azuma slid over to make room for her and beckoned her across by patting the seat. MiJa thanked her, filled her large plastic bowl with fresh water, and started to scrub off her dead skin. She noticed that the Azuma next to her smelled of Sabon soap. It was the same kind her mother used, and memories of her first day at school came flooding back. It was true that you only miss something once it has gone. That life had disappeared forever now, but for the moment, it was still a vivid picture in her mind.

'Will you scrub my back, please?' asked the Azuma.

'Sure,' said MiJa snapping out of her daydreaming. 'Sorry, I was miles away.'

'Thinking about the election?' Korea was to hold its first ever election and the whole of Korea, north and south, would have say in how the country was governed.

'Oh, no,' said MiJa. 'I don't qualify to vote.' She began to scrub the Azuma's back and thought about who she would vote for if she did have a vote. She was old enough to vote, and women were allowed to vote, but only if they were landowners or taxpayers. In villages, the headman voted for the entire population.

'Harder,' the Azuma said.

'Who will you vote for?' said MiJa as she scrubbed harder.

'The National Association for the Rapid Realisation of Korean Independence,' said the Azuma. 'Quite a mouthful, isn't it? NARRKI, for short. The trustees are taking too long to sort things out.'

MiJa scrubbed the Azuma's back until no more dead skin came off. 'All done,' she said.

'Turn around,' said the Azuma. MiJa sat on the floor with her knees together, and the Azuma scrubbed her back with a rough hemp cloth until the skin rolled up into thin, light grey strings of exfoliated cells that looked like noodles. 'Soba noodles tonight,' said the Azuma and laughed. MiJa was embarrassed even though it was a standard bathhouse joke.

. . .

Bok-nam arrived at the bathhouse later in the afternoon, and as she sat soaking in the hot tub, she too thought about the election. What if the Yangban were returned to power as was rumoured? They would look after their own. She started to dream.

In the male section of the bathhouse, Dol-soi thought about everything the People's Committee had achieved already. They had finished digging the irrigation ditches, the rice was growing well, and all the signs indicated they were in for a bumper harvest. The school was open again, it was free, and they were teaching a Korean curriculum. They had built this bathhouse, and it was free. The committee system was working. He started to dream.

CHAPTER 25

BUDDHA AND THE GENERAL
ELECTION

M iJa and Yung-soo had never seen anything so dazzlingly beautiful and held their breath. They were mesmerised by the thousands of crepe paper lanterns — a glittering kaleidoscope of translucent reds, pinks, golds, blues and greens shimmered and lit the way ahead, like a guiding rainbow that you could almost reach out and touch. Each lantern had been handmade and formed a globe-shaped lotus flower. It represented the belief that wherever the young Buddha stood, a lotus flower would miraculously sprout from the ground.

It was 16 May 1948, and all over the country Koreans celebrated the Buddha's Birthday for the first time since the Japanese occupation. State-sponsored Shinto was dead. *Hae Guk Sa* temple had been restored to its previous magnificence and was a popular choice for the celebrations because its name means *The Country Owes You*, in reference to the monks who fought the Japanese invasion in 1592. Everybody wanted to celebrate being Korean, and this once outlawed religion seemed so colourful and vibrant after the drabness of the Shinto shrines.

MiJa held her brother's hand tightly, and they flowed with the crowd of faithful along the lantern-lit path until they came to the main prayer hall. She was impatient to see this new god, but first she stood back and watched how the others paid their respects. When she was confident, she removed her shoes and kowtowed three times, making sure that her forehead, knees and elbows always touched the ground. She peered into the main hall and was underwhelmed: there was nothing but a small golden statue of Buddha in the centre of the hall. He was flanked on both sides by a pair of flickering candles, and to his left stood a stack of books containing his teachings, the Buddha Dharma. In front of the statue was a tray of freshly-picked flowers, and the petals had already started to turn brown and curl at the edges, adding to her disappointment. This new god did not look very powerful — how could he help?

A group of shaven-headed monks, dressed in saffron robes, sat behind a row of tables serving the food. They handed MiJa a large bowl of plain steamed rice, mixed with wild vegetables, and two wooden spoons. She gave one to her brother and asked the monks what their colleagues were doing. She pointed to a group of monks furiously scribbling on pieces of paper.

'They are writing out prayers for the people.'

'Can they write one for me?'

'Of course.'

The monk smiled and said, 'I will need the name and the date of birth for those you wish to pray for.'

MiJa removed a few tarnished and bitten coins that were no longer currency from her pocket. 'Will this be enough?' she said. 'I need two prayers.'

The monk looked at the coins. 'That will be plenty,' he said.

'One is for Choi Mi-soon, born on 7 June 1922, and the other, for Kim Jung-sik, born on 15 August 1925.'

'What would you like me to write?'

'I want the Buddha god —'

The monk put down his pen and placed his palms together. 'Lord Buddha is not a god,' he explained.

'He isn't?'

'No, he was no different to you and me, except that he was born a wealthy prince. But everywhere he went, he saw nothing but suffering and death and he wondered why it had to be like that. Then one day, he gave up his privileged life and went in search of the truth. He lived as simple a life as he could, but he nearly died from starvation. That convinced him that extremism was not the answer. He needed to find another way and then one day, whilst sitting under a Bodhi tree, the answer came to him. We call this his moment of enlightenment, and that is why we light candles at the temple, to light the way ahead.'

'I see,' said MiJa.

'Do you know what the answer to end all suffering was?'

'No,' said MiJa, eager to hear the answer.

'The cure for all of our problems lies in our thoughts and actions.'

'Is that it?' she asked. 'So simple.'

'Yes,' said the monk, but he could see that she still looked puzzled. 'What is it, child?'

'If Buddha is not a god, what is the point of writing out prayers for him?'

'It is like this. People sing in the bath when no one is listening because it makes them happy. It is the same with prayers. You don't need a god for them to work. Sometimes, all we need to do is organise our thoughts and emotions to find out what is troubling us. What would you like me to write?'

'I want you to write that I hope my sister and boyfriend aren't suffering.'

'Where are they now? Are they dead?' asked the monk.

'No, I don't think so.'

The monk thought about this for some time and said, 'When you prayed to Buddha did you notice the tray of flowers?'

'Yes. I think you need some fresh ones.'

'You are very observant,' said the monk. 'All things must fade and die. Nothing is permanent.' He handed MiJa the written prayer and a lantern. MiJa thanked the monk and she took the lantern, attached the prayer to it and hung it with the thousands of others.

'Buddhism is very simple,' said the monk. 'Live with a pure heart. Do not harm any living thing. Train your mind to curb your desires and be wise. A wise man is always selfless.'

Earlier in the week, on 10 May 1948, Korea had held its first general election. The UN called for an election for the whole of Korea, but the north, with far fewer people, feared a landslide so they prevented the UN mediators from entering. There was temporary hope when the USSR proposed that all foreigners leave the country to let the Koreans run the elections, but the USA rejected it. They wanted their Korean puppet, S M Lee, in power as a backstop against the communists. Some politicians boycotted the election because they knew that Korea would be permanently split and become a puppet state. The poor boycotted the elections because they feared that the old Yangban class and Japanese collaborators would be elected. They were right. The National Association for the Rapid Realisation of Korean Independence won the election, and S M Lee got his paws on power. From there things moved rapidly:

. . .

On 20 July 1948, S M Lee bribed the National Assembly of MPs by promising not to purge their ranks of Japanese collabora-tors if they elected him as President. He was elected President, and his first job was to reinstate the Yangban class to key govern-ment positions.

On 14 August 1948, Sohn Kee-chung led the Korean team out at the closing ceremony of the XIV Olympiad in London. He had won a gold medal for Japan in 1936, and today he was the flag bearer but it was no ordinary flag. It was the Korean flag — the first time it had been seen in any Olympics. He said later that it was the proudest moment of his life.

On 15 August 1948, S M Lee declared the birth of the Republic of South Korea with him as President of the whole of the Korean Peninsula. In response, the North appointed Kim Il-sung as the glorious leader of The Democratic Republic of North Korea. He also claimed authority over the whole of the Korean peninsula.

Then one day, the people woke up in the morning and found that their dreams had vanished in the night. The politicians took the golden opportunity that had been handed to them on a plate and promptly turned it into a sow's ear, as is their wont. The country broke apart. The power stations and bulk of the industry was in North Korea, whilst South Korea was mainly agricultural. The North switched off the power and plunged the South into darkness. In the springtime, the fertiliser from the factories did not arrive, so there would be a food shortage. Hopes for unified and independent Korea faded fast, and some feared it would never again be united. Korea had become a pawn in the Cold War, and anger filled the people's hearts. The whole country was a dry powder keg. All that was needed now was a spark.

CHAPTER 26

THE PRESIDENT AND THE PASTOR

J eju-do, a semi-tropical island idyll 100km off the south coast, provided that spark. In the thirteenth century, the Mongols used the island to breed horses and not much had happened since. Ancient stone statues like the ones found on Easter Island are found all over Jeju, but these grandfather figures do not gaze out over the ocean. They look inwards, keeping a watch over the sacred land as if the old guard knew that trouble would come from within. When the People's Committees were disbanded on Jeju and replaced with local government, the locals saw the hated Japanese collaborators and the Yangban class returned to power. They rose in protest, and when the South Korean police horses trampled their families underfoot, killing and maiming many including their women and young children, the anger burst out of their hearts and exploded onto the streets.

The President of South Korea had a problem: the people on Jeju Island were openly rebelling against the government, and when they started cutting the phone lines and destroying bridges and roads, he feared that, if left unchecked, the plague would reach the mainland and infect everybody. The new country would eat itself, and he needed to act quickly.

He picked up one of the files that he had ordered from the Korean Central Intelligence Agency and flicked through it. Inside was a black and white photograph of Mr Song: an elementary school teacher in Mun-gyeong Good Citizen School. Recruited by a Japanese colonel and changed his name to a Japanese one. Trained at the Japanese Military Academy in Tokyo and served in Manchuria. After that, he served in Burma under the Japanese, and when the war finished changed his name back to his original Korean one and enrolled in the Korean Army with the rank of Major.

President Lee closed the file and leaned back in his chair. It looked like he had found his man. A man who is full of ambition and switches allegiances so easily would be easy to control. But could he trust him?

The very next morning, a government black sedan swept along a curved avenue fringed with dwarf Korean pine trees on the way to the Blue House. Major Song pushed himself back into the plush leather seats. He could get used to this sort of luxury, he thought. Chance plays a part in the affairs of men, but why take the risk? He grinned. The old adage was true — it's not what you know, it's who you know. To receive a summons from the President of South Korea could only mean one thing: promotion to a colonel in the South Korean Army. Yes, he had come a long way from his teaching days and had done well by sucking up to the Japanese. Follow orders and you will go far, the Japanese recruiting officer had told him, and it had proved to be good advice. It would be another step forward in his army career, and it would be plain sailing now that the war had ended. He had a new boss now, but he was not so different. As far as he was concerned, the new South Korean President was foreign too, an American with an Austrian wife. If he was honest with himself he preferred the Japanese, but he had worked all his life to get this far and wasn't about to throw it all away. He would kiss ass, follow orders and keep his nose clean. Who knew where that would lead? Maybe he would try his hand at politics, and the Korean people would finally have a proper Korean in charge? But first, he needed to get to the top of the South Korean army. One step at a time, he told himself.

They cleared security and went through a set of wrought iron gates. The sedan swept past manicured lawns with cosmos borders and pulled up outside the steps that led to the Presidential palace — a complex of traditional Korean houses with blue-tiled roofs that gave it its common moniker, The Blue House.

He was led to an anteroom by two bodyguards and shown to a seat. After a while, the double doors opened and an aide led him to the presidential office.

'Come in Major Song, and take a seat,' said President Lee and pointed to a seat opposite his desk, flanked by two armed guards. Two newly designed South Korean flags hung behind the Presidential desk.

'Thank you, Mr President,' said Song as he removed his military cap and sat down. His heart raced.

'Shall I call you Major Song?'

The major was puzzled. 'Of course, Mr President.'

'Or should I use your Japanese name?'

There was a slight delay before he responded. 'I was always Song. I only changed my name to a Japanese one to survive under that regime. I hope you understand, Mr President.'

'I do. I do,' said the President. 'You served in Manchuria, I believe.'

'Yes, sir.'

President Lee tapped the manilla file on his desk. 'It says in your file that you apprehended Korean nationalists who were active in the north of the country and turned them over to the Japanese. Is that correct?'

'I was just following orders, Mr President.'

'I see,' said the President. It was exactly the words he wanted to hear. He was looking for somebody who could follow orders, even if they were unpleasant and involved betraying your fellow citizens.

'That sounds like treason to me,' said the President.

Song shuffled on his seat and fiddled with his collar. 'I thought I was doing the best thing for Korea at the time. They were nobodies, and I didn't feel it was the right time to unite the country. It was better to let the allies defeat the Japanese first and then unite the country.'

'I see. But you see my problem, don't you? I don't know who I can trust. Especially those with links to the North, like those who served in Manchuria, for example. How do I know they are not sympathetic to North Korea?' The President paused to let the implications sink in. 'I hate to do this Song. I really do, but you leave me no alternative. There is no easy way to say this: I am relieving you of your duties in the South Korean Army.'

'But I always did what I believed was right for the country. I was only following orders.'

'Well, you will be following my orders from now on. I think it is clear that you are a traitor to South Korea, and you know what that means?'

Song did. It meant the death penalty. 'Is there nothing I can do, Mr President? I will do anything ...'

The President leaned back in his chair and smirked. He put his hands together as if in prayer. 'You must have gathered a lot of intelligence during your time in Manchuria. Maybe you can share some of it?'

The President wanted the names of all the communist

sympathisers, and he was sure that Song would squeal on his friends and colleagues to save his bacon. He did.

In the master bedroom of The Blue House, a rather plain and plump Austrian woman removed her make-up and listened to her husband recollect his day.

'You was right about Song. He is singing like a canary now.'

Francesca Lee, his secretary, wife and now the First Lady of the Republic of South Korea, looked in the mirror and smiled.

'He betrayed everybody. All his friends. His former brothers-in-arms, communist sympathisers, Japanese collaborators and Korean nationalists. We have quite a list. Nobody was sacred to him. He would sell his own grandmother if it helped further his career.'

'You should be wary of his ambitions.'

'I have thought of that and given him a chance to redeem himself.'

'Oh? How?'

'He is on his way to Jeju Island, right now as we speak.'

'To quell the rebellion?'

'Precisely.'

MiJa was disturbed from her sleep by the loud grunts from the old sow, followed by a squeal of alarm, more heavy grunting, and the heavy footfall on the staircase that made the hayloft tremble with fear. The trapdoor flung open, and a beam of light swept the room. She instinctively held up her forearm to protect her eyes from the torchlight and the dust and debris that fell from the rafters.

'Police. Where is Dol-soi?' said an officer.

'Here. What is it?' said Dol-soi and sat up in his pallet bed.

MiJa whispered to her brother to keep still and pulled the grubby blanket over them both for protection.

'You must come with us,' said the officer.

'Why? I haven't done anything wrong,' said Dol-soi.

'He hasn't,' said Bok-nam.

The officer shrugged. 'Presidential orders. We have orders to take everybody who served on the People's Committees down to the police station and lock them up for their own protection. Get dressed.'

In the morning, Bok-nam, MiJa and Yung-soo visited the police station and demanded to see Dol-soi. 'He has visitors already,' said the desk sergeant, much to their surprise. 'I had better take that,' he said and pointed to the bowl of steamed rice that Bok-nam had made for Dol-soi.

MiJa thought that her stepfather had aged ten years, overnight. He was busy explaining his predicament to a Korean translator. Another man looked on, a strange-looking man in Western dress. He had large round blue eyes with flecks of grey in them, and his black hair had flashes of grey at his temples. In his hand, he carried a thick book, bound in leather, with a brass clasp on the side.

Yung-soo pointed at the man and said, 'Look, he is wearing a collar like Silverbell.' He looked closely for any sign of a silver bell hanging from his white-collar and was disappointed, but he did have a large gold cross hung around his neck.

Pastor Matthews had swapped his cassock for a cloak-of-compassion a long time ago when he joined the American missionary movement to Korea. He saw his role as guiding those who needed it most, and his focus was on this world, not the one after it. His church educated the young and provided food for the hungry. Dol-soi explained to the pastor that all he was trying to do was build a better life for all Koreans, and all he received in return was the clang of a metal door slamming in his face. The pastor tried to comfort him as best he could. He also knew that Dol-soi belonged to the torturing class, and a confession was waiting in the wings. It was only a question of timing. The pastor promised that he would do all he could to get him released, and until then he would look after his family. They should attend his church every Sunday because if they followed the same religion as President Lee, nobody could accuse them of being Communists.

CHAPTER 27

A NEW RELIGION

'Do you really think this God Wesley will make any difference? What can he do that Hirohito and Buddha could not?' said Bok-nam. She was sceptical about everything new; to her, the old ways were always better. This new religion did not blend harmoniously with nature like the mountain shrines of Shinto. It did not have the vibrant colours, intoxicating smells and sounds of a Buddhist temple. Christianity seemed a bit bland. What was the attraction?

MiJa shrugged and said, 'If it keeps us safe, what's the harm? Maybe one of those miracles will happen to us? At least we get fed.' But she could see her mother's point of view. Why did Koreans come here to worship? What was the attraction? It didn't feel spiritual. They worshipped an emaciated white man with long dirty hair that looked like he had suffered all his life. He wasn't even Korean. What did he know about Korea? Could he even speak or understand their language? What was the point of heaping prayers on a God that couldn't even understand you?

Maybe it was the temporal advantages: it provided food

and shelter and English language classes. MiJa threw herself into English lessons and showed an unusual aptitude for the language. Every day, Pastor Matthews taught English from the King James Bible and MiJa would practice her conversational skills. She would arrive early morning and help to tidy the church and within a year she could hold a conversation, read a newspaper and question the Pastor directly about the bible passages. She enjoyed the bible stories at Sunday School, especially the gripping gore of the Old Testament. The Garden of Eden, Noah's Ark, and especially Moses and the plagues of Egypt: the blood, the locusts, the frogs, the slaughter of newborns. The miracles of the New Testament and Jesus being born in a barn. It all sounded familiar, but two stories resonated with her. The first was when Moses set his people free, and they argued amongst themselves and got lost in a desert. The second was that Christianity offered something different: it promised everlasting life and reunion with loved ones. All you had to do was believe in Jesus and all your sins would be forgiven. Maybe that was where she was going wrong? At a Shinto shrine or Buddhist temple, you washed away your sins with water. Maybe it wasn't that simple?

One day she picked up a newspaper somebody had abandoned on one of the oak pews and read an article on its front page.

East Asia Daily 07 April 1949

Communist Agitators Commit Atrocities on Jeju Island

Trouble erupted again on Jeju Island today as the civil unrest continues. The Communist agitators first initiated civil unrest almost one year ago by attacking government property, and it has been raging ever since. They have cut telephone lines and destroyed bridges, roads and railway lines, but today their violence was directed against South Korean citizens for the first time. Eyewitness accounts report brutal acts of violence that include summary executions, torture, and the mutilation of ears, noses and other body parts. One eyewitness account even reported the brutal gang rape of a group of young schoolgirls, followed by their summary execution. The South Korean President said that the current situation he inherited from the trustee government, led by the United States, is unacceptable. He can no longer stand idle and watch the slaughter of innocent Koreans. He had no alternative but to mobilise the South Korean Army and order them to crush the rebellion and restore peace to Jeju Island.

It was nothing to worry about: Jeju Island was miles away and might as well have been a foreign country on the other side of the world. It had nothing to do with her life in Mungyeong. She folded the newspaper in half and threw it in the bin.

CHAPTER 28

CHRISTMAS EVE

Everybody agreed that the 1949 Christmas Eve communion service was remarkable. Pastor Matthews rounded up his flock using his usual combination of old-fashioned bribery and Old Testament fear, and he delivered the Festival of Nine Lessons and Carols with his usual spiritual fervour and panache. What nobody was expecting was a miracle.

MiJa thought about the service and sighed. It was all so confusing, and none of it made any sense. A talking snake tricked a woman into eating the fruit from the Tree of Knowledge. If you could get past the talking snake, why was gaining knowledge a sin grave enough for God to expel Adam and Eve from Paradise? She decided to ask the Pastor, but he was busy chatting to her mother and a man she hadn't seen before, and every time she glanced in their direction, she caught the stranger staring at her.

The sermon got even more bizarre when God told Abraham to sacrifice his only son as an act of faith. What sort of God would do that? And this all-powerful God, who could do anything he wanted, devised a plan to send his only son to earth where he was born in a barn, lived a short, tormented life and died an agonising death nailed to a cross. It didn't seem like a well thought out plan for somebody with unlimited power and resources. A living God descended to earth. Where had she heard that before? It sounded a lot like the Japanese Emperor God.

She went to the altar and lit three candles. It was all too incredible, and she could not believe that any of the characters were real, except perhaps one: the King who had ordered all the new-borns slaughtered, she could believe in him. He sounded plausible enough. What was his name? Herod.

'MiJa, come over here,' shouted her mother, and beckoned to her. 'There is somebody I would like you to meet.' She was still speaking to the stranger — a well-groomed middle-aged man who seemed to be doing a lot of preaching of his own.

MiJa slowly trundled over to her mother and put her arm around her baby brother.

'This is Mr Jang,' said her mother.

MiJa gave him a slight bow but avoided eye contact.

'Mr Jang is the Member of Parliament for the Mun-gyeong district,' said her mother with starry eyes, full of scheming.

Jang nodded, and an oily, unctuous smile spread across his face and betrayed his insincerity. 'I am sorry if I was staring at you just now, but your mother was telling me a little about you. I hope you didn't think I was rude?'

MiJa unconsciously took a small step backwards. She didn't like the way his wandering eyes undressed her.

'May I ask why you lit those three candles?'

'They were for my step-father, elder sister and a boy I used to know.'

'I am so sorry for your loss.'

'Oh, they are not dead. I lit the candles so that they may find their way home. Will you excuse me?' said MiJa, 'I need some fresh air.' She clutched at Yung-soo's hand and made for the door.

'Sorry, but she is at that awkward age,' said Bok-nam. 'What she needs is a husband. One with good prospects.'

'I understand. I understand perfectly,' said Jang, but his mind was elsewhere. He had been a minor government official based in the north when the purges started. The Koreans in the north were fiercely nationalistic, and they had never forgiven the south for selling out to the Chinese and Japanese. They wanted their revenge, and when the lynchings started, he fled south. A travel ban was in force, but he knew how to work the system and bribed the officials at both sides of the border. He believed in gold, not God as the saviour, but the church did have its advantages. He joined the same Methodist Church as President Lee and lost no time making it known that he was from good Yangban stock and a loyal government official fleeing the communists. The President had no problem reinstating the old guard, even if they were Japanese lickspittles, and appointed him to a local government position in Mungyeong. He had asked the government for help to purge the communists from Mun-gyeong.

Once outside the church MiJa thought she heard a distant crack of a whip but thought no more about it. Eventually Bok-nam joined them and made their way home. It was dark after the midnight mass, so they stuck to the main thoroughfares, but something didn't feel quite right. After about five miles they came across an horrific scene: the streets were a melee of chaos and confusion, and the bodies of the old, the infirm and children littered the streets. People stooped over the bodies, beating their breasts and tearing out their hair in bloody clumps. MiJa rushed to help one woman who was clutching a dead child tightly against her body. He had a gaping gunshot wound in the back of his head, but his mother was talking to him lovingly as though he was still alive.

'What happened here?' asked MiJa.

'The soldiers said we were filthy communist scum, and we must die. Look what they have done.' She held the little limp body up in her arms. 'Does he look like a communist? How can a child be a communist?'

MiJa wanted to ask more questions, but some soldiers appeared from around the corner and started bocking the main road. They were ordering people to stay inside their homes.

Yung-soo emerged from behind Bok-nam and shouted, 'Follow me I know a shortcut.' He led them onto a dark foot-path that ran alongside the Mojeoncheon stream. The fight or flight instinct kicked in, and adrenalin coursed through their veins and drove them on at an ever-faster pace until they were almost running, but they were not alone. When their eyes adjusted to the ambient light, they could see that the stream was full of bodies drifting with the current. A few must have been still alive, revived by the icy water, and their feeble cries carried on the darkness until they fell silent.

They walked in silence until they reached the desolate safety of the hayloft. Sleep was impossible. MiJa closed her eyes and tried to sleep, and she tried to un-see what she had seen but it was no use. The images embedded deep into her mind, and the ghosts followed her home. She could see them still: their sallow waxy skin, twisted faces, accusing eyes. The ragged gore of the bullet wounds and the impossible angle of their twisted limbs.

In the morning, the papers reported on the Mun-gyeong Massacre of the Innocents. The government said communist rebels had slaughtered the innocent civilians. Most of the dead were the elderly frail women and innocent children.

Yung-soo said, 'I hate all communists, and when I am old enough, I will join the South Korean Army and kill them all.'

MiJa put her arm around him and asked, 'Did you see any communist soldiers?'

'Who else could have killed all those people?' He started crying.

MiJa realised that the only soldiers she had seen were wearing cap badges, marked 3rd infantry division, South Korean Army. It was a communist purge by the South Korean government, and it had turned into a massacre. Nobody would look for a communist in a church. Maybe it was a miracle they survived.

CHAPTER 29

CHRISTMAS DAY

A brood of mothers, dressed in their Sunday best, garnished with fur stoles and sable hats, dabbed at their misty eyes with dainty lace handkerchiefs and let their emotions get the better of them.

'Aren't they adorable?' said one.

'Like little angels,' sniffled another.

The crib service held at Seoul Methodist Church on Christmas Day, 1949, was a school nativity play. The stable was anything but stable and wobbled precariously every time a child accidentally brushed against it. It had authentic straw for bedding and a wooden crib that contained a swaddled baby doll. Mary and Joseph knelt at prayer beside the crib whilst three wise men, dressed in the gaudy colours of Quality Street wrappers, looked on and couldn't resist opening the gifts they had brought for the baby Jesus. The shepherds watched their flocks of cotton wool sheep and fiddled with the tea towels draped over their heads whilst a band of angel-faced cherubs, dressed in crisp white bedsheets with cardboard wings and gold tinsel halos, flashed a missing-milk-teeth smile at the audience. It started with the entire ensemble singing *Away in a*

Manger and finished with *Hark! The Herald Angels Sing*, and a wish for peace on Earth.

After waiting for the applause to fade, the Elder said, 'Let us pray.' In the front pew sat the President of South Korea and the First Lady. In the other pews sat most of their cabinet, their wives and children, security service personnel and selected guests, including the editor of the *East Asia Daily*.

The President lowered himself onto the kneeler in front of his pew and bowed his head. The recent atrocities on Jeju Island and Mun-gyeong hadn't troubled him in the least. With great power comes great responsibility, and he knew his Bible. He knew that it was acceptable to kill his enemies. He knew it was acceptable to kill women and children and checked it in Ezekiel 9:5-7. He knew it was acceptable to slaughter entire villages from Deuteronomy 13:13-19. He also knew it was acceptable to slay sons for the sins of their fathers — it said so in Isaiah 14:23. If the people of Jeju Island and Mun-gyeong had any sense, we'd have no more civil disobedience, he thought. Sometimes you had to be cruel to be kind, and it was always better to be feared than loved. Now he could refocus on provoking border incidents with North Korea. Would it come to war? He doubted it, but if it did, he knew they were ill-prepared. The USA did not allow South Korea to arm itself. They had no heavy armour, and who knew what North Korea was planning with their Soviet allies? No, it wouldn't come to war. It was called a Cold War for a reason. Besides, South Korea had the military might of the USA behind them. If it came to war, there would be only one outcome: the Communists would capitulate, and he would be the President of the whole of a united Korea. It was his destiny.

'Amen,' said the congregation.

CHAPTER 30

A RADIO ANNOUNCEMENT

By late June 1950, a tidal wave of panic rippled down the Korean peninsula that would not stop until it met the southern ocean. Rumours of a North Korean invasion filled every soju tent, galbi house and dinner conversation throughout the land. For the last year, the *East Asia Daily* had been filling South Korean minds with news about the terrible atrocities committed by the Communists, and reason deserted them. Fear and ignorance filled in the voids left by the media.

The poor lost no time and fled south. It was easy for them because they had nothing to lose, so they gathered up their meagre belongings and headed as far away from the border as possible. But for some, the tie of ancestral lands, livelihood and sense of place was too strong a bond. Doubt crept into their minds. Were the rumours even true? Was there any need to leave at all? Why so soon? The South Korean Army would defend them, and they had the backing of the Americans. Boknam decided she would wait and see, and the following day news arrived in the village that the President would make an announcement on the radio.

MiJa, her mother, and brother merged into the large crowd gathered outside the post office to listen to the communal radio set. The electron tubes hummed and glowed behind the Bakelite case and the air crackled with tension and anticipation as they waited for the South Korean President to make his announcement. You could hear a pin drop, but suddenly the airwaves crackled into life with a static burst, and a faint, ethereal voice addressed them: 'My dearest Korean People, this is your President, S M Lee, speaking.'

The people strained their ears and stared at one another in dumbfounded silence. MiJa had never heard the President speak before and was shocked by his poor grasp of the Korean language. Worse than that, he sounded like a bleating lamb, a frightened animal, one that was about to be slaughtered, but he reassured them. There was no need to worry. The rumours of a North Korean invasion were untrue. Everything was normal. There was no need to panic. If North Korea ever made the mistake of ever trying to invade, the South Korean Army would be waiting for them and would defend their country to the death — to the very last man. They were to rest assured that the South Korean Government was fully prepared for war and would remain in Seoul. All loyal and brave citizens should stay where they were.

When the Presidential announcement was over, the crowd dispersed and MiJa could hear their mutterings: how right they were to stay put and not abandon their property; I told you so; rumours were only rumours, and only the crazy acted on them; everything was going to be fine, they had everything under control.

The following morning when MiJa turned up to clean the church she was surprised to see Pastor Matthews in a fluster and hurriedly packing his belongings.

'Have you heard?' he asked MiJa.

'No. What is it?'

'The North Koreans have invaded.'

'But, the President said on the radio —'

'There is no time to lose, MiJa. It was all a lie. The first casualty of war is always the truth. It was a tape recording. The President fled to Busan last week.'

'It can't be true.'

'It is. He has abandoned his citizens to their fate and destroyed all the bridges over the Han River so they can't leave. The President has taken the South Korean Army with him and fled south to Busan. There is nothing to stop the North Korean advance. We must go at once.'

MiJa shook her head. Her place was to stay in Korea with her family. The last war had little impact in Korea and so what if North Korea had invaded. They were all Koreans and, in some cases, the same family. 'I must stay here with my family.'

'I want you to take these,' said the pastor. He removed the gold cross from around his neck and hung it over her head and pressed his bible into her hand.

'I can't accept this gold cross.'

'It is yours now. It will come in handy if ever you need money and if you are ever lost you will find your way in the bible. Remember, in your hour-of-need just call out for Jesus and He will be with you.'

'Thank you,' said MiJa and she watched dumbfounded as the pastor finished packing.

'I must leave now so take care of yourself and I hope to see you again, one day.' He gave MiJa a hug and they said a prayer together. When he turned to leave he said, 'One more thing MiJa. If you want to protect your brother, hide him. The South Korean Army are conscripting every male they can find.'

'Yung-soo is not old enough to join the Army.'

'They are conscripting anybody who can hold a gun, whatever their age. God bless you all.'

CHAPTER 31

AN EXECUTION

I n Mun-gyeong prison, Dol-soi and the other political prisoners were woken up before dawn and loaded onto a covered truck at gunpoint. Their wrists and ankles were bound with strong thin cord using hojojutsu techniques, borrowed from the Japanese, and they were driven into the remote countryside, accompanied by an armed guard. They were told they were going to dig a trench for a new water main and after about an hour the truck drew to a halt and the engine was turned off. Everybody remained silent and Dol-soi noticed a fleeting look of apprehension pass over the guards' faces. The tailgate was thrown open and one of the prisoners was led away. A few moments later Dol-soi heard a shot ring out. There was a commotion in the truck, but the guards poked their rifle barrels into the prisoners faces and told them to be quiet. So, it had come to this thought Dol-soi. The last order the President had issued before fleeing south to Busan was to execute all the prisoners. One by one they were removed from the truck and led away for the coup de grâce to be delivered until only Dol-soi was left.

'Jump down,' instructed the guard.

Dol-soi jumped down from the truck and was frog-marched across a field. It was still dark and Dol-soi had to step over the lifeless bodies that lay like bloody ragdolls along the side of the trench. Dawn was breaking and the first rays of the sun threw up the silhouette of a bulldozer at the far end of the trench. There appeared to be a forest up a slight incline on the horizon. The guard kicked Dol-soi in the back of his knee and he fell to the ground on his knees.

'Please don't do this,' he said to the guard.

'Shut up.' The guard had heard it all before. What could he do? He was carrying out orders. If he didn't, he would be next. All the guards knew that. They were nothing more than the pawns of their political masters. Beside these people were traitors to South Korea and treason is treason. They must pay the price.

Dol-soi was weak from weeks of overwork and starvation rations. He tried to retch, but nothing would come up. 'Please. I have a wife and children. You could aim to miss and leave me here. Nobody will know. I'll play dead.' He felt the still hot muzzle of the gun barrel touch the nape of his neck.

'Be quiet.'

Dol-soi tensed and heard the pistol click but nothing happened. It must have misfired.

'Hurry up. Get on with it,' shouted one on the guards. 'The North Koreans will be here if you hang about much longer.'

'Get in the truck. I will join you shortly.'

'Well don't take too long or we'll go without you.' The other guards left him to it and got back into the truck.

Dol-soi heard the engine start. He was going to die. There was nothing he could do except accept his fate. He was Buddhist and death was a natural part of the cycle of life. It was nothing to be feared. The spirit does not die. He will be reborn. Death was not the end. He felt the prod of a barrel on the back of his head again. He tensed his body and closed his eyes, but he did not hear the shot.

Then suddenly his bonds were loose. He was free. It seemed surreal. He seemed to be watching himself from afar. He crawled into the muddy ditch and squirmed on his belly along the trench. The strong smell of freshly-dug earth filled his nostrils and, somehow, he found the strength to get out of the ditch and reach the safety of the forest. He glanced back at the truck. Why did they not hunt him down? Even the forest seemed otherworldly. It was eerily quiet. There was no sound from any animal and he couldn't even hear himself breathing. His thirst raged and his head throbbed. His whole body was racked with pain and hunger, and it seemed like he had wandered for days in that ethereal forest. Just when he felt like he would be trapped there forever he found a logger's track.

When he emerged from the forest, he found himself outside the entrance to his master's house and Gil-soo was there to welcome him. They talked of old times and how much Korea had changed. North and South had been united, and the old class system had been disbanded. The economy was booming, and healthcare was free for all. A tear rolled down Dol-soi's cheek. Then there was a thunderous noise and his head jolted backwards. He saw a flash of vivid red, a bright white light, and then eternal darkness as the bullet smashed through his skull burrowed through his cerebellum and frontal lobe and exited his right temple.

The bulldozer engine sputtered into life, and it pushed the corpses into the trench and backfilled it with soil.

CHAPTER 32

THE SACRIFICE OF PRESIDENT LEE

'What, in there with the pig?'

'Yes. Jesus lived in a barn, didn't he?

'Yes, but why do I have to?'

'How many times do I have to explain it? It is for your own good.'

'But I want to join the Army.'

'You are not old enough. Now get in there.'

'Can I come out to eat, or do I have to share the trough too?'

'Now, don't be silly. I will bring your meals to you. All you have to do is make sure you hide well. Think of it as a hide and seek game, but you must hide so well that nobody will ever find you.'

The morning calm was broken two days later by the grunts of a disgruntled pig, whose slumber had been rudely disturbed. MiJa peered through the chinks in the weatherboards and pulled her face back in shock. Soldiers. They were wearing a much lighter uniform than the South Koreans, with red flashes on the collars and soft kepi hats. They were North Korean Soldiers, and they were busy searching the pigsty.

They would find her brother. Her heart was in her mouth. What should she do? She had heard rumour that the North Koreans would kill all the men and rape the women, but her mother had refused to leave. She wasn't going anywhere. There was no way she would leave her ancestral home. It rightfully belonged to her son, and she would stay in Mun-gyeong until they returned it. If she left now, she knew she would never get it back.

MiJa quickly dressed and ran down the rickety wooden steps. The soldiers raised their rifles and took aim. She raised her quivering arms and yelled, 'Don't shoot. What took you so long. We have been expecting you.'

The North Korean soldiers laughed. 'Oh, really?' said the patrol leader as he indicated to his men to lower their rifles. He sent one of the patrols to search the hayloft, and he returned a short while later with Bok-nam. The leader looked around at the squalor.

'Is this how you live in South Korea? Like animals?' The pig grunted and nodded in agreement, and the soldiers laughed and licked their lips. MiJa knew she had a chance.

'Where are all the men?' asked the patrol leader.

One of the soldiers answered. 'Maybe they have all run away and left their country to be defended by little girls and old women?'

MiJa scoured the pigsty, trying to see any signs of her brother. The soldiers had rifled through the straw-bedding and turned over the palette-bed, but there was no sign of him. He must have buried himself deep under the straw and mud, thought MiJa, and she began to panic. She must keep them preoccupied. Somehow.

'It's true. The men all ran away. There is nobody here but me and my old mother. We are delighted you have come to free us from the Americans. We have been saving this pig for just such an occasion.' MiJa rushed over to the sow and grabbed it by its ear. The soldiers couldn't stop laughing at the ensuing tug-of-war contest between a fat sow, squealing in protest, and a determined but willowy young Korean woman.

'Here, take it,' said MiJa and she handed the soldier the pig. She noticed a note pinned to one of the wooden support posts. Yung-soo must have left it. They must not find it — it would lead them to her brother. She thought her heart would explode and blurted out, 'I bet you can't guess his name?'

The soldiers stopped laughing and frowned.

'You named a pig?'

'Of course. He is called President Lee.'

'He does look like a pig but he sounds like a bleating goat.' The soldiers doubled over with hysterics and slapped their thighs until tears streamed from their faces. A short while later, a pistol shot rang out, and the soldiers slung the pig from the floor beams, slit its throat and let the blood run into a galvanised bucket. They butchered the carcass with their machetes. Now and again they broke into laughter, and MiJa could hear them muttering 'President Lee'. She was aching to read the note, but that must wait for later.

When the soldiers finally left MiJa found her mother hiding under the straw in the loft.

'You can come out now, Mother. They've gone.'

Bok-nam had heard the rumours how the North Koreans raped the women and thought it better to hide until they had gone but she was more worried about them taking her son and her only link back to the ancestral home. If he had been taken, she would never get it back.

'Where is Yung-soo? Did they take my son?'

'No, Mother,' said MiJa. 'He had already left but he did leave a note.' She read it to her mother with trembling fingers and a trembling heart.

Sister, Yung-soo here

*I don't want to play your childish game of hide-and-seek
anymore. I am not a child, and I have run away to join the
South Korean Army. I felt so ashamed hiding away in a pigsty
when all my friends have joined the Army.
Tell mother not to worry. I will be safe. I was charmed with a
long life when I chose the thread on my first birthday, and I am
still only seventeen.*

See you soon when we have beaten the Communists.

Bok-nam wept at the loss of her son and MiJa hid her anger.
Her baby brother thought he had grown into a man, but he
was still a child in her eyes, and an idiot.

In the evening the North Koreans returned. MiJa was
surprised when they gave her a chunk of cooked belly pork.
She thanked him and gave half to her mother, and they sat in
silence and chewed the crispy pork until the fat ran down their
arms. What should they do now? They talked long into the
night. One thing was clear: they must survive this Korean War.

PART THREE

THE KOREAN WAR

CHAPTER 33

THE ROAD TO BUSAN

Every household had to billet a soldier from the North Korean People's Army, and their hayloft was no exception. MiJa suspected that it would be a long way down the list of choices, but there seemed to be an endless stream of new arrivals as the spearhead pushed south at an alarming rate.

The North Koreans had driven the combined American and South Korean forces to the port of Busan in the far southeast corner of the peninsula. It was here that President Lee, his government and his favoured cronies had fled, leaving his citizens to fend for themselves. He hid behind the remnants of the South Korean Army and arranged them in a multi-layered defensive ring called the Busan Perimeter. He was careful to leave the route to the ocean clear, and a South Korean Navy destroyer was on standby if he needed to flee again.

In Mun-gyeong, the North Koreans put the people left behind to good use: the women were set to work cleaning and cooking for the soldiers whilst the men repaired any damaged property so it could house the North Korean soldiers. MiJa had at first feared the North Koreans and imagined the enemy as barbarians who would beat the men and rape the women. But they seemed no different to the South Korean men. Why should they be? They were of the same blood, the same family. They looked the same, ate the same food, spoke the same language. The only way MiJa could tell them apart was from their uniforms. Maybe that was why they put them in uniform, to make them think they were different from their brothers. Her early apprehensions slowly waned, and she began to feel more at ease. She was surprised that the leaders were the same. Kim Il-sung and President S M Lee were Methodists, like Pastor Matthews. The soldiers never stayed long anyway and were continually replaced as the North Korean Army advanced. There was a steady influx of replacements, and it all became quite normal and sometimes even felt peaceful.

Of course, there were good and bad people on both sides. The North Korean Army sequestered all their food and left the villagers to fend for themselves. The villagers tried to grow what they could in every piece of unclaimed land. Every available patch of soil had something edible growing in it, tended each day and jealously guarded, but the Army took this too. Most of the wildlife had been decimated, eaten along with all the nuts, berries and wild fruits. Even the trees had been stripped of their bark and drained of their sap for food. MiJa was sure that the South Korean Army would have done the same, and they decided to stay put and sit out the war in Mungyeong, but one evening she changed her mind.

The senior officers were billeted in the farmhouse and they summoned MiJa to serve them dinner. She noticed a blue ribbon and a small silver bell lying on the kitchen table.

'Where is Silverbell?' she asked the kitchen staff.

They avoided eye contact.

When MiJa cleared the dinner table, the group of officers were in a heated conversation. The senior officer patted his belly and said, 'That was excellent bosintang. Nothing beats dog stew for virility.'

The other officers laughed.

'I feel like a new man already. Like a dog with two dicks. And we have the prettiest girl in the village to serve us.'

After dinner the North Korean officers grew quite excited and animated in their conversation about how South Korea had always been a traitor to a unified Korea. They were bragging about how North Korea would soon win the war. They had Russian T34 tanks whilst the Americans had none. They didn't even have any anti-tank weapons. It was too easy. They would soon drive the enemy into the ocean, and all of Korea would be under the red flag. It would all be over by August. MiJa choked down her fear. What would happen to her brother if South Korea lost the war? MiJa decided that they must leave and head south.

One moonless evening when the heavy seasonal rainfall had finished, MiJa shook her mother awake. 'Here, eat this,' she said to her mother and handed her a large bowl of steaming rice.

'Are we leaving now?'

'We must leave under the cover of darkness and what we can't physically carry we must carry in our bellies.' MiJa had retrieved Dolsoi's rickety wooden A-frame rucksack and crammed into it as much as she could. It contained blankets, clothes, and enough rice bowls, chopsticks, and spoons for all the family members when they were re-united. She also packed food that wouldn't perish on the journey: partly steamed and dried rice, small quantities of salt, soya sauce, bean paste, chilli paste, dried noodles, roasted barley and dried fish. She had managed to pilfer two old water canteens from the North Korean soldiers and filled them with cold barley tea that had been boiled. When the tea ran out, they would have to take a risk and fill the canteens from the nearest stream.

'Put on as many layers of clothes as you can and still be comfortable,' she told her mother.

Bok-nam did as she was told and stuffed her pockets with her secreted supply of dried ginseng roots, powdered deer antler, dried seahorses, cinnamon bark and sang hwang dried mushrooms in case they would need medicine for the journey. She watched MiJa tie her Bible and her Korean history book together with twine. Hidden inside the leaves were the pressed flowers from the picnic at the waterfall with Jung-sik and the farewell note from her brother.

'Do you really need those?'

'Yes, why not?'

'Well, they are heavy for one thing, and what use will they be?'

MiJa ignored her mother as she rolled up a tarpaulin sheet, tied it with twine, and tucked it under her arm. 'You will have to carry this,' she said and handed her mother a cooking pot that she had filled with glutinous rice balls and cooked sweet potatoes for the journey. They took a last look at the hayloft that had been their home for more than half a decade, closed the door on their past and slipped out into the cold, clear night.

They walked in silence. Bok-nam could feel the sharp edge of the photo frame of her son that she had hidden under her blouse stab at her heart with each step and dreamed of the day they could move back into their ancestral home.

MiJa thought about this giant leap into the unknown. What would they find in the Busan? Would she find her brother? Where would they live? How would they survive? She stared to the heavens for an answer, but the velvet blanket of the night was punctured only by faint starlight and the distant cries of children. They turned south and joined the stream of refugees heading towards a better future, burdened by all their worldly goods. That was not all they carried. They carried their family histories, a lifetime of memories and perhaps the heaviest burden of all — their hopes and dreams for the future.

When dawn broke, so did MiJa's heart. The darkness of night had protected her eyes and emotions, but the harsh light of day spared her nothing. A biblical scene unfolded before her: a long line of refugees stretched as far as she could see, all wearing the same uniform of dust, mud and despair. This trudge of humanity snaked across the landscape like lost souls marching on Hades. The adults said little, even when their children complained they were hungry. They ignored them because they were too tired or had run out of food, or they feared the consequences of delay. The sight would be branded permanently into MiJa's mind, but what cut the deepest was the waifs of war: an army of children who wandered, lost and alone, amongst the endless stream of refugees. Their bewildered faces, with eyes too large for their heads, scoured the faces of the adults hoping that they would see a familiar face, but they never did. Others just sat at the roadside and stared motionless into the dust as if they could find an answer there. MiJa tried to speak to them, but there was no reply. She didn't need one: their pitiful rags, extended abdomens and pleading eyes told all. She tore open a packet of dried noodles, broke off a small piece and gave it to one of the waifs. The small boy stared back at her vacantly.

'It's no use, MiJa,' said her mother. 'There are too many.'

MiJa ignored her mother and delicately coaxed the morsel of dried noodle into his mouth. He chewed on it and smiled. Encouraged, MiJa broke off some more. The other waifs mobbed her, clutching at her clothing and silently begging with their eyes. Soon all the food she could give them had gone, and the first child was vomiting. His stomach had refused to accept the food.

'What did I tell you? You foolish girl.'

MiJa ignored her mother and gave the boy a sip of barley tea. She held him in her arms and buried her face into his frail body to hide her tears and sobbed until no more tears would come because she knew her mother was right. She couldn't save them all. She couldn't even save one. She had to be selfish and move on, no matter how bitter the taste was in her mouth. Every day she wished for darkness so that she wouldn't have to look at the suffering. But when it came, it brought no relief. The skeletal ghosts of the day with accusing eyes stalked her dreams. The worst part was that she knew tomorrow would bring more of the same, day after day after day. Who knew when it would end? MiJa fingered the gold cross hidden under her clothes. She thought about selling it but who would buy it? She couldn't trust anybody and what would they spend the money on anyway? Without trust, money was nothing.

She looked for answers in her Bible and her heart hardened. She blamed God. Where was He? How could He let this happen if He was omnipotent? Then anger raised its ugly head and stuck in her craw. Why should the innocent pay the price of war when they had the least to gain? What did war ever achieve? Old men started the war because they could not change or would not compromise, but it was left to the young men to sacrifice their lives, and when it was all over, the women had to pick up the tattered remnants of their lives and make do and mend.

Sleep did not come that night, and in the morning, when MiJa picked up her load, she added guilt, shame, anger and a feeling of uselessness to the things she had to bear. This river of anxiety oozed slowly south to the ocean. Many would never make it. All carried their worldly belongings on their backs, but the things they left behind were just as important. They left behind their humanity as the thin veneer of civilisation was scraped away and exposed the raw, ugly, feral instinct under the surface. Law and order collapsed, and the dark side of humanity was laid bare. Fights broke out and theft was common. The strong stole from the weak. The young stole from the old. The dead were left unburied on the roadside, and disease walked hand in hand with the Grim Reaper. Fear was endemic. Not from the ever-closer explosions, they had grown used to those. What they really feared was their fellow refugees. Everybody looked out only for themselves. Nobody dared to eat or drink in the open, and those that still had food or drink ate it at night, where they could hide their guilt under a cloak of darkness.

Two weeks later they arrived in Daegu. The town was a lifeless pile of rubble and bodies littered the streets. They made their way through the war-ravaged ruins, and MiJa thought that even the buildings looked starved, hollow husks that no longer knew what their purpose in life was. Some were still on fire, and she saw one collapse and die. Some said that the North Koreans had destroyed the town. Some said that the Americans and South Koreans had done it to prevent refuge to the rapidly advancing North. Who knew what was true? There were no rules of war anymore. MiJa watched a squadron of B-29 bombers fly overhead like a wake of vultures gathering to pick over the bones of a wasteland.

About a month after they had first set off, MiJa had her first glimpse of American soldiers. On 3 August 1950 she joined the steady stream of refugees crossing the Nakdong River over the Waegwan Bridge, just west of Busan. A chaos of khaki whirled to-and-fro across the bridge, shouting orders at the men and at the refugees in a language they couldn't understand. A few tanks rumbled past, churning up the road with their caterpillar tracks and belching black, aromatic diesel fumes as they made a hasty retreat. The American soldiers chewed gum, flashed smiles crammed with too many white teeth, and watched them with contemptuous, intolerant eyes. They were talking about closing the bridge to stem the flow of refugees.

'Hurry up, mother,' yelled MiJa as a squadron of RF86 Sabres streaked overhead,

howling like shamans and streaming water vapour trails across the sky.

'What?'

'I said hurry! The Americans are going to close the bridge.' They were lucky. They had just moved onto the bridge when the Americans erected a barricade behind them and started yelling at the Koreans to stay behind the barricade. It didn't work. The refugees soon breached it and flooded back onto the bridge. The Americans yelled at them to stay back. They were going to destroy the bridge, and they tried, again and again, to clear the bridge, but each time the refugees paid no heed. MiJa realised that most of the refugees couldn't understand English and began to yell to them to stay put in Korean. It made no difference. What choice did they have? MiJa grabbed her mother's arm and pulled her across the bridge.

They had just made it across when MiJa heard and felt an earth-shattering explosion. She looked back in horror. Hundreds of women and children were still on the bridge when it detonated and were either killed by the explosion or fell into the river and swept away by the cold swirling waters. She collapsed to the ground exhausted and watched the dust settle. Refugees were still crossing the ruined bridge clinging on twisted girders and trying to get to the other side. Many fell into the water below and were swept away.

They had no choice but to continue. A week later they could smell Busan before they saw it. The smell of humanity and raw sewage mingled with the sweet smell of the salty ocean. It carried on the wind and assaulted the nostrils. MiJa and her mother set down their burdens and collapsed onto the ground, spent. MiJa wondered if they had made the right decision. They had set off with food, drink, belief and hope, but along the way, they lost them one by one. Their clothes fitted like sacks filled with bits of leftover skin and bones, but when a Busan perimeter guard let them into the city and directed them to the refugee camp, a faint glimmer of hope was rekindled.

CHAPTER 34

AMI-DONG

Ami-dong was the name given to the monstrous carbuncle that grew on the face of a mountainside that overlooked the port of Busan. It was a shanty town built by the refugees, on the site of an old Japanese graveyard. The enterprising residents lost no time recycling the scrap material that others had discarded, and almost overnight a sprawl of shacks had sprung up. Old pallets were scavenged from the dockyards and used as walls. A fortunate few used empty rice bags that they crammed full of earth and stacked, one on top of the other. Old oil drums, beaten flat or reeds cut from the estuary or abandoned corrugated-iron sheeting, became a patchwork of leaky roofs in various shades of brown oxide. Abandoned polythene sheeting became windows or was wedged into cracks to offer a semblance of protection from the wind and the rain. Even the gravestones found a use: they were removed and became foundation stones to stop the wooden walls from rotting on the damp earth, or they became steps, set into the many tortuous paths that wound around the village.

In this labyrinth, people scurried along like rats, going

about their daily business without complaint for this was no de-gentrified slum. This was not permanent housing that had fallen into disrepair and despair. This housing was only a temporary solution, and hope hid in the cracks, gullies and other dark places. Nobody dared speak its name, but it was there, dormant, waiting for a chance to grow, waiting for sunlight, waiting for the warmth of spring.

The refugees had built a town from leftover scraps, and they helped MiJa and her mother find the crates and sandbags they needed to build a home. They hauled the tarpaulin MiJa had carried from Mun-gyeong over the shack to make it water-tight, but the most valuable thing they constructed was a community spirit.

'What are the toilet arrangements?' asked Bok-nam.

An old hand explained. 'If you follow the footpath downhill you will come to a fork in the trail. Turn left and it will take you to the communal cesspit. It's only open for one hour in the morning so be sure to empty your yogang —'

'We don't have one,' explained Bok-nam and flashed a glance at MiJa.

'You don't have a pot to piss in?'

'We forgot,' said MiJa and flushed red.

'I'm sure we can find one for you. The cesspit is guarded, and you must pay each time you empty your yogang. As I've said already. It's only open for one hour in the morning before they throw some earth over the filth and cover it with straw matting to keep the stench down.'

'What about work?' asked MiJa. 'Is there any work available?'

The old hand shook his head. 'The Americans drop off some food every day so you won't starve. You can live on it, but it tastes like shit. There is always work in Kangkangee if you are that desperate.'

'Kangkangee?' asked MiJa. 'What a strange name. Why do they call it that?'

The man laughed. 'If you follow the others down to the port in the morning, you will find out soon enough.'

When morning came, MiJa found a broken pot that somebody had left outside their door. Well at least we have a pot to piss in thought MiJa and she made a metal note to tell her mother not to sit on the sharp edges. She followed the steady stream of workers until they came to a small shipyard, framed by the iron-grey ocean that was indistinguishable from the leaden grey sky. A sea fret hung heavily on the shore, and the rusty iron hulks of ships jutted out of the fog like the peaks of a mountains range. The pervasive odour of the ocean and rotting bladderwrack enveloped everything. When she got closer, she could see the soft underbellies of the hulls, alive with encrustations of mussels, barnacles and seaweed, were heeled over as if suffering from some form of sickness. Somebody thrusted a scraper and small hammer into her hands, and all day long she scraped away at the fouled hulls, chipping away at the crusted, calcified life, inch by inch, yard by yard, until the hooter sounded the end of the day. In the evening she returned home with aching arms and cut and blistered hands. The dead smell of the sea still clung to her, and the relentless noise was still ringing in her ears. She was surprised to find that dinner was waiting for her on the upturned crate they used as a table.

'Where did this come from?'

'A truck stopped by at the village,' said her mother. 'You take an empty bowl, and they fill it with food.'

MiJa stirred the stodge with her spoon, and her stomach churned. It didn't look very appetising and smelled strange, but beggars can't be choosers.

They ate in silence until Bok-nam said, 'It's the slops the American forces leave on their plates.'

MiJa pushed the bowl away, half-eaten. 'The Americans eat this? Our neighbour was right — it does taste like shit.'

Her mother finished her bowl. 'Did you find out why they call it Kangkangee?'

MiJa laughed, 'It's a joke, I think: the endless Kang, Kang, Kang from the hammers banging on the iron hulls. There is no escape from it. I can still hear it now.'

The next day MiJa woke up with tinnitus ringing in her ears and cramps gripping her intestines. Her mother was already awake and handed her a cup of medicine she had made from powdered deer antler and dried mushrooms.

'Drink this. I have been shitting since four this morning, and we have run out of toilet paper. I used the last sheet of the *East Asia Daily*, so I tore some out of the back of your book.'

'My history book?' yelled MiJa.

'No, the one with gilt edging.'

'The Bible?'

'The paper was lovely and soft. It was a revelation.'

'Mother, have you no shame? You will go directly to hell.'

'I think we are already there. When I opened it, this fell out.' She handed MiJa a white envelope, still sealed, with her name handwritten in English on it.

'What is it?' asked her mother.

MiJa didn't answer her. She tore open the letter and read it.

'Well, hurry up. I need to go again.'

'Here take this,' said MiJa, and she handed her mother the envelope. When her mother had gone outside, she re-read the letter to make sure she had understood correctly. It was from the American pastor. Why hadn't he told her about it before he left? He must have forgotten about it in his haste. It was an introduction to the Red Cross Hospital in Busan. She was to take the letter to the hospital and present it to one of his colleagues who would offer her work in the hospital.

CHAPTER 35

THE SWEDISH RED CROSS

An arched sign with a red cross painted in the centre marked the location of the Red Cross Hospital. Above the arch, a light blue flag with a gold Nordic cross fluttered in the breeze. It didn't look like a hospital, thought MiJa, more like a military camp with its regimented lines of tents and trucks, covered in khaki canvas. She showed the gate sentry the letter from the American missionary, and he directed her to a solitary Nissen hut.

She knocked on the door, and a muffled voice coughed and said, 'Enter.'

A man in a white coat, with a shock of blond hair and a matching beard, sat behind a desk.

'Dr Samuelsson?' asked MiJa, unable to stop staring at the first blond hair she had ever seen.

'Ja,' he replied. 'And who are you?'

'Choi MiJa, sir.' She handed him the letter.

After reading the letter, he said, 'How did you meet Pastor Matthews?'

'Through his church. That's where I learned English. I can speak Korean too, er obviously.'

The Swede was delighted. Very few Koreans could speak English, no foreigners could speak Korean and it was well known that even the American military had no interpreters.

'Perfect. You have arrived at just the right time, MiJa.' The Swede explained that they were building a field hospital. It would have 200 beds, treat all combatants, regardless of nationality, and would be paid for by the Swedish nation. 'I need somebody to translate to the Korean construction crew. Do you think you can do that?'

'Sure.'

The hospital opened on schedule on the 10th of September 1950. At that time, Busan port was a frantic bustle of activity as the Americans imported all the arms, weapons and food they needed to re-arm South Korea and take the fight to the enemy. Those Koreans with money and the right contacts made a cosy bed with the politicians and made their fortunes from the war. It was here that the Chaebols were born: the family-owned conglomerates that would be funded with risk-free government capital and become household names in the eighties.

On the 15th, great excitement swept the camp and infected everybody: there was rumour of a South Korean counterattack. A maverick American General called MacArthur had landed his troops on the mudflats at Incheon, in the north-west, and attacked the North Koreans from the rear. The next day the Americans broke out of the Busan Perimeter and caught the enemy between a hammer and an anvil. The North Koreans crumbled and fled north in utter chaos.

By the time the first Swedish doctors and nurses arrived in Korea on the 23rd of September, the American military had already reached Seoul. The Swedish Red Cross Hospital was re-designated as an evacuation hospital, and MiJa saw the first patients arrive from the MASH units. The Mobile Army

Surgical Hospitals followed the front line as it pushed north-wards. They provided life-saving surgery and stabilised the casualties until they could be moved to the evacuation hospitals by helicopter, ambulance truck or hospital train.

MiJa scrutinised the face of every Korean casualty, half expecting to see her brother. If the patients were well enough, she asked if they had seen or heard of him, but the answer was always no. Once she thought she recognised him, but her mind had tricked her. The casualty was so seriously injured it could have been anybody, and after that she hoped never to see him in the hospital. It was better if he returned after the war intact.

She absorbed herself in her work and worked as many hours as she could. It was easy, now that life had some purpose, some goal to achieve. Her primary duty was to collect information from the Korean casualties and translate it into English for the doctors and nurses and sometimes for military intelligence. Sometimes the hospital was so overwhelmed that MiJa helped with the nursing. She enjoyed that part the most and she thought about Mi-soon in Japan and wiped a tear from her face. Her elder sister would be so proud of her.

The most seriously injured would be evacuated by fixed-wing aircraft to Tokyo General Hospital, and occasionally MiJa would accompany the casualties to the American airbase in Busan. The USAF, Busan East, K9, Air Base was in the Haeundae district of Busan, one hour away from the hospital, by ambulance. Douglas C-54 Skymasters had been fitted out with scaffold and shelving so that the litters could be placed directly onto the support frames without moving the casualties from the stretchers. MiJa would help transfer the hospital litter from the ambulance, strap them down and hook up the IV drips.

One afternoon she was having trouble with one of the catheters that wouldn't stay in place when suddenly the doors were closed, and the aircraft started taxiing down the runway for its return flight to Tokyo.

'Wait, I'm still in here,' shouted MiJa and started banging on the fuselage door.

'It's too late now,' said one of the cabin crew nurses and pointed to a bulkhead chair. 'Just strap yourself in there, and you'll be fine.'

MiJa strapped herself in for the flight. She was nervous and had heard from the other nurses that this sometimes happened, so she was prepared. She removed a short length of bamboo with a hollowed-out centre and clamped it between her teeth.

'What on earth are you doing, MiJa?'

'It's for the pressure when the aircraft gains height.'

'For your ears?'

'To stop my head exploding.'

The stewardess nurse laughed. 'Is that what the other nurses told you?'

MiJa blushed, removed the bamboo and thrust it back in her pocket. She was angry with herself for being so gullible but soon forgot all about it when the aircraft left the ground, and she got a glimpse of the world through God's eyes. After that, she felt like she could do anything.

When she returned home that evening it was late, and she was greeted at the door by her angry mother.

'Where have you been? I couldn't wait for you. I've had dinner. Those Yankee trucks have been around again. This time it was Specially Processed American Meat, called SPAM, and chocolate bars, but I wasn't quick enough to get the chocolate. The young varmints got them all.' The children chased the food distribution trucks all over the city, like gulls following fishing boats, and swooped down on the tins of SPAM and Hershey chocolate bars regurgitated from the back of the truck. It was all part of the American hearts and minds campaign.

'I've made budae jjigae,' said Bok-nam. An Ami-dong staple that everybody called army base stew. It was made from bite-sized pieces of SPAM, a tin of baked beans and whatever vegetables were at hand. 'Next time I will try to get some hot dogs to make it. Americans like dog meat too. So, where have you been all this time?'

'Japan.'

'Yes, and I suppose you flew there.'

MiJa just smiled. 'Eat your budae jjigae.'

'Do you like it?'

'It's not too bad,' said MiJa, unaware that they would live on it forever.

'I got this too,' said Bok-nam and produced a can of Coca Cola from its hiding place.

They sipped the warm Coke from the tin, and MiJa said, 'I've been thinking. If Yung-soo did manage to join the South Korean Army, he must have followed them here as they retreated. Tomorrow, I will go to the Army headquarters and ask. They must keep records and should know where he is. For all we know, he could still be here in Busan.'

CHAPTER 36

THE BATTLE OF MUN-GYEONG

'It is a great and glorious thing to die for your country,' said the South Korean army officer as he pushed himself, with a leathery squeak, into a well-worn Chesterfield chair that was as far away from the frontline as it was possible to be, and still be in Korea. 'I hope you realise what a great opportunity this is. When I was your age, I would have jumped at a chance like this. A chance to do something important for your country. Do you understand what I am saying, Private Choi Yung-soo?'

'Yes sir, perfectly,' said Yung-soo with the kind of look on his face that showed all too well that he did. He would have been quite happy to sit out the rest of the war in Busan. He knew that Seoul had been re-captured on the 28th of September 1950. By the 30th of September, the Americans had reached the Yalu River, and it looked to all the world like South Korea would win. But MacArthur had miscalculated when he crossed the Yalu River into China and dragged them into the war. In December, the Americans had their own Dunkirk moment and evacuated North Korea, and by January

1951, the Chinese had pushed the front line back down to Mun-gyeong.

'Mun-gyeong must be held, at all costs,' said the officer. 'If it falls, then all of South Korea will fall. Once the Great North Road is open, Daegu will fall, and then Busan. Understand?'

'Yes, sir,' said Yung-soo. His ears pricked up at the sound of his hometown. Was it still intact? Maybe he would get a chance to see his mother and sister.

'You know the territory better than anybody. Your role is to gather intelligence, so you won't see any fighting. Any questions?'

'No, sir.'

'Then, there is no point in delaying you any further. Good luck Choi,' said the officer, and he shook his hand and dismissed him, knowing full well he was probably sending him to the frontline and a bloody death. 'I wish I was going with you. Keep this to yourself, but there may be a medal in this.'

Yung-soo hardly recognised his hometown. The school was no more, and large swathes of Mun-gyeong had been flattened and reduced to scattered piles of rubble. It was a common theme: as the war ebbed and flowed up and down the penin-sula, the country was scoured clean with each wave until only the debris and detritus remained, and both sides paid a heavy price for control of the rubble left behind.

The North Koreans had orders to hold their position in Mun-gyeong, but only the injured and fearful did so. Every soldier who could walk disappeared into the safety of the Sobaek mountains during the day. At night, they swooped down into the town, like a murder of crows, to steal food and harry the enemy. The Americans ordered the villagers to build a defensive stone wall on the northern approaches to the town and destroyed all the houses lying beyond it to deny refuge to the North Koreans.

Yung-soo may not have recognised his hometown, but the bitterly cold northern winter was all too familiar. It was minus twenty degrees Celsius — the sort of winter that froze the marrow in your bones and solidified the jelly in your eyeballs. White frosting clung from his eyelashes and eyebrows, like fondant sugar, and the cold nipped at his flesh like crabs picking over a still-warm corpse. The ground was too hard to dig, so Major General Son, the area commander, instructed his troops to re-use the existing foxholes dug last summer. Intelligence had warned him that an attack was imminent, so he rallied his troops.

'We've got them where we want them now, lads. Enemy to the right, to the left, forward and behind. There's no way they can escape, now.'

The soldiers grimaced at the general's gallows humour, but he wasn't a man to wantonly waste the lives of his men and the last order he issued was, 'If you want to stay alive, stay in your fucking foxholes.'

Yung-soo climbed into his ready dug grave. It was like climbing into a freezer, so he followed the lead of the other soldiers and stripped the thatch from the roofs of the houses and filled the foxhole with it. He stuffed his clothing with strips of the *East Asia Daily* and burrowed into his nest, like a small mammal preparing for long winter hibernation, and awaited his fate. He had grown up far too quickly. He had needed to, to make it this far. He shook his head with disbelief when he recalled his childish wargames with a watermelon hat on his head and a head full of dreams and glory. The reality of war had turned out to be something very different.

He checked his rifle and ammunition level. All he had to do was shoot himself in the hand or the foot. There was minimal risk. He would be evacuated to the Red Cross

Hospital in Busan and sit out the rest of the war, but he knew he could not. In the heat of battle, it hadn't taken him long to discover that he was a coward. He decided that it was better to survive and go home to your family than go home in a body bag, with a letter full of lies and a piece of tin with a coloured ribbon attached to it. He wasn't going to take any unnecessary risks. As far as he was concerned, bravery was a form of temporary madness.

He awoke in the night to the crack of sniper fire. He peeked out of his foxhole. Snow had started to fall and lay thick on the ground. Then all hell broke loose as the North Koreans launched an attack. He fired until he was out of ammunition, fixed his bayonet, plugged the foxhole entrance with straw to stop the snow falling in and braced himself against the earthen trench to await whatever God had planned for him.

The morning was eerily quiet. When the all-clear siren sounded Yung-soo cleared the foxhole entrance from the straw and accumulated snow and crawled out of his protective cocoon. The word was that the North Koreans had fled back to the mountains, and he wasn't surprised to see that the South Korean soldiers had piled up the frozen dead in front of the foxholes as a protective barricade, as solid as any sandbag. It was standard practice: the earth was iron-hard — too hard to dig graves — so the dead might as well fulfil a practical purpose and protect the living. A soldier's practical solution. Hard but fair. An order was issued to rebuild the defences, but first Yung-soo had to pay a call of nature, so he made his way to a small copse of trees that he used to play in as a kid. When he had finished and was pulling up his fatigues, he heard the crack of a twig and felt the prod of cold steel in his back.

'Don't shoot,' said Yung-soo, and he trembled with the cold and the fear.

'You're coming with me,' said a voice, as steely as the

bayonet pressed into his back. When Yung-soo turned around, he saw an oversized North Korean soldier dressed in a thick padded winter uniform, like a Michelin man. He was bleeding heavily from a wound in his thigh. He leaned clumsily on Yung-soo for support, jabbed the bayonet he was holding in his hand into the space between his ribs and growled, 'You will take me back to North Korea. Let's go.'

CHAPTER 37

THE RIVER OF THE DEAD

22 APRIL 1951

T he South Koreans call the Imjin River, The River of the Dead because of the numerous bodies swept down from the North. It is a wide river with swift, deep currents and is flanked on both sides by steep limestone gorges until it merges with the Han River, just north of Seoul. It is unbreachable for most of its length, but there is a shallow section at a small rural settlement called Jeokseong Myeon. If the Chinese came, they would cross the river there.

Nearby, on Hill 235, an army medical officer filled his canteen from the cool water of the Seolmacheon stream and waited for the purification tablet to take effect. He stuck three, six-inch nails into the soft ground and placed a chipped enamelled mug on top of the nails, filled it with water, powdered milk, two teaspoons of sugar and a NATO standard teabag. He adjusted it until the liquid was level, lit the solid fuel tablet under the mug, stirred like crazy and wondered if he had done the right thing.

Who named these bloody hills anyway? Couldn't they have come up with a more imaginative name than Hill 235? Had he done the right thing? That was the question, the one that wouldn't go away. He should never have left under a cloud. They had both said things that were better left unsaid, and now it was too late. It was the National Service conscription that swung it, he told himself. When India gained its independence in 1947, there had been a shortage of men enlisting, so the government introduced forced conscription for all males between the ages of seventeen and thirty. They had to serve for two years, got minimal training, and for the unlucky few that got posted to Korea, they risked their lives on the front line for the princely sum of £1.40 a week.

Maybe it was the guilt of surviving when so many had not? He had served in the last war and had seen plenty of action in Burma. When he returned home to Cheltenham, he had qualified as a doctor and married his childhood sweetheart. It had seemed like a good idea at the time, but now it seemed like he was probably just swept up in the euphoria at the end of the war. He had tried to explain to her that he had a duty to do and couldn't just stand by idly at home and watch all those young kids die on a remote hillside for want of medical attention.

Inevitably she asked him about his duty of care to her. She pleaded with him to stay. He had done his bit in the last war, and now his place was beside her at home. He was selfish. What about their plans? Weren't they trying to raise a family? He said that there was plenty of time for that later, and they blamed each other for their lack of children. The argument ended with him storming out of the house, and a week later he joined HMS Belfast after her refit. In January 1951, he arrived in Korea and deployed to the front line with the Gloucester Regiment to provide a buffer zone to protect the capital, Seoul.

The tea was ready when the fuel pellet expired. The water hadn't boiled and the milk powder hadn't dissolved. It never did, but nobody would waste another pellet of fuel on a cuppa. He took a sip. It was wet and warm, all he had really expected, and he walked over to join the others.

'Morning,' he said to one of the National Servicemen who was staring into his lunchbox with apprehension.

'It's not as bad as they say,' said the medic. 'Sometimes it's even edible.'

The national serviceman laughed.

'What's in the horror bag today?'

'Same as yesterday, sir. The usual suspects: one egg mayo sarnie, stale. A mystery-flavoured bag of crips, stale. A can of Coke, warm. And a KitKat, melted.'

'You've got everything you need, right there, for a growing lad, but I recommend you don't eat it, on medical grounds. I'll have one of these instead.' He tapped out a cigarette, lit it, and stared at the towering Gamak San on his right. They had recce'd the mountain last week and found it hard going. Steep limestone cliff faces rose to over 2,000 feet above sea level, and the upper reaches were treacherous with ice and snow. The lower reaches were dense impenetrable pine forest, and there were no signs of life. No humans. No animals. No birdsong. Not even the sound of scurrying small mammals fleeing in the undergrowth. It was a silent, eerie place, like the dark side of the moon, and they concluded that it was impossible to cross.

The medic drained his tea and threw the dregs on the ground. When he had first arrived, it was mid-winter, but now that spring had arrived, the blue-green pine needles were showing light-green sprouts of new growth. The whole mountainside was a beautiful verdant canvas intermittently splashed with the pinks, yellows and whites of blossom trees.

'Don't worry lad,' he said to the national service man. 'Nobody is going to come over that mountain. They would first have to traverse the narrow river crossing, and we've got it covered with enfilading fire. The Royal Artillery are on the other side of that mountain with their 25 pounder mountain guns, and the Septics will arrive tomorrow. There is nothing to worry about.'

But the medic was worried. They hadn't bothered to dig in because they didn't expect to be there long, and they were running low on ammunition. The sneaky beakies back in US Intel had told them that the Chinese were massing on the other side of the river, a small force of not more than a few hundred men. But they had been wrong before, and the only thing that stood between them and Seoul was a small detachment of 600 men. And they were about to discover that freedom does not come free.

CHAPTER 38

THE GLORIOUS GLOSTERS

That night, the sky lit up with Chinese flares. It was the favoured Chinese method of attack: a barrage of flares to light the way, followed by the piercing cries of bugles and the dull thud of mortars. It was a cacophony designed to confuse and intimidate the enemy, to put the fear of God into them, but all it did was provide advanced warning of an attack. The Chinese usually attacked as a column and focussed their strength on any perceived weakness in the defensive line by attacking, wave after wave until the enemy succumbed to attrition or ran out of ammunition.

A few moments later, the unmistakable splutter of Bren machine gun rattled in the night, and tracer rounds streaked the sky as the Glosters raked enfilading fire into the gorge. Once they had radioed in the enemy position, the Royal Artillery barrage started, and exploding shrapnel shells started to find their range and shake the earth with angry thunder. All the while, the sharp intentions of Chinese bugle calls carried on the wind.

The medic's stomach churned — he knew what was coming. The waiting was the worst part, the anxiety, the frustration, the feeling of inadequacy. He retrieved the bags of saline that he had been keeping warm in his sleeping bag and hung them on the makeshift gantry over the makeshift beds, scrubbed up as best he could with cold water and carbolic, and snapped on his latex gloves in a cloud of chalk. He didn't have to wait long before the first stretcher-bearers arrived with their gruesome loads. His first job was to remove the casualty's weapons and grenades. It wasn't unknown for an unconscious soldier to revive, and in his disorientation fire on his own men; a dead medic was no use to anybody.

The first casualty had a sucking noise in his chest and bright red frothy blood on his lips. Chest shot.

'What happened to you?' asked the medic. The casualty just pointed to his wheezing chest and uttered an illegible reply, but at least he was conscious. The fact that he could understand the question and attempt a reply told the medic that his airway and brain were still functioning, and he wouldn't die just yet. He moved on to the second casualty who was in cardiac arrest. He moved on to the third: his lower right leg hung at an impossible angle, and he didn't respond to any questions. The medic cut away the blood-soaked trousers with his surgical shears just above the knee to assess the wound. The leg was partially amputated, a shredded mess of veins, arteries, muscle, and shattered bone hung from the stump. Bright red blood was spurting out with each pump of his heart. This man had lost a lot of blood and was already in hypovolemic shock as his heart pounded away, faster and faster, to try and circulate what little blood he had left to his vital organs. He would soon go into cardiac arrest.

The medic opened a sterilised bandage pack and folded it into a two-inch-wide cravat. He taped some padding four inches above the wound and wrapped and tied the cravat over this. Then he took a splint and tightened the tourniquet until the artery ceased leaking the casualty's life away. He secured the tourniquet to prevent it slipping, took an indelible marker, and wrote the letter T on his forehead and the time. It was the 23rd of April, 02:53 hours. He would dress the wound later.

He turned to the chest casualty next because he could save him. It was too late for the unconscious soldier in cardiac arrest. He could not waste time with CPR whilst the other men bled out and died. Triage was brutal, doubly so when there was nobody to help, and he hated deciding who should live and who should die, like some impotent God. It was better not to think about it, but the one thing he could not do was waste time and let them all die. He cut away the casualty's uniform to inspect the chest wound. There was no sign of any exit wound, just the familiar cloying metallic smell of blood, sweat and fear. This man would die soon if he continued to suck air into his chest. He used the sterile plastic wrapping from the bandages to form a seal over the puncture wound, taped the edges closed and then placed a field dressing over it and bandaged his chest.

The stretcher-bearers returned with more casualties.

'What's the current situation, Private?' asked the medical officer.

'Grim. There's a lot more of these to come, Doc. The latest estimate is that thirty thousand Chinese are trying to cross the Imjin River, and our ammunition is low.'

'Any sign of the American reinforcements?'

'None.'

The medic hid his fear. All he could do was save those that could be saved and get the most seriously injured evacuated to the MASH hospitals in the morning because the choppers couldn't fly at night.

'Get that dead body out of here.' He pointed to the soldier who had died of cardiac arrest. 'We need all the beds available.' The dead would be stored outside until there was time to bury them.

. . .

When dawn broke, a ghostly silence nestled over the gorge. The medic was exhausted and had worked all through the night. He looked at the clouds that hung low in the sky, enveloping the hills in a ghostly shroud, and sighed. The evacuation helicopters could not land, but that was not the worst of it. The Glosters had all retreated over the Seolmacheon, an icy stream, and had their backs to Hill 235. Only the Gamak San mountain protected their eastern flank. It got worse. The radio confirmed that the American column of reinforcements had set off but come under heavy fire. They had tried to break through the Chinese lines but failed in three attempts. The situation was desperate: the enemy was at the door, and the reinforcements weren't coming.

In the afternoon, the remnants of the regiment unanimously decided that they would make a last stand. They would fight until the last bullet, and when the ammunition ran out they would fix bayonets and fight hand-to-hand. If they were going to die, they would die hard and not give away their lives cheaply. The lull in the fighting allowed them to bury the dead.

The medic continued with his work. By now, the makeshift hospital tent was full: full of the groans of the suffering, full of the smell of disinfectant, blood and foisty canvas; full of the dead and dying. He patrolled this living hell-on-earth and checked the vitals of each patient. He applied splints to broken bones to minimise internal bleeding and ease the pain. He changed the field dressings until he ran out. He had learned the hard way to leave the soldiers fully dressed to keep warm and only cut off enough clothing to assess the injuries. If they got cold, their heart rate increased to make up for the lack of blood volume, and cardiac arrest and death would soon follow. He continued his rounds. The casualty with the chest wound was critical. He was still conscious, but the veins in his neck were engorged, and his trachea was displaced. It was an obvious sign of tension pneumothorax: the pressure was building up in his chest and putting pressure on the other organs. It was a life-threatening scenario, so the medic took a catheter with an attached needle and inserted it into his chest between the second and third ribs — the sound of air exiting his lungs confirmed his diagnosis. He gave him a shot of antibiotics and morphine and moved on to the next casualty.

The soldier with the partially amputated leg was losing consciousness. He was confused and aggressive. The medic removed the morphine auto-injector from his thigh. Either he had administered it himself, or somebody had given it to him in the field. Tourniquets were extremely painful, and it wasn't uncommon for a patient to remove the tourniquet themselves and bleed to death. He gave him a fresh shot of morphine to help with the pain and flushed the wound with saline. He debrided the opening. It was beginning to smell and would have to come off if it got any worse. He hooked him up to an IV line to keep his blood pressure stable and moved to the next casualty. It was the National Serviceman, the one he had told not to worry so the medic felt the guilt even more intensely. He was still conscious and coughing up dark blood. He had an abdominal wound and swelling that indicated internal bleeding. The medic hooked up to the last IV drip and gave him shots of antibiotics and morphine and collapsed.

When darkness fell, the fighting stopped and the men carried the medic to his cot and cut the boots from his swollen feet. He started to object, but he had played at God for far too long and was exhausted and fell into a deep sleep, devoid of screaming, groaning and that blood-spattered hellhole. He awoke to the sound of the Chinese bugles heralding another attack. It was the morning of the 25th of April, and the

Glosters were soon on the receiving end of a battery of mortar shell fire and heavy machine gunfire. The Chinese were very close now and, in desperation, the Glosters called on their artillery to fire on their position to keep the enemy away. They waited for the onslaught. The medic checked that his Webley Mk IV service revolver was loaded: as a non-combatant, he could only use it to defend his patients from abuse, but the expected attack never materialised, and by nightfall the order had come through that they were to break out and try and get back to safety. It was every man for himself.

The medic lit a Camel cigarette. Maybe if he had received the letter from home in time, he would have made a different decision. Maybe not. Who knows what makes some men flee in the face of certain death, and some men stay and face their fate with a cool head. The Padre sat down next to him.

'I'm going to stay behind and look after the injured,' said the medic.

'I'm staying too,' said the Padre. 'To look after their souls.'

'Aren't you scared?'

'No. We all owe God a death.'

'That's true,' said the medic, 'but I was hoping mine would be a long time into the future.'

The men sat alone with their thoughts for a while.

'I want to ask you something, Padre.'

'Go ahead.'

'Some of the casualties aren't going to make it. Is it a sin to end their days in the euphoria of a morphine-induced sleep, or is it better to let them die in agony or at the hands of the Chinese?'

'God always forgives you if you confess your sins. You are a brave man.'

'I'm not sure if brave is the right word ... Maybe foolish is a better one?'

'The word you are looking for is brave.'

'Bravery didn't do them any good, did it?' said the medical officer as he pointed over to the dead and dying. 'It's a crazy world we live in where dishonour is feared more than death, and honour valued more than life. I can't remember who said it first, but there's no point in dying for a word. Bravery is just that, an empty word. Nothing more than air. All those sick and dead were brave, but where did it get them? It got them killed. That's where it got them.'

'It was Shakespeare,' said the Padre. 'Henry the Fourth.'

The medical officer checked his supplies of morphine and wandered over to the casualties. The amputee was unconscious. The medic inspected the dressing, and there was a crackling sounder under the skin when palpated and the unmistakable smell of gas gangrene. This man would die a painful death, and nothing could save him now. If he left him to the enemy, they would torture him. They wouldn't waste their limited medical supplies on the enemy. The medic removed his red-cross armband. He was not allowed to do this as a doctor so he would do it as a compassionate soldier. He filled the syringe with an overdose of morphine. His hands were shaking as he tried to find a vein and a few seconds later it was over. It was the first time he had killed a man. It was easy but was he justified? Had he made the right choice? He knew worse was waiting. Much worse. His supply of morphine was almost exhausted. Would he be able to do it? He moved on to the next casualty. It was the young the National Serviceman. He was fading in and out of consciousness, and the internal bleeding worsened. His blood pressure was falling quickly, and all the saline was gone. The medic injected an overdose of morphine into the soldier's vein, asked for his forgiveness, and told him he was sorry. He was no more than a boy and hadn't even had a chance to live his life. Another family destroyed by war. The medic fought back the anger and the tears. Once you had crossed the line and freed yourself of emotional baggage it was easy to become a monster.

That was the last of the morphine. He checked his Webley service revolver. Five rounds. Should he save one for himself? Shooting somebody was different to administering an injection. The medic retched up bitter bile and spat it on the floor. It wasn't fair to be lumbered with such a burden of responsibility. Was he strong enough to deliver a coup de grâce? He would soon find out. They were in severe pain. They had no chance of survival. Surely, they would welcome relief from pain sooner than later? He covered the patient's head with a pillow, so he didn't have to look, and pushed the barrel of the Webley into the pillow to stop his hand trembling. He closed his eyes and squeezed the trigger. It was over. Four more to go.

When he had finished, he returned to the Padre. There was nothing else to do now except sit and await his fate. He attached his Red Cross armband to a stick and put it in a prominent position where the enemy couldn't miss it.

'Do you think that will help?' asked the Padre.

'They must have heard of the Geneva Convention?'

'I doubt it, but we'll soon find out,' said the Padre.

'Anyway, haven't you heard? We are not officially at war. Our politicians have designated this a police action, not a war, so the Geneva Convention doesn't apply.' He passed the medic his last cigarette and said, 'I advise you to forget the Geneva Convention and anything else man-made and put your trust in God. Only He can help you now.'

CHAPTER 39

STALEMATE

The war seemed to drag on forever, and every day MiJa felt confronted by endless work and endless bowls of budea jjigae, and she promised herself that once the war was over, she would never, ever, open another tin of SPAM. When they had first moved to the graveyard village, legend had it that once you had crossed the Bridge of Doom into Ami Dong you would never leave, but in reality all it took was for somebody to care. MiJa and her mother moved onto camp, and the family became part of the hospital community. MiJa even attended the church services, not as a true believer, but because she believed that working together, as a community, would achieve success.

Hospital admissions were fewer and fewer, so they accepted Korean civilians. MiJa loved the work and had become a competent nurse and translator, but her favourite part of the day was lunchtime. She enjoyed the full smörgåsbord of Swedish food and the chance to catch up on the latest gossip. Today was her favourite, meatballs and mashed potato.

'You couldn't make it up, could you?' said one of the young Swedish doctors. 'They are bogged down at precisely the same place they were when they started this bloody war.' There was a consensus of shaking heads around the table. 'I mean, what have they achieved in three years? Nothing. Nothing at all.'

'Except the death of millions and all this suffering,' said one of the nurses.

The war had become a war of attrition. The initial enthusiasm and battle cry of *Let's drive the enemy onto the sea* was watered-down to, *Let's drive the enemy back to the 38th parallel.* As the war bogged down, it became protracted and ever expensive. The peace talks began, but they could not agree on a solution. They lacked the noble ability to compromise and let their vanity trump their humanity. The military leaders wanted a ceasefire, perhaps because they were nearer to the action, but their Korean political leaders on both sides were aloof and distant. Both leaders wanted a last throw of the dice. They weren't risking their lives, and they wanted control over the whole of the Korean peninsula. Each believed that they could still win the war, and each was only too willing to sacrifice their men for a chance to add their name to a footnote in a dusty history book.

On Sunday of 1 March 1953, MiJa attended the camp church service. The South Korean War Office had confirmed that her brother was Missing-In-Action and that his last posting was to Mun-Gyeong. MiJa prayed for a miracle, and that very same evening a short, elderly Georgian peasant called Ioseb retired to his bed, had a cerebral haemorrhage, pissed himself, and died. He was better known to the world as Joseph Stalin, The General Secretary of the Communist Party of the Soviet Union. His successor wanted a quick end to the Korean War, and in the early summer of 1953, the armistice discussions started.

Once again, the dithering cronies could not agree on what to do with the prisoners of war. In the ensuing political pissing match, President Lee released 27,000 North Korean prisoners who had decided that they wanted to stay in South Korea. The Chinese and North Koreans were enraged and decided to teach the South a lesson. The punishment of the innocent would continue.

On 27 July 1953, the military leaders had had enough and agreed to the 'Cessation of all hostilities until a peace settlement can be agreed.' The President of South Korea refused to sign the armistice agreement, so both sides withdrew their troops and created a four-kilometre-wide sterile no-mans-land, called the demilitarised zone. Three million people had died for nothing, and many still lay where they fell, grim reminders of their failure to compromise. The leaders turned their attention to agreeing to the peace treaty, searching for the guilty and heaping praise and reward on those that played no part. The first would never start, the second and third would never end.

The Korean War was over, and many had paid the ultimate price and lost their lives. All had lost something and some everything. The survivors had lost their past, present and future. Children had lost their parents. Families had lost their relatives, sometimes by death, sometimes by being on the wrong side of a line on a map. But it wasn't all bad news.

President Lee was guaranteed the Presidency of South Korea for life and presented a golden opportunity to drag his country out of the mire of war and redevelop it as a modern economy. Mr Song, the one-time schoolteacher and Japanese collaborator, finished the war as a Brigadier General of the South Korean Army and was sent to the USA for training. The Chaebol families, who got their start sheltering behind the Busan perimeter, would become the wealthiest families in South Korea and were rewarded with contracts to rebuild the country, financed by risk-free, incestuous, government-backed loans. In time, life on the peninsula would return to normal. But its leaders and the future incumbents had forgotten, 'That nothing is ever settled until it is settled right.'

'Well, I think we should leave,' said Bok-nam.

'But what about my life here?' said MiJa. 'The hospital said that I can take my exams and qualify as a nurse.'

'It's not all about you, MiJa. What about your brother?' Bok-nam's thoughts were with her son. She must find him. He had the right to the ancestral property, and she felt sure that it would be returned to its rightful owners now the war had finished. 'His last posting was to Mun-gyeong. What if he returns home, and nobody is waiting for him? Don't you want to see your brother again?'

'Yes, of course I do,' said MiJa. After all, blood is thicker than water, and the force to return home is a strong one and who knows, maybe Mi-soon will be waiting for us. War may destroy buildings and infrastructure, but the indomitable human spirit remains. It was time to make a new start. 'Let's go home.'

PART FOUR

THE PEACE

CHAPTER 40

THE MUDANG

The Mudang's house was easy enough to find. A festoon of coloured lanterns hung from the eaves, and a tall bamboo flagpole planted in the yard bowed under the weight of the pennant flags that trilled lightly in the breeze as they channelled energy from the spirit world.

'This is it! This is it!' said Bok-nam, barely able to contain her excitement.

MiJa fingered the gold cross at her neck and wondered if they had done the right thing. When they arrived back at their ancestral home in the fall of 1953, they found it occupied by a wealthy Chaebol family who owned legal title to the property and refused to move out. Bok-nam was furious but they had no choice but to move back into the rickety, stilted hayloft. MiJa consoled her mother: when Yung-soo returned he would go to the hayloft first because that was where he would expect them to be living.

Bok-nam received no news of her son and as the days turned into weeks, she grew impatient. One day she heard of a new Shaman who had just moved to the area. He was a young child and unadulterated by sin and therefore pure, and he came highly recommended by all who had visited him. That sealed it. Every day she nagged MiJa to do something about it. But what could MiJa do without money? Her mother was insistent and suggested that MiJa barter her gold necklace for news of her brother, and in the end, she agreed.

When they entered the house, they were greeted by three stooped old cronies, dressed in black sackcloth with extra-long sleeves like wings, and hoods that drooped over their heads and hid their faces. They reminded MiJa of three black ravens. The bird of bad omen. Thrice. She knew she should not have come and was about to leave when one of them cawed, 'Looking for somebody?' She clicked her tongue and cocked her head to one side, birdlike.

'Yes, I'm looking for my son. My only son,' said Bok-nam and wrung the blood out of her hands until they were white.

'What is his name?' said the second raven. As she spoke, she raised her head, and the hood slipped back slightly revealing her face.

MiJa winced. She had been wrong about the ravens. They were harpies, ones that made vultures look like birds of paradise.

'Choi Yung-soo.'

'And when was he born?'

'The 15th of August 1935.'

One of the ravens removed an old chart from a drawer, held it an inch away from her face, and studied it closely.

'At what time was the birth?'

'I'm not exactly sure,' said Bok-nam. 'But it must have been before dawn because I didnt hear the rooster crow.'

The old raven intently studied the sexagenary chart that had been divided into the twelve Chinese zodiac animals. She made regular clucking sounds and murmured when the chart revealed something auspicious. 'Hmmm, Midsummer. Before dawn, and a pig ... How unfortunate. A rabbit would have been better.'

'How will you pay the bok-chae? Blessings cost,' asked the leader in a wheezy breath from the dusty depth of her lungs.

Bok-nam stared at MiJa and nodded. She removed the gold cross from around her neck, the one the American missionary had given her, and put it into the bony outstretched claw that protruded from under the baggy sleeve. The old harpy seized the necklace and examined it closely, nodding. Eventually, she said, 'Ready to meet our miraculous mudang?'

They were led into a dark room and MiJa squinted her eyes to see who or what was squatting behind a lacquered table in the centre of the room. She could make out a small child, no more than five years old. Whether it was a he or she was impossible to tell because the child was wearing a multi-coloured dress in all the colours of the rainbow. The mudang was wearing makeup: a light luminous foundation, red lipstick and kohl eyeliner. Fierce black eyes shone brightly and unblinkingly and seemed to burn into her very soul. The mudang talked in tongues, and in its left hand, it held a paper fan which it was wafting toward itself and sniffing the air as if to catch prophecies from the spirit world. The mudang studied Bok-nam's face and ears and said something to the head raven.

'What does he say?' asked Bok-nam.

The head raven translated: 'What is it that you really seek? The return of your son or the return of your house?'

Bok-nam's mouth dropped open as if her jaw muscles had lost all their power.

'He sees everything. Everything in you,' said the head raven.

'My son,' lied Bok-nam and a cold shiver ran through her. How did he know?

'Deep, deep in the earth,' said the mudang.

'Is he dead?' said Bok-nam and braced herself for the answer.

'Let's find out now,' said the three cronies.

The unholy trinity formed a huddle. There was much wailing, tutting and sharp intakes of breath. The leader removed a small gong from her clothing and started banging it with a soft mallet, softly at first but gradually upping the tempo and volume until it filled the small house with an uncomfortable, deafening cacophony so the spirits would have nowhere to hide. The other two cronies lit three joss sticks in each hand and began to fan every nook and cranny to smoke out any lurking spirits.

They began ululating and flapping their arms as they circled the floor like possessed creatures. The macabre dance slowed down and sped up until they began whirling like demented dervishes. Their cries pierced the thick atmosphere, and the gong beat a frantic rhythm until they collapsed, exhausted, in a heap onto the floor and started shaking in spasms with their eyes rolled back into their heads, so only the whites showed.

Eventually, one of the ravens slowly raised herself from the floor with a crack of old dry bones. She had five bamboo sticks clutched in her hand, and she offered them to Bok-nam.

'Choose one,' she said.

Bok-nam pulled out one of the sticks to reveal a green flag.

There was a gasp from the others. The head raven added another flag to the ones in her hand and said with a toothless smile, 'Try again.'

Bok-nam pulled out a stick. It was black.

'You poor poor woman,' said the raven. 'First green, then black.' She glanced at the others. 'Blue means help is coming from the east, white means a spirit will bring help from the west, red brings luck from the south, and yellow means an ancestor will help you from the centre. But green or black is cursed. The cold north brings only death. The obangsing-janggi never lie.'

'No. No. No. It can't be,' said Bok-nam. 'Say it's not true.' She swooned, but MiJa caught her before she fell to the floor.

'I've had enough of this nonsense,' said MiJa. 'This is nothing but a sham. Give me my gold cross back, right now!'

'Quiet!' said the head raven.

'Come to me my God. Come into me.' The mudang started to shake a stick adorned with small silver bells. The stick continued to jingle like sleigh bells for a while, and then suddenly, it stopped. 'It is God's will that your son is buried deep under the earth.'

The mudang put down his bell stick and picked up a knife shaped like a small billhook. He placed it on the floor and spun it around three times. Each time the tip of the knife pointed at Bok-nam. The mudang turned around to distance himself from Bok-nam and spoke to the head raven.

'His God wants you to leave now and take your sins with you,' translated the head raven. MiJa and her mother turned to leave, and the young Mudang threw a fistful of rock salt at Bok-nam's head.

'Not you,' said the head raven and pointed at MiJa. 'You must stay.'

When Bok-nam left the room the mudang spoke directly to MiJa, 'The answer is in your book. Seek, and ye shall find.'

When they returned to the hayloft, MiJa hunted everywhere for her Bible.

'Mother, have you seen my book?'

'I hung it up, next to the toilet.'

'Oh no. Not again, Mother.' MiJa found the Bible hung over a loop of string. She snatched it off the nail and went outside into the light. Her mother had torn out many pages and it fell open at John, Chapter 11. She sat down and read it. It was a story about two sisters who called upon Jesus to come and save their brother, who was at death's door. Jesus delayed his journey and the brother died. It didn't sound very promising, thought MiJa, but she read on:

Lord, Martha said to Jesus, If you had been here, my brother would not have died, but I know that even now, God will give you whatever you ask. Jesus said to her, Your brother will rise again. Martha answered I know he will rise again on the Resurrection Day. Jesus said to her, I am the resurrection and the life. He who believes in me will live, even though he dies, and whoever lives and believes in me will never die. Do you believe in this? Then Jesus called in a loud voice, Lazarus, come out. The dead man came out, his hands and feet wrapped with strips of linen and a cloth wrapped around his face. Jesus said to them, Take off his burial clothes, and let him go.

And MiJa understood that for Christians, death was not the final word and it could be defeated.

CHAPTER 41

A RESURRECTION

Seventy-three feet under a South Korean Mountain, the dim light from an oil lamp hissed in the dark, dank air as it trundled along the rough granite passageway. A man crawled along on all fours, pulling a cart behind him on a narrow-gauge rail track. He held the lamp in his left hand as high as he could to cast the pool of light as far forward as possible and steadied himself with his other hand on the smooth metallic rail.

It was hot and humid, and he was naked except for a cloth wrapped around his loins and the strips of linen on his hands and feet. As he gained purchase with his feet on the sleepers and pushed forward, the leather harness bit into his shoulders, and the sweat trickled down his back, like crawling spiders' feet, and stung his shoulders where they had been rubbed raw by the chaffing of the harness. When he stopped, he fell to his knees and the jagged rocks stabbed through the improvised padding and spurred him on. So, inch by inch, like a grubby subterranean caterpillar, he advanced into the tunnel.

How long had he been here? Who knew? He had lost track of time, but it never got any easier. Every time felt like the first time, and the ever-present claustrophobia squeezed the life out of him like a giant boa constrictor, getting tighter and tighter the deeper he went. At first, he thought he could conquer his fears: the fear of a tunnel collapse that would crush him to death; the fear of being buried alive; the fear of drowning if the tunnel filled with water; the fear of asphyxiating from the foul gases released from the bowels of the earth and the blasting. But he was wrong; the fear grew in intensity with every step. When he reached the tunnel face, the bitter taste of the sulphurous blasting fumes stung his throat, and the salty sweat ran down his face and made his eyes sting. He wiped the sweat away with his forearm and accidentally rubbed the fine gritty granite into his skin until it left a permanent grimy tattoo.

He piled the rubble into the cart and could feel the tracks vibrate under his hand as if they were trembling in fear. It meant the haulier had set off. The haulier would take the full cart back and empty the muck on the North Korean side. He was also supposed to fetch stout wooden props to support the roof, but they stopped shoring up the tunnel when they fell behind schedule. He could hear and smell the haulier before he could see him. The rasping breath reverberated along the tunnel, and the rank body odour filled the confined space. He watched a pinprick of light bob up and down, glinting like a distant star or lost firefly.

'Hey Comrade, found any coal yet?' said the haulier as he squeezed past the cart, put his lamp down, and pressed his back into the wall.

Yung-soo laughed, 'No, Comrade, but I think we may hit a rich seam today.' They were supposed to be mining for coal, but nobody had ever seen any. It was an open secret that they were tunnelling under the DMZ to infiltrate South Korea, but nobody dared speak about it, even down here; everybody gossips. The haulier had an airline slung across his shoulder, and he hooked it up to a rudimentary ventilation duct: a section of rusty pipe, drilled with random holes, suspended above their heads. The air hissed into the tunnel, and they greedily feasted on it and chewed the fat for a while.

'Well, I suppose I better get back before they miss me,' said the haulier as he connected his harness to the spoils cart. Yung-soo pushed the spoils cart to help the haulier overcome the inertia, and he watched the light from his lamp fade into the sea of blackness until he was alone again with only his thoughts for company. He checked the level of oil in his lamp. Not much left. He would ask the haulier to bring some more. He didn't want it to go out. The fear of the dark. The ghosts. They often heard crying or wailing in the tunnel, but nobody would admit to it, so stories of ghosts filled their imaginations. Enough people had died down here, so some of them might have stuck around with unfinished grievances to resolve.

Long ago when he was captured by the North Koreans, he had accepted that he would never leave here. He would work here, live here and die here, and had seen many people do just that. He had watched them drag the bodies out into the morning sunlight and dispose of them without ceremony, and he hoped that when death came for him, it would not be a lingering death. There was no way he was getting trapped underground and dying of thirst. He checked the knife that hung around his neck from an old bootlace. All the miners carried them, a weapon of last resort that was their only remaining freedom: the freedom to choose. They could force him to dig his own grave, but when the time came, the choice of how he died would be his.

He placed a square of canvas across his mouth and nose and secured it with two ragged strips of cloth tied behind his head, shoved some cotton wool into his ears, and pressed the pneumatic drill into the rock face. Even with earplugs inserted, the sound was deafening, and the vibrations shook his arms and every internal organ, bone and muscle in his body. At the end of the shift, it would take him several hours to stop shaking. He could taste the fine granite dust as it filled the air and clogged his face mask, making breathing difficult. His job was to drill one-inch diameter holes about three feet deep in a regular pattern into the rock face.

The blasting engineer arrived, he checked the depth of each hole with a bamboo stick, loaded a stick of dynamite and a detonator into each hole and sealed it with a plug of clay to focus the direction of the blast into the rock face. Then they would evacuate the foul air from the tunnel using extractor fans, clear the rubble and start all over again. The blasting engineer also brought lunch: it was the same every day, an overcooked potato with leathery skin as chewy as a hundred-year-old squid, but it was better than nothing. When they had finished lunch, the blasting engineer said, 'I reckon we are close to the surface now. You know what that means?'

'They might hear us?'

'Unlikely. According to my surveying and calculations, we are under a wooded area just south of the DMZ. I have never told anyone this before, but I've got a family in the South. I don't suppose I will ever see them again, at my age.'

'I have a family in the South too,' said Yung-soo.

'Fancy getting out of here, son?'

Yung-soo didn't respond at first because he was afraid to commit himself. He had heard of other people trapped this way by using informers.

The blasting engineer sensed his fear. 'I ain't a snitch,' he said. 'There is nobody down here but us. Understand?'

Yung-soo nodded his head.

'Now get yourself behind the blast wall while I light these damn fuses.' When they had first started digging, everybody evacuated the tunnel when they were blasting. But the project fell behind schedule as the tunnel got longer, so they built temporary blast shelters. Yung-soo scurried along like a rat leaving a sinking ship and had only just drawn level with one of the temporary refuges, sealed behind a stack of old truck tires when there was a flash of light, as bright as a thunderbolt. The rapidly expanding cloud of noxious gas knocked him to the ground and dislodged his oil lamp, and he watched the flame die just a few feet beyond him as though he was watching his life ebb away, and then all was black.

Yung-soo had no idea how long he had lain unconscious. When he regained consciousness, it was as dark as pitch in the tunnel and eerily quiet, except for the continuous ringing in his ears that made him feel like he was underwater. He had no idea where he was and thought he was asleep in the hayloft in Mun-gyeong and called out for MiJa. Gradually it came back to him. He was in the tunnel. They had just set off the explosion. The engineer. Where was he? What had happened? There was usually plenty of time to get back behind the blast wall. Maybe the engineer had set the wrong fuses, or the explosive had become unstable over time?

When his head cleared, he realised that he had to get out. This wasn't going to be his grave. He crawled along in the dark and placed his hand on something wet and clammy that felt like warm meat. He pushed it away in disgust when he realised what it was. He found more pieces of the blasting engineer as he crawled further into the tunnel until he came across a rock that blocked his way. He was trapped.

Panic set in, his heart raced, and his breathing tried to catch up. Then it dawned on him. He had gone the wrong way. He was at the work face. He was about to turn around and head in the other direction when he noticed something strange. The tunnel air was clearing, and he could make out the surface of the walls, and motes of dust danced before his eyes. They must have turned on the extraction fans. But the dust was travelling the wrong way. It was being carried on a stream of fresh air into the tunnel, towards a shaft of light. Then it dawned on him. They had broken the surface.

He tried to squeeze past the fallen rock, but it was so tight that he could only get his head through the gap. He could see daylight, and the cool air that brushed his face was so delicious he gulped it in and tried to wriggle his way out of the fissure. He sucked in his breath, but his shoulders would not fit through the gap. Then he remembered the drill. As he rushed back for it, he could see the body parts of the engineer, and it made him retch, but it also spurred him on.

He had a chance to escape, but he didn't have long. The search party would soon be here as soon as they had evacuated the gas and the dust. He heard the ventilation fans start. He collected the engineer's body parts together and piled them up so it would be the first thing they found. That should delay them. Then he derailed the cart and worked like a madman, moving all the rock spoil into the cart and around the tunnel until it blocked the way ahead. There was only one way out now. If he didn't make it, he could wait until rescue arrived. It was a risk worth taking.

He picked up the jackhammer, wrapped the pneumatic line around his waist and over his shoulders and dragged it to the rock obstruction. If everything went to plan, he would soon be free. He squeezed the trigger of the drill — nothing happened. The airline must have been severed or turned off, and his initial elation sank into dark despair. He was so close, and yet so far. He had gambled and lost. There was nothing to do now except await rescue, and that would take time. Unless he did it the old way. He removed the drill bit, steadied it in his hand, and pounded it with a rock. His hand was bleeding, but he didn't stop. The smell of sweet air was just too tempting, and eventually he managed to break off a sliver of rock. He tried to fit his body through, but it was still too tight. He heard voices in the tunnel.

He would try one more time, only this time he rolled in the wet slippery mud on the floor, sucked his breath in and held it in, stretched his arms out like a diver and wriggled like a porpoise with all his remaining strength. He was through. All that lay before him now was the soil, loosened by the explosion. The light above him spurred him on. Freedom was in sight. He dug, using both his hands as shovels like a crazed mole, and swam for the surface. His head broke the surface. He was free. And then, suddenly, he could go no further. He was stuck fast. Something was holding him back. Panic set in, and he writhed like an eel trying to free himself. Then it dawned on him: the airline, tied around his waist. It must have jammed tight in the struggle. The knife. The knife. In an ironic twist of fate, the knife he wore around his neck to end his life would now save it. He unhooked it from his neck, cut through the umbilical, and pulled himself back into the world.

Yung-soo lay spread-eagled on the earth with the rain spattering off his face and grinned like a village idiot. He was free. He licked his parched lips and savoured the sweetest drink he had ever tasted. The old blasting engineer had been spot-on with his surveying; he emerged in a clump of the pine forest and, for the moment, was well-hidden. So well-hidden that the infiltration tunnel, to be used for North Korea's invasion of the South, would not be discovered until 1972 by South Korean soldiers investigating the steam rising out of the trees.

He tried to stand up, but tinnitus and tunnel vision conspired to make him fall over. He tried again with the same result, so he forced himself into a sitting position, propped his back against a tree for support, and laughed at his good fortune. When he had adjusted to his newfound freedom, he stood up, stripped off his rags of linen, raised his arms and face to the heavens, and let the rain wash away all the grime and filth. He felt born again, as though he had freshly returned from the dead. The heavy burden he hadn't realised was there was suddenly removed from his shoulders, and he felt as light as air. All the anguish and torment he had suffered and bottled up inside him all these years gushed out in a flurry of emotion, and he sobbed like a baby until the rain and tears merged, rolled down his face in rivulets and soaked into the earth. When he had recovered, he thought about what he should do next. He crawled to the edge of the wood and could see the lights from the border post behind him and laughed. He couldn't believe his luck — he was in South Korea. He thought about surrendering himself to the South Korean Army. He could show them the tunnel, but he realised he didn't have any identification and they would probably shoot him as a North Korean spy. Once night had fallen, he would get as far away from this place as possible, so he got dressed back into his newly-washed rags and waited.

When night came, he felt like he was seeing the heavens for the first time and was rooted to the spot, mesmerised by the eternal beauty of the stars. Then he did something he hadn't dared do for years: he dreamed about seeing his mother and his sisters again. He dreamed about living his life again and pointed his feet in the direction of home.

CHAPTER 42

THE GUI-SHIN

On the night of 16th of June 1954, MiJa awoke from a dream, drenched in sweat, and kicked off the covers to let it evaporate. She lay still and listened to the wind howling around the shack, rocking the stilted building to and fro until it groaned in protest. Occasionally a bank of rain would lash against the clapboarding and run down the inside walls. She glanced across at her mother. She was lying perfectly still except for her slowly heaving chest. MiJa tried to go back to sleep, but the roof started leaking and the water dripped onto the floor next to her yo, with an annoyingly regular rhythm.

She decided to get up and fetch a bucket to collect the rainwater. Was the storm as bad as it sounded? Often the imagined storm was much worse than the real thing, especially when you live in a hollow wooden box. She peered through one of the gaps in the timber cladding but couldn't see anything through the swirling rain. She strained her eyes trying to focus through the gloom, and she thought she caught a glimpse of something moving in the distance. She must have imagined it, she told herself. Nobody was crazy enough to be wandering about on a night like this, but it had piqued her curiosity.

She unbolted the trap door that led to the staircase and tentatively poked her head out for a better look. There was nothing there. She had imagined it and was about to close the hatch again and go back to bed when she glimpsed it again. There was something out there. A blurred figure seemed to float through the rain, but it was no ordinary figure. It was pale, dressed in rags, and had something other-worldly about it like an emaciated corpse wearing a sumo loincloth — but it was also familiar.

A cold fingertip of fear traced down MiJa's spine, and she shuddered as though somebody had walked across her grave. She had heard the stories about the Gui-shin but had always thought they were old wives' tales from long ago when tigers used to smoke. The Gui-shin were wayfaring ghosts who had died before their time and wandered the land and tormented the living until their grievances were satisfied.

Maybe this thing, this apparition, hadn't seen her. She was about to close the door and go back inside when this apparition, this ghost, whatever it was, raised a hand and appeared to beckon to her. Fear paralysed her for a moment, but only for a moment. The fight or flight instinct kicked in and she jolted into action. She slammed the trapdoor shut, dived under the safety of the covers, pulled them tight over her head and held her breath. She tried not to make a sound, but her pounding heartbeat must surely betray her. She strained her ears for what seemed like hours, but in fact could only have been a few minutes. There was no sound except for the wind and rain. Whatever was out there had gone.

Then she heard a squeak on the staircase, followed by the heavy thud of a step. She gripped the covers tighter until her knuckles showed white through the skin. The stairs creaked and thudded, and she counted them off one by one. When she got to nine, she remembered that she had forgotten to slide the bolts on the trap door. She lifted the blanket ever so slightly and watched as the trapdoor slowly opened and a head poked through. She screamed.

'What is happening?' yelled her mother, who leapt out of her bed, struck a match and lit the kerosene lamp. Bok-nam screamed, too, and said, 'It can't be. It can't be.'

MiJa recognised the withered face in the light of the kerosene lamp and mumbled, 'It is... It. Is.'

'Mum, I'm home,' said Yung-soo and collapsed.

For the next few weeks, MiJa doted on her brother and stared at him continually, afraid he would disappear if she stopped looking. She was anxious to know all that had happened to him, but he was cagey about many things and had not straightened them in his mind yet. So she told him of their decision to go Busan, her work in the Kangkang shipyard and her work as a nurse in the Swedish Red Cross Hospital. She told him how their stupid mother had decided to consult a Shaman to find out where he was and demonstrated the scene by running around the room, flapping her arms with her sleeves pulled over her arms and cawing, like the three old cronies.

'They said you were buried deep in the ground. Which was true, I guess, but Mother thought you were dead.' Then she told him about how her mother had been using her Bible as toilet paper, as though it was the *East Asia Daily*, and the next page happened to be the story of Lazarus. She told Yung-soo the story of Lazarus and how she knew she would see him again after reading it.

'I was in Busan too until they sent me back here,' said Yung-soo. 'I fought in the Battle of Mun-gyeong. I say fought, but perhaps hid, would be a better description. I dug a hole in the ground and stayed there until it was all over. Like a frightened rabbit.'

'You hid?'

Yung-soo nodded his head. 'We were ordered to stay in our foxholes by the colonel. I would have been alright, but I had to pay a call of nature in the morning. I thought that the North Koreans had returned to the mountains, but an injured soldier caught me with my pants down and took me prisoner. He made me carry him back to North Korea, and we ran into a North Korean Patrol. They taunted me about being just a child and was that all South Korea could muster as soldiers. They threatened to shoot me, but the injured soldier told them what I had done for him and pleaded for my life. Another argued that I was fit and young and should work in the labour camps. I ended up digging an infiltration tunnel into South Korea. The first time I tried it, I realised that I had just traded a slow death instead of a quick one. But one day there was an accident and I escaped. It was a miracle, and I kowtowed in the rain and prayed to God. What day is it today?'

'The 17th of June 1954,' said MiJa.

'Really?' said Yung-soo, and he became withdrawn again, lost in thought. He was trapped in the tunnel again and wondered where all the time had gone.

'Any news of Mi-soon?' he asked.

'No,' said MiJa, and the gloom descended on the room and made itself comfortable in familiar surroundings. She noticed that her mother looked away to hide her shame.

Yung-soo thought of the similarities between Lazarus and himself. He had stripped off his linen rags and come back from the dead. 'Maybe if we really believe in Jesus, He will return Mi-soon back to us.'

MiJa shrugged.

'It worked before, didn't it? I came back.'

MiJa was unsure, but Pastor Matthews had told her that if you believed in Jesus, then she would be reunited with her sister in heaven. She had nothing to lose. She might have to change her life a little bit, attend church and change her beliefs, but it was a small price to pay for a place in heaven, so she agreed. They decided to make a fresh start and join the Methodist Church.

They were both surprised when Bok-nam announced that she would also join the church. She had other plans that involved the local politician Jang-Jun-pyo, and she knew just where she could find him.

CHAPTER 43

A BAPTISM

A special church service was held on the banks of the Yeong River on Sunday, 4 July 1954, and the entire church congregation had gathered to witness the baptism of the new believers. Even the passers-by stopped and wondered what all the fuss was about, but a circus was a circus and free entertainment was in short supply so they tarried and craned their necks to see.

The Elder finished his sermon of Mark 3:16-17 and Rome 6:3-4 and asked MiJa, 'Do you believe that our Lord Jesus is the Son of God?'

'I do,' said MiJa. Last week the family had taken a test on their knowledge of the gospel and even Bok-nam had passed much to MiJa's surprise.

'And do you believe that He died for your sins to save you from death?'

'I do.'

'Do you believe in the resurrection?'

'I do.'

The Elder stepped into the river until his waist was

submerged, turned around and signalled for the ceremony to start. Two Deacons led MiJa by the arms into the river and the choir struck up the spiritual:

I've got peace like a river
I've got peace like a river
I've got peace like a river in my soul ...

'Oh God,' said MiJa as she stepped into the river, and immediately apologised. The river was always icy cold from the mountain snowmelt, whatever time of year. She lost all feeling in her toes, and the numbness slowly crawled up her legs. The rocks were slippery, so she grabbed onto one of the Deacon's shoulders for support.

The Elder said, 'Based upon your profession of faith in the Lord Jesus Christ, I now baptise you in the name of the Father and Son and Holy Spirit. Buried with Him in the likeness of His death. Raised with Him in the likeness of His resurrection to walk in the newness of life.'

'Amen,' said MiJa. The Elder leaned MiJa backwards until she was fully submerged under the freezing current. When she resurfaced she took a sharp intake of breath, and paralysed by the icy water, began shaking uncontrollably. When the Elder raised her again, she felt that the water had scoured away her old life and swept her sins downstream. It felt like she had died and been reborn. She inhaled deeply like it was her first-ever breath, the breath of a new-born. She was a new woman now and ready to start a new life.

As she climbed up the riverbank she began to shiver violently. The two Deacons were waiting with towels to dry her but before she could reach them Jang Jun-pyo held out a towel of his own. He smiled. MiJa's thin cotton clothing clung to every contour of her naked body and left nothing to the imagination. She self-consciously covered her breasts with her hands. Jang wrapped the towel around MiJa and started to rub her body vigorously. 'Congratulations, MiJa. Welcome to the Church of God. We'll soon have you warmed up.'

MiJa winced. He had been staring at her body for longer than was decent, and now his hands were wandering as much as his roving eyes.

'I'm fine now. Thank you, Mr Jang,' said MiJa as she ducked away from his groping hands and glared at her mother.

In the following weeks, Jang was a frequent visitor to the Choi residence and spent a lot of time talking to Bok-nam. MiJa noticed that her mother had perked up a lot, especially when Jang brought joints of beef and bags of rice. Slowly he revealed his motivations to Bok-nam. There was an upcoming election, and to be electable he needed to be married.

Bok-nam had been waiting for this moment. Her plan was coming to fruition, and she knew Jang would not find a better bride in this town.

'I don't think that would be wise,' she said.

'Why?'

'How could somebody of your stature marry someone that lives in a hayloft? It's such a shame because MiJa is of good Yangban stock.'

'What should we do?'

'If only there was some way to return my ancestral home. Rightfully, it belongs to my son but if you could find a way to restore it to the family, then things might be different.'

And so, it was agreed. When Jang had won the election, he would restore the property to her son in return for the hand of MiJa in marriage.

'Shall I arrange the marriage then?' asked Jang

'You can announce your engagement, but the *marriage*

can only take place *after* you have won the election,' said Bok-nam.

'Will MiJa object?' asked Jang.

'Yes, probably, but leave that to me,' said Bok-nam. She knew she would have to browbeat MiJa until she overcame her objections and accepted her filial duty. After weeks of nagging and lecturing, MiJa reluctantly agreed to sacrifice her future for her family.

But the plans of mice and men don't always run smooth. Jang lost the local election to Jung-sik's father and was fuming. Bok-nam refused to let him marry MiJa and the red mist descended. 'How can the people be so stupid? They fell for all his election promises. There was no way the charcoal train would be diverted to stop in Mun-gyeong, yet they swallowed it hook, line and sinker. And as for reuniting the families with the wartime missing in action. Did they really believe that would happen? Dreams. Nothing but daydreams. How could he show his face in the town ever again? People would point and stare. There goes that man who lost the election. Well, my life isn't the only one that will be ruined. I will leave here, but not alone. I want a souvenir.

A week after the election, MiJa was drawing water from the well and was surprised to hear a familiar reptilian voice behind her.

'Hello pretty MiJa. I have been looking for you everywhere. I thought I would find you here.'

She glanced over her shoulder. 'Hello Mr Jang. What are you doing here?' She thought he had left town last week after the election results were posted. She was so relieved when Jung-sik's father had won.

Jang stared at her, trying to decipher her thoughts.

MiJa noticed that he had a picnic hamper in his hand and a rolled-up blanket tucked under his arm. The last picnic she had was with Jung-sik before the Japanese had spirited him away.

'How could I leave without saying goodbye?'

'I am sorry you lost the election and I wish you good luck with your new life.'

'Shall we have a last supper together?' He raised the picnic basket as evidence. 'Fancy it?'

MiJa did not, but it was only polite to accept. Besides, what harm would it do? She would have lunch with him and then he would be out of her life forever. 'Okay,' she said. 'But I can't stay long.'

Jang led the way up the hill until they came to a gnarled old tree that was rumoured to be 700 years old. It looked it too. The villagers believed that the spirits that lived within it protected them from evil. Jang spread the blanket under its shade and unpacked the hamper. 'I made it myself, especially for you.' He handed MiJa a roll of gimbap.

The bloody liar, she thought. It was the same texture and taste as the ones she had bought at the open market. 'It's delicious. It must have taken you ages to make it.' MiJa blushed.

'It's an old family recipe,' said Jang and smiled at the thought of fooling her. His ruse had worked. 'How about a drink?' Jang produced two green glass bottles of soda water. 'Surprise.'

'What is it?' asked MiJa.

'7Up. It's similar to Coca Cola.'

MiJa's mouth salivated. She loved the crackling sensation and sweetness of Coca Cola. 'Why is it called 7Up? Is it seven times better than Coca Cola?'

'I'm sure it is. Why don't you try it and tell me.'

MiJa took a small sip. It was the first time she had ever tasted lemonade.

'How does it taste?' asked Jang.

'It's got a strange taste. Slightly bitter. I think I prefer

Coca Cola.' She took another sip and started feeling light-headed and giddy. Then everything seemed to be in slow motion. She complained about feeling unwell. She heard a disembodied voice say, 'Finish it all, like a good girl.' After that, everything went hazy, and her speech slurred. She remembered shouting, 'No,' and she remembered trying to push Jang away, but he was too strong. Then everything went black.

CHAPTER 44

MUKHO

To some, heaven is all pearly gates, gold-paved streets, jewel-encrusted mansions, clouds filled with string-plucking cherubs, and endless worship. MiJa's heaven, the one in which she now found herself, was different: there were no gates to keep people out, no streets paved with gold and not a single cloud in the sky. The only jewels to be found were an endless lapis lazuli sky and an ocean of topaz and sapphire. The crystal waters gently lapped at the shingle shore, and MiJa watched a solitary white seabird soar effortlessly, just above the waves, thinking it would glide on forever. She sighed, and her breathing rose and fell with the sound of the ocean crashing on the shore until their rhythms were perfectly synchronised, and it felt like she was controlling the cadence of the sea and was at one with the world. The seabird suddenly dived into the ocean, and the dream was over.

To some, hell is a bottomless dark pit filled with sinners, sorrow and wailing, fiery flames, torment, the gnashing of teeth and everlasting punishment. MiJa's hell, the one in which she now found herself, was different: heaven and hell can be the same place, and just like the allegory of the six-foot chopsticks: it is the people who make the difference. When MiJa first glimpsed the ocean, she thought she had died and gone to heaven; she soon discovered otherwise. Her head throbbed, and her body ached all over. She felt spent and wet, and there was pain and blood in her underwear and on the sheets. Slowly she realised what had happened and dragged herself out of the bed she found herself in.

She ran to the open doors that overlooked the ocean and screamed at the sky. There was nobody to hear, so she went back into the room and ran a hot bath. She scrubbed herself clean until the water turned cold, but she still felt dirty and degraded.

In the late afternoon, Jang Jun-pyo returned, drunk. MiJa panicked and pretended to be asleep. It didn't make any difference. His hot breath smelled of alcohol and lust, and she tried to fight him off, but she was too weak, and in the end, she just submitted to his violent act. After he had finished, he threw some money on the bed, like she was a cheap whore.

'Why don't you be a good wife and fix some dinner?'

MiJa was relieved when he left, and she quickly dressed in the only clothes she had. She could not bear to put her old panties on, so she would have to buy new ones from somewhere. But where? She thought of running away, but where would she go? She had no idea where she was and felt trapped. The tears came again, hot and heavy. Proper tears of anger and she wailed in despair, tried to rip the hair from her scalp, and beat her head with her fists. She was so angry with the world.

When she went outside, the natural beauty of the ocean took her breath away. It wasn't a dream. It was real, but so was the pain. On the outskirts of the town, she came across a small village store. 'I am looking for women's underwear,' she reluctantly asked the man behind the counter, without making eye contact.

The man bent down and retrieved a packet from under

the counter. 'We only have one kind. No choice. But I think they will fit you.' He looked MiJa up and down and tried to catch a glimpse of her face.

MiJa paid and rushed out of the shop. She plodded on, following the winding coastal path until she came to a small fishing port. A collection of colourful fishing vessels bobbed in the harbour, and market traders were trying to outshout each other for attention. A group of old weather-beaten women, wearing battered wetsuits and battered faces, were rinsing out some terracotta-coloured plastic buckets with fresh seawater.

MiJa had heard about the Hae-nyeo in her childhood but had never really believed that they existed. To the people that lived inland, who had never even seen the coast, they were the stuff of legend: an old wives' tale or something you told to scare the children. A myth created to while away the long hours of boredom and plug the gaps in human knowledge, yet here they were. Like all good stories, they had their fertile roots buried in reality. The tales used to terrify MiJa as a child. Some said that the Hae-nyeo were half woman, half marine mammal, and lived all around the Korean coastal towns. Some said that they had actually seen them and that they spent a large part of their lives scouring the ocean floor for food and could breathe underwater. When night fell, they would return to the land, shed their skin and become human again.

'Excuse me, can you tell me where am I?' asked MiJa.

'You are in Mukho, sister,' said one of the Hae-nyeo.

'Where?'

'On the east coast of South Korea.'

'I am Choi MiJa.'

'Yes we know who you are,' said the elder Hae-nyeo. 'Don't we sisters?'

'You do?' said MiJa in a state of confusion.

'We do. Do you want to know how you got here?'

MiJa shrugged her shoulders. 'Yes,' she said, not sure what to expect. The Hae-nyeo finished gutting and filleting their fish, swilled them with fresh seawater, and tossed the blood and guts over the harbour wall. They arranged the upturned rubber buckets in a semi-circle and beckoned MiJa to sit. The others joined them, and one of them pushed a steaming bowl of fish stew towards MiJa.

'Eat up,' she said, and the head Hae-nyeo told MiJa how she had first arrived in Mukho. 'We had sold our catch for the day, so we decided to head along to the soju tents as is our custom. We work hard and play hard, don't we sisters?' The others nodded in agreement, and the leader gave a dirty laugh and slapped her thigh.

'The soju tents are those makeshift, orange plastic tents with clear windows you see over yonder.' She pointed to a small shanty town of tents erected on the harbour wall, not far from the fish market. Inside were white plastic tables and chairs and stacked crates of soju: a spirit made from distilled rice wine, cheap but effective.

'We had just finished our first round of shots and were about to order another and some seafood pancakes because you shouldn't eat on an empty stomach when in walks a stranger with an enormous hunch on his back. So, we looked at each other and cocked our heads, waiting to see what would happen next. The man ordered a glass of soju and then removed his coat and revealed the source of the bulge. A woman was lashed to his back, just like we carry our children, only this woman was unconscious. We looked at each other and thought, what is going on here? He untied the woman and laid her on the floor. Then he ordered another shot for himself and one for each of us and said, "Gambei. Meet my new wife, MiJa."

'Of course, we never believed his story that you were

simply tired from the journey. You had better watch that one, MiJa.'

When MiJa left the market, she had two whole fish for dinner and still had money in her pocket. About halfway home, it started raining, and it seemed to her that the very sky was crying.

CHAPTER 45

THE HAE-NYEO

MiJa settled into her daily routine of visiting the Hae-nyeo in the market. She was there at the crack of dawn to greet the boats as they came in and helped them wash down the boats and land their catch. The Hae-nyeo made their living by catching abalone, octopus, sea cucumbers, sea slugs, seaweed and everything else that was edible and lived or swam in the ocean.

Nobody quite knew how this group of women had come to dominate this way of living. Some believed that women excelled at this cold-water work because of their increased body fat. Others maintained they were forced into it as a means of survival when their husbands perished at sea, but the simple truth was that they had outlived the men and needed to create some income in their widowhood.

They showed MiJa how to clean, prepare and cook the catch so that it retained all its flavour and health benefits, using the same methods their mothers and grandmothers had passed down to them. MiJa was glad of the company and the chance to learn something new, and fully immersed herself in their world. She would rush home to make her dinner for her husband, in case he returned, but he rarely did. In the evening, she would hurry back to the market and listen to the Hae-nyeo recount their tales of adventure in the soju tents.

The Hae-nyeo were natural raconteurs and knew how to embellish a story. Freediving was not an occupation without risk, and MiJa was enraptured by their incredible tales of encounters with right whales as they migrated through the ocean. Tales of hungry sharks attracted to them by the splashing on the surface, their underwater activity, and the smell of the disturbed seabed. Tales the women lost in the fog or swept away by the tidal current, never to be heard of again. Tales of nitrogen narcosis as women entranced by the raptures of the deep lost their bearings and drowned. But most of all, MiJa was enchanted by their way of life: their freedom, their bond of friendship, their close matriarchal society, and she welcomed the opportunity to speak to somebody with the experience and wisdom that comes with old age.

One frosty September evening, MiJa pushed aside her hot stone bowl of seafood stew. 'I don't think a seafood diet suits me.'

A few eyebrows raised at this sacrilegious statement. 'What makes you think that?'

'I'm not ungrateful. It's just that I don't think it agrees with me.'

'What do you mean, it doesn't agree with you? How exactly?'

'It makes me feel sick.'

'When do you feel this sickness?' asked the head Hae-nyeo.

'On a morning.'

'Every morning? When was your last monthly magic?'

The penny finally dropped and MiJa stared at her feet.

'You poor, foolish, innocent girl,' said the elder. 'Don't you know that you are pregnant?'

Jang Jun-pyo continued to come and go as he pleased, and when he was home, the abuse continued. One evening he pushed some papers across the table.

'Sign this,' he said.

'What is it?' asked MiJa.

'Our marriage papers.'

Jang had been forced to withdraw from the elections in Mun-gyeong for an undisclosed criminal record. He was transferred to Mukho and told to keep his nose clean for a few years, and then, and only then, would a position be found for him somewhere more civilised. He planned to do just that, but his boss had found out that he was living with a woman who was not his wife and that she was expecting a child. He was ordered to get married and be quick about it if he still wanted a job in government, or anywhere else for that matter. He never did find out who informed his boss, but since fishing was the most important economic activity in Mukho, he felt it must be somebody who worked in that industry. Somebody senior. Somebody with power, but little did he realise that the Hae-nyeo knew everybody in the business.

MiJa told him she would think about it: her anger had softened with time, and she could think about her future rationally, but she was still angry. Why should she have to marry her kidnapper? Why should she marry her rapist? If there were any justice in the world, she would report him to the police, and they would punish him for his crime. But the world wasn't like that: in a fair world, she would have married Jung-sik and had his child. Even if she did report it, she knew they wouldn't believe her. Deep inside, she knew the answer. She remembered what her teacher had told her about Confucius: to starve to death is a small matter, but to lose one's chastity is a great matter. Confucian society was a trap: a woman could not choose who to marry, could not divorce, and could not remarry, even if widowed, because that would be unfaithful to the memory of her husband. When a woman married, all her property became her husband's property, and she did not even own the right to her own body. The simple matter was that she had no choice. Nobody else would want to marry her now, and she had to put the unborn child first. It was innocent and should not pay for its parent's selfishness. There was also the matter of God. He must have chosen her for a purpose. So, she signed the marriage paper, and on a chilly day in February 1955, MiJa gave birth to a daughter, Jang, Soon-hee.

The following year the Hae-nyeo held a small party for Soon-hee's first birthday. They paid for a photographer to take her picture; MiJa treasured it and always carried it in her purse. Soon-hee did not choose any of the objects that determined her future. The Hae-nyeo made a cash gift instead.

'To make your mother rich,' they said.

MiJa laughed and said, 'Thank you, but I don't think that will ever happen.'

'You never know,' said the Hae-nyeo. 'We have a gift for you too, MiJa.'

'Really?'

'Yes, really. We have been thinking about it for a long time now, so now you have nothing better to do. How would you like to train as a Hae-nyeo diver?'

MiJa was puzzled, 'How can I when I have a child to look after?'

The Hae-nyeo laughed and slapped each other on the back to relieve the hysterics. 'We have an army of grandmothers who have raised countless children and have a lifetime of experience. They will look after your daughter. Having a child does not mean that your life stops, MiJa. So how about it?'

CHAPTER 46

ULLEUNG-DO

A few months later, in the ungodly hours of the morning, MiJa huddled around a shoreside fire and listened to the excited chat of the Hae-nyeo. In the red glow of the fire, she watched their faces as they bragged about who would catch the most fish, the biggest fish, and who would make the most money, but most of all they talked about the weather.

Occasionally MiJa caught them casting a furtive glance to the east, over the silent brooding ocean, hoping for the first signs of daybreak. They were anxious to start work. Many started diving when they were eleven years old but still remembered their first dive like it was yesterday, and even though some were now in their eighties and the youngest members in their mid-sixties, the thrill was still there.

When the faintest crack of red light appeared on the horizon, the leader said, 'It's time. Are you ready, MiJa?'

MiJa nodded, and the anticipation of a new adventure and a step into the unknown made her body tingle with excitement. She edged down the rocky slopes to the seashore with the others and watched the leader launch a small straw boat filled with offerings for the Sea Gods. She watched the small boat drift away on the ocean current until it was just a speck on the horizon and disappear into the darkness. It was time.

The diesel engine thumped its way out of the harbour, and the small wooden boat pitched, heaved and rolled its way out to the open ocean. When they cleared the harbour wall, the skipper opened the throttle, and the hull slapped and scudded over the waves. MiJa steadied herself by placing a hand on the gunwale, and the cold spray of the salty water stung her face and ran down her back like icy fingers. Her senses were fully awake now, and it felt good to be alive.

When the sun rose fully, it revealed the vast ocean that lay before them: an endless virgin world begging exploration. They smiled at each other and their hearts filled with joy. They glanced at the sea with a knowing look glinting in their eyes. Who knew what hidden treasures they would find today? The waiting was over — this is what they were born to do.

Today they were heading to the shallow waters around Ulleung-do, a volcanic, semi-tropical island, two hours east of Mukho. The locations of the best fishing grounds were jealously guarded and passed down to the next generation by word of mouth. The Hae-nyeo called the hunting grounds sea farms, but they were natural wild areas. They usually worked the sea farms closer to their home port, but the head Hae-nyeo had decided to give the local farms a chance to recover their depleted stocks.

They navigated to a shallow sheltered bay, dropped the anchor and cut the engine. The throbbing vibration of the boat stopped, and all was silent except for the dampened sloshing of the sea, slapping against the wooden hull with its playful caresses. MiJa was amazed at the natural beauty of Ulleung-do: a series of verdant volcanic pinnacles jutted sharply upwards out of impossibly turquoise waters. Here and there, the turquoise ocean was blotted with deep pools of indigo as if somebody had dipped in a fountain pen. MiJa looked over the side of the boat into water that was so clear she could see the rocky seabed twenty metres below the surface. It was teeming with life.

The boat bobbed and rocked violently, now they had lost the forward momentum through the waves, and MiJa felt sick. The Hae-nyeo kitted up quickly and in silence. They helped each other zip up the back of their wetsuits, put on their gloves and strap heavy lead weights around their midriff to counteract the buoyancy of the wetsuits. They donned their fins, spat into their circular full-face masks, and smeared it across the glass surface to stop it misting up, and stepped off the boat with one giant leap.

One of the Hae-nyeo handed MiJa a wetsuit and helped her to peel it on. The peculiar chemical smell of the wet neoprene, and the rocking of the boat, made her nauseous until she vomited over the side.

'Keep your eyes on the horizon,' said her instructor. 'Don't worry about being sick. It's more food for the fish.'

She handed MiJa a bottle of water. 'Rinse your mouth with this and get into the water as soon as possible. Once you are underwater, you will be fine.'

MiJa stepped over the side of the gunwale and splashed into the ocean. A boat hand passed her an L-shaped piece of metal, with a spike at the end, for prying shellfish off rocks and weeding seaweed, and a conical shaped, suspended under a small buoy to store their catch.

MiJa practised her deep breathing exercises to expel as much carbon dioxide from her lungs as possible and maximise the oxygen uptake in her bloodstream. Then she bent her body double, hinging at the hips, slipped under the surface and entered another world: silent, still and weightless. She could see the seabed below. It looked so close in the gin-clear water that she felt all she had to do was reach out and grab a handful. The browns, greens, reds and purples of the soft corals softly undulated in the current and beckoned her.

She kicked her fins to descend faster and scattered clouds of iridescent fish. Their flanks flashed like ingots of silver. She could almost touch the seabed when she felt a pain in her left eardrum, and her head buzzed with a constant tone like water was being slowly poured into her head. She tried to equalise the pressure in her eustachian tubes by jutting her jaw forward because the full-face mask that the Hae-nyeo favoured prevented access to the nose. Her ears would not clear, and the pain became acute. She signalled to her instructor that she would return to the surface and finned upwards as fast as she could. She could see the hull above her, a dark shadow silhouetted against the diffused rippled light that scattered off the ocean surface.

Once at the surface, she gasped for breath and spat out the intense saltiness of the ocean. She was being buffeted against the hull and hung onto the gunwales. The Hae-nyeo tending the boat asked her if she needed a hand getting out of the water, but she refused. She would try again in a minute.

'Ready?' asked her teacher.

MiJa nodded her head. This time she tried to clear her ears earlier in the dive, where the pressure differential was lower, and her ears made a light pop. Her teacher grabbed her hand and finned vigorously, dragging her to the bottom, twenty meters below.

MiJa hunted around, and just as her lungs were fit to burst, she saw an abalone shell only a few meters away. She prised it off the rock with some effort and was surprised how well it clung on to life, but in her moment of triumph, she dislodged her face mask and it filled with water. The sudden loss of vision made her panic, so she dropped her weeding tool and made a mad dash for the surface, still clinging to the precious abalone.

In the afternoon, the Hae-nyeo's keepnets were bulging with fish, conch, octopus, sea urchins and a type of brown seaweed that would be salted, air dried and served with beer. They were careful to take only a limited amount of this natural bounty, and as soon as their nets were full of produce, they returned to the boat and waited for the others. It was good business to let the sea life recover. That way, it would still be there for future generations.

They transferred their catch to plastic buckets filled with seawater. The seawater would be changed at regular intervals on the journey home because the seafood had to be kept alive. Nobody would buy dead seafood. If anything died on the journey home, they prepared it sashimi style and ate it there and then. One of the elders held up a gaebul, a type of sea worm, about a foot long and two inches in diameter, and let it droop over her hand.

'Reminds me of my husband,' she said and gave a filthy cackle.

'So big?' asked one of the younger ones.

'No, so limp,' she replied.

'I'm surprised you can remember at your age.'

'I have a good memory,' she said. 'It's the only true source of pleasure we have as we grow old. Hear that, MiJa? Make all the memories you can whilst you are still young.' She looked around to see if MiJa was listening but found her hanging over the stern of the boat.

'She's feeding the fish again.'

The Hae-nyeo laughed.

'They have been well-fed today. Imagine how big they will be next time.'

The head Hae-nyeo cut up the live gaebul, washed it in the fresh seawater, and handed it around. They ate in silence, and the head Hae-nyeo wondered what to do about MiJa. She wasn't cut out for a life at sea.

When the lights of Mukho harbour twinkled into view, the head matriarch's thoughts turned to the market and the hard-drinking session in the soju tents that would follow. They moored next to a squid boat preparing to leave, and the head Hae-nyeo smiled and nodded her head. She asked permission to board and ducked beneath the rows of bright lanterns festooned on every piece of available fixed rigging. The squid boats only fished at night, and the bright lights attracted the squid until they were close enough to catch with dragnets.

The next day, the Hae-nyeo gave MiJa a wooden crate full of fresh squid. They showed her how to split the body and squeeze the black ink out, remove the hard beak and entrails, taking care not to damage the skin. Then the squid was washed in seawater and stretched across two slivers of bamboo arranged as a cross and dried in the air like so many kites flying in the wind. The winters in Mukho were crisp, sunny, and dry, and anything left outside for too long withered and dehydrated to a crisp. Every house in the village used this to their advantage to preserve food; dried seaweed, dried fish and dried squid hung from every washing line and everywhere else that was available. A faint whiff of mummification hung in the air.

The Hae-nyeo leader arranged with the skippers of the squid boats to make some of their catch available to MiJa. The Hae-nyeo provided the capital and guaranteed the payments for the squid. They set MiJa up with a stall in the market, next to their own, and the business thrived. When the Oriental Brewery opened its first bars in Mukho, it decided to provide the dried squid snack free to its customers because it made them drink more. Soon MiJa was buying the entire catch from the squid boats and getting her neighbours to dry it on their washing lines. In return, they could keep a percentage for their use. Business was good, and life was good. The only downside was that her husband still visited whenever he took the fancy and spent the night with MiJa. But the squid-drying business had an unexpected advantage: he always complained about the smell and never stayed long.

MiJa's house was perched high on a hill that overlooked the harbour where five years later they would build Mukho lighthouse. She panted with the effort of carrying her daughter and could feel the cold, dry air rasp on the back of her throat. She propped the box of squid, tucked under her arm, up against the house. The last few desiccated petals of hot pink cosmos still clung to life and provided a vivid contrast to the grey stone and daub walls. The rest had turned to seed as if they knew they would not survive the winter, and so put all their faith in the next generation.

MiJa moved a heavy earthenware pot to retrieve her key, and the last petals fell to the ground. She knew the neighbours would be watching. They always were and could hear their barbed gossip about a woman's place being inside the home. The outside world, and all its affairs, was strictly for the men. A woman's place was to serve men: first their father and later their husband. If they were good wives, they would produce male heirs.

The Hae-nyeo told her to ignore them; they only said those things to hurt her because she was a successful businesswoman. So what if she hadn't given her husband a son. Who cared? But MiJa did care, and she finally silenced her critics on the 8th of May 1959, at 22.19 hours, when she gave birth to her first son, Jang Seok-joon. It was Mother's Day.

CHAPTER 47

GIMJANG SEASON

The tenth moon of the year marks the beginning of gimjang: the kimchi-making season. The entire village had gathered to prepare the cabbages so they would last over the long, lean winter months. The weather in the autumn of 1959 had been perfect for farming and the napa cabbages had grown firm and fat, like giant pale green bok choi. The farmer cut off a cabbage at the stalk, split it in half lengthways, and handed MiJa a section of the pale-yellow heart. She popped it into her mouth. It was crunchy, with a natural sweetness. She nodded. She would barter her dried squid in return for 5000 cabbage heads. Her business was thriving, and she was even supplying the fashionable bars that were springing up in Seoul. She had paid back the start-up capital to the Hae-nyeo and was now generating enough income to support herself and her growing children. It was time to pay back their generosity.

The Hae-nyeo organised gimjang day with military precision. MiJa had joined the first column at zero-four-zero-zero hours as they gathered on the shoreside. 'Yong-cha. Yong-cha. Yong-cha,' chanted the team of women as they hauled on the rope like a squad of Volga boatmen. Each net contained two hundred cabbage heads that had been sliced in half lengthways and left to soak in the ocean, to brine overnight. It was heavy work. They removed the cabbages from the nets and stacked them onto the waiting rickshaws to drain. One of the Hae-nyeo took a sample of cabbage to check the seasoning.

'Is that salty enough for you?' she shouted at the ocean.

'Who is she talking to?' whispered MiJa to the woman standing behind her.

'Her husband.'

'Her husband? I didn't know she had a husband.'

'Dead. Drowned decades ago.'

'Is it seasoned enough this time?' she yelled at the ocean and shook her fist. 'You bastard.'

'She's as daft as a brush. She does the same thing every year,' whispered the Hae-nyeo. 'She lost her husband at sea. Must be forty years ago now, but she still can't forget. Nor can she forgive. Her husband only ever complained about her kimchi-making abilities once.'

MiJa covered her mouth with her hand to hide her laughter.

'Don't laugh,' said the leader. 'Some things in life are unforgivable, and not being able to make tasty kimchi is one of them.'

'At least she is free of her husband,' said one of the younger women in her sixties. 'Mine is still alive. I asked him to come along and help pull the nets in. Do you know what he said? That gimjang was women's work, and if he did that, his balls would fall off. I told him they might as well for the use they get.'

The other Hae-nyeo started laughing and muttering half-forgotten complaints about their long-dead husbands as they moved on to the next net and got back into their stride. 'Yong-cha. Yong-cha. Yong-cha.'

When they had finished pulling in all the nets and stacked the mountain of cabbages on the rickshaws, they pulled them to the village well and rinsed them off until they were clean and just slightly salty. They pulled the sloshing cabbage trucks through the streets to the agreed rendezvous point and stacked the cabbages on a bamboo drainer. When they had finished, dawn was breaking and so was their backs.

The second column was at the rendezvous point by zero-seven-one-five hours. Their first job was to light the fires at the far end of the courtyard, stoke the wood-fired ovens, and simmer sweet glutinous rice, in vast cast-iron cauldrons, until it broke up into a paste. After that they would cook the evening meal: thick slabs of pork belly, thinly sliced and wrapped in fresh kimchi cabbage leaves. No washing up was required — the day was full enough.

The third column, the Grandmother's Own Yeomanry, set off at zero-eight-zero-zero hours, with a steely determination burning in their eyes and their chopping boards tucked under their left arms. In their right hands, they clutched their freshly sharpened kitchen knives, tips glinting in the morning sun. Others balanced buckets on their heads and some banged a mortar and pestle percussion to keep marching time. When they reached the rendezvous point a buzz of excitement rippled through the camp.

The head matriarch opened the proceedings. She sat on the sill of her door to address the team. Behind her, some young children were poking their heads through the gap in the sliding doors. 'Shoo. Go back inside and keep warm with the other children,' said the elder, and she slid the door closed. They had converted her courtyard into a makeshift kitchen, and a pavilion made from blue plastic sheeting sheltered a mountain of napa cabbages, mooli radishes, bunches of spring onions and chives, and piles of garlic bulbs and root ginger. The women sat on the ground on a large linoleum sheet. They rested their chopping boards on their buckets, knives at the ready.

The Commander-in-Chief addressed the troops. 'I would love to help you all, but as you know, I'm too busy looking after these varmints.' She nodded her head in the direction of her house and now a makeshift creche. 'Anyway, you all know what to do by now. It's not like it's the first time, is it?'

The women laughed, and the leader gave the order, 'Showtime. Let's make kimchi!'

There was a loud cheer, and the knives were out.

'Who does she think she is?'

'Who?'

'That blue-eyed American woman in the Blue House,' said one woman, referring to the Presidential Palace in Seoul.

'Have you seen how she dresses?'

'She is supposed to be our First Lady, and she's not even Korean. She's Australian.'

'Austrian,' corrected another.

'She can't even speak Korean.'

'She never will as long as her eyes remain blue.'

The women cut all the vegetables into matchstick size and mixed them into the rice paste with handfuls of vivid red chilli flakes, crushed garlic, ginger paste, fermented shrimps, salty fish sauce, and freshly squeezed pear juice for sweetness. They rubbed the marinade between each cabbage leaf. Occasionally they would add freshly caught abalone, small gutted whole fish and squid to macerate in the sauce that would later be sliced up and eaten as sashimi. When the day was over, they allocated each woman her share of the kimchi. She would take it home in her bucket, transfer it to an earthenware pot and bury it in the ground, up to its neck, to prevent the kimchi from freezing and allow it to slowly ferment and gradually become sourer as the lactobacillus got to work.

'Thank God Typhoon Sarah spared us.'

'That's not a nice thing to say. I heard it killed 900 people in the south. I don't know what we would have done if we were out at sea.'

'Drowned probably.'

The others ignored her gallows humour, and one of the Azuma's nodded to the older children who were running around outside, giddy with the festive atmosphere and lost in their own world of adventure. They were kicking up whirls of dust. 'It looks like we've got our very own mini-typhoons here, judging by the amount of havoc and destruction they leave behind.'

The others nodded in agreement and laughed.

In the afternoon, the Commander-in-Chief ducked back inside her house. She was feeling peckish and had put two sticks of rice cake, skewered on short rattan sticks, to heat on the stove like toasting marshmallows around a campfire. It should be ready by now, she thought and drooled in anticipation, but when she looked at the stove, only a sticky toasted residue remained.

'Who has stolen it?' she shouted.

'Soon-hee, took it,' said one of the children, eager to avoid the blame.

'Where is she?'

'Over there,' said the child and pointed to a large, shellacked medicine chest in the corner. 'She's hiding behind that chest.'

'Is she? Well, we will see about that.'

'I think she is dead.'

'What?' The old woman hobbled over to the child. Soon-hee's lips were turning blue so the old woman checked her throat. She couldn't see any blockage so she picked up the limp body and struggled to the door and screamed, 'MiJa. MiJa. Oh, no. MiJa!'

Everybody stopped work and stared.

MiJa took her pale and unconscious daughter and patted her hard on the back, but there was no response. Please don't do this to me. She stuck her fingers down her throat and couldn't feel any obstruction. She pounded her fist on her daughter's back out of frustration and panic. The nearest doctor was thirty minutes away so she strapped her daughter onto her back and ran all the way to the doctor's surgery. She was panting and sobbing, and her clothes were smeared with blood-red streaks, as though she had just murdered somebody.

The doctor stared in disbelief at this wild-haired, wild-eyed madwoman until he noticed the child on her back. He rushed over to her side but could see immediately that it was too late. There was nothing he could do. The girl's lips were blue, her tongue swollen and black, lolled out of her mouth, and her eyes rolled back into her head. He unstrapped the child and gave MiJa a sedative. The baby had been dead at least an hour, and there was nothing more he could do except to find out what had happened. Later, he carried out a more detailed examination and wrote out the death certificate. *Name: Jang Soon-hee. Sex: Female. Age: 3 years and ten months. Date of death: 5 December 1959. Time of death: 16:14 hours. Cause of death: accidental choking on sticky rice cake.*

On 5 December 1959 at 16:14, MiJa's husband checked into the Prince Hotel: a gaudy squat building painted a tasteless shade of pink and arranged over four floors. A red sign buzzed away in throbbing neon. The sign said, *Hotel*. It wasn't.

Jang Jun-pyo read the sign in reception displaying the room rates: a lower one for a *Rest* and a higher one for a *Stay*. He opted for stay and slid the money under the frosted glass barrier between them and the anonymous receptionist. The receptionist didn't need to see the clientele. They were three types: inquisitive, young couples who couldn't wait until they got married; married couples who wanted to have an illicit affair, and married men looking for a good-time girl. The Prince Hotel was known all over town as the Four Floors of Whores. The receptionist slid the keys under the divider without a word, and Jang took his escort to the fourth floor.

A king-sized bed dominated *The Ocean Room*. It was round with blue satin sheets and scattered on top were red cushions in the shape of hearts and some pink artificial cosmos petals. The walls were painted azure and had fish tanks built into them, full of tropical fish of every hue and shape.

'They are so beautiful.'

'They make me hungry,' said Jang.

'Hungry?' asked the girl.

'I feel like Tantalus watching a conveyor belt of sashimi that he can't reach.' Jang laughed whilst his escort visited the bathroom.

The bathroom had pink neon lights around the mirror, bottles of toiletries, and some large conch shells with convoluted, shiny pink insides.

Jang laid back on the bed. He didn't care what his work colleagues said. He had been fortunate to meet this beautiful young Korean girl, even if she did have a North Korean accent. 'Hurry up,' he shouted. 'What are you doing in there?'

Later, when Jang flicked the lights off and was amazed to see an array of moons and stars above his head. Somebody had stuck childish glow-in-the-dark stars to the ceiling since their last visit.

'Have you seen the stars?'

'Fuck the stars, I want a cigarette,' said Jang. He got out of bed and walked to the window.

'I have got something important to tell you.'

Jang knew what was coming next. Later that night, he gazed up at the sickly green constellations above him and cursed the day he'd met her. Her every movement annoyed him but what kept him awake all night was the problem of what to do with the baby when it was born.

CHAPTER 48

THE FOUNDLING

MiJa had found the loss of her daughter too painful to bear and lapsed into a state of denial. She built a wall between her and the truth and sank farther and farther from reality. The Hae-nyeo visited every day and made sure they didn't starve to death. Weeks passed, and they feared she would never return to normal, but then one cold February day the spell was broken.

'Mom. Mom. Mom,' said Seok-joon. He grabbed his mother's ears, pushed his face into hers, and stared straight into her soul. They were the first words her son ever spoke, and MiJa snapped out of her trance and returned to reality. Oh my God. Where the hell had she been all this time? She asked herself. She jumped to her feet and squeezed her son.

'I'm sorry. I'm so sorry, baby. Mummy was lost.' The room was freezing cold. She checked the heating stove, and the charcoal was nearly out. She must go to the market. Immediately. She bound the son to her body using a woollen scarf and threw on her husband's coat. She retrieved the last of her money from its hiding place under the oiled paper flooring, scrunched it tightly up in her hand to make sure that it could not escape, and set off for the market.

When she reached the market, darkness fell, and so did the temperature. She pulled the overcoat closer to her body and increased her pace to keep warm. It was the bitterest winter she could remember, but the market was the usual bustle of activity and full of tempting, tantalising smells and tempting, tantalising talk. She paid them no heed and headed directly to the charcoal seller. Her cash was nearly gone, but she would say a quick thank you to the sisterhood and head directly home; it was not an evening for lingering.

The Hae-nyeo were delighted to see MiJa up and about. They had kept her squid-drying business running, and it was ready for her to take over whenever she felt up to it. They shared their fish stew with her and fed her son small pieces of hot sweet potato, blown on until it was just the right temperature.

No matter how much MiJa insisted, they would not let her leave empty-handed, so when MiJa set off home, with the two stacks of charcoal slung from her hands, she had a bag full of live whelks and a fat flounder that fluttered on her breast like a palpitating heart until it froze solid.

MiJa said her thanks and climbed the steps up the harbour wall. She stared out to the dark ocean. The waves crashed on the wall, and the cold spray whipped her face and stung her eyes. She licked the salt from her lips. As she set off for home, she glanced back towards the haven. The orange lights of the soju tents glimmered faintly like fireflies, and she thought how fortunate she had been to be adopted by these matriarchs of the sea. Chance and circumstance often gave life direction and meaning. She thought about her past. Had any of it had really happened? It all seemed like a dream now. The big house of her childhood, with servants to tend to her every need. How different life was back then, when everything was shiny and new, and the future was full of endless opportunities. Her childhood had room to dream, room for hope, and room to grow. How quickly all those opportunities had withered on the vine. One by one, the open doors that looked so inviting were firmly slammed shut and locked forever.

She thought about her school days. Her Japanese name and wondered if Yoshiko's life would have been any better. What had happened to her school friends? She thought about her father and wondered if anybody had tended his grave. She thought about her sister. Was she still alive? Did she still have her necklace? She thought of her brother and her mother. She thought of Jung-sik, and she thought about her son. What sort of future could she offer him now? But most of all, she thought about her daughter. Why did she have to die? Was it her fault? If so, what had she done wrong? Where was God? There were so many questions, but one thing was clear: nobody would ever replace her.

When she was nearly home, the beam from the newly built lighthouse stroked the ocean with a regular rhythm that she found soothing. She watched it for a while. Somebody had told her that it allowed sailors to work out exactly where they were in a vast ocean of nothingness. She liked that because once you knew where you were, it was a simple matter to work out what you needed to do to reach your destination. The beam of light swept the door to her house, and she noticed that somebody had left a bundle of cloth on her doorstep. Probably her husband's dirty laundry. She was going to leave it there until morning, when she noticed, out of the corner of her eye, that it moved. She opened the bundle and saw it was a new-born infant.

She looked up and down the street. All was dark and silent. The foundling had a label attached to it. *Born 1960, Feb 29. Up to You?* So, the rumours were true. That bastard of a husband had produced a bastard of his own. She was a fool.

The anger raised in her gorge, and red mist fogged her brain. If he thought for one moment that she would look after his illegitimate child, then he had better think again. It was no concern of hers. She would leave it there to die. But what if the neighbours had seen him leave it there? They always hung their noses out of their doors. She picked up the bundle, brought it inside and put it in the corner of the room next to a cold draught.

That night she huddled under the blanket with her son but, try as she might, sleep would not come. Occasionally she stuck a foot out of the blanket and nudged the interloper towards the crack in the wall but soon pulled it back under when she felt the icy wind chill her toes. What was she so concerned about anyway? It would be better for everybody. Better for her, and better for her husband. The child never made a sound, and she must have dozed off. When morning came, all was quiet, and she could hear the sound of her own thumping heart reverberating off the hard floor. She glanced over at the bundle and strained her ears. Still. Silent. The foundling must be dead. That was one problem solved. She would have to report the death as an accident, and she would have to pay the price that much was certain.

Eventually, she plucked up enough courage and crawled over to the corner of the room. She slowly peeled back the blanket, expecting to see another blue-faced baby like her poor daughter, and the baby smiled at her and blew some bubbles. MiJa was shocked that the baby was still alive. How could it be? There could be only one explanation: it must be God's will. She picked up the child and burst into tears. She prayed for God's forgiveness, and slowly it dawned on her that she was supposed to have this child. When she found out it was a girl, it all made perfect sense. It was a heaven-sent replacement for the daughter she had lost.

CHAPTER 49

A COUP

On 28 April 1960, President S M Lee and his Austrian First Lady were flown out of South Korea by the CIA, the same organisation that had arranged to fly him in, fourteen years earlier, and instal him as the first President. He had been caught rigging the elections and was under investigation for war crimes. A trial would have embarrassed the USA and revealed its complicity. They knew the President would do anything to hang on to power, even spill more Korean blood, so they convinced him that the noble thing to do, the diplomatic thing to do, was to resign. His punishment for his crimes was early retirement to Honolulu, Hawaii, with all expenses paid for the rest of his life, courtesy of the Korean taxpayer. Now the question on everybody's lips was who would replace him?

One man was sick of the inaction caused by the political infighting, the corruption, and the state of the economy. It was clear to him that the country needed to be saved from itself, and it needed an iron hand to guide it. That man was Mr Song, the former elementary school teacher at Mun-gyeong

Elementary School for Good Citizenship, former Japanese collaborator that served in the Imperial Army in WW2, and Korean war veteran. He had returned from his training in the USA and was now a Major General in the South Korean Army.

On 16 May 1961, Major General Song launched his coup. He ordered the South Korean Army to storm the Blue House, the KBS TV studio, and all the government buildings in Seoul. The coup was a success, and he took the country by the scruff of the neck, installed himself as President and ruled with an iron fist. But the more things change, the more they stay the same: his cronies were promoted to the governing class to replace the Yangban, but now, instead of owning the land, they controlled the Chaebol family businesses. They provided the families with state aid, granted them a monopoly to eliminate all competition, and guaranteed them access to USA markets and technology. In return, all they asked for was a little baksheesh, to oil the wheels of industry and political support.

The government granted the Chaebol families risk-free loans that launched an industrial revolution that set them, and their future generations, up for life. Funds flowed in from the USA, and business boomed. Demand for food, textiles, petrochemicals, shipbuilding, steel, electronics, and construction rocketed, and the race to build the country's infrastructure began. It is a well-known fact that *Behind every great fortune, there is a crime*. But Honoré de Balzac's famous quotation only holds true if the government passes the necessary laws to make it a crime: they didn't.

It is also true that nothing in life is free, and when the horse-trading began, the USA wanted something in return. They wanted President Song to send South Korean conscripts to fight their war in Vietnam. The South Korean President was an ex-military leader and was used to sending men to their deaths purely for the honour of dying for their country, so he had no problem sending men to their deaths for hard cash. So the poor got to die, and the rich got to live, and that summer, Yang-soo was conscripted into the South Korean Army and put on a plane bound for Vietnam.

CHAPTER 50

A VISITOR CALLS

When the poliomyelitis epidemic hit Korea in the May of 1964, the fear spread faster than the disease. It was helped on its way by a hysterical media, desperate for a sensational headline, and MiJa was at her wits' end. Her husband had failed to register the birth of his daughter, which meant Jae-hee didn't officially exist so she could not attend school nor have her childhood vaccinations. As a mother she could not register Jae-hee as her daughter, so she had no choice but to write to her husband and plead with him to register the birth, but there was no reply. When Jae-hee was old enough to start school, she wrote again, but her letters still went unanswered. Her son, Seok-joon, had received all his childhood vaccinations, but her daughter had not. She could not endure the loss of another daughter, especially one sent from God, so when the first case of polio hit the town she kept her son off school to prevent him bringing home the disease and wrote to her husband yet again in desperation.

There was no reply for two months, then one fine summer day, like a bolt out of the blue, the village witnessed an unprecedented event. It arrived on a cloud of dust and left a

trail of screaming children in its wake. Heads poked out of
every door and window to get a glimpse of the fantastic
machine. MiJa went outside to see what all the fuss was. It was
the first time a motorcar had visited the village, and she grew
alarmed when it started heading towards her house, so she ran
inside but left the door ajar. The car stopped outside, and
MiJa's heart pounded. She peeped through the gap in the
door. A miniature government flag flew from the bonnet, and
she could see her house reflected in the car's lovingly polished
glossy black paint. It was obviously somebody important and,
as if to prove a point, a grey liveried chauffeur got out of the
car and wiped the dust from his cherished bodywork. He
opened the rear passenger door and out stepped MiJa's
husband.

MiJa caught her breath. When the car door opened, she
could see that in the back seat of the car sat a young woman, a
beautiful woman, dressed in a silk traditional Korean dress.
She had clear, even skin, kohl eyebrows, ruby red lips and
silken hair, like polished ebony, fashioned in the latest style. In
her arms, she cradled a baby wrapped in a pure white wool
blanket. It was contented, asleep, and MiJa could see its long
eyelashes and milky, angel-bow lips. She pulled the door
tightly closed and wanted to hide from the world. She felt so
ashamed: ashamed of her appearance and ashamed of how far
she had fallen in the world. She hid behind the door cowering.
She could hear her husband complaining to his chauffeur
about the state of his car and what people would think if a
government official drove around in a dirty car. MiJa
wondered who would clean the dirt from him.

The memories of her childhood flooded back, and she
thought about everything she had lost. No. Lost was wrong. It
had been stolen and she trembled with rage. There was a
knock on the door. What should she do? Just ignore it was her
first reaction. She didn't want her husband to see her like this.

He would only compare her to that perfect woman in the car and congratulate himself for making the right choice. No, that wouldn't do. She must have courage. She hadn't done anything wrong. She straightened her hair the best she could, wiped her eyes dry, took a deep breath, and opened the door.

'Yes, what do you want?' she said.

Her husband smiled like a politician. 'I want a divorce,' he said and handed her a set of papers and a stamp. 'All you have to do is stamp the papers here.' He pointed to where she should make her mark. 'You can keep the house.'

'Why didn't you reply to my letters?'

'Which letters?'

'You know which letters. The ones about your daughter. She needs to go to school, and she needs her vaccinations.'

'My daughter is in the car.'

'No. I'm talking about the daughter you left at my doorstep. Her name is Jae-hee if you are interested.' MiJa shook the divorce papers in his face. 'I will only sign these if you agree to register her as your daughter.'

'But, there will be fines to pay ... for late registration. A man in my position —'

'That's your problem,' said MiJa and shrugged her shoulders.

Her husband thought for a while, and in the end, the Right Honourable Jang Jun-pyo did the right honourable thing and agreed to register his daughter in return for the divorce. Once he had what he came for, he turned to leave.

'Would you like to see them? Your son and daughter.'

'No, not just now. I'm too busy,' said Jang, and he stormed off muttering something about fines for late registration, muddy backward villages and everything else that was wrong with the world.

CHAPTER 51

AN EDUCATION

'Ahh. I can't go any further,' said Jae-hee, and she seemed to grow roots in the ground that firmly anchored her to safety.

'Why not?' said Seok-joon, somewhat amused. 'Are you too scared to go to school?'

'No, I'm not a child,' said Jae-hee. 'It's those.' She pointed to the ground and gathered in the hem of her pleated school skirt.

'There are hundreds of them.'

'What? I don't see anything.'

'Those! They're disgusting.' The overgrown meadow was still wet with the morning dew, and the grass rippled with jumping frogs. Jae-hee tensed and gave a little shriek with every unpredictable, jerky leap. She didn't like the look of their wet, slimy, warty skin, and she knew that if she touched one, God forbid, it would feel as cold as death. They had revolting bloodshot eyes that bulged out of their heads and seemed to swivel in their sockets and follow her every move. One opened its gaping cavernous mouth and let out a sound, the croak of death, and the rest of the army joined in the chorus.

'What these?' said her brother, who had managed to catch one and stuck it under her nose. The skin touched her lips.

Jae-hee screamed, 'I'm going to tell Mother.' She fought back the tears. 'I'm going to tell.'

'Don't be silly,' said Seok-joon. 'They won't hurt you.' He put the frog down and told his sister to jump onto his back. He carried her piggyback across the meadow, leaping like a frog, and every time her ankles brushed against the dewy grass Jae-hee, gave a little squeal of alarm that so startled him that he nearly dropped her. After that, he started brushing her legs against the wet grass on purpose.

School proved to be less of a challenge than getting there, and gradually the children's initial excitement, enthusiasm and expectations waned until they conformed. They learned their lessons in rote fashion: slowly brainwashed until they could recite, by heart, their multiplication tables and all the key dates in history, but they had no idea how to create or think for themselves. The teachers killed the joy of reading by having each pupil read out a line from the book in turn, until the story became fragmented, lost its rhythm, and became an exercise in public humiliation if any pupil mispronounced a word. In this manner, the teachers transferred their faults and failures onto the children and quelled their natural curiosity, but thankfully it was only constrained to the classroom. What they learned outside school was a different matter, and when the home time bell rang, their real education began.

Summertime was the season for learning, and it provided a rich and varied classroom. The days were long, and the golden hours dripped by slow until it seemed like the holidays would last forever. They would rise early and head into the sun-dappled woods, alive with nature's bounty, cool tinkling streams, the rip-saw rasp of the cicadas and the smell of wild garlic. It seemed like they had the whole world to play in, and their games were limited only by their imagination.

There was no rush — they had all day. If they wanted to know the time, they just looked at the sun or blew on a dandelion clock. Even hunger would not send them scampering home. There was no need. In the sweet fat days of summer, they collected wild berries and gorged on them until their maws were stained glossy and purple, like gaping hatchlings. When they had had their fill, they continued to cram the precious berries into tin cans and any other container they could find. The arrival of dusk signalled the end of the day and they reluctantly set off home under the gaze of the watchful stars and an enormous copper moon that filled the sky.

'Why is it following me?'

'Why is what following you?'

'The moon. Every time I turn around, it's there. Following me.'

'Because you're special,' said her brother.

Jae-hee smiled, and they chatted all the way home, recounting their adventures so they would be committed to memory and never lost. When they got home, they presented their trophies to their mother, with thorn-torn hands, stained blood red and purple, and sticky with sugar. That night they slept the sleep of the tired and the innocent and dreamed of all the adventures they would have tomorrow.

Sometimes they would catch dragonflies and marvel at their dazzling array of colours: iridescent sapphire blues, shimmering green emeralds and luminous ruby reds that seemed too vivid for this world. They were like living jewels but with facets too perfect to have been polished by the hand of man. The colours shimmered and sparkled with the changing light and the vital spark of life that flowed through their bodies. They gazed at the wondrous beauty they held in their hands that proved beyond all doubt in the existence of a creator. After a while, they let them go because it seemed a mortal sin to kill something so beautiful. Other animals were not so fortunate, and when the time was right, the hunt would begin.

They would rise early and arm themselves with a piece of netting, a plastic bag, and an old jumper. On the way to the hunting ground, Seok-joon found a clump of bamboo, cut off a thin culm with a knife and split it into skewers about a foot long. When they arrived, they gazed at the overgrown meadow. Its long grass spikelets shone like burnished gold in the low morning sun, and here and there were patches of white, pastel purples, and the dull yellows of the Asian fawn lily, starworts and cosmos in full bloom. They watched the meadow undulate gently in the breeze like the rippling waves of an ocean that invited them to dive in and discover its treasures.

Jae-hee went to one end of the meadow, armed with a bamboo stick in each hand. Her brother went to the opposite end of the lea and spread the net above his head.

'Ready,' he shouted.

'Ready.' Jae-hee ran toward him with feline grace, beating the long grass as she went with the bamboo culms, and above her head, the quarry took flight. Hundreds of grasshoppers took to the air, and she let out an involuntary squeal of delight.

Seok-joon caught as many as he could with the net, and together they carefully untangled them. They pushed the thin strip of bamboo into the gap between the hard shell-like carapace of the head and the start of the abdomen. When the grasshopper straightened its head, it would trap itself onto the skewer, still alive and unharmed.

By mid-morning, they had caught enough grasshoppers for a good snack, so Seok-joon gathered some kindling wood and tied them into faggots, using strips of dried grass. Once home, Seok-joon found an old oil drum and knocked holes in its sides, at the base, to make a brazier. He lit a fire inside and fed it with small twigs until it got well established and then added the larger branches. The smell of the smouldering wood smoke set them both drooling in anticipation. He put a steel mesh on top of the drum, and once it was sizzling hot he put the skewers on the grill. The intense heat crisped up the grasshoppers straight away, and the wonderful smell, reminiscent of barbecued shrimp, filled the air. They breathed it in greedily and could not wait for them to cool, so they juggled them in their hands whilst they peeled them and savoured the nutty roasted flavour.

'You know what these taste like?' asked Jae-hee.

'Grasshoppers.'

'No, sky shrimps.'

When MiJa returned home, she laughed. It was a rite of passage for most Korean children that lived in the countryside, and she was transported back to her childhood. The roast smell of flesh evoked memories of President Lee: the pig she sacrificed for the North Koreans. The smell of crispy crackling and the sound of fat spitting over an open flame came back to her; some meals last a lifetime.

June brought the rains to Korea, and with it, squadrons of freshly-hatched, hungry mosquitoes, but even that could not dampen their spirits. The rainy season also brought new opportunities and new games to play. Elasticated rubber plimsols had recently arrived from Japan and were part of the school uniform. They were cheap, functional and waterproof and also made excellent boats.

Wherever there was a muddy puddle, there was a naval battle. Seok-joon and Jae-hee would re-enact the famous Royal Korean Navy battles and always had the same argument.

'I'm Admiral Yi Sun-sin, and this is my turtle ship,' said Jae-hee as she launched her plimsol over a large, muddy puddle. 'You can be the Japanese pirates.'

'I don't want to be the Japanese,' said Seok-joon.

'Well, somebody has to be. And I said it first.'

Seok-joon launched his boat, and the battle commenced.

'You can't sink my turtle ship,' said Jae-hee. They had been taught about Admiral Yi's sixteenth-century armoured turtle ships. He never lost a single battle to the Japanese.

'We'll see about that,' said Seok-joon, and he pitched a rock at Jae-hee's plimsoll.

'Yes! A direct hit. You are sinking.'

'You idiot,' said Jae-hee. She removed her other plimsol, hitched her skirt up, and waded into the puddle to retrieve the sunken ship. As she did so, Seok-joon threw her other plimsol into the water. She tried to catch it, but as she did so, she let go of the bottom of her skirt, and it fell into the muddy water. 'Look what you've done now! I'm going to tell,' yelled Jae-hee. She grabbed her brother plimsol and threw it back at him.

'Thanks. I needed that,' said Seok-joon. He put the wet plimsol on and ran off. 'I'm going to tell first.'

'Oh no, you're not because I am going to kill you first,' shouted Jae-hee. She put on her wet plimsols, hitched up her skirt, and ran after her brother with squelching feet.

In the morning, their clothes had been washed and ironed, and their plimsols were dry, as if by magic, and a new adventure awaited.

CHAPTER 52

A NEW ADVENTURE

One late-autumn evening in 1965, MiJa returned from work, opened the door and was surprised to find all her furniture pushed to the perimeter of the room. In the centre of the room stood Seok-joon. He was holding his sister's hands and spinning her around the room as fast as he could rotate. Jae-hee was skating around the room at an alarming rate, and on her feet she was wearing her school plimsols and lashed to the bottom, with sticky packing tape, were a pair of school abacuses.

'What the hell are you two doing?'

Seok-joon, shocked by his mother's sudden entrance, let go of his sister's hands, and she flew into the furniture and collapsed in a heap of limbs, makeshift roller-skates and tears.

'She made me do it,' he said, changing his face from glee to a guilty sulk in an instant.

'Stop it right now,' said MiJa. 'Stop it this instant, or I swear I will tan your backsides like they've never been tanned before.' She noticed that Seok-joon had a bloody nose and a black eye. 'You see what happens when you fool around? Just look at your face.'

'That wasn't from the roller skating,' said Jae-hee, thinking she was helping the situation.

Seok-joon handed his mother a note from the headteacher. They had both been sent home early for causing trouble, and Seok-joon had been fighting with the other children. The headteacher wanted to see her first thing tomorrow morning.

'Is this true?' asked MiJa.

'Yes, Mother,' said Seok-joon.

'Then you had better tell me exactly what happened.'

'It wasn't my fault. Some boys said that Jae-hee wasn't my real sister. They said she didn't have a father and started calling her a bastard, so I hit them.'

'Watch your swearing young man. I will go and see this headteacher in the morning. You two tidy up this house whilst I make dinner.'

The school meeting didn't start well. MiJa could see that the teacher was expecting a gift as a peace offering, but she arrived empty-handed. The teacher claimed that he had seen the entire incident and Seok-joon was entirely at fault. When MiJa questioned him about the taunting her son received from the other children, it went rapidly went downhill.

'Children will be children,' said the teacher, and he shrugged his shoulders and added, 'Sometimes, they blurt out the truth without thinking. By the way, where is your husband?'

MiJa couldn't believe her ears. 'What kind of children do you educate here? Ones without any manners? Ones who can call other children bastards and not expect any response. I am not at all surprised with you as their teacher.'

'The parents of the child your son hurt are threatening to call the police. What do you want to do about it?' said the teacher, and he let it sink in for a moment before continuing.

'I might even have to expel him, and they would be a fine or compensation to pay. Maybe both. And a police record. Of course, I could keep it all hushed up, but it would take time and money.'

MiJa decided that she would not give him the pleasure of expelling her son, and she certainly wasn't going to pay any bribe. She had recently heard of a government-sponsored housing scheme in Paju and had been giving the matter some thought. There was an American military base in Paju, which meant no Koreans wanted to live there. To attract people to the area, the government had set up a scheme whereby you could rent a house for five years and purchase it at a bargain price, and with her English language skills, she could probably find work on the base. If she sold the house and her business in Mukho she could afford to send her children to a decent school, and there was nothing to keep her here especially since the matriarchal leader of the Hae-nyeo had died. The decision was suddenly an easy one. She let him have both barrels and when she had finished, she said, 'This meeting is over. I wouldn't want my children to be educated in this school if you were the last teacher on earth.'

When she returned home, she hugged her children and told them she loved them. She told them they hadn't done anything wrong and that tomorrow they were all going on a big adventure: they would leave this place and start a new life in a new town.

CHAPTER 53

MARILYN

The town of Paju lies just south of an oxbow bend in the Imjin River, not far from the shallow ford where the Gloster Regiment made their last stand in the Korean war. The local government had not finished the construction of the Rent-to Buy apartment blocks, so they housed MiJa in a shack close by the river, built from stone boulders that had been worn smooth by time and current. It had a blue corrugated iron roof, compacted mud steps and an outside toilet. It wasn't much, but it was home, for now, and it gave them a chance to make a fresh start. And at least the school was not far away. MiJa had enrolled both her children in the local Christian school, not for any ideological reason but because it was the best school in the area, and it was also strict. But she still had nagging doubts. Had she done the right thing? Only time would tell. At least the location was peaceful and close to nature. Maybe too close.

The first night they spent in the shack was uncomfortable: they were woken up at regular intervals by the rapid trill of soft pink feet skittering across the hot tin roof. In the morning, the bar of hard soap in the bathroom had tell-tale gnaw marks scraped into it. The second night they were ready. Jae-hee and Seok-joon lay in the dark and listened to the patter of tiny feet scurry along the roof in short bursts. Whenever the pattering stopped, it was followed by a loud thud, a squeak of alarm, and the sound of vegetation rustling, as the rat leapt off the roof.

It became their regular night-time routine, and when they did finally drift off to sleep, Jae-hee would dream of her new school whilst Seok-joon dreamed of the traps he would check in the morning. Sometimes when they woke in the morning, they would find their mother still slumped in her chair, her head drooping to her chest, still clutching the broomstick in her hand that she used to bang on the roof to scare off the rats. But far more often, they awoke to the sound of their mother yelling, 'Come on, you two! Get up for school. You'll be late.'

Seok-joon usually dragged himself into the bathroom first, still half asleep, until the cold water, freshly drawn from the river, stung his face and set his heart racing. 'Mum, I need a new bar of soap.'

'Look for it. It will be in there somewhere. Unless the rats have taken it again.'

Seok-joon found it hidden behind the water bucket. He lathered up the soap trying his best to ignore the gnaw marks in it, but at least the soap was still there. Sometimes when the rats had whittled it away it would be light enough for them to haul the whole bar away and hoard it their larders.

When he went back into the room, Jae-hee was sitting at the breakfast table. 'I have finished in the bathroom. It's your turn now.' When Jae-hee left the table, he helped himself to her breakfast.

'Stop that, this instant,' said MiJa with a stern scowl.

After breakfast, they dressed into their school uniforms, and Seok-joon ran outside to check the traps. Jae-hee tried to join him, but her mother was tidying her hair and smoothing down her uniform. Eventually, she managed to struggle free and ran outside to join her brother.

'Did we get one? Did we get one?'

'Yes, just one. Look,' said Seok-joon and held up a dead rat by the tail.

'Fantastic. Can I have the tail?' asked Jae-hee.

'Maybe.'

'But you promised me.'

They took the dead rat to their mother. MiJa cut off its tail with a carving knife and wrapped it in an old sheet of the *East Asia Daily*. They marched off to school together, and once they were out of sight of the house, Seok-joon unwrapped the parcel and held the rat's tail in his outstretched hand, making sure it was out of his sister's reach.

'Can I see? Can I see? Show meeee, show meeee,' said Jae-hee as she jumped up and down, trying to snatch the prize.

'No,' said Seok-joon and stuffed it into his jacket pocket as if it was a precious relic. The Ministry of Agriculture had launched a coordinated campaign across the whole country to try and reduce the rat population. Posters were put up in every school and other public places with headlines that stated, "Let's Catch Rats" or "Rats are getting Fatter: Humans are getting Thinner." They issued each household with 20 grammes of rat poison with instructions not to eat it. For every rat tail the students brought to school they would be given a pencil as a reward and within a few months Seok-joon and Jae-hee held the school record.

About a month later, when her children had settled into their new school, MiJa decided to enquire about a job at the US military base. It was a long shot, but sometimes chance lends a helping hand. She was walking past some prefab plywood shacks that had been erected outside the military base for convenience when a voice called out from behind, 'MiJa!'

MiJa stopped and turned around and saw a woman propped up against the door of one of the shacks. She was a complete stranger. She was about the same size and age as MiJa, but she had a shock of platinum blonde hair, a figure shaped like an hourglass, and her ample breasts were much too large for her slight frame. She was standing with one hand on her jutted-out hip and put a cigarette to her pouting lips that had been painted a shade of fuck-me-red.

'Excuse me, do I know you?' asked MiJa, wide-eyed.

'Oh my God it is you MiJa. It's me, Bunny.'

The only Bunny MiJa could remember was a buck-toothed butcher's daughter from Mun-gyeong, and this exotic creature was definitely not her. She tried not to stare, but her eyes were drawn upwards to her teeth: they were dazzling white and perfectly straight.

'Bunny? Is that really you?' asked MiJa.

'Sure thing, Hun. Well, they don't call me that anymore. I'm Marilyn now,' she said in a drawling American accent.

MiJa, none the wiser, said, 'Marilyn?'

'You know,' Bunny said and lifted her short white mini-dress as though a subway updraft had caught it. There was still no recognition in MiJa's eyes, so Bunny rolled her eyes and said, 'Marilyn Monroe.'

'Who? ... But why? What happened to your teeth?'

'Oh, I fixed those ages ago, Hun.'

MiJa laughed. 'It is you, Bunny. What on earth have you been up to?'

'If you've got an hour to spare, I'll tell you, Hun.'

The summer of 1969 marked the Summer of Love in San Francisco and the first time MiJa had ever been to a public bar. The bar was called *Mama's*, and it was packed full of US servicemen and silicon-enhanced Korean girls in symbiotic relationships. 'Gimme a pint of gin and tonic,' said Bunny. 'What are you having, MiJa?'

'Just a Coke for me, please.'

MiJa looked around the bar. It was only mid-afternoon, but everybody seemed drunk already, and the music was even louder than the Americans dress sense. The people on the dance floor looked like they were having a synchronised epileptic fit. Bunny explained: it was the latest dance craze from America called the Nitty Gritty.

She introduced MiJa to all her friends. There were too many foreign names to remember, but MiJa knew that she met a Mary Jane, a Jenny, a Brandy and a Coco. They all looked vaguely similar.

'Are you all related?' asked MiJa.

'No,' said Bunny, and laughed. 'We all use the same beauty tips. The same make-up techniques and we pad our bras out with socks or cotton rags. Hell, some of the girls even use chicken breast fillets so they feel realistic, you know. A few have even been to America and had silicone implants inserted into their breasts.'

'Isn't it dangerous?'

'They can do anything over there. Breasts enlarged, sagging butts lifted and enlarged, teeth straightened and whitened, eyes made rounder, folds of skin added to their eyelids, noses reduced, chins and jawlines altered, and lips engorged.'

MiJa thought about her time in the Red Cross hospital and the surgical procedures she had seen carried out to save lives. How could anybody spend a fortune paying for an operation that wasn't necessary? It was crazy. 'Why do they do it?'

'To get a man. Some even get married and go and live in the States.'

'What is wrong with looking like a Korean, anyway?' asked MiJa.

'Nothing, but the Yanks want a bit of fantasy. Why buy a plastic sex doll when you can have a living, breathing one? That's what my boyfriend says.' Bunny lit a cigarette, inhaled the smoke, and when she exhaled, said, 'So Hun, what brings you to Paju? Are you going to become a Yankee Princess too?'

MiJa laughed. 'No, I don't think so. No offence. I'm looking for a job in the Army base. Any job.' Fifteen minutes later, Bunny introduced her to the camp administrator. He was impressed with her nursing skills and her command of the English language, but the only vacancy he could offer was for a maid.

MiJa started her new job the following day. She worked every day from 6 am to 9 am and earned seven cartons of Marlboro cigarettes per month. It was illegal to sell foreign cigarettes, one of the few laws the government managed to pass, but the Yankee Princesses showed her how to sell them on the black market; she got 2000 Won per packet, compared to 100 Won per packet for Korean cigarettes. She could also barter the cigarettes for food at the US Army-run PX grocery stores. As a thank you gesture, she washed the Yankee Princesses' clothes and altered them to meet the latest fashions, which usually meant shortening their skirts. In the seventies the government passed a law banning miniskirts and demand rocketed.

CHAPTER 54

THE MIRACLE ON THE HAN RIVER

T*he Miracle on the Han River would never have happened if it had not been for the foresight of President Song. In just a few short years, the President has turned the traditional agricultural society of South Korea into a modern Asian Tiger economy based on heavy industry, technology, and exports. Democracy is all very well, but its endless arguments and debates get you nowhere, and when all is said and done, a lot more is said than done. Sometimes you need a dictator to get things done. Sometimes you need to make a decision and move on; it will soon become apparent if that decision is wrong. It is good news for everybody in South Korea because the wealth created for the country will trickle down to the very poorest in society.*

The *East Asia Daily* ran that article in the winter of 1971, and the remarkable thing was that it was partially true. The trickle-down economy was working, and the jobs that nobody else wanted trickled down to those who had no choice. When MiJa finished her work at the American Army base, she clocked on at a local toffee factory that made yeot: a sweet, caramel flavoured cinder toffee. Her job was to fetch the trays of boiling toffee and carry them to the next stage in the process. It was hot, heavy work, and in her first week she underestimated how heavy the trays were, slipped on the wet floor, and spilt the boiling sugar onto her arm. She carefully hid the wound and did not report it because she knew they would fire her if she did; it had happened to others.

The burn needed medical attention. She decided to see a doctor next month when she had enough money for the consultation fee. Then there would be ongoing costs and medication costs. Everything was so expensive now. Her son played baseball for the school and had shown quite an aptitude as a pitcher, and he wanted a bat, glove and ball. Jae-hee had asked for piano lessons. She hated to say no, but it was so expensive. It would take a long time to become proficient, and she needed to buy a piano for practice. Jae-hee would get over it when the school moved on to the next craze. What was the latest one? American sneakers, the ones with the tick mark. Why were they so expensive? She wasn't paying that price for a pair of shoes!

MiJa finished her shift at the toffee factory at 5 pm. She rushed home to make dinner and made sure the children had done their schoolwork and were tucked up safely in bed before she dashed out again to the vegetable market. When the market closed, the traders left behind all the fruit and vegetables that had been pawed over and rejected because it was cheaper to leave them than take them home. Every evening an enterprising group of middle-aged women swooped down on the market. They sorted through the produce, removed any damaged outer leaves, cut out any bruising, and peeled individual garlic cloves and fresh ginger root. They sold the salvaged produce directly to the restaurants before they opened in the morning, and what the restaurants refused was used to feed their families.

MiJa sorted through a pile of Korean chives, removed all

the rotten ones, picked off the debris and outer skins and placed them in a bucket of cold water between her feet to refresh them. She enjoyed the work. It gave her time to think, and the camaraderie reminded her of the Hae-nyeo, but most of all, she enjoyed taking treats home to her children. She knew they would be still awake when she got home, eager to see what she had brought. Today she had a box of tangerines.

'What have you got there, Mother?' asked Jae-hee.

'Nothing.'

'Behind your back. It looks like something.'

'Have you done your homework?'

'Yes, Mother,' said Jae-hee.

'And what about you, Seok-joon?'

'Yes, Mother.'

'It's just a box of tangerines.'

'What is a tangerine?'

'A type of fruit from China.' She opened the box and gave one each to Jae-hee and Seok-joon. They ate in silence until MiJa asked, 'Is it any good?'

'Uh, uh,' said Jae-hee. 'It tastes like an orange, but it's smaller and sweeter and easier to peel.'

'Can I have another?' asked Seok-joon.

'Not tonight because it's too late. You had better get to sleep now. I don't want you both falling asleep in school tomorrow. You can have another tangerine tomorrow.'

In the morning, MiJa rose early, as she did every day, and prepared the children a breakfast of congee and dried fish. 'Get up, you two. You can't lounge around in bed all day. Hurry up. I have got to go to work,' she shouted as she stirred the sweet rice porridge and added the pieces of air-dried fish and soya sauce to season it.

'My stomach hurts,' said Jae-hee.

MiJa checked on her daughter and tripped over the empty

tangerine box lying on the floor. 'Where have all the tangerines gone?'

'My stomach hurts,' said Jae-hee.

'I don't care. Get up and get to school, this instant. I don't care how you feel. Get up now and get dressed.'

'But mother, there is a sharp pain inside my tummy. I can't stand the pain. I don't think I can walk to school.'

'Not today. Jae-hee. I don't want to hear any more excuses. Do you hear me? I won't tell you again. Get dressed, eat your breakfast and get along to school or I will fetch the bamboo cane.'

Jae-hee struggled to get dressed, so Soek-joon helped her. 'We shouldn't have eaten them all,' he whispered to her.

'Do you feel ill?' asked Jae-hee.

'I feel fine,' said Jeok-soon.

'Hurry up, you two.'

'Mother, I feel sick,' said Jae-hee. 'I can't eat my breakfast.'

'I can't afford to waste good food. You can eat it tonight, for dinner. Do you understand?'

'Yes, mother, but it hurts so much.'

'No more, Jae-hee. It serves you right. I hope you and your brother have learned your lesson. Eating a full box of tangerines between the two of you is nothing but gluttony, and that's a sin. Did I ever starve you two? I hope you are sick. Both of you. Now get along to school.'

Later that morning, at 11:10 am, an announcement came across the company Tannoy system. 'Would Choi MiJa please report to the manager's office immediately,' said a disembodied voice. MiJa's heart skipped a beat and fluttered. Had they found out about the accident? They would dismiss her, and that would be that. Her mouth was dry, so she wet her lips as she made her way to the manager's office.

'Mrs Choi MiJa?'

'Yes.'

'Please sit down. The school just called.'

MiJa breathed a sigh of relief but then absorbed the words she had just heard. 'What happened at the school?'

'It's your daughter —'

'What happened?'

'She has been rushed to hospital with a burst appendix. She is in surgery now, so you had better leave immediately.'

When Jae-hee woke up from the operation, she saw her mother sitting in the chair opposite. She had been there for over an hour, stewing away and slowly filling with anxiety and regret until it had overflowed into an uncontrollable sobbing fit. Her head drooped onto her chest, and she shook violently.

'Mother, what's wrong?'

MiJa sat up and wiped at her eyes. 'I'm so sorry, my baby. I should have listened to you and not sent you to school. I should have taken you to the hospital straight away. I'm so sorry. Please forgive me.'

'The pain has gone now. What was it?'

'Appendicitis.'

'What did they do?'

'They took it out. It had ruptured. How do you feel?' She stroked her daughter's lank hair.

'A bit sleepy still.'

'You go to sleep then. I will stay here until you feel well enough to go home. I brought you this.' She handed Jae-hee a shoebox with the all-important whoosh mark on the lid.

CHAPTER 55

A FUNERAL

Jae-hee recovered in record time, and within a week was back at school. The operation was a success, but MiJa had to pay the medical fees in advance, and it had eaten up most of her savings. At least she still had three jobs, and she calculated that if she worked hard and lived frugally, she could manage to put a little money away each week for the next rainy day. It came soon enough, the following winter, with that most harmless of events: a knock on the door.

When MiJa answered the door, she reeled back with shock. A skeletal wraith stood before her: an ancient ghost of a woman with roughly shorn hair that was falling out in clumps, and sallow skin, the colour of old rice paper left in the sun for too long. Her angular cheekbones looked like they would poke through her skin at any moment, and a pair of dead eyes stared accusingly into her own. MiJa felt afraid and was about to ask how she could help when she realised, she was looking at her future, her own death, and when the wretched wraith opened her mouth and spoke, there could be no doubt.

'Don't you even recognise your mother?'

MiJa was speechless. She had not heard anything from her mother since she was abducted and taken to Mukho and had hoped to keep it that way.

'Well, are you going to leave me shivering in the cold all day?' said her mother.

MiJa paused and said, 'Of course not, Mother, come in.' She slid the door open.

'I wouldn't have bothered you, but I have nowhere else to go. The cancer has got me.'

MiJa guided her inside and helped her sit on the floor, resting her back against a cushion. 'How do you know you have cancer? Have you been tested?'

'Tested? Ha. Don't make me laugh. I've no money for testing, but a mother always knows. A mother knows. I can feel it in my bones.'

'You can stay here,' said MiJa as she started to make up a bed in the corner of her room. 'I will take you to the hospital first thing tomorrow morning and get you tested. You can sleep here, for now. Get some rest whilst I make dinner. The children will be home soon. Are you hungry?'

'No.'

'How is Yung-soo?'

'Your brother is dead, otherwise I would have gone to stay with him. I don't want to be a burden.'

'What! My brother is dead. What happened?'

'He died in 1968. Fighting for the Americans in Vietnam.'

'My brother died in 1968, and you never thought to tell me?'

Her mother smiled at her as if she enjoyed inflicting pain on her daughter. 'If you hadn't run away —'

'Don't, Mother. Just don't.'

'He didn't want to go to Vietnam, but the government conscripted him in return for blood money to line the politician's pockets. Politicians like your husband.'

'He is not my husband any more, and I didn't run away. He kidnapped and raped me. Happy now?'

'Mi-soon has abandoned me too.'

'Really! I thought you abandoned her?'

Her mother didn't answer, and the children returned from school, so the bitching was bottled and saved for later. MiJa felt trapped again and tried to control her anger by deep breathing. Her mother had stolen her childhood. Now she would steal her future. But she was still her mother. What else could she do? She would let bygones be bygones, but she was determined not to let the poison leach from her mother, seep into the walls of her home and infect her children.

'I am afraid the cancer is at stage IV,' said the doctor. 'Colorectal. The prognosis is not good. Maybe a month. Two at the most. I am sorry, you should have brought her to me sooner.'

'Is there nothing you can do?' asked MiJa.

'We can make her last months as comfortable as possible, but the analgesic drugs are expensive. Foreign made, so we have to import them.'

'How much will it cost?'

'It depends on how long she lives. I would say not less than a million Won per month. It would need to be paid for a month in advance, in a case like this. Can you afford it?'

'Yes, I think so. Until my savings run out.'

'Well, as soon as you bring the money, we can start the treatment.'

The weeks dragged on, and the medical bills chipped away at MiJa's savings, and she found it harder and harder to watch her mother eat her children's future, like a familial parasite. Her anger rose in her gorge time and time again until it nearly choked her, but what could she do? Family was family, but the burden of care proved to be too much, and she found herself secretly wishing that her mother was dead. Sometimes she imagined that her mother was just spitefully hanging on to life, trying to make it as painful as possible for everybody around her.

Cancer ravaged Bok-nam. Her body was racked with pain and sapped her strength, but she could always summon up enough energy to curse Jae-hee, and she secretly pinched her skin until it bruised in purple welts. Jae-hee didn't understand why her grandmother was so cruel to her, so she stayed away from her, and because she understood that she was very ill, she never told anybody about it.

February arrived, hungry and howling, with a biting wind. It was so cold that the Imjin river froze, and icicles hung from the eaves of the houses. The thinned blood that coursed through Bok-nam's veins seemed to turn to water, and she heaped more and more charcoal onto the burner.

One evening when MiJa returned from work and entered the house, she could immediately smell burning. It slowly dawned on her what was causing it, so she rushed to the corner of the room and frantically pulled back the linoleum, sank to her knees and cried. She clawed at the paper fragments as if in disbelief and rubbed them between her fingers, and let the ashes fall to the floor. The blackened, charred paper was no longer recognisable as money. 'Look what you have done, you stupid woman.' Some of the serial marks on the notes were still legible, so MiJa went to the bank and tried to exchange the scraps of charred paper for new banknotes, but they refused: they were very sorry. There was nothing they could do. They would like to help, but it wasn't up to them. The government made the rules; they just followed them.

With no money for drugs Bok-nam's life slowly ebbed away, but her evil streak and vindictiveness showed no signs of relapse. One day, just after MiJa had gone to work, she said, 'Jae-hee, come here. I want to tell you something.'

Jae-hee walked to her bed but stayed far enough away to avoid being pinched by her.

'Come closer,' urged Bok-nam. 'It's important.'

Jae-hee took a step closer.

'Come closer. I feel so weak.'

'What is it, Grandmother?'

'Your mother is not your real mother.'

'She is. Of course, she is. What are you talking about?'

'She is not. Your natural mother was a whore who abandoned you at my daughter's door. That's why she doesn't love you. She only feels sorry for you.'

Jae-hee started to cry and yelled that it wasn't true.

'It is true,' said Bok-nam over and over until she became so exhausted she nodded off to sleep with a smile on her face.

When MiJa returned home, she found Jae-hee still crying in the corner of the room. 'What is wrong, baby?'

'Don't speak to me.'

'Why?' asked MiJa as she removed her coat and shoes.

'Don't speak to me. You are not even my real mother.'

'Oh, and who told you that? That bag of cancerous bones, I suppose. Spreading her poison everywhere.' She raised her voice so her mother could hear and said, 'I wish she would do us all a favour and just die.' MiJa went and sat down next to her daughter and put her arm around her. She took out her purse and removed a photograph. She gave it to Jae-hee. 'What do you see?'

'Is it me?'

'No. That was my first daughter, but she died when she was very young. I was heartbroken. I knew I would never get over it, but one day a baby was left at my door. A gift from God. You know who that baby was?'

Jae-hee shook her head.

'It was you.' Then MiJa said quietly, 'You are my daughter from heaven. God took my older daughter because he needed her more than me, but instead he sent me a perfect daughter. No matter what anybody says.' She raised her voice and added, 'I know how to be a mother.'

Bok-nam lost her tenuous grip on life a few days later and slipped over to the other side to meet her maker. Only three mourners attended the funeral, and that included the priest. Iron-grey clouds loitered low in the sky and chopped the heads off the distant mountains, and a fine drizzle of rain fell onto them and soaked their clothes. Jae-hee shuffled her feet to keep warm and wanted to get back into the warmth.

MiJa was embarrassed when she couldn't afford to pay for the funeral, but that was the only emotion she felt. She did not cry. The tears just would not come, however hard she tried. She dabbed away the rain on her face with a handkerchief for the benefit of the priest. The priest conducted a very basic ceremony, paid for by the local council on the grounds of public health. He felt sorry for the family. Where was everybody? How could somebody live for so long and not have any friends? There was no mourning that day, no tears shed. Instead, the cold hard rain ran down their faces and dripped onto the hard icy grave. Then the rain stopped as if the sky refused to cry too, and MiJa felt relief that it was all over.

CHAPTER 56

THE FOREIGNER

MiJa checked the handwriting on the letter and smiled: it was from her son. He never forgot to send her a gift on her birthday, at Chusok, and the Lunar New Year, but today she was not expecting anything. She checked the postmark, 16/06/79. She tore open the letter and breathed a sigh of relief. Everything was fine: her son was doing well at school and was going to university.

'Jae-hee. Fantastic news. Your brother has an unconditional offer to study at Seoul University.'

'Wow! That really is good news,' said Jae-hee whilst she towel-dried her hair and grinned at her mother. 'What is he going to study?'

'Philosophy, Politics and Economics,' said MiJa. She had mixed feelings about it. It was great that her son had got in at the most prestigious university in South Korea, but he was following in the footsteps of his father. What if he turned out to be like his father? She remembered the day her son left, just a few weeks after her mother had died. Misery loves company, and sure enough, Jang darkened her door one cold crisp morning with hoar frost still on the ground, a day that was so cold the politicians had their hands in their own pockets.

The lies came freely and eloquently: it was everybody else's fault, of course. His wife couldn't have any more children, and he wanted a son and heir. It wasn't fair. MiJa kept a cool head and asked for time to consider his offer and concluded that he was right. What sort of life could she offer her son? It would be better for him if he went to live with his father. Besides, there was nothing she could do about it anyway. In the register of births, her son was a Jang, and she was a Choi so his father could take him away legally. That was the law. So, she agreed to give up her son if Jang transferred the government-owned house into her name.

MiJa's thoughts turned to her daughter. She knew she would lose her soon. Jae-hee seemed to bloom brighter with each passing spring, and within a few short years, she had matured into a beautiful woman. She was clever, too, and blessed with a likeable personality, and by the time she left school she was head girl. MiJa knew she could not keep her forever and rued the day she would stretch her fledgling wings and taste all the world could offer. She stared at her daughter. Her natural mother must have been a beauty, and she wondered why she had abandoned Jae-hee at birth. There must have been a good reason.

'Jae-hee, I am going for a walk along the river. Do you want to come along?'

Jae-hee knew that her mother liked to walk when she wanted to be alone and think things over. 'I have got some things to do this morning, Mother. I will catch up with you in the afternoon?'

'Fine. Meet me by the old war memorial.'

MiJa took a shortcut through the wooded mountainside. The carpet of pine needles crunched under her feet, and she inhaled the citrusy turpentine smell and felt clean and refreshed, and her spirits soared. God had blessed her with an intelligent son and a beautiful daughter. The sun hung low in a cloudless sky, and she shielded her eyes from the flickering bars of light, cast by the tall pines, and felt like she was in an old movie. She made her way down to the ford in the river. The cherry blossom was out, and the birds dived in and out of the slender branches, dislodging the blossoms, oblivious to the problems of the world, busying themselves only with the thoughts of raising the next generation.

She sat on one of the river boulders and dipped a toe into the icy stream, checked her breath and immediately withdrew it. She tried again a few moments later, gradually inserting her feet until they were comfortably numb, and she could fully immerse them. She thought about her life and how time was a great healer. Time eroded everything. Even the jagged rocks in the stream had mellowed over time and had become smooth and shiny until they offered less resistance to the onslaught. It was the same with life thought MiJa. Her pain had lost its sharp edges, eroded by time. All memories fade, and in time, all will be forgotten.

She dried her feet, put her shoes back on, and made her way to the war memorial. It was in a shady valley next to the Seolmacheon. She climbed the stone steps, mottled with lichen, and sat beside the monument, which was no more than a stacked of grey granite stones with their back pressed into the mountains. Engraved into bronze plaque were these words:

Battle of Solma-Ri – April 21 to 25, 1951
This memorial on Gloster Hill commemorates
The heroic stand of the 1st Battalion the
Gloucestershire Regiment and C Troop, 170
Light Mortar Battery, Royal Artillery.
Surrounded and greatly outnumbered they

Fought valiantly for four days in the
Defence of freedom

It was always peaceful there; even the birds refused to sing, and she never saw anybody. Occasionally, a gaggle of grand-mothers would pass by hiking their way up the mountains, and they would say their hellos and pass on their way, but usually, she didn't see another soul. Today was different: a young man crossed the stream and began to walk up the track towards her. He was heading straight towards the memorial and what was even more surprising was that the man was a foreigner.

MiJa nodded to him. 'American?' she asked.

'No, I am British. I'm working as an engineer at Hyundai shipyard in Ulsan. You speak English very well.'

'Thank you. I used to work in a Red Cross Hospital in the Korean War. I was a nurse.'

'My father was a medic in the regiment,' he said and pointed to the war memorial. 'I have come to pay my respects. He served here with the Glosters.'

'You must be very proud of him,' said MiJa. 'It was an important battle for South Korea.'

'Yes, of course, but I never met him. He didn't even know he had a son. I was born when he was serving in Korea. My mother sent him a letter to tell him all about me, but it was returned unopened. I still have it.' He rifled in his backpack and took out an envelope with *Missing in Action* stamped on it. It was stained with watermarks as though heavy tears had dropped onto it. He took the letter from the envelope and read it, even though he knew it by heart.

Dear Hubby, 11 April 1951

I hope that this letter finds you well and you are not having too hard a time. I'm sorry about our arguing before you left. I think about it every night and looking back now, I see that it was so foolish of me, and I promise to make it up to you when you get back.

Spring has finally arrived in England, at long last, and the snowdrops are out in the garden. They have really bloomed this year. I visited your parents yesterday, and they were fuming at the budget statement. Everybody will have to pay for spectacles and dental treatment from now on. The government needs the money to pay for the Korean war, and everybody is up in arms.

The reason I visited your parents was to tell them the good news. I was waiting for the confirmation before telling anybody. I am finally pregnant. You heard right, it finally happened, and there can be no mistake this time. Maybe you will have the son you always wanted? Your mother has started knitting already, and they are so excited about being grandparents, and I have been buying a few small things for the baby already.

I worry so much about the future now, so please look after your-self and come home safely. Do you think you will be allowed home for the birth? I do hope so, and we can choose a name together. I know you are very busy but please write as soon as you get this letter.

I miss you terribly and love you till the oceans turn to sand and the camels come home on skis.

All my Love
Valspar xxx

'It arrived too late,' he said and folded the letter and put it back in the envelope. 'The regiment said that he had volun-teered to stay behind and look after the sick. After that, he must have been captured and taken as a prisoner of war by the

Chinese Communists. My mother never heard from him again. He must have died there because he never came home after the war. Died a hero, the regiment said, but I would rather he died a father.'

'I'm so sorry for your loss,' said MiJa.

They sat in silence for a while, each lost in their thoughts and united in grief. All notions of countries, languages, races and nations vanished, and all that remained was an umbrella of humanity and peace, and for a brief time, the world made sense and was a unified whole. The medic's son broke the silence. 'I'm sorry. Where are my manners? I don't even know your name,' He offered her his outstretched hand and said, 'Mark.'

'MiJa.'

'MiJa. What a coincidence. The world really is a small place.'

'Why? Do you know another MiJa?'

'You probably won't believe this but before the Korean War my father served in Burma and he wrote about a girl called MiJa, in his diary. A Korean girl.' He rummaged around in his backpack and withdrew something heavy, made from stone. He handed it to MiJa. It was a stone necklace with a simple leather strap and scratched onto the stone in a childish scrawl, were some Korean characters. 'It says MiJa, I think.'

MiJa was dumbstruck. Was she dreaming? It was the necklace she had made for her sister. She began shaking, and tears streamed from her face and fell to the floor in hot molten globules. She struggled to get the words out.

'Where did you get this? I made this necklace, and I gave it to my sister, Mi-soon, when she left for Japan to train as a nurse. I scratched my name onto the necklace so she would never forget me. I never heard from her again.' She broke down and sobbed until no more tears would come. When she recovered, she poured her heart out to this total stranger and told him all that had happened to her. After a while, she asked, 'Why was the necklace found in Burma?'

'My father was posted there. One day he was sent to a hospital that the Chindits had captured from the Japanese ...'

'You mentioned a diary. Do you still have it?'

'Yes,' said the medic. He knew everything written in the diary but wasn't sure if he should read it.

'Please read it. I want to know what happened to my sister.'

25 May 1943. Summoned by the commander. He is sending me to the front line. The Chindits have finally had some success, and during the push forward, they captured a Burmese village called Paungbyin. There is a hospital there, and they need my help.

26 May 1943. Arrived in Paungbyin the following afternoon, and the hospital in a wretched state. It stinks of death and rotting flesh. There are more than a hundred casualties, and they are all dead, or soon will be. It is a hopeless situation. There is not enough medicine and only one nurse. She is from a place called Mun-gyeong, in South Korea. I don't know how she managed to cope for so long in these dreadful conditions.

27 May 1943. Today, I had a long chat with the Korean nurse. She told me that she loved her job and thought it was her true calling in life. She told me that it was great to find a purpose in life. It made it so much more meaningful when you had a reason to get up each morning. She struck me as compassionate and very brave. She had seen the full horror of war and didn't once shirk from her duty. She told me that she had tried her best to help soldiers and civilians of all nationalities whenever she could. She visited a nearby PoW camp as part of her duties and smuggled in food and medicine for them. She even helped some escape so that they could fight the Japanese again.

28 May 1943. The Japanese found out about her activities, but before they could carry out the execution, they came under heavy machine gunfire. Before they left, they took all the medical supplies with them. She hid under a hospital bed, but they found her, dragged her out, and thrust a bayonet in her stomach. Then they hurriedly finished off the sick and dying patients, still helpless in their beds, and fled the scene.

29 May 1943. I found out she patched herself up and never said a word. I did my best to try and save her, but I was too late. Septicaemia had set in, and the only drugs we had did not work. We ran out of time, and she died the next day. Her dying words were that she wished she could see her sister and brother one more time. She was sure she would meet them in heaven.

'I'm sorry my father could not save your sister,' said the medic.

'Is that the last entry?' asked MiJa.

'No, there is one more. Shall I read it?'

MiJa nodded her head because she was choking on her tears.

30 May 1943. In the morning, I buried Mi-soon in the hospital grounds under the shade of a cypress tree. I said a few words from the bible and placed a simple wooden cross on her grave with these words carved on it: Choi Mi-soon. 30 May 1943. Cherry blossom falls at its moment of perfection.

They both sat in silence for a long while, lost in their thoughts, until the medic donned his backpack and said, 'It was a pleasure to meet you, MiJa. I have a long trip back to my hotel and must get going.' He offered her his outstretched hand. 'Goodbye.'

MiJa ignored him. She had seen her daughter walking up the mountain path, and she smiled and said, 'Don't go just yet. There is somebody I would like you to meet.'

Epilogue

One thing is for sure: there is no justice in this world. When I was a young girl, I was taught by the Japanese that I should live my life according to the Bushido Code, the Way of the Warrior. I have tried to live my life with courage, compassion, and honesty, and I have always done what I thought was right and put my family first. How did that turn out? What reward did I get? Nothing. It all turned out it to be bullshit. It seems to me that the opposite is true. Take the man who taught me those principles. President Song. Did he follow his own teachings? Did he live his life with honour and integrity? I don't think so. Yet, he rose to the top of the Army and became the President of South Korea. Corrupt business leaders and government officials, like my ex-husband, all seem to profit by not following the rules.

I tell you, there is no justice in this world, most of the time. But sometimes there is. I read in the newspaper about the assassination of President Song on 26th October 1979 by his lifelong friend and head of the Korean Central Intelligence Agency. It just goes to show that you can't trust anybody in this world, and everybody gets their comeuppance, eventually, whether in this world or the next.

Of course, the obituaries were all lies: loved by his people who elected him four times. He could not do enough for his country. Responsible for the Miracle on the Han River. They said nothing about being a traitor, working for the Japanese, his military coup, making South Korea a dictatorship and ordering the soldiers to shoot demonstrating students. There was nothing in the article explaining why the head of the KCIA shot him, but everybody knows he lost a son in those riots. What comes around goes around if you ask me, and if you can't remove a leader democratically, people find another way.

Will his death change anything? I don't think so. The more things change, the more they stay the same. I am old now and can see the past in everything. I have seen the Korean Yangban ruling class replaced by the Japanese and then by the Chaebol families. Did any of them deliver justice and fairness? Was my family property ever returned to its rightful owner? No. What really changed? Nothing. Just the colour of the boot trampling you down. The way I see it is that there must be a higher level of justice where truth prevails. I guess that forms the basis for my belief. I don't know if I deserve a place in heaven or not. Only time will tell, but I've tried my best and, if anybody does, then I think I do.

I hope my children can find the happiness in life that eluded me. I hope so. Maybe happiness is transmitted in the genes, and it sometimes skips a generation. The future looks promising. My son has graduated from Seoul University and will run for MP in Mun-gyeong. My daughter is married and lives in England now. I know that I don't know much, but one thing I do know is this: when she met the medic's son, and they looked at each other in the eyes, something sparked. It was their destiny like a meeting of souls forged by the same hand.

He does seem to be a caring young man, and it was kind of him to make up that story about my elder sister, but I didn't believe a word of it. I think he forgot that I could read English. I know what happened to her, but the real tragedy is that the world doesn't care, and the longer time drags on, I fear the collective memory will fade and die with them. It would be terrible if the last of the Comfort Women died and the wrongs had not been put right. They are not asking for money: they only want an apology.

When I look back on my life, it seems like I have only had one moment of happiness. I locked the memory away in a secret chamber in my heart where I hoped it would remain forever young, even as I grew old. When I was young, I could easily access those memories and frequently did. But with each passing day, the memory fades a little, and the reality and the memory become blurred. Was it possible to fall in love with a memory? Maybe that is all we ever do? Fall in love with our mental image of somebody instead of the actual person. The memories can be rekindled though and made vivid again.

When I saw my daughter's face light up, when she met the medic's son for the first time, my heart skipped a beat too, and the hairs or my arm stood erect. The dying embers hidden in my heart flickered into life and burnt brightly again, and I was transported back in time. For the first time in years, I felt alive. It is ridiculous, I know. I am fifty-two years old now, but in my mind, I still feel like I am a nineteen-year-old girl. The heat of the sun. The coolness of Seven Angels Waterfall. A watermelon army hat, birds twittering, the sweet summer smell of a clover ring and bracelet. I still have it somewhere. The aroma has long gone, but it is lodged in my mind as sweet and heady as if picked yesterday.

I have an image in my mind of a boy's face that will remain

forever young and long to see him again. But for now, I will have to live in that no-man's-land between living and dying until my time comes, and now that I believe in God, I have hope: if Jung-sik did die in Hiroshima, I know he will be waiting for me in heaven. So, one day, I know I will see him again, and I have a curious feeling that that day will be soon — very soon.

THANK YOU!

I hope you loved reading *MiJa* and found it interesting. I believe word-of-mouth is the best form of advertising and would really appreciate it if you would take the time to leave an Amazon review:

Review MiJa

Acknowledgments

When I first started writing *MiJa* in the winter of 2018, little did I know the journey that lay ahead. My wife suggested I write the opening scene for a writing competition, and I was selected to read it to a group of publishers and agents. There was considerable interest, but I only had the first chapter. Four years later, the research had taken me to some dark places, and imagining some of the scenes left deep scars, but I also learnt more about Korean history, folklore, and culture.

I underestimated the effort required, and I would like to thank my wife for editing the manuscript, explaining Korean customs and folklore, checking the female characters acted convincingly, and checking the cultural authenticity of the story. Some scenes were impossible to translate to English or left a different impression in the reader's mind than I intended, so we resorted to acting the parts, which led to much hilarity on both sides.

I would also like to thank my advanced review team for taking the time to review the early drafts and add the final polish to the manuscript.
The few remaining Comfort Women that are still alive are still waiting for justice, recognition and an apology. If you would like to donate to their cause you can at:

https://remembercomfortwomen.org

About the Author

MARK ATKINSON was born and raised in York, England but has spent much of his life living, studying and working in Southeast Asia, and has spent over a decade in South Korea. It took him four years to research and write his first novel, *MiJa*. You can find more about the author, join his book-club, and download a Korean language version by visiting:

www.bookmark-publications.com

Book Club Questions

Q1. Was MiJa's life really blighted by the Chinese curse, "May You Live in Interesting Times"?
What role does chance play in people's lives? Can you avoid your fate? Was it Yung Soo's fate to die as a soldier, or Jung-sik's to die in Hiroshima?

Q2. MiJa experiences State Shinto, Buddhism and Christianity. Did this religious journey help or hinder her journey through life? Was MiJa correct in her assumption that because there's no justice in the world there must be a higher power in the afterlife?

Q3. How did Confucianism shape the role of women in Korean society? Why did Bok-nam object to educating MiJa? Why is having sons so important in Korean society? How has Korean society changed?

Q4. Different nations have different version of history. How can we reach a consensus? Should past events that reflect poorly on a nation be suppressed? Should history be preserved, or should we rewrite the history books to suit modern sensibilities?

Q5. Mi-soon is sold by her mother under the pretext of being trained as a nurse but is sold into sexual slavery. This was very common, and the victims have never been compensated. Why does Japan find it so difficult to apologise for forcing these Korean women to work as sex slaves?

Q6. When Bok-nam returns to live with MiJa she impoverishes the family with her medical bills. Should Koreans be burdened by looking after elderly or sick parents, or should there be a Welfare State, funded by taxation? Modern Korea has the highest number of cosmetic surgery procedures per capita. Is cosmetic surgery ethical? What part does K-pop play in increasing demand?

Q7. Can a foreign author accurately represent Korean characters, culture, and nationality? How are women depicted in the novel? Are the characters stereotypical?